AF241600

GODFREY BEFORE THE PHOENIX

MARK HOWARD

WARRINGTON
PUBLISHING

Danbury, Connecticut

Godfrey Before the Phoenix
Copyright © 2026 by Mark Howard

Published by Warrington Publishing
Danbury, CT
www.warringtonpublishing.com

All rights reserved. No part of this publication may be reproduced, stored in a retrieval system, or transmitted by any means – electronic, mechanical, photographic (photocopying), recording, or otherwise – without prior permission in writing from the author. For such requests, contact the publisher directly at www.warringtonpublishing.com.

Printed in the United States of America
First Edition
ISBN: 978-1-969359-16-3 (paperback)
978-1-969359-17-0 (hardcover)
978-1-969359-15-6 (ebook)

Cover designed by JD&J Designs
Edited by Mike Waitz at Sticks & Stones

This book is a work of fiction. Names, characters, places, and incidents either are products of the author's imagination or are used fictitiously. Any resemblance to actual persons, living or dead, events, or locales is entirely coincidental.

ALSO BY MARK HOWARD

The Griffin Legends

Godfrey's Crusade
Godfrey Under Siege

To Cathy, for inspiring me to dream bigger!

The Kingdom of Lortharain

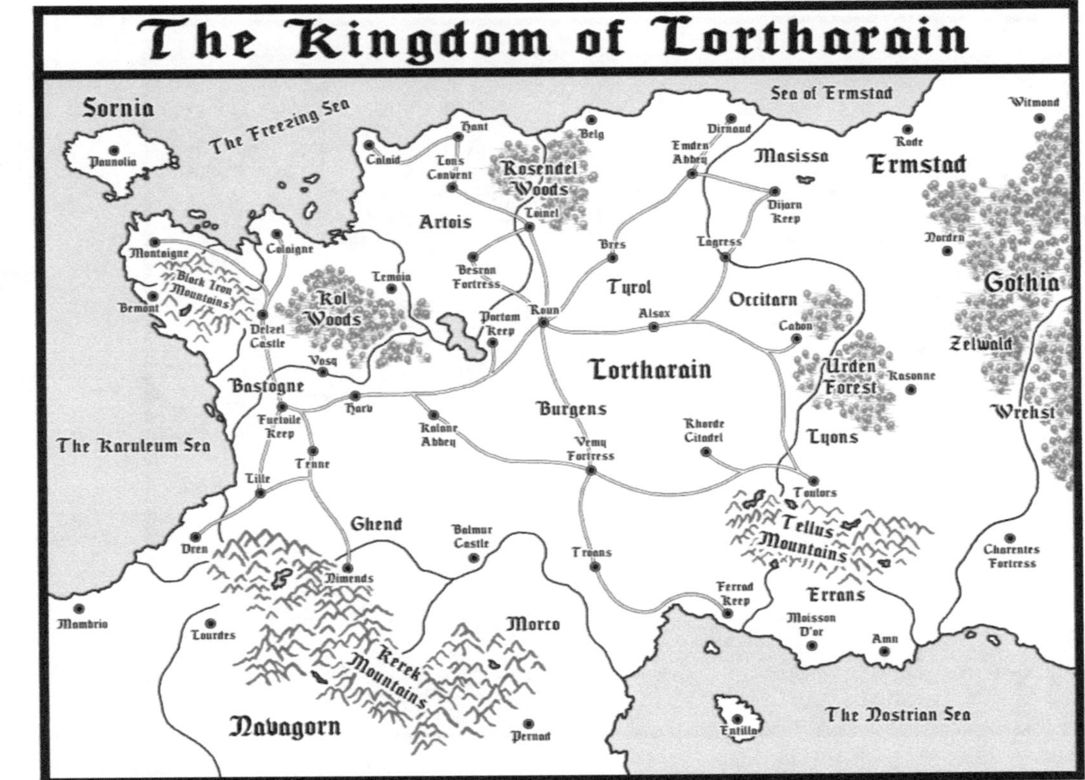

The Nordslands
Troll Lands
Cyclops Tribes
Wyrmwind Peaks
Bergred Citadel
Vasag
The Bosvian Sea
Sigtun
Zemel
The Five Clans
Westranorg
Drammon
Orcish Tribes
Gorgon Heights
Kovdor
Brismarik
Vorot
Olsa
Northern Marches
Kirnu
Mendelpav
Hydra Gulf
Pskov
Pavik
Ohlaru
Skasgun
Rorku
Novod
Friodlad
Helsirki
Epsberg
Tisgu
Smosten
Asgald
Narlstad
Blighted Lands
Odsha
Mirtys
Austlad
Troms Mountains
Vindholm
Eastern Marches
Lublain
Durstfold
Gotlad
Royal Domains
Smaalad
Biorkon
Lakt
Sval
Kalscroft
Petty Kingdoms
Sudvall
Mirborg
Fiord
The Freezing Sea
Istad

Chapter One

Urzg's hot breath steamed from his mouth and nostrils as his heavy footfalls crunched through the cold, frosty hills. The night was starless, but Urzg's orcish eyes were well-adjusted to the dark. He strained his ears, clenching his teeth hard.

Through the trees, a hunched figure emerged. Urzg instinctively took a step back, drawing his ax. He was about to unsling his shield from his back when the figure held up a hand and waved at him. Releasing a long breath, the orc chieftain lowered his weapon.

"Oath-warrior Trosh," Urzg hissed.

"Yes, Chieftain," the other orc answered.

Trosh drew his worn and tattered cloak about himself and hobbled to Urzg. Trosh's chainmail hauberk, a prize ripped from the body of a fallen knight at the siege of Olso, clinked with each step he took. The oath-warrior shot glances here and there as he approached. Fear gripped him as it did the Chieftain.

"We should have stopped Alvir before it was too late." Trosh shook his head as he stopped just in front of Urzg. "That satyr, Rogith, was right. Alvir dabbles in powers that cannot be controlled."

"None of us knew the full extent of his madness." Urzg gestured with his ax. "Or his lies."

"You were part of his inner circle." Trosh pointed an accusing finger. "You should have known. You should have known what powers he communed with."

"I *am* part of his inner circle," Urzg snarled. "Our pact with the Five Clans still stands regardless of High Warlord Alvir's madness."

"It won't for much longer," Trosh scoffed, "once the orc tribes learn what that mad high warlord of yours awakened in the Blighted Lands!"

"The rumors are true?" Urzg shuddered.

"Come and see." Trosh gestured to the woods he had emerged from. "*You* will see."

Urzg replaced his ax on his belt loop and cautiously sniffed the air. No orc was above treachery, no matter the circumstances. Once satisfied that nothing smelled unusual, Urzg stalked after Trosh.

They crept slowly through the forested hills. As they ascended a particularly steep incline, Trosh silently gestured for them to crawl the remaining few paces to the top. Complying, Urzg wriggled up the slope beside his companion. The musk of wet, dead foliage filled his nostrils.

As they crested the hill, Trosh froze in place. Urzg stopped just beside the oath-warrior, who pointed down to the glen several yards beneath them. Urzg's gaze focused on the sight below, his heart pounding.

In the middle of the glen, a pale, skeletal figure in a dark, hooded robe stood. A thick mist surrounded it, obscuring its body up to its waist. The creature was motionless. Not even a breath escaped its lips.

"Necromancer." Urzg swallowed hard as he tried to keep his voice down to a whisper.

"It's Nera." Trosh's whisper grew frantic. "It's the Great Witch of the North back from beyond the grave."

"Nonsense." Urzg shook his head. "I promise you this has nothing to do with the High Warlord or that witch."

Urzg sniffed the air again. They were downwind, and their hiding spot was good. The skeletal creature gave no indication she was aware of their presence.

He and Trosh stared at the necromancer for a long moment. Urzg could only speculate who she might have been in life. Perhaps she was a very beautiful woman at some point, but now all that was left was a withered husk, cursed with undeath. Such was the fate of all who sought to extend their lives by pleading with Athanatos, Belnor, or other dark powers.

"Our rangers speak of other undead monsters prowling the forests," Trosh continued. "A dark mist always precedes their kind."

"Why do they stir?" Urzg wondered aloud.

The oath-warrior was about to answer, but went pale at the sound of a barely audible voice rasping through the slumbering trees. Urzg's heart froze. It was a feminine voice chanting in some long-forgotten language he could never hope to understand.

The Chieftain's eyes were fixed on the hooded necromancer as she gently swayed to the rhythm of her eerie song. Soon, a moaning creature slowly limped towards the undead woman through the misty glen. Then a second. Then a third. It took only a few moments for more than a dozen more to appear.

They were all corpses in various states of decay. They shambled to the necromancer in moldering peasant garb as pained groans escaped their lips. The stench of death was upon them. Urzg's mouth went dry. He had been here for far too long.

"Zombies." Trosh gulped. "The necromancers are gathering all the dead they can before leading them to the Blighted Lands."

"It's time to go," Urzg insisted as the mist around them grew thicker. "We need to warn the Prilka Tribe and the others. Warn Alvir and the Nordsmen. Let them know what's happening."

Trosh nodded in agreement, slithering back down the hill the way they had come. Urzg turned to follow but found himself staring into the lifeless eyes of a zombie just a few feet in front of him. A putrid scent wafted from its slack mouth. More zombies emerged through the dark mist. Urzg and Trosh were surrounded. Trosh let out a horrid shriek that pierced the night as a zombie's fetid maw clamped onto his shoulder.

Lances splintered with sharp cracks as the colorful, mounted knights passed each other on the open ground. Though his horse continued to gallop at full speed, one of the cavaliers, clad in a green and gold surcoat, slipped from his saddle. He hit the packed earth hard amidst both cheers and groans from the crowd gathered in the stands set on the sides of the tournament field outside of Pskov's thick walls.

Godfrey and Madeline sat next to each other in the raised lord's gallery above the scene. Godfrey pumped his fist and cheered at the knight who still remained atop his steed. The victorious knight, in turn, raised the remains of his shattered lance in triumph. His heraldry consisted of a red lamassu against a white field, easily identifying him as Sir Jordan, one of Godfrey's barons. The other knight, whose squire was helping him onto his feet, loosely held onto a green shield featuring a gold tyger passant as its charge.

"Too bad, Torcul!" Godfrey cupped his hands around his mouth as he shouted down at the green- and gold-clad knight, who was dusting himself off.

"Why don't you come down here, and I'll put you in your place?" Torcul of Cumbria shook his fist at Godfrey. "I don't care if you slew a dragon. You can't joust worth a cheap musimon stew!"

"The griffin doesn't catch flies," Godfrey shot back.

Torcul waved dismissively and stomped away from him. Smiling broadly, Godfrey turned his attention to Madeline in the seat next to him. Her expression was dour as she crossed her arms. Apparently, she either did not approve of his banter with the Ogleddish lord, or something else was bothering her.

Pensively, Godfrey cleared his throat and gave her a long, uncertain glance. Madeline stared at the tournament field as the next contestants prepared to compete. He sighed. He was in no mood for drama.

"I'm surprised at how well Sir Jordan has done so far." Godfrey indicated the baron as his horse trotted off the tournament field. "That's a new horse. You'd think he would need more time to break it in."

Madeline nodded but remained quiet.

"When he beat Sir Felgid in the first match," Godfrey continued, "I knew we were in for a treat."

"He's very good," Madeline confessed. "Do you think he'll win the whole competition?"

"He will certainly be a close match to Melcho of Elgun if they face off in the next round." Godfrey scratched his chin. "But Karl the Hammer beat Melcho before and can probably do it again today. Karl's the best jouster in all of Bastogne, maybe all of Lortharain. It will be interesting to see how he does against the Azgaldian knights Duke Ivo invited to Pskov for the Therismos Festival."

Madeline shrugged indifferently. Godfrey let out a long breath. Was she really this uninterested in the games, or was it something more serious?

"What's wrong?" Godfrey asked.

"Nothing." Madeline tightened her lips.

Godfrey cringed. He did not know much about women, but his experiences with his betrothed had taught him that when she said nothing was wrong, *something* was certainly wrong. And it was probably his fault.

"Are you sure?" Godfrey pressed.

"Why would something be wrong?" Arius leaned in between Godfrey and Madeline's seats from the row behind. "It's not like you have anything to be *ashamed* of."

"You only spent all summer moping in your room while Olso Fortress was under siege," Berig added as he leaned in from Godfrey's other side.

Silently, Godfrey cursed. It did not take long for him to see why Madeline preferred not to have her twin half-brothers around. They were mentioned to him only briefly a couple of times before arriving with Madeline's father to relieve the siege of Olso Fortress. Since then, their antagonism seemed to be their defining characteristic. Even thinking about them was enough to cause a headache.

"Don't forget how you let the *Book of Elder Wisdom* possess our dear sister." Arius gave Madeline an overly dramatic look. "She almost died because of you."

"I saved her." Godfrey raised an eyebrow. "I didn't know anything about the book."

"Exactly," Arius and Berig chorused. "You were too concerned about yourself. It was irresponsible!"

Creasing his lips into a deep frown, Godfrey squirmed in his seat and lowered his eyes to the floorboards. He did not see how this last charge was his fault. Yet he had a duty to Madeline. Should anything happen to her, he could never forgive himself.

"Twins!" Madeline huffed. "Will you two stay out of this? It's none of your business, so leave us alone."

Arius and Berig feigned shock as they retreated to their seats in the row behind Godfrey and Madeline. She glowered. Godfrey's stomach sank as the twins' words echoed in his mind.

Godfrey refocused his attention on the joust. A knight clad in a solid black surcoat with a shield also painted completely black faced off against some other cavalier that

Godfrey had seen in the crusader camp only a few times. The second knight was tall and broad. His shield displayed a blue unicorn set against a white field, suggesting some relation to House Sleus. The black knight, however, bearing no heraldic charge on his shield, never once removed his menacing great helm and remained a mystery.

"Who is that?" Godfrey pointed to the enigmatic figure sitting in the saddle of a grey mount whose caparison was also plain black.

"The herald just introduced him as *the black knight.*" Madeline shrugged. "I don't know anything else except he's got a reputation as an excellent horseman."

"I know he's a black knight." Godfrey stirred in annoyance. "But who is he? What house is he from? Was he banished from his home, or is his exile self-imposed? Surely, there's some rumor, at least."

"I told you I don't know," Madeline insisted as the two knights prepared to charge across the field for their first pass. "Black knights are rare in Azgald, but more than one has traveled through this kingdom."

Godfrey frowned at Madeline's brusque response. He was about to reply, but whipped his head around at the sound of a lance's heavy thud striking a shield. The crowd cheered. The knights' steeds slowed as they reached opposite ends of the field.

Godfrey released a frustrated sigh. He missed it. How could he miss the joust?

After consulting with a pair of squires who had been watching the action from different vantage points at the edge of the tournament field, the herald hustled to the center next to the wooden rail that bisected it.

"Strike to the shield," the herald bellowed. "One point for the black knight. No contact made with the lance. Zero points for Elwond the Rosendelian."

"Who did Sir Elwond come on crusade with?" Madeline asked. "I don't know his coat of arms."

"I think it was Phillip d'Artois," Godfrey answered. "His heraldry is similar to House Sleus', and Rosendel Woods borders the Duchy of Artois."

"Right," Madeline agreed with Godfrey's assessment. "Duke Phillip's house has a red unicorn instead of blue. Are you planning on changing your coat of arms now that you're the duke of Kovdor? It's your prerogative to change your heraldry now that you're a lord in your own right."

Glowering, he looked down at his tabard. The white griffin rampant of House Cretus was emblazoned across the breast, set against a blue field. He bit his lip.

"I don't think so." Godfrey sighed. "There aren't many members of House Cretus left alive anymore. I want to keep it as is to remember my father."

"You slew a dragon," Madeline countered. "You could replace the griffin with a dragon. Your own deeds are worth honoring."

"I only defeated Vozzab with Spathi's help," Godfrey noted. "I would not have provided the dragon much of a challenge without riding a griffin in that battle."

With a vexed look, Madeline returned her gaze to the joust as Elwond and the black knight readied for their second pass. Godfrey clenched his fist as he looked down into his lap. Why was Madeline acting this way?

"The House Cretus coat of arms was fashioned to honor my griffin knight ancestors," Godfrey explained. "Now, by some twist of Tyche's thread, I am a griffin knight as well. I think my heraldry is more than fitting already."

"You're the duke of Kovdor." Madeline rolled her eyes. "The lords of Azgald would find a dragon more prestigious, but you can do as you like."

Dumbfounded, Godfrey opened and closed his mouth a few times without finding the right words to reply. A thunderous crash, followed by the crowd's raucous cheering, forced Godfrey's eyes to dart back to the field. He missed it again.

Elwond lay sprawled on the ground as the black knight banged his lance against his shield, saluting the crowd from atop his steed. Elwond's squire rushed to the knight and tried lifting the big man to his feet. Elwond, however, remained limp and proved too heavy for the adolescent squire to lift alone. Panting, the squire removed his lord's great helm, revealing the knight's dazed expression. At least he was still alive.

"Elwond the Rosendelian is unable to remount his horse and must forfeit the match," the herald boomed. "Victory to the black knight!"

Focusing on the remainder of the joust proved difficult for Godfrey. Though many skilled champions from both the ranks of crusaders and Azgald took to the tournament field in a gallant display of arms, his thoughts kept returning to Madeline. She had remained aloof ever since they had endured the siege of Olso together. It was not his finest hour, and he had temporarily lost the Sun's blessing when his holy blade, Uriel, reverted to an ordinary longsword during a disastrous sortie against the Clan army. However, Uriel once again sparkled with the light of Helios now that he had redeemed himself. He could put the past behind him. Could he not?

"When we get back from Pskov, we should talk with your father about a new wedding date." Godfrey practically shouted in Madeline's ear to be heard over the applause as Karl the Hammer was declared victor against Arthur of House Drechov. "You still want to marry me, right?"

"Of course I do," Madeline replied with what sounded more like vexation than zeal.

"Is he bothering you, my lady?" Arius popped his head between Godfrey and Madeline's seats again.

"We can teach him some manners if he's not behaving," Berig joined in from Godfrey's other side.

Godfrey fumed. Arius and Berig were just a little older than him, and they had no great feats of arms to speak of. They had not slain any dragons, vampires, or other particularly dangerous monsters as far as he was aware. Still, they bore a striking resemblance to Madeline's father, and that man's gravitas could not be ignored.

"You may be Duke Tancred's sons," Godfrey muttered through gritted teeth, "but I am your lord and have not yet parceled out your fiefs."

The twins exchanged worried glances before returning once again to their seats. Madeline appeared to have largely ignored the discussion and continued to sit with her arms crossed. If she did not want to tell Godfrey what was bothering her, there was little he could do about it now.

Yielding *that* contest for another time, Godfrey focused on the tournament field in front of him. A hush fell over the audience. The Sun began to lower in the sky as the herald strode to the center of the field to announce the final two contestants.

The days had steadily grown shorter in recent weeks, but Godfrey had hardly noticed until now. He was vaguely aware of the cooling temperatures, but he almost always wore his cloak outdoors anyway. His shortcomings, flaws, and the siege of Olso were of far greater concern and were ever-present in his mind.

"After a long day of witnessing many glorious spectacles," the herald barked, "the Therismos Festival's joust brings us down to two last competitors."

The crowd cheered in response.

"First." The herald raised his index finger to the sky. "Karl the Hammer, one of our selfless crusaders from the Kingdom of Lortharain, has the honor of taking the field with his faithful steed, Epono."

Even Madeline joined in the ovation at this announcement. Karl was not only the greatest jouster Godfrey knew, but he had proven both a ferocious warrior and a loyal retainer to him while in the Nordslands. He should not have been surprised in the slightest to see Karl make it this far.

"His opponent." The herald gestured to the enigmatic black knight's dark grey stallion as it twitched its tail. "Without lord, land, or even a people to call his own, this knight has none but his warhorse to call friend. When I asked their names, he replied *the black knight and the Night*. So, that is what they have been called here today!"

The audience hooted. While the idea of not having a lord or land unsettled Godfrey, martial games cared far less for pedigree than they did for ability. Whoever this black knight was, his skill was superb from what Godfrey had seen, and the mystery surrounding his identity only elicited excited whispers among the stands.

"Without further delay." The herald raised a small flag bearing the black winged lion against a yellow field, the heraldry of the lords of Pskov, before glancing at both knights on the field in turn. "To the first pass!"

The herald swiftly lowered his flag, and both mounted knights galloped towards each other. Godfrey gripped the edge of his seat so tightly that his knuckles ached. This promised to be a good one.

Karl aimed for what appeared to be the center of the black knight's torso, but his opponent deflected the blow with his lance before slipping the shaft of his own weapon under Karl's shield in the same motion. Grunting, Karl dropped his lance as the black knight struck his side. Godfrey blinked incredulously. It was almost too much to take in at once.

Praise erupted from the stands. The herald consulted with the two squires in the middle of the field for a long moment as Karl and the black knight assumed their starting positions for the second pass. All eyes were on the herald as they excitedly gestured at what they had just witnessed. The crowd buzzed. Godfrey could hardly believe it.

"Strike to the torso *under* the shield," the herald announced after he and the squires resumed their places. "Two points for the black knight. Dropped lance. Minus one point for Karl the Hammer. Score: two to minus one. Black knight leads!"

The herald signaled the second pass, and the knights once again charged each other. Karl's lance struck the black knight's shield, but the black knight's slid up Karl's shield and shattered against the face plate of his great helm. Gripping the reins so tightly that Godfrey feared they might snap, Karl barely remained mounted.

Karl wobbled in his saddle for a long moment as Epono slowed to a trot. The black knight, however, appeared completely unaffected by Karl's blow. Even after the knights assumed their positions for the third pass, Karl sat just crooked enough in his saddle for Godfrey to notice. It was a miracle he did not fall off Epono.

"He's just toying with him." Godfrey leaned over to Madeline amidst the chattering in the stands. "I've never seen someone outdo Karl the Hammer like that."

"Strike to the shield," the herald called out after consulting with the squires. "One point for Karl the Hammer. Strike to the head. Five points for the black knight. Broken lance. Minus one point for the black knight. Current score: six to zero. Black knight leads!"

"I can't believe it," Godfrey murmured more to himself than anyone else. "For Karl to win, he needs to dismount the black knight. That's his only chance now."

The herald signaled the final pass. The horses thundered down the muddy field. Godfrey held his breath. Karl had to pull this off.

Karl aimed for the black knight's head, but the nameless cavalier raised his shield to deflect the blow. His lance skimmed against the shield's upper rim while the black knight's weapon struck the side of Karl's helmet. The glancing blow was not enough to shatter the lance, but it did send Karl careening off his horse.

For a short moment, the audience froze where they were. Not a sound escaped anyone in the crowd as all eyes fell on Karl's inert, twisted form in the mud. Finally, Karl groaned as he struggled to stand.

"Karl got *hammered!*" a peasant jeered.

Raucous laughter followed from the audience.

"Was that allowed?" Madeline asked Godfrey over the screaming of the ecstatic crowd. "When the black knight raised his shield?"

"Some tournament rules specify you must hold your shield in place," Godfrey explained. "But if they don't say one way or the other, then the old rules let you move your shield where you want."

"And the head strikes?" Madeline grimaced at Karl as he staggered to his feet.

"The priests are pushing to change the rule from a score increase to a penalty." Godfrey scoffed. "They say it encourages too much violence."

"They're not wrong." Madeline pursed her lips as Karl limped to his steed. "People die in jousts sometimes."

"People also get hurt or die just riding their horses." Godfrey rolled his eyes. "They also die in hunting accidents or on sailing ships. A little risk is what makes the games fun."

"All I know is I'm beginning to understand why Walaric didn't want to come along with us," Madeline said as the black knight was declared the tournament's winner.

"He has business back at Olso." Godfrey shook his head. "He would have come if it weren't for that paladin, Izold.

Anyway, let's go down to Karl and get him cleaned up before the feast. Shall we?"

A minstrel's song played from the middle of the great hall in Pskov's citadel, but the lively singing and the lute's bright chords could not hold Godfrey's attention. Instead, a dark-haired maiden with bronze skin caught Godfrey's eye from the opposite end of the chamber through the noisy feast. She wore a fine veil and wimple, and her deep blue gown accentuated her figure as she went to join a table of other gossiping young women. Their eyes met for a long moment before he swallowed hard and shook his head.

Blushing, Godfrey looked back at Madeline sitting beside him at their table. Briefly, she frowned at him before turning back to her meal. He grimaced.

Taking a bite of the venison on his plate, Godfrey tried to forget his momentary lapse. He chewed and swallowed. Madeline ignored him. She still would not tell him what was wrong. The music and chatter continued around them, oblivious to the tension.

Torcul of Cumbria sat on Godfrey's other side, and he took a long swig of wine from the brass goblet in his hand. Melcho of Elgun and a few other Ogleddish knights, Karl the Hammer, Sir Jordan, and some noble ladies whom Godfrey had only briefly been introduced to occupied the other seats at their table. Most gossiped about the black knight's performance during the joust. Some said they saw him ride due south straight for Friodlad after collecting his prize money. Others wondered if he had dropped his disguise and was sitting among them unbeknownst to all at the feast, even now. Karl glowered in his seat. So far as Godfrey could tell, he did not want to hear another word about the black knight.

Torcul glanced between Godfrey and the maiden he had locked eyes with a moment ago. It took only a minute for Arius to approach her, just as Berig exchanged a broad grin with the blonde damsel next to her. Godfrey's muscles tensed. Madeline was not the only one to notice his wandering eye.

"That's Sophia de Logreno." Torcul subtly indicated the maiden Arius was now flirting with. "She has come all the way from Navagorn to visit her uncle, the Count of Dagdlia. Rumor is she's looking for a husband."

"Dagdlia is just a little southwest of here," Godfrey noted. "She has some relation to House Loridan?"

"Possibly," Torcul conceded. "House Loridan has a large presence in this duchy, but I don't know how all these Azgaldians are related to each other. What I was trying to say is to watch out for her, if you still want to marry Madeline, that is."

"Of course I do!" Godfrey's heart jumped.

"You do what?" Madeline leaned in to join Godfrey and Torcul's conversation over the din.

Godfrey's tongue grew heavy. His jaw tightened. Why did he not know what to say?

"I was saying I thought Karl did everything he could in that last joust," Godfrey answered a little too quickly. "That blow to the head really shook him up during the final pass, though."

Madeline replied with a pensive expression. Godfrey's hand trembled ever so slightly. He should not have lied. Why did he do that? He was having trouble thinking over all the noise.

"If you don't mind my saying, I think you should have participated in the joust, Lord Godfrey." A young woman with golden red hair sitting near Melcho of Elgun gestured to him. "I bet you would have done splendidly."

"Thank you, Isbeil of House Perch." Godfrey cleared his throat as Madeline glowered between them. "But I only have my griffin, Spathi, to ride, and I think that might not make for a fair competition."

"But someday soon, consider it." Isbeil smirked.

Godfrey murmured something indistinct before turning his attention back to Torcul of Cumbria. Isbeil was beautiful—even more than Sophia de Logreno—but he had promised himself to Madeline. And she was more beautiful than either of them when she was not so angry at him.

"Well." Torcul gave a low whistle. "Your man, Varin, won the archery contest earlier, at least."

"There is that," Madeline agreed.

"He hasn't been right since the siege." Godfrey rapped his fingers over the table.

"Has he ever been right?" Madeline raised an eyebrow at him.

"Not really," Godfrey confessed. "But I think he's gotten worse. I think he lost some friends in the final assault on the castle. I was hoping the Therismos Festival would cheer him up, but I haven't seen him since this morning."

"I didn't know he had any friends." Madeline bit her lip. "Poor Varin. What a shame. A man like that can't afford to lose even one."

The minstrel's tune changed to something a bit slower and more somber. Godfrey did not recognize the melody. It must have been some old Azgaldian song.

"I don't know what to do for him." Godfrey sighed.

"You can't do much for a ranger like Varin." Torcul took another long sip of his wine. "He got a large enough bag of prize money. Maybe he will find some consolation in one of Pskov's shops or taverns before we go."

"Where is the crusade going next?" Godfrey asked eagerly. "Brismarik? Kirnu? Westronorg?"

"What do you mean?" Torcul shot Godfrey a perplexed look.

"High Warlord Alvir is reeling after this latest defeat." Godfrey gestured beyond the doors to the great hall. "We need to hit him again while he is unbalanced. If we can convince Baldwin de Ghend and Phillip d'Artois to go to Westronorg, I can bring at least four thousand men from Kovdor."

"Don't get too far ahead of yourself, lad." Torcul waved his free hand. "Winter is fast approaching, and it's supposed to be a bad one."

"Right," Godfrey conceded. "So, we wait until spring and then we…"

"Didn't you hear?" Torcul shook his head.

"Hear what?" Godfrey asked.

A sense of dread washed over Godfrey. What could postpone the expedition beyond spring? Surely, the Clans did not have another offensive left in them. The crusaders might break if they had to endure more attacks so soon.

"After Conrad the Wolf retook Skasgun," Torcul explained, "he and Henry the Pilgrim declared the crusade a success. We just received the news, and Phillip and Baldwin are eager to leave before the weather gets worse."

Godfrey's jaw hung open. His eyes shot to Phillip d'Artois and Baldwin de Ghend in turn. They sat at their tables surrounded by food, their retainers, and beautiful women. They laughed and sang and ate to their hearts' delight. They certainly acted as though the crusade had come to a glorious conclusion.

"No one thought to tell me until now?" Godfrey's hand shook more forcefully. "What about you or King Lothar? Does he agree the crusade is over?"

Torcul did not answer at first. His eyes seemed to look past Godfrey. Taking a taste of the wine from his own goblet,

Godfrey braced himself for what was about to be said. The wine was sour. Bitterly, he swallowed it.

"It's over." Torcul set down his goblet after a long swig. "This crusade accomplished a lot. It did a lot more than the last few crusades in living memory. We won."

"But the Clans are still a threat," Madeline cut in. "High Warlord Alvir has not been vanquished. They will need time to regroup, but Alvir is not finished with Azgald."

Torcul nodded soberly. He drained the last of the wine from his cup and set it down on the table. Letting out a long sigh, he stretched in his seat before tapping his finger against his empty plate to the rhythm of the minstrel's latest song. It had a pleasant enough melody, and Isbeil of House Perch quietly swayed in her seat to the tune. Godfrey clenched his jaw as he tried to reconcile the minstrel's harvest tune against the news he was receiving.

"But are the Clans finished with a high warlord who can't win battles?" Torcul asked.

Godfrey and Madeline exchanged a glance. There was merit in this idea. No one wanted to fight a war they could not win.

"Besides," Torcul continued, "we've suffered our fair share of losses too. I don't know if you've looked around here, Godfrey, but there are not many Ogleddish knights left in the crusader camp. Baldwin and Phillip's armies fared worse, and the men have done nothing but speak of returning home since the last battle. It's over. Let's call it a victory while we still can."

Godfrey stammered but could not find the words to refute Torcul. For months, most of his own men had been speaking of returning to Bastogne. He had tried to entice as many as he could to stay in his new realm of Kovdor, but surprisingly few took him up on his offers of lands, titles, and other honors.

"Bastogne is home," Godfrey muttered.

"What?" Madeline's eyes grew wide.

Godfrey bit his lip. Was Bastogne still home, or was it Kovdor now? Maybe it just took time to get used to the change.

"Something Turpin said a while ago." Godfrey stared at a tapestry on the far wall as he invoked the deceased chaplain's name. "Crusaders don't vow to stay on campaign perpetually. We promise to help, a goal is decided upon, and then we either win or lose. Most of us didn't volunteer expecting great treasures, and, even when the gods smile upon us with their magnanimous gifts, it seems most of my knights would rather go home."

"Even the most battle-hardened knights grow weary of war and yearn for the embrace of their wives and children." Torcul rose from his chair. "The gods gave us great success on this crusade, and they will still watch over you here, Godfrey de Bastogne."

Godfrey silently nodded in agreement.

"Don't forget," Torcul added, "Loxias gifted you a magical sword. I believe he expects you to put it to good use as the new duke of Kovdor."

Torcul took a few steps towards the great hall's exit before turning back to Godfrey and Madeline. He cleared his throat before looking Madeline in the eye. His expression grew more severe.

"My lady has also been gifted strange powers we all rightly fear." Torcul's jaw grew tight. "But my lady has also used these powers to drive back the nightmares that would consume us. Keep using these gifts to serve Kovdor, and your realm will prosper. Gods be with you both."

"And the gods be with you." Madeline bowed her head. "Safe travels back to Cardigal."

"Safe travels," Godfrey echoed.

With that, Torcul made for the large double doors leading out of the great hall. Melcho of Elgun and most of the other

Ogleddish knights soon followed, giving their own brief farewells. However, Isbeil of House Perch lingered in the great hall, chatting with some other kinsmen. Madeline's expression softened as Isbeil's attention drifted away from Godfrey, at least. A few at a time, other lords and knights began to excuse themselves from the feast as the music died down.

Soon, the host, an older man sitting at the head of the high table, apparently sensing the festivities were coming to a close, rose from his seat. He wobbled for a moment but quickly steadied himself. All fell silent as he cleared his throat.

"That's Sir Jordan's father," Madeline whispered in Godfrey's ear. "He's Duke Ivo."

Godfrey looked from Ivo to his baron. Beneath the duke of Oblarv's long, grey beard and aged face, there was a mild resemblance to Sir Jordan. Like Godfrey and some of the other younger nobles, Jordan kept his face clean-shaven. However, with a few years added and some extra facial hair, his resemblance to the head of House Loridan would be unmistakable as far as Godfrey reasoned.

Duke Ivo said a lot of things about the sacrifices made at Pskov, the heroes who had fallen on crusade, and Azgald's special duty to act as the bastion against Nordsman invasions and worse. Interspersed within this long-winded speech were all the usual harvest festival sentiments hosts tended to convey at such feasts. Godfrey stretched in his seat as he tried to focus on Ivo's words, but his eyelids grew heavy. He had heard many such speeches before.

At last, Duke Ivo's monologue came to an end, and the remaining guests applauded before beginning to file out of the great hall or offer a quick word to their host before doing the same. Sir Jordan rose from his seat and cut to the front of the line of those wishing to speak with his father. Karl the Hammer was now engaged in conversation with a fair maiden with dark hair and brown eyes. Godfrey previously saw her at Sophia de Logreno's table, and he silently smiled at Karl's good fortune. Madeline wandered off to find Arius and Berig, leaving Godfrey to himself.

"I guess I will go check on Spathi," Godfrey said to no one in particular.

Departing the chamber, Godfrey made his way through the dark candle-lit corridors of Pskov's citadel to the open doors leading to the palatial courtyard. Any of Ivo's guests who were not staying at the duke's residence were dispersing into the high city beyond the citadel's walls to find lodging for the night.

The air was crisp. Godfrey's breath billowed out into the starry night as he traversed the courtyard. A single delicate snowflake fell on his nose before it melted against his skin. Winter would be here soon.

Godfrey stopped in front of the large stable and unlatched the heavy wooden doors that protected the horses from the elements. A footman or stable hand might normally have stood watch here in a large burg like Pskov to let Godfrey in to see Spathi, but not tonight. The Pskovians had suffered heavy losses against the Clans, too, during their invasion and the subsequent crusade, so they must not have found a replacement to take on this duty yet.

Godfrey let himself in through the stable door, walked past a few stalls, and stopped as his eyes adjusted to the darkness. A man in a chainmail hauberk stood in front of Spathi's stall. He was older, Godfrey guessed in his late forties, and had short hair and a closely trimmed beard, and a deep scar that ran from his forehead down his cheek. He wore a tabard depicting a twin-headed wyvern that was half blue and half white, while the per pale blazon mirrored those colors. There was something familiar about this man Godfrey struggled to recall.

"Uncle Badian?" Godfrey asked.

"No." The man chuckled. "I am Roltar, your cousin. Remember me?"

"Roltar?" Godfrey stared blankly for a moment.

Suddenly, comprehension dawned on Godfrey. It had been years since he heard the name Roltar of House Hracour. He had only ever given it a rare thought at best. Even then, his parents had always been the first to conjure the name of his cousin.

"What are you doing here?" Godfrey gestured to Roltar. "I thought House Hracour went extinct after the Clans razed Skasgun all those years ago."

"Most of us died there, yes," Roltar agreed, "including Uncle Badian."

"I'm sorry." Godfrey gazed at Roltar incredulously. "I didn't think I had any family left here."

"Well, I haven't seen you in about ten or twelve years." Roltar smirked. "You were maybe three or four years old the last I saw you."

"It has been a long time," Godfrey agreed.

"Your parents could never be bothered to travel back to Azgald after their marriage." Roltar snorted. "And House Hracour's treasury all but vanished after the loss of Skasgun, so a visit down to Bastogne has been out of the question."

Godfrey shifted awkwardly from one foot to the other. He felt pity for the fate Tyche dealt Roltar, but his cousin was practically a stranger to him. His condolences could only stretch so far.

"But look at you now." Roltar shook his head. "You've grown into a man."

Godfrey squinted at some movement behind Roltar.

"This is Mauger." Roltar stepped to the side, revealing a younger man in the shadows also bearing House Hracour's coat of arms. "My son."

Mauger gazed into Spathi's stall for a long moment before turning to Godfrey. He was maybe five or six years older than him and kept a short beard like Roltar. He carried a riveted spangenhelm beneath his arm with a flared nose guard very similar to the helmet Godfrey wore in battle.

"What a magnificent creature," Mauger whispered as he indicated the sleeping snowy white griffin in the stall. "Spathi is what you call it?"

"Yes." Godfrey nodded. "I recognize you. You went up against Arthur of House Drechov in today's joust."

"If I were going to lose to anyone at the Therismos Festival." Mauger blushed. "Let it be to no less than one of Friodlad's victors of the great hunt."

"It was a very close contest," Godfrey insisted.

"We can speak more about jousts and tournaments later," Roltar cut in. "But we came here tonight from a very long way to ask a favor as kinsmen."

"Go on." Godfrey swallowed uncertainly.

"Skasgun has been retaken for the Kingdom of Azgald," Roltar began. "But Conrad the Wolf has installed Davin, a member of his household, as the estate's new lord. Skasgun was founded by Louis the Blue. It belongs to House Hracour, not House Talhout. By the gods, we cannot let this stand."

"While there is no love lost between Conrad and me," Godfrey answered slowly, "I'm not of House Hracour. How can I help you press your claim?"

"You're not only the duke of Kovdor but a hero too," Mauger hastily exclaimed. "You destroyed a vampire, drove back the Nordsmen on crusade, and slew Vozzab, one of the last great wyrms known to man. If you don't have King Lothar's ear, who does?"

"Right." Godfrey frowned. "So, you want me to plead your case before his majesty to remove Davin and restore you to your ancestral lands?"

"We are your kin." Roltar looked Godfrey in the eye as he grabbed Mauger by the shoulder. "We beseech your aid, and you have a duty to answer us."

"Of course," Godfrey agreed. "But before we can speak with King Lothar, I have to return to Olso Fortress. I have a wedding to plan."

"Then we will go with you," Roltar answered. "First light tomorrow."

Chapter Two

Walaric's steamy breath slowly rose through the frigid night air as he peered into the darkness. His heart raced as he watched several emaciated figures through the bushes. Nine or ten bony creatures were digging at the frozen earth before them with long, clawed fingers. Their clothing had been reduced to little more than filthy rags girt about their loins, and their skin was a pale purple.

"Ghouls," Walaric whispered to Izold as the larger man crouched beside him.

Walaric took little comfort in the sword at his belt or the shield strapped to his arm as he knelt in the brush, but Izold's presence steadied him. Izold bore the full panoply of war, and his great helm's scuffed and scratched appearance attested to its long use. His Gothian war hammer was already drawn in one hand and his heater shield in the other. The shield's face was painted with alternating yellow and green stripes with a green fleur-de-lis occupying the center. Izold was a grizzled paladin, and that gave Walaric some modicum of courage in their present danger.

"This is not their usual hunting grounds," Izold grumbled as the ghouls continued to dig.

"Was it the runestone of Athanatos that brought them here?" Walaric asked.

"I brought *you* here to tell me," Izold countered. "I've heard rumors of undead multiplying in other parts of the Nordslands. I destroyed a small cult worshipping Athanatos near Kirnu on the northern borders of the Blighted Lands, then another along the Irelven River, and that led me to Olso."

Walaric's jaw tightened as he pondered the undead creatures for a few tense heartbeats. Soon, they began pulling blackened bones from the earth and gnawing on them. They were feasting on all that remained of the Nordsmen, orcs, goblins, and satyrs who had died during the final assault on Olso Fortress.

"Well." Walaric gestured to the ghouls as they began crunching on bones with their jagged teeth. "There's your answer. They came to devour the Nordsmen we buried here. Can we go back inside the castle now?"

Walaric gazed longingly at Olso's thick walls in the distance beyond the serfs' fields and hovels. Ghouls were opportunistic scavengers. They would not attack a heavily fortified position such as Olso Fortress.

"Don't be so insolent," Izold huffed. "We saw Lord Godfrey destroy the runestone in the Clan encampment. We need to *know* why they are here."

Squinting, Walaric turned back to the ghouls. He had studied undead under Bishop Clovis before the crusade. If his heart had not been pounding so loudly in his ears, he might have been able to think of a better answer.

"Ghouls are attracted to the stench of death," Walaric began. "They also gather where there is a strong presence of evil. Maybe the runestone left some lingering aura behind."

"How can we undo such a curse?" Izold's gaze was stern as he tightly gripped his war hammer.

"A sprinkling of holy water can cure unhallowed ground," Walaric suggested. "In the morning, I can bless some and pour it over the grave, and where the runestone was erected.

A ritual like that done in the full light of day should clear the taint."

Walaric began shuffling back towards Olso's walls, but Izold remained firmly planted where he was. His expression was hidden behind the cold steel of his great helm. From what he could see, the paladin showed none of the fear Walaric felt. Stopping in his tracks, Walaric gave him a quizzical glance.

"Those villagers are in danger if the ghouls decide they hunger for more than just charred bones." Izold indicated the serfs' meager huts clustered on the far side of the frost-covered fields.

Slowly, Walaric nodded and drew his sword. As a priest, his duty to the people was mostly spiritual, but could he forgive himself if he turned his back on them in this hour of need? His training with arms and armor amounted to little more than a few rudimentary lessons under Leon de Valois. Would it be enough?

"The gods saw me through this last siege." Walaric kissed the four-pointed star engraved in the circular pommel of his sword. "May they protect us tonight!"

"Amen." Izold kissed the strange amulet he wore around his neck.

Walaric strained his eyes at the golden image etched in the paladin's amulet. Though heavily stylized after the manner of the Estmen, it clearly depicted a constellation of seven stars. Drawing in a sharp breath, Walaric recognized it at last. Of course, a paladin would choose this as his patron deity. He should have known it at once.

"Arktos?" Walaric asked.

"The Northern Bear." Izold nodded.

"May her constant light guide us to victory." Walaric made a pious gesture.

"Amen and amen!" The paladin rose to his feet.

Bellowing, they charged at the ghouls through the bushes. As if confused at the strange reversal of their normal role as ambush predators and scavengers, the hideous creatures ceased chewing on the bones they had dug up from the mass grave and gawked at Walaric and Izold. However, the shock soon left their faces, and the ghouls rushed to meet them.

Izold's war hammer connected with a ghoul's skull and smashed it to pieces with a sickening crunch. Two more ghouls rushed him, but he leapt away from one as he blocked the other's attack with his shield. Another strike from his war hammer sent an undead creature tumbling onto its back.

One of the ghouls reached out to Walaric with a clawed hand, but he bashed it with his shield. Swinging his sword in a wide arc, Walaric severed the monster's arm as it tried to reach past his shield. The ghoul grabbed the shield with its remaining claw, opened its jaw wide, and lunged at him.

Screaming, Walaric reeled back to avoid the ghoul's bite. He thrust his sword into its gut and severed its spine. The revenant dropped, and Walaric plunged his blade through the top of its skull before it could swipe at his legs.

The remaining ghouls quickly surrounded Walaric and Izold. The young priest stood close by the older paladin. Turning his back to Izold, Walaric focused his efforts on blocking the attacks in front of him while Izold struck the monsters out of Walaric's field of view. Amidst the terrors of fighting the undead, Walaric ceased thinking but found himself automatically repeating the movements he had practiced with Leon de Valois at drill.

Izold's heavy blows continued to break bones and knock down enemies with every attack, but Walaric's slashing took a bit more effort to destroy the hungering beasts. Was Izold simply a more experienced fighter, or were swords not the right weapons to take against these creatures? The ghouls did not care about deep gashes across their chests or even the loss of limbs. Walaric gritted his teeth as he tried to subdue his fears.

Lashing out at three ghouls before him, Walaric sliced his blade through one of their jaws. The horrible thing collapsed in a heap, but the other two lurched at him simultaneously. Raising his shield, Walaric stopped one of them, but the other's claws ripped into his habit.

The monster knocked Walaric to the ground before diving on top of him. Its filthy claws stabbed into his gut. The cold, sharp pain made Walaric's eyes go wide. Fear turned his heart to ice as he watched the ghoul lower its head to sink its teeth into his flesh.

With a yell, Izold swung his war hammer at the ghoul on top of Walaric. The momentum of Izold's blow sent the monster spinning to Walaric's side, trailing putrid ichor from the wound left behind. Izold stepped over Walaric and slammed his shield into the other ghoul assailing the priest. Another strike brought it down. Aside from Izold and Walaric's heavy breathing, the night was now still.

Returning the war hammer to the loop on his belt, Izold cocked his head to face Walaric. He clasped Izold's extended hand and struggled to his feet. Wincing, Walaric grabbed his sword from the hard earth and put it in his scabbard. Gingerly, he touched the bleeding scratches left behind by the ghoul that had tried to rip open his belly.

"We'll need to clean that out with some wine as soon as we get back inside." Izold removed his helmet and knelt to inspect Walaric's wounds. "We don't want it to get infected. The taint of undeath might set in if it's not properly treated."

With Walaric leaning on Izold, they made their way back through the fields to Olso Fortress. The castle rested on a hill surrounded by two layers of high walls. The outer gate faced the more distant Wyrmwind Peaks, but the mountains were vague snow-capped lumps in the darkness to Walaric's eyes.

Soon, they entered the great hall of Olso's keep. The hearth crackled dimly in the quiet hours before dawn. Upon entering the chamber, Walaric and Izold were swiftly met by one of Madeline's maidservants, Elja. She was a beautiful young woman with curly blonde hair, the same age as Walaric. She dashed to him from the far end of the room. However, her joyful expression immediately changed to concern as her green eyes narrowed on the bloody stomach wounds Walaric still clutched with his hand.

"You're hurt!" Her muscles tightened.

Elja pried Walaric's hand from his belly and inspected the cuts more closely. She pursed her lips in concentration. Forcefully, she grabbed his hand and led him to one of the nearest feasting tables.

"Lie on your back," she ordered.

Walaric grunted as Izold took the shield he still gripped and helped him up onto the long table. After he had lain down, she ripped open his already torn habit. Walaric was too weak to protest.

"Thieda," Elja called out to the kitchen. "Fetch some wine. Walaric's hurt!"

Bleary-eyed, Thieda hurried from the kitchen with a large clay pitcher in one hand and some fresh rags in the other. Like Elja, Thieda was tall and fair-skinned, but her blonde hair was straight, and her eyes were brown. Walaric found Thieda to be the more serious of Madeline's two handmaidens. She always managed to busy herself with some chore even when others had finished the day's labors.

"What did this to you?" Thieda asked as she handed the rags to Elja.

"Ghouls," Walaric muttered.

Elja gulped.

"As we feared," Izold confirmed. "They were devouring the bones buried at the far side of the fields."

"But we got them," Walaric reassured Elja as Thieda poured a splash of wine over his exposed belly.

The wine stung Walaric's wounds, but Elja soon mopped it up with her rags. The bleeding had diminished. The wounds were not so deep.

"I don't think it's too bad now that I can see it in the light," Walaric said.

"I'll get some bandages," Thieda insisted.

Elja's gaze followed Thieda back to the kitchen, but she soon focused on Walaric and Izold again. Walaric's heart melted as his eyes met hers. No. He was a priest dedicated to Helios. He could not indulge in such feelings.

"I've never heard of ghouls coming this far west before." Elja pressed some clean rags against the scratches on Walaric's stomach.

"I think it has something to do with the runestone of Athanatos High Warlord Alvir erected during the siege," Walaric guessed.

"But Godfrey destroyed the image," Elja countered. "It shouldn't hold any more power."

"That's what we were thinking," Izold interjected.

"Could it have something to do with the Great Witch of the North?" Elja wondered aloud.

"A powerful witch can make for a powerful ghost," Walaric said. "And powerful undead attract more undead. Godfrey told me he thought he saw Nera's shade when he destroyed *The Book of Elder Wisdom*. I'll consult with Sister Vanya and see if there is anything in the library that can give us more answers. If Nera's haunting these lands, I might need to perform an exorcism over the whole castle grounds and surrounding farms."

Walaric sat up as Thieda returned with the bandages. Elja frowned at him. She blushed and looked away. Walaric blushed and looked away, too.

"Take it off." Elja pointed to Walaric's torn clothes.

"Huh?" Walaric blinked.

"We need to bandage you," Elja explained. "Take off your habit. Okay?"

Groaning, the priest tugged at his sleeves with some difficulty. Izold helped him pull his habit over his head. The young man was left in just his trousers and shoes. Well, not just his trousers and shoes. He still had the sword in its scabbard hanging from his belt and a bronze pendant shaped like a four-pointed star dangling from a silver chain around his neck. Regardless, Walaric was unsure how he should feel being in young women's presence like this.

Thieda and Elja wrapped the bandages tightly around Walaric's wounds. Was Elja concealing a smirk as she touched his bare skin? Did her fingers linger over his flesh any longer than necessary?

Walaric bit his lip. Real or imagined, whatever feelings were between him and the maidservant could not be realized. A priest dedicated to the Sun could be bound to no others. It was tradition.

"Thank you, ladies." Walaric bowed his head as Elja and Thieda finished their work.

"Leave your habit with me," Elja instructed, "and I'll have it washed and mended in the morning. All right?"

"All right." Walaric blushed.

Averting his eyes again, he handed the crumpled, bloody garment off to Elja. The handmaiden's cheeks turned a bright shade of pink as she quickly glanced him up and down before scurrying away with her friend.

With a sigh, Izold helped Walaric to his feet, and the two made for the great hall's exit. The paladin's expression grew stern as they entered the darker corridor beyond the great hall. Walaric cringed at the thought of what he was certainly about to hear.

"Madeline's maidservant seems fond of you." The paladin glowered. "Elja certainly does not lack in the attention she gives you."

"She's a friend." Walaric bit his lip.

"Indeed." Izold's gaze bored into him.

"We've been through a lot together during the siege," Walaric explained. "She's a friend. Nothing more."

"Priests dedicated to the celestial gods are forbidden from entering any romantic relationships." Izold handled Walaric a little too gruffly as they hobbled towards the spiral stairs.

"I know." Walaric sighed. "But she's clearly in love with me. What do I do?"

"Don't return that love." Izold stopped in his tracks. "You are in control of your actions, if nothing else. Do you want me to talk to her?"

"No." Walaric gasped. "I-I'll do it."

"Will you?" Izold persisted. "The longer you two entertain these fantasies, the deeper the heartache will be for both of you."

Walaric's jaw tightened. Certain members of the priesthood were allowed special dispensations regarding clerical celibacy. If he became some sort of demon hunter or something similar, maybe Bishop Manfred would grant him such a dispensation. He rolled his eyes. How sure was he about following such a dangerous vocation after tonight?

"I said I'll speak to her," Walaric blurted more forcefully. "It should be me. I'll make the time for it."

Izold scoffed before leading him up the spiral stairs to the top floor of the keep with only the occasional candle to light the way. They did not say much else as they climbed the stairs. At first, Walaric had little difficulty, but by the time they reached the second floor, the pain in his stomach was steadily growing with each step. By the time they reached the fourth floor, Izold was practically carrying Walaric up the stairs.

"Thank you," Walaric panted as Izold set him against the wall of the fourth-floor landing.

"Get some rest," Izold admonished. "It's an early morning tomorrow."

Izold continued up the stairs to one of the keep's adjoining towers, where he had been given a room to sleep in while he stayed at Olso Fortress. Leaning against the wall, Walaric closed his eyes and took several deep breaths. His mind wandered between thoughts of Elja, the hideous ghouls they had destroyed earlier that night, and the dark possibilities that brought the undead here.

Stretching, Walaric made his way down the corridor past Madeline's bed chamber on his left and one of the empty guest rooms on his right. There were a few other unoccupied bed chambers on the fourth floor reserved for guests, both expected and not. Godfrey had initially offered one of these to Izold, but the paladin said he preferred to have the more commanding view provided by the footmen's billets in the towers. After the siege, there was certainly no shortage of beds to choose from.

Walaric stopped in front of the door next to Madeline's room. Furrowing his brow, he gazed at it through the darkness. This door had not been opened in a long time. He let out a sigh.

"I hope you've found peace, Chaplain Turpin." Walaric made a pious gesture towards the door.

Kissing the bronze star pendant around his neck, Walaric continued to his own bed chamber next to Turpin's. Melancholy numbed his senses as his thoughts dwelled on Turpin. The grizzled chaplain was captured during a sortie in the middle of the siege, and High Warlord Alvir sacrificed him to Athanatos. It was a grisly display meant to goad Godfrey into launching a foolhardy attack in response. Enraged, he fell into Alvir's trap, and they all suffered for it.

Walaric's bedroom door creaked as he pushed it open. The room was completely dark. As he took a step inside, his eyes slowly adjusted to make out the dim shapes of his furniture scattered about the otherwise empty chamber. He yelped and jumped back in surprise.

The grey form of a veiled woman hovered over Walaric's bed. Her skeletal features were as ethereal as they were undefined. She was little more than a grasping shadow. He blinked, and she was gone.

"The Great Witch of the North," Walaric hissed.

Frantically, the young priest held his holy symbol aloft on its chain as his eyes darted from one end of the room to the other. There were no other signs of any ghosts or spirits that Walaric could see, but the air immediately around his bed was frigid. However, the feeling soon dissipated. Had Walaric just imagined it all?

His whole body shaking, Walaric stood still for a long moment. He eventually snapped out of his paralysis and cautiously changed into his night clothes. Occasionally, his eyes would dart to some shadow in the corner of the room, or his heart would stop at the slightest noise. All of these proved to be false alarms, and Walaric slowly regained his nerves. He spent a long time in prayer at his bedside, all the same.

It was not yet dawn when Walaric, Izold, Vonig the Cold, Sir Rodair, and a few other retainers from Godfrey's household trudged back across the fields to the mass grave where they had buried the Nordsmen. Izold, Vonig, and the other knights all wore their chainmail armor and carried their weapons and shields. Erikur and a couple of other serfs, whom Walaric did not know by name, wore thick tunics and trousers while carrying shovels. Walaric himself was dressed in a fresh habit and carried a large vial of holy water. All wore heavy cloaks to keep the chill from their bones.

Walaric stopped in his tracks. A single pale ghoul hovered over the remains of one of its fellows that had been destroyed in the night. It picked at the flesh and bones, but it froze and twisted its head as Walaric's party approached. The foul creature soon turned and scurried off towards the woods to the south. It was out of sight just as the sun touched the frosty ground before Walaric.

"Kolsmarden Forest." Erikur gestured to the woods. "You can bet dozens more ghouls are hiding in those trees right now."

"If there were ever a reason not to hate this place," Rodair muttered, "I can't think of it now."

"Aye," Sir Warmann agreed.

Ignoring the murmurs, Walaric stood over the mass grave. Parts of it had been dug up by the ghouls the night before, and bits of blackened bone, some with tooth marks, were now exposed to the Sun. The remains of the destroyed ghouls also lay scattered about the area where Izold and Walaric had fought them.

Walaric uncorked the vial of holy water and raised it in the direction of the rising Sun. He cleared his throat and began chanting the ritual of purification as he sprinkled the holy water across the ground. The others present bowed their heads as Walaric spread the vial's contents from one end of the mass grave to the other.

He repeated this two more times before emptying the last of the holy water on the ground. Satisfied, Walaric turned back to the others he had brought with him. Their faces were uncertain.

"Make sure the bones are covered with earth again," Walaric told Erikur. "Bury what remains of the ghouls, too. If Loxias favors us, that's the end of this."

Erikur and the other serfs took their shovels and got to work. Meanwhile, the knights kept their eyes on the distant tree line with hands on the handles of their swords, axes, and other weapons. Carrying his great helm under his arm, Izold approached Walaric. With a brooding gaze, he looked the young priest up and down.

"You seem unsure about the ceremony," Izold noted. "The men see it in your eyes."

At first, Walaric said nothing. Gazing at Kolsmarden Forest, where the ghoul had retreated to, he took a long breath. He could not keep this to himself.

"Last night, I saw Nera's ghost above my bed." Walaric shuddered. "I prayed a long time and found no comfort. She haunted my dreams, and my abjurations had no power over her."

"The Great Witch of the North was rightly feared in life." Izold met Walaric's eyes. "It may take more than a priest's simple prayers and a sprinkling of holy water to undo her curse."

"I began a fast this morning," Walaric added.

"That could help." Izold nodded. "But we may need a true exorcist if this continues."

"We had one come from the Temple of Spes when we first captured Olso Fortress," Walaric explained. "He destroyed all of the Nordsman idols he found and sent Sister Vanya here to investigate the books in the library."

Izold grunted.

"But the sacrifices, pentagrams, and the runestone were after he left," Walaric continued. "Maybe there's more to uncover. I still need to talk with Sister Vanya."

"See that you do," Izold agreed, "but be sure to begin your research with a prayer. You will need all the help you can get from the gods in this task."

"I'd better get to it then." Walaric began marching back to the castle.

The serfs continued digging as Walaric waved farewell to them. None of them seemed eager to touch the remains of the ghouls as they tentatively prodded the corpses with their shovels. Walaric could hardly blame them for their timidity. What if one was not as dead as it appeared? That was what Izold and the knights were here for, Walaric reminded himself.

Eventually, Erikur used his shovel as a lever to roll one of the broken ghouls into a pit they had dug. The serfs quickly filled the pit with dirt before moving on to the next broken revenant. With a sigh, Walaric turned his attention back to the castle beyond the fields and the serfs' hovels. They could take care of things from here.

After offering a short prayer in the keep's chapel, Walaric made his way up the spiral stairs to the library on the third floor. Books were rare treasures that held many secrets. Few castles could boast of having even a modest library. Little wonder the Order of the Ivory Chalice had sent one of its sisters to Olso as soon as it fell into the crusaders' hands.

Pushing open the door to the library, Walaric discovered numerous shelves filled with scrolls and codices. Some were written in elvish, others in the old Nordsman tongue. Still more were written in languages Walaric could not even identify. Only a few volumes were written in celestial or in Ostman from what Walaric had seen.

At a large wooden desk near the front of the chamber sat an older woman in a nun's white habit. Even she was while reading a book, Sister Vanya's intimidating aura gave him pause. Swallowing hard, he took a determined step forward.

Though his steps echoed through the library, Sister Vanya did not look up from the book she was reading as Walaric drew nearer. Only after he stopped directly in front of her desk and cleared his throat did she set down the tome in her hands. Her piercing gaze met his, and Walaric swallowed again.

"S-sister Vanya." Walaric forced a smile.

"Good morning, *Father* Walaric." A tight smile curled the nun's lips.

Walaric shifted uncomfortably. The irony of Sister Vanya's tone was not lost on him. Others had jokingly or otherwise questioned Walaric's maturity in filling the role of Olso Fortress' resident priest. However, his youth did not seem to be much of an issue at first. Then Turpin died.

"What can I do for you today?" Sister Vanya pulled Walaric from his thoughts.

"Do we have any books on exorcisms?" Walaric gestured out to the library shelves. "I have a basic primer in my room, but I think I will need something more advanced for this problem."

"More ghouls?" Sister Vanya pursed her lips.

The old librarian rarely showed any emotion outside of her usual pretension, but only a fool would not be afraid of the undead. Every year, their power grew stronger. Every year grew closer to Ragnarok.

"That's part of my concern," Walaric admitted. "After all the trouble caused by *The Book of Elder Wisdom* and other bad omens as of late, I wanted to be sure we gave Olso a very thorough cleansing."

"What other bad omens?" Sister Vanya asked.

"Nera's ghost may be haunting the castle." Walaric gave the librarian a dark look.

"That is serious." The color disappeared from the Sister's already pale face. "Let me see what I can find. We should have a copy of *Conjurations of Father Amroth.*"

"That would be good." Walaric nodded. *"Seals and Protections* by Saint Bede was what I was hoping to find."

"I know we have Saint Bede's works," the librarian said. "This way, please."

Sister Vanya rose from her desk, and Walaric followed her through the narrow aisles between the shelves. Her brisk steps echoed through the chamber. She was surprisingly nimble for a woman her age.

The librarian plucked a musty book off a shelf and dropped it into Walaric's hands, quickly followed by a second and third volume. Without a word, she moved on to another shelf in an adjacent aisle. After scanning the shelves for a moment, she dropped two more tomes on top of the stack Walaric was carrying just as he caught up to her.

"That should do it," Sister Vanya said as she placed one last codex on top of the stack in Walaric's arms. "Saint Bede, Father Amroth, and a couple of other authorities on the topic of exorcisms you may find helpful."

Walaric grunted in reply. The weight of the books and his recent wounds strained his muscles, and he struggled to carry them to the nearest desk. Finally, he dropped them onto the wooden surface with a muffled thud. They spilled out across the table, and the librarian curled her lip into a frown at Walaric as she deftly caught one of the books before it could hit the floor.

"Careful, *Father* Walaric," Sister Vanya chastised him as she put the book back in his hands. "These books are ancient, and we don't have a scribe to replace anything that gets damaged beyond my basic skills to repair."

Walaric blushed as he stammered out an apology.

"Start with this one." The librarian pointed to a dusty, leather-bound codex.

"*From the Book of the Dead.*" Walaric frowned.

"It was written by Saint Horic after he purged some banshees from Cromant," Sister Vanya explained. "He was a renowned exorcist, and every library in the Cardigalian Islands had a copy of this book a hundred years ago."

"It's hard to argue against that." Walaric pulled out a chair from the desk. "Thank you."

The librarian soon left Walaric, and he began reading through Saint Horic's work. Though it was written in celestial, the script on the pages was thick and blotchy. There were also several Ogleddish phrases sprinkled throughout the text that Walaric had to use context clues to decipher. It took him a long time to not make it very far.

Walaric scribbled down notes with a quill on a blank sheet of parchment as he read. At first, the information seemed rudimentary enough, but perhaps some small but critical detail would emerge as he continued. He bit his lip. If only Bishop Clovis or Chaplain Turpin were here.

After a few hours at this, Walaric's stomach began to grumble, and his mind increasingly wandered. Much of Saint Horic's advice on exorcisms proved to be knowledge he already had. Still, there were specific variations of the exorcism rituals that were more effective against particular kinds of incorporeal undead. How was Walaric supposed to know if what he saw last night qualified as a specter, poltergeist, or phantom?

Eventually, Walaric put his quill down in its ink bottle, set his notes aside, and pushed his chair back from the desk. He stretched as he stood. More progress would have to come after a good rest.

After several days of studying the books Sister Vanya had given him, Walaric decided the best course of action would be to try any and all of the different exorcism techniques that seemed appropriate. One of them was bound to work, he decided. Yet none of them felt right after trying.

"I don't get it," Walaric complained as he sat at the high table in the great hall with Izold and Sister Vanya at breakfast. "I've tried everything, but I still feel uneasy."

"How often do you feel uneasy?" Izold asked as he stabbed a sausage link with his fork.

"Not every day," Walaric admitted.

"Sometimes the memory of evil spirits lingers longer than the spirits themselves." Sister Vanya picked at the eggs on her plate. "Perhaps that is what vexes you."

"But it's not just a memory," Walaric insisted. "I've woken up in cold sweats. Members of the household tell me they hear strange noises at night…"

"It could be more ghouls," Izold suggested. "The serfs tell me they've spotted more in Kolsmarden Forest to the south at dusk ever since we first encountered them."

"Great." Walaric sighed. "How do we put an end to all of this madness?"

"If there were an easy answer to cleansing the world of evil, it would have been done long ago." Izold took a bite of his greasy sausage.

Walaric's gaze wandered to Elja as she served Sigibald of Fulda, Vonig the Cold, Sir Magnus, and Candac more scrambled eggs from a hot iron skillet at their table. Sir Taran and Garic's spots among them remained conspicuously empty. How was Candac holding up after his master's death?

The table Berimund the Brash had sat at during meals in the past largely remained full, though the absence of Berimund's crass humor left the remaining knights noticeably more sullen. Walaric bit his lip. Normally, Sir Paschal would have occupied the spot nearest to where Berimund used to sit, but the young knight now ate his breakfast alone in an empty corner of the chamber.

"He's been taking Berimund's death pretty hard?" Walaric subtly indicated Sir Paschal.

Izold and Sister Vanya shifted slightly in Paschal's direction before turning back to Walaric. Clearing his throat, Izold shook his head. The grizzled paladin gave Walaric a weary look before turning back to his plate.

"They tell me after the final assault on the keep ended, they found Paschal hiding in the stables," Izold grumbled. "He's dishonored."

"Nonsense." Sister Vanya clicked her tongue. "He was hit with a crossbow bolt and dragged himself into that stable. I tended to him myself."

"Others fought in worse shape," Izold countered.

"I saw him during the final assault that night," Walaric recalled. "He was fighting in the midst of some levies and footmen. They were cut off, and I thought he was as good as dead."

"However it happened," Izold said, "Sir Paschal's honor was lost that night. And, once lost, most knights find it's not so easily recovered."

"I might need to speak to them." Walaric's focus returned to Berimund's old table.

"No." Izold scolded. "Let warriors handle warriors' affairs. Sir Paschal will redeem himself in time."

Crossing his arms, Walaric slumped back in his chair. His duty was to see to the spiritual welfare of his flock. If a knight was treated unfairly by his peers, was it not Walaric who should set them straight?

The remainder of breakfast passed quietly enough for Walaric. Having given up on his fast some time ago, he finally got around to eating his biscuits and gravy. However, they had grown cold and stale by the time he put them into his mouth. Slowly, the knights and footmen began shuffling out of the great hall to their various duties while Elja and Thieda cleared away the dirty dishes.

Walaric's heart skipped a beat as he caught Elja's eye. He still had not found the right words to tell her they needed to bury their feelings. In truth, he feared he could not bring himself to say it at all. Thankfully, Izold was too preoccupied with ghouls to follow up with Walaric on this.

Giving Elja only a simple smile, Walaric pushed his chair back from the high table and stood. Nervously, he reached into a pouch on his belt and began fidgeting with a heavy, pointed amulet within. He had business in the mint to take care of before the day got away from him.

He bustled to the great hall's exit without even giving Elja another look. Brusquely, he made his way to the stairs leading down to the dungeon and mine. He would have to deal with his feelings for her, and soon, but not yet.

After descending the first set of dark, damp stairs, Walaric passed through the silent dungeon. Grimacing, he stared into the poorly lit cells as he hurried along. He had not spent much time in this part of the castle since the goblins were imprisoned here after their rebellion during the siege. He preferred to keep it that way.

Soon, Walaric found himself among the dwarf coin-makers in the mint. They sang merry tunes in their native tongue as hammers rang out among the other sounds of their industry. He smirked at the sight of the dwarves at work. Their faces were much brighter since the goblins were driven out of Olso.

"Dachlann?" Walaric called out. "Dachlann?"

A squat dwarf with a large blonde beard hustled from the far side of the chamber to Walaric. He wiped his hands on his thick, stained apron before clasping Walaric's arm. A broad smile creased his face.

"What can I do for you, Father Walaric?" The dwarf beamed. "I'm afraid you've made no converts of any of my miners or minters yet. Lithos and the ancestors, they know well. Loxias, they do not."

"I'm not here to preach today." Walaric shook his head. "I've written Bishop Manfred, and he says Lithos is not a dark god. You're free to maintain your people's traditions as you have up until this time."

"Grateful for your permission to keep doing what we always have." Dachlann scoffed. "My father was patriarch of the dwarves at Olso before me and his father before him."

"I have a request." Walaric cleared his throat. "Can you make something for me?"

"If it's metal or stone, I can do it." The dwarf nodded. "What do you need?"

Walaric produced the amulet from his pouch, which he had been fidgeting with up in the great hall. It was a large, four-pointed star pendant very similar to Walaric's holy symbol. However, what was in his hand was more ornate and shone brighter than Walaric's star in the mint's light.

"Is that pure gold?" Dachlann's jaw dropped.

"This was Chaplain Turpin's," Walaric explained. "I need you to melt it down."

"Melt it down?" Dachlann gasped. "Have you lost your mind, lad?"

"It is pure gold." Walaric handed the star pendant to Dachlann. "I need you to melt it down and make a coin out of it. Can you do it?"

"I already said yes, I can, but why spoil such a beautiful thing?" The dwarf frowned at the pendant in the palm of his hand. "Aside from such exquisite craftsmanship going to waste, won't your gods be upset at turning one of their holy symbols into money?"

"I found it in Turpin's room upstairs," Walaric explained. "I never saw him wear this pendant. I don't think he cared for such ostentatious things. Besides, it's not a common gold piece I'm asking you to make. I need it to be a funerary coin. Give it an image of the star of Spes for its face and the gates to the afterlife for its tail. It will still serve the gods."

"Understood," Dachlann muttered. "The four-pointed star of the celestial gods on one side, and the gates of the underworld on the other. Who died?"

"No one yet," Walaric clarified. "Not recently, at least. But I've been reading about something called the Keeper of Souls, and I have a hunch I may need the gold."

"I'll make your coin for you," the dwarf agreed after a long pause. "There should be plenty of material to work with here. What do you want done with the excess?"

"Keep it." Walaric waved his hand. "The laborer is worth his wages, and the gods will smile on it."

"I'll start working on the mold right away," Dachlann reassured him.

"All right," Walaric answered. "Try to finish it as soon as you can. I may have to leave here soon."

"I'll let you know when it's done." The dwarf clasped Walaric's arm once again.

Walaric returned the gesture before turning away from the mint. Hastily, he made his way back up the stairs and through the dungeon and store rooms. He breathed a sigh of relief once he returned to the ground floor. Now he could turn his attention to the outside world again.

Exiting the keep, Walaric squinted hard in the bright morning sun. On the towers and walls surrounding the inner courtyard, a few guards stood sentinel with heavy cloaks wrapped around themselves, but no one seriously expected another attack so soon. With the year's meager harvest already over, there was little activity in the garden near the stables. However, smoke billowed from the chimney of Drogon's smithy. Curious, Walaric made his way towards the shop next to the inner gatehouse.

"Father Walaric," Drogon greeted him warmly.

Walaric grinned in reply. Drogon was an older, portly man. He was bald and not particularly handsome by Walaric's estimation, but he was an honest craftsman and had managed to win a wife and young son out of his humble life so far. He and some of the other commoners did not seem to question Walaric's youth in his priestly role, at least. It was nice to know some people had faith in him.

"What are you and Evroul working on today?" Walaric crossed his arms.

Drogon hit a small steel ring sitting on the corner of his anvil with a hammer. Several similar rings sat in a pile in the center of the anvil. The strike flattened the ends of the heavy wire that formed the ring and emitted a high-pitched pinging sound. Briefly inspecting his work, Drogon picked up the partially flattened ring before setting it at the opposite end of his anvil. Meanwhile, Drogon's scrawny, young apprentice, Evroul, wound more of the same steel wire around a thin wooden rod.

"We're making chainmail." Drogon struck another ring with his hammer. "Lord Godfrey ordered a dozen hauberks, and it's going to keep us busy for a long while."

"What happens after you flatten the ends like that?" Walaric asked.

"Then we punch some holes through them," Drogon explained in between chiming hammer strikes. "After that, we start linking the rings together and riveting them closed."

"Sounds tedious." Walaric grimaced.

"Evroul's getting better at things around here," the blacksmith noted. "I've been showing him how to do more of the harder parts, and I think we can get each hauberk done in just a few weeks."

"That's good." Walaric smiled.

"We're going to need them." Drogon frowned as he hit another ring. "A lot of levies didn't have enough armor during that last siege. If the Nordsmen come back…"

The blacksmith's words trailed off as he resumed his work. The sound of the hammer hitting the rings was pleasant in Walaric's ears. There was probably a sermon somewhere in this about forging spiritual armor one metaphoric chainmail link at a time.

The blast of a trumpet from one of the towers pulled Walaric from his thoughts. He cleared his throat. Turning his gaze from the blacksmith's work to the inner courtyard, Walaric strained his ears.

"Lord Godfrey and Lady Madeline return," a herald cried from the battlements.

"Excuse me." Walaric left the blacksmith's shop before he could hear Drogon's reply.

Walaric passed through the stone inner gatehouse and made a sharp turn to his right as he hurried through the courtyard. A small crowd gathered at the entrance as Godfrey's party made their way through the open portal. Though at first, the crowd clustered around the gatehouse, they quickly pulled back as Godfrey entered the castle grounds astride his snowy griffin steed. Walaric had never seen Spathi lash out at anyone Godfrey did not wish him to, but that was no reason to chance a carelessly placed hand or foot now.

Madeline and the knights who accompanied her and Godfrey immediately followed on horseback. Karl the Hammer and Sir Jordan were among Godfrey's party, but there were two Azgaldian knights with them whom Walaric did not recognize. They began talking excitedly as Walaric drew nearer the crowd.

"The crusade is over at last?" Sir Berold, one of Godfrey's younger knights, exclaimed.

"Good," Rodair replied over the commotion. "I can't wait to leave this place!"

Chapter Three

Resting her cheek against her palm, Madeline sighed as Sir Rodair and his squire, Polig, approached her and Godfrey at the high table in the great hall. Rodair was a dark-haired man of medium build. Though his ruddy complexion hinted at a man still in his youth, his short, grizzled beard placed him closer to Karl the Hammer's age in Madeline's mind. The two were friends, so it was easy enough to imagine them being the same age, at least.

Rodair's expression was hard. Taking a deep breath, Madeline gripped the armrest of the chair she sat in. She knew what was coming. The dejected look on Godfrey's face told her he knew it too.

"My lord." Rodair bowed his head.

Polig also bowed as he stood back a respectful distance from the knight he served. Polig was a few years younger than Godfrey, but a few years made a big difference when Godfrey himself had only turned eighteen years old over the summer. Few crusaders had brought squires with them. Even fewer brought squires with them who were not yet flowering into manhood.

"Speak, Sir Rodair." Godfrey gestured for the knight and his squire to lift their heads.

"We have fought long and hard in the Nordslands," Rodair began. "Biorkon, Epsberg, Olso, and every foot of ground in between knows our blood. Now that the crusade has been declared a success, and others are returning to their homes back in the Ostlands, I beg your permission to also return to Bastogne with my squire."

Godfrey squirmed in his seat and did not immediately answer. He exchanged a glance with Madeline as if she would have the words he was searching for. She could only sulk in reply.

"Sir Rodair." Godfrey swallowed. "You have been a great help to us. You are one of my strongest knights, and Kovdor would surely suffer without you here by my side. Is there no way to persuade you to stay?"

"My crusading vows are fulfilled." The knight shook his head. "I need to go home."

Godfrey took a breath as if he were about to speak more, but Rodair's expression grew fiercer.

"Sir Euric is gone, and Berimund the Brash is no more," Rodair lamented. "I need to go home to tell Berimund's family why he couldn't keep his promise to return. Let not another knight be required to tell my family why I could not come home too."

Godfrey folded his hands over the high table and rested his chin on them. He wore a dark expression as if storm clouds hung over his head. Madeline tensed as she wondered what he would say next.

"Your crusading vows are fulfilled," Godfrey said at last. "Your duty to me is over, and I release you from my service. Go back to Bastogne, and serve *Duke Simon* well for as long as he holds Fuetoile Keep."

Something in the way Godfrey mentioned Duke Simon made Madeline's skin crawl. Rodair flinched, apparently reading all the same undertones in Godfrey's voice that Madeline did. She shifted uncomfortably in her chair. For a moment, no one spoke.

"My lord." Rodair coughed. "It is not lightly that I go to serve Duke Simon and House Gramon."

"But King Wilhelm stole Godfrey's birthright," Madeline interjected. "How could you go to serve that house after they betrayed him like that?"

Rodair's lips creased into a frown. Another long moment of silence followed. How could any respectable knight even answer such a question?

"Bastogne is home." Godfrey nodded in understanding. "None of us planned on staying in the Nordslands forever. Your duty to me is over. You must go back to fulfill your duty to your family now."

"You are most gracious, Lord Godfrey." Rodair began to exit the great hall and gestured for his squire to follow. "We must leave immediately before winter sets in. May the gods bless you in your new realm, and may they prosper you forever."

"Gods be with you on your journey." Godfrey's expression softened a little as his face caught the rays of the morning light filtering through the chamber's windows. "Should Bastogne under House Gramon prove to be less than what it was under House Cretus, remember us. I will remember your service to my father and me, and you may yet find a place here in Kovdor."

A faint smile crossed Sir Rodair's lips before he and Polig left the great hall. Godfrey gave Madeline an uneasy look. She squeezed his hand.

"We'll manage," Madeline said. "Some will leave, but others will stay. There is an opportunity to be had in a new realm such as this."

"I hope more come than leave," Godfrey added wistfully. "Sir Rodair won't be easy to replace."

Before long, Sir Magnus and Sir Berold entered the great hall and marched to the high table. They were both among Godfrey's younger knights, though Magnus still had at least a few years over Godfrey. Berold, however, looked closer to Godfrey's age.

"And what can I do for you two?" Godfrey asked.

Godfrey tried to keep his tone pleasant, but Madeline sensed he was still recovering from Rodair's departure. It could not be called desertion. The crusade was over. Still, it did not feel right for a warrior to leave his lord.

"We wanted to know what was next now that the crusade is over," Magnus said.

"Are we going home?" Berold's expression grew anxious. "Are we going to retake Bastogne from King Wilhelm now that we're done here?"

"We're not going to fight King Wilhelm or try to remove Duke Simon from Bastogne." Godfrey set his jaw. "I thought I made that much clear earlier."

Madeline rolled her eyes. Godfrey was not acting as the decisive lord he should have been. *Someone* would have to salvage the situation.

"Listen, you two." Madeline leaned forward in her chair earnestly. "There is still much to do in Kovdor. We have a lot of opportunities right here. If you stay with Godfrey and me, you will be well taken care of. There is enough silver embedded in the rock beneath us to support generations of knights."

"Lady Madeline is right." Godfrey cleared his throat. "Opportunistic lords from all over Azgald and beyond are sure to come seeking advantageous marriages for their beautiful daughters soon enough."

Averting his eyes, Sir Berold blushed at the mention of beautiful maidens. Madeline was sure that was enough to convince the young knight to stay. Sir Magnus tilted his head and looked askew, perhaps less convinced.

"The Nordsmen weren't beaten for good." Magnus crossed his arms. "They'll be back. And what about these ghouls? We've seen them almost every night since the siege ended. It doesn't bode well. The undead are a bad omen."

"Perhaps High Warlord Alvir has been beaten badly enough to agree to a lasting truce," Godfrey speculated. "As for the ghouls, I don't know where they're coming from, but we will eradicate them. You have my word."

Godfrey indicated the sheathed sword hanging from his belt. The blessed blade, Uriel, was a gift from the Sun that had considerably boosted Godfrey's popularity among the crusaders. At least, it had boosted Godfrey's popularity among some of them for a while.

Sir Magnus and Berold contemplated Godfrey's sword as if they had need to be reminded that a magic weapon was in their presence. Madeline pursed her lips. How quickly doubt gripped men's hearts.

"Don't forget you are also under a sorceress' protection." Madeline smirked. "If all of this is for you, who can be against you?"

Though she and Godfrey exchanged reassuring smiles with Berold and Magnus, Madeline silently prayed that Magnus would not seriously try to answer that question. There were hosts of malignant powers Madeline barely understood and could not hope to defeat of her own accord. She frowned at Godfrey. Would he grow into the man she first thought he was? The gods had smiled upon both of them thus far…

"We await your next command, Lord Godfrey." Sir Magnus bowed his head.

Sir Berold also bowed before following Magnus out the door. Godfrey cracked a genuine smile at Madeline. The gesture was too rare as of late.

"We can do this." Madeline frowned, finding her resolve. "With the gods' help, we can do this."

Other knights came to visit Godfrey and Madeline in the great hall throughout the day, either in small groups or individually. Some were able to be bought with gifts and promises. Most, like Rodair, had already decided upon going home and could not be persuaded to stay.

At some point during these exchanges, Godfrey's kin, Roltar and Mauger, entered the great hall. Mauger entertained himself easily enough by idly chatting with Thieda as she served him food and drink at one of the tables. Roltar, however, prowled back and forth near one of the walls at the far side of the chamber.

"What do you know of House Hracour?" Madeline whispered in Godfrey's ear.

"Not much," Godfrey confessed. "My mother was of House Hracour but rarely spoke of it."

"Their house was founded by the paladin, Louis the Blue, after the first crusade to the Nordslands," Madeline explained. "He founded the realm of Stormsud and built Skasgun at its center. While he performed many great deeds during Azgald's early years, his descendants struggled to hold onto what he had gained. Slowly, they lost their lands to the Clans until Skasgun was finally razed to the ground."

"I remember hearing about that back in Bastogne," Godfrey said. "My uncle, Badian, died defending that castle. Mother was very upset when she heard the news. Roltar is my cousin, but I don't really know him well."

"Since they lost Skasgun," Madeline continued, "House Hracour has been a shell of its former self. Roltar has been obsessed with regaining the fortress since the Clans rebuilt it, but he has not had the means to see his ambition come to anything."

"I might have guessed as much." Godfrey's gaze followed Roltar across the room. "He asked me to press his claim on Skasgun when I first met him at Pskov."

"Men in Roltar's position are dangerous." Madeline gripped Godfrey's arm. "Think carefully before agreeing to anything he asks of you."

"I won't do anything unreasonable for him, even if he is family." Godfrey met Madeline's eyes.

"House Hracour has spent years scheming in the shadows," Madeline clarified. "You may think Roltar is asking one thing of you, but it may be a ruse for some other purpose. Understand?"

"I'll be careful." Godfrey's jaw tightened.

Madeline's gaze drifted back to Mauger and Thieda. The young knight was clearly trying to engage Madeline's handmaiden in conversation, but Thieda's responses were curt and her posture aloof. Why did men always have so much trouble understanding when a maiden was not interested? Finally, she found some excuse to go back to the kitchen, leaving Mauger despondently crossing his arms.

"You've lost a lot of knights today." Roltar approached Godfrey and Madeline.

"The crusade is over." Godfrey gritted his teeth. "The men want to go home."

"That won't help our position when going to King Lothar's court." Roltar's eye twitched ever so slightly. "A lord's sway at court depends on the knights he commands."

"Give me time to formally organize my vassals." Godfrey raised his hand in a placating gesture. "That should help attract some new knights to Kovdor."

"Forgive me," Roltar started, "but while you plan your wedding and organize your vassals, Davin of House Talhout grows all too comfortable in Skasgun. Stormsud belongs to House Hracour."

Clenching her teeth, Madeline balled her fist. They had only been back at Olso for less than a day and had still said almost nothing about the wedding since the siege ended. Who was Roltar to accuse Godfrey of not being a gracious host?

"We'll leave for Vindholm as soon as we can," Godfrey insisted. "Please be patient, cousin."

"I am nothing if not patient." Roltar bowed his head. "Just understand that there is some urgency here as well."

Roltar nodded to Madeline before marching out of the great hall. Seeing no other young women to flirt with, Mauger leapt from the bench at his table and followed his father. With the evening meal still an hour or so away, all was quiet in the chamber for a moment.

"I told you he was persistent," Madeline said once she and Godfrey were alone.

"I don't see any harm in Roltar's request," Godfrey mused. "I'll go with him and Mauger to Vindholm, request an audience with King Lothar, and plead his case. If the King listens, House Hracour can reclaim its inheritance. If he doesn't, then maybe we could find a place for them here in Kovdor. We need more knights."

"You can't go to Vindholm yet," Madeline protested. "Father should be back here any day now."

"Don't worry." Godfrey smiled. "We will get the wedding plans finalized before going anywhere else."

Madeline twisted the engagement ring on her finger. It was an emerald set in an intricate band of pure silver. The jewel was a gift from Leon de Valois, one of Godfrey's vassals, while the precious metal had been mined from the tunnels beneath the castle. Both the emerald and silver had been worked by the dwarves in their craft shops in the lowest levels of Olso's dungeons, just above the mines proper. Their labors resulted in an exquisite ring that Madeline could not help but idly stare at from time to time. Yet now she frowned. Was she really ready for marriage?

Godfrey was strong, brave, and handsome. He was pious and kind, but he did not always give her the attention she felt she deserved. Her father certainly felt she could do better, and there had been other suitors before Godfrey or Conrad the Wolf came on crusade.

Madeline shook her head. Cedwyn of Twyl and Tybalt of Norfulk were not coming back for her hand. Besides, she and Godfrey had been through so much together, and she had fought tooth and nail to finally gain Father's approval. She could not go back now. Could she?

Finally, Elja, Thieda, and a few other servants began bringing in food for the evening meal. They set plates of hot beef, venison, and bread across the tables, and a steaming pot of stew found its way to the center of every one of them. The luscious aroma attracted Godfrey's retainers and guests from all corners of the castle.

"We might have prepared too much for tonight." Madeline tugged at a strand of her dark hair nervously as she swiveled her head towards Godfrey.

Godfrey's eyes darted to Sir Rodair's old spot, Sir Warmann's, and about a dozen other knights who would not be joining them for dinner tonight or any other night again, so far as Madeline knew. The crusade was over. Their vows were fulfilled, and they now traveled south before winter could trap them in Azgald until spring.

"There's a familiar face at least." Godfrey gestured in Sir Halinard's direction as the older knight found his seat.

Sigibald of Fulda, Sir Chlodion, and Vonig the Cold also soon found their seats. Sir Munderic, Sir Eozen, and Crocus the Entillan were not far behind. Madeline raised an eyebrow at Sir Paschal as he found his spot away from the other warriors.

"I thought he might have taken the opportunity to quietly slip away," Madeline whispered.

"Well, he didn't." Godfrey shot Madeline a reproving look. "And I'll take him over an empty place at a table as things stand now."

"Sir Magnus, Segeric, and Berold are all on watch now?" Madeline asked as the ranger, Varin, slipped into the great hall to grab his meal before making a swift exit.

"Right," Godfrey said. "Sir Corbus is on duty too."

"Then the rest of your retainers are all here." Madeline gestured to the men in the chamber. "You're going to need a lot more knights than this to defend Olso."

"I know." Godfrey eyed the squire, Candac, sitting at Vonig the Cold's table. "Let me see what I can do about that. Give me a moment."

Godfrey rose from his chair and strolled towards Candac. Karl the Hammer and Sir Jordan briefly exchanged greetings with their lord as they found their places near the end of the table. Soon, they filled their plates and were stuffing their faces with savory meats and wine.

Before long, Arius and Berig led Sister Vanya to the high table. Madeline tensed as the old librarian's eyes narrowed on her. A scowl crossed her face as she sat down, while the twins smirked as they took their places.

"No one thought to tell me you were back already." Sister Vanya wagged her finger.

"We just came back this morning," Madeline explained. "Godfrey and I had a lot of business to attend to here in the great hall as soon as we came in."

"Well." Vanya huffed. "Now that you're back, you're under my stewardship again."

The librarian turned to Arius and Berig before grabbing her goblet that Elja had already filled with wine when the table was set.

"Thank you, boys, for keeping her safe on your trip to Pskov." Sister Vanya's tone was far sweeter than Madeline had ever heard before. "I'm really getting too old to be doing much travel when it starts getting cold like this."

"Our pleasure." Arius gave a hearty smile.

"Anything for our dear sister." Berig grinned.

Madeline twitched in annoyance. The twins were always trying to do something to get under her skin. She had never imagined that making friends with the castle's librarian would be one of them.

Before Madeline could reply to the twins, Godfrey resumed his place at the high table. Arius and Berig quickly shut their mouths as if afraid of being heard in Godfrey's presence. At least they respected Godfrey's authority as a duke.

"Candac will stay." Godfrey indicated the squire. "I will knight him first thing in the morning. He served well on crusade, and he played a big part in putting down the goblin rebellion down in the mine. The honor is overdue."

"Shouldn't he have to complete some quest to prove he is worthy of being knighted?" Madeline asked.

"That's true in many cases," Godfrey confessed. "I had to slay a vampire at Kurl Keep to prove my worth, but Candac has seen plenty of combat while on crusade. Besides, after Sir Garic's death, I think being knighted will raise his spirits."

"My lord couldn't think to send Candac on some token errand to prove his valor?" Berig quipped. "The boy can't be more than fifteen years old."

"Tomorrow happens to be Candac's sixteenth birthday." Godfrey tapped the table emphatically. "I think knighting him tomorrow is an appropriate celebration."

"Look around." Arius gestured to the chamber before them. "Lord Godfrey has fewer than a dozen knights here at the evening meal. If he doesn't do something quick, he'll need to start elevating peasants to knighthood."

Berig sniggered. Godfrey blushed but made no reply. Madeline's eyes darted between him and the twins. Godfrey would not stand to see Madeline vexed by Arius and Berig, but the twins were quickly learning what boundaries they could push with Godfrey himself. Madeline gave Godfrey an earnest look. His humility would cost him.

"Kovdor's lack of knights is your problem too," Godfrey said at last.

"Father should be coming with at least a hundred," Berig answered smoothly.

"They will help keep *our* counties safe from the Clans." Arius smiled wryly.

"Godfrey hasn't given out your fiefs yet," Madeline reminded the twins.

Arius and Berig's expressions grew more somber, though the effect was not as great as the first time Godfrey had threatened to give them poor fiefs. He had also told Roltar and Mauger, who were now filling their plates at the high table, that he would be reorganizing the duchy soon, so that line would not work for much longer anyway.

"My understanding was that Duke Tancred was installing you as counts under me for the express purpose of protecting Madeline." There was a dangerous weight behind each of Godfrey's words. "I will make sure you do not fail in that duty."

The twins exchanged worried glances. Mouthing some unheard reprimand, Berig shoved Arius' shoulder. A line had been crossed, and they all knew it.

"Anything for our dear sister," Arius said with more sincerity than Berig did the first time.

At last, Walaric and Izold found their way into the great hall and up to the high table. Both hung their heads low and said little as they filled their plates. Godfrey, apparently unaware of their subdued attitudes, practically jumped from his seat at the sight of Walaric.

"Where have you been all day?" Godfrey threw his hands out in exasperation.

"The library," Walaric answered gravely.

"For what?" Madeline leaned forward in her chair as her interest was piqued.

"We have an undead problem," Izold explained.

"I was told about the ghouls." Godfrey crossed his arms. "I thought destroying the runestone should have been the end of it all for us."

"There's more at work here." Walaric swallowed hard. "I saw Nera's ghost."

Everyone at the high table fell silent. They all turned to Walaric expectantly. Arius' and Berig's mouths hung open while Roltar's and Mauger's eyes went wide. Jordan and Karl stopped eating for the first time since they sat down at the table. Even Godfrey went pale at the mention of the Great Witch of the North's name. Only Izold and Sister Vanya appeared unaffected.

"Where?" Madeline's mouth gaped.

"In my bedroom." Walaric's lip quivered.

"That was days ago," Izold hastily added. "Walaric performed several rites of exorcism and hasn't seen anything in the castle since then."

With that clarification, the color returned to Godfrey's face, and the others relaxed somewhat. Jordan and Karl swallowed the food that had been sitting in their mouths since Walaric first mentioned Nera. Arius and Berig rolled their eyes, and Madeline sighed in relief. Even though the tension had lessened, everyone's focus still firmly remained on Walaric and Izold.

"But we fear the ghost's reluctance to move on to the afterlife, and the presence of ghouls so close to Olso Fortress is a sign of something worse," the paladin continued as his gaze met Godfrey's. "The undead are beginning to stir throughout all the Nordslands. I have seen it. We need answers."

"Could Ragnarok be drawing near?" Godfrey swallowed hard. "The legends say it's supposed to get colder and the undead grow more restless as we get closer to the end of the world."

All fell silent. No one wanted to consider the final freezing doom of the world that had been prophesied so long ago. Most believed the end of the world to be many generations away. Yet there were doomsayers, and omens could not be ignored.

"Did you find any answers in the library?" Madeline wondered aloud.

"Nothing promising yet." Walaric gave a heavy sigh.

"Patience," Sister Vanya spoke up. "There are many books to consult in the library still. More may yet be revealed. Have patience."

Madeline cocked an eyebrow in surprise. It was rare for her to agree with something the old librarian said. It was rarer for her to find genuine wisdom in her words.

The meal continued quietly for some time. Eventually, Elja, Thieda, and the other servants began clearing away dirty dishes from the table as Godfrey's retainers and his guests slowly departed for the night. Squeezing Godfrey's hand, Madeline gave him a brief kiss before excusing herself to her bed chambers. Sister Vanya only gave the subtlest disapproving look at this gesture.

Rosy-fingered Dawn came early the next day. Madeline blearily rubbed the sleep from her eyes as she, Godfrey, and Walaric stood in front of the keep's entrance in the inner courtyard. Before them knelt Candac on the snow-covered ground. Madeline frowned as the squire shivered. The snow was only a foot or so deep. It should hardly have been enough to bother him.

If it had been actively snowing or raining, Godfrey might have held Candac's dubbing ceremony in the great hall or the chapel, but tradition held that cold and heat were not sufficient inconveniences to move this rite indoors. A knight's duty was to endure hardships for his lord.

All of Godfrey's retainers gathered in the courtyard, as well as his guests and some of the serfs who lived closest to the castle walls. They all held their cloaks tight against their bodies as a chill wind swept through the crowd, but those not native to the Nordslands reacted the worst to it. Madeline scoffed. They were just not used to the cold yet.

A few dwarves from the mines, including Patriarch Dachlann, also shivered as they watched the ceremony. Madeline pursed her lips at the dwarves huddling closely. They were also native to the Nordslands, but their kind was more accustomed to the underground, where fierce winds could not bite their noses.

After Walaric offered an invocation in the celestial tongue, Godfrey took a step towards Candac with a drawn sword. He tapped Candac's left shoulder and then the right with the flat of the blade before doing the same to the top of his bowed head.

"With this sword which has been consecrated for the purpose of destroying evil and preserving that which is holy," Godfrey began, "I dub you, Sir Candac, knight of the Duchy of Kovdor."

"I, Candac, swear fealty to you, Duke Godfrey," Candac replied. "Furthermore, I pledge my services to the Duchy of Kovdor for as long as I shall live."

"In return for that service," Godfrey answered, "I grant you a place in my household as my retainer until such time as the needs of the duchy require your services in another office. Take your sword and arise a knight."

Candac stood and took his sword from Godfrey's hands. He sheathed it in the scabbard on his belt as the crowd applauded. Godfrey and Candac briefly embraced and exchanged a few words too quiet for Madeline to hear over the cheering. A light returned to Candac's eyes that had been absent since the death of Sir Garic. There was hope.

A banquet was held back in the keep's great hall to honor both the dubbing ceremony and Candac's birthday. It was not as elaborate as some feasts Madeline had witnessed accompanying the knighting of other nobles, nor were there nearly as many guests, given Candac's lack of kin beyond Bastogne. In fact, much of the food was just leftovers from yesterday's dinner. However, spirits were high among the relatively few who were there at Olso. They needed something to celebrate after so many losses in recent months.

The next day, Leon de Valois arrived at the castle with a few of his knights at Godfrey's request. He was only average height as far as Ostmen went, but he was broad and muscular, filling the doorway as he entered the great hall behind Arius and Berig. Madeline grinned at the sight. Leon had defected from Conrad the Wolf's camp to Godfrey during the crusade between their capture of Olso Fortress and the Clans' attempt to take it back. He had proven a loyal vassal and a strong warrior. He even taught Walaric some basic swordplay techniques during the siege. Yes, Leon de Valois was a welcome sight.

Karl the Hammer entered the chamber next with a small group of his own retainers. He was a grizzled veteran who had long served Godfrey's father, Ulric, back in Bastogne. Godfrey recently granted Karl a larger fief and a handful of knights in Kovdor as a reward for his loyalty. He was a particular favorite Godfrey often spoke highly of.

Then, Count Osvald marched through the great hall's doors shortly after Karl. He was tall, fair, and had fiery red hair. Osvald still wore a Nordsman gilded spectacle helm over his chainmail armor, but he now also wore an Ostman surcoat. On this surcoat was a new coat of arms Madeline did not recognize: a voided blue dragon passant against a white field.

"You are looking at the heraldry of House Rime Wyrm," Godfrey explained as he followed Madeline's gaze.

"*House* Rime Wyrm?" Madeline raised an eyebrow. "When he broke off from Clan Black Dragon, Lord Osvald was calling his people *Clan* Rime Wyrm."

"The missionaries have been making some progress over in Upplad." Godfrey shrugged. "With a new religion comes a bit of *cultural exchange,* as Walaric put it."

"Maybe not too much progress." Madeline frowned as a few of Osvald's wives followed him to the high table.

Lastly, Godfrey's three barons, directly under him, Sir Jordan, Renaud of Vosg, and Sir Govran, entered the great hall. Sir Jordan, Madeline knew from House Loridan before Godfrey had arrived in the Nordslands, but Renaud and Govran were crusaders she had met only briefly before now. Her betrothed had quickly granted these latter two titles and fiefs when he was first named duke of Kovdor, and they had mostly stuck to their estates since then.

The lords Godfrey had summoned, and as many members of their entourages as could, assumed their seats at the high table with Godfrey and Madeline. However, the high table quickly grew crowded, and Sir Jordan and Godfrey's other barons, Renaud of Vosg and Sir Govran, were forced to stand behind the chairs. With a reluctant scowl, Sister Vanya stood in one of the corners of the chamber. Though she watched Madeline like a carrion bird, the old woman was not confining her to the library anymore, at least for important discussions like this.

Roltar and Mauger, though not summoned to this council with Godfrey's vassals, still found places to quietly observe the meeting from the minstrel's gallery. Madeline was unsure of Mauger, but she grimaced at the sight of Roltar. House Hracour had an unfortunate, if not bad, reputation in the Western regions of Azgald, and Roltar's single-minded obsession with Skasgun did nothing to improve that view.

"Welcome, everyone." Godfrey cleared his throat as Walaric bustled into the chamber with a roll of parchment in one hand and a bottle of ink and some quills in the other.

Walaric forced his way to Godfrey's side, and Madeline huffed as she scooted her chair to accommodate him. Exhaling loudly, the priest spread his parchment across the table in front of him, uncorked the bottle of black ink, and dipped the point of one of his quills into it. Finally, he exchanged a brief nod with Godfrey. Now they were ready.

"Many promises were made over the last few months after the birth of the Duchy of Kovdor," Godfrey began as Walaric transcribed his words onto the parchment. "Some of these arrangements have been formalized through holy rite and ceremony. Others have not. My intention today is to solemnly and publicly rectify this and declare each of your titles and estates. I have asked all of you to bring trustworthy witnesses, and Father Walaric is recording these proceedings for posterity."

A general murmur of assent followed. Furiously, Walaric scribbled down the words almost as quickly as Godfrey spoke. Madeline took pride in her skill with languages and letters, but she soon lost track of what Godfrey was saying as she watched how speedily Walaric performed his task.

"To Lord Osvald of House Rime Wyrm." Godfrey rose from his seat. "The council recognizes his title of count and his possession of the County of Upplad. He is to answer directly to me as his lord, but he is free to further organize baronies within Upplad as he sees fit. Long may be his just reign as he seeks to please the celestial gods."

"Hail Count Osvald, lord of Upplad." Madeline raised her goblet before taking a sip of wine.

"Hail Count Osvald, lord of Upplad," the others chorused with raised goblets before also drinking to him.

"To Lord Karl the Hammer," Godfrey continued after everyone set down their goblets, "the council recognizes a new fief and a new house. The Southwestern region of Kovdor, known as Bormheld, shall now be known as the County of Bormheld. Lord Karl shall be its first count, exercising the same rights and privileges as Count Osvald, and he shall be known as the head of House Bormheld. May his reign be long and prosperous."

"Hail, Lord Karl the Hammer, Count of Bormheld." Madeline toasted Karl as she had Osvald.

The others repeated the toast.

"The council now recognizes the County of Mosjen as Leon de Valois' fief, as he was formerly granted this estate and its accompanying title," Godfrey said as he indicated his next lord. "His rights and privileges shall be considered equal to my other counts. May all my vassals prove as loyal as he and find joy in their reward."

The toast was repeated again. Madeline looked down into her goblet. About half of the dark wine was left. No matter. Only a few vassals still needed their estates assigned.

"To Arius and Berig." Godfrey indicated the twins. "I grant to you the counties of Trondhelm, which is situated between Bormheld and Mosjen, and the northeastern County of Dovard bordering the Volgon River. Take joy in these realms and titles, and serve me well."

Madeline raised her glass to offer a final toast, but Arius shot to his feet. Berig was just a moment behind. Indignation contorted their faces.

"Trondhelm is the smallest region in Western Kovdor," Arius spat.

"And Dovard doesn't border my brother's realm," Berig added.

Godfrey's face also flashed with rage, but he almost instantly regained his composure. His hand trembled slightly, but his expression was placid. Madeline would have expected some objection from the twins. Godfrey apparently did too.

"Most of these fiefs were allotted before Duke Tancred granted me your services." Godfrey clenched his teeth so subtly that Madeline barely noticed. "Show gratitude, and *enjoy* the same rights and privileges as my other counts."

For a moment, Berig's face contorted as if he were about to shout. However, Arius grabbed his brother by the shoulder. The twins exchanged a glance. It was as if a great deal was being communicated through a few brief and slight gestures, but they soon sat down. The twins rarely needed more than that to understand one another.

Madeline smirked as she offered her toast. She may not have understood all that they had conveyed to each other, but she knew her brothers well enough to recognize an element of defeat in their body language. They would not ruin this despite their best efforts.

"As for me," Godfrey said after a moment's pause, "I shall retain the central portion of Kovdor and the Southern peninsula of Vardo as my personal estates with Olso Fortress as the capital. The barons Sir Jordan, Renaud of Vosg, and Sir Govran shall continue to serve directly under me and hold the fiefs previously bequeathed to them."

"Hail, Lord Godfrey de Bastogne, Duke of Kovdor." Madeline raised her bejeweled goblet before draining it into her mouth. "May he lead Kovdor to a glorious future!"

The toast was repeated one last time, and the guests emptied the remaining wine in their goblets. Hastily, Walaric finished his transcription, blew on the drying ink, and rolled the parchment back into a scroll. He handed it off to Sister Vanya, who would undoubtedly store it somewhere safe in the library archives later. Madeline shifted her chair closer to Godfrey, and Walaric awkwardly took his usual place on Godfrey's other side.

"There is a bright and glorious future for Kovdor and the Kingdom of Azgald," Godfrey loudly proclaimed. "Our arms have been tested by the sword and our faith by fire, but we have endured. We still endure, and we will continue to endure!"

A hearty cheer rose at the table.

"If we stand united against the Clans or whatever else may come our way, we will drive them back as we have already." Godfrey thumped his chest with a closed fist.

"Aye!" Leon shouted.

"Aye!" the others chorused.

Madeline's heart swelled at Godfrey's words. This was the leader she knew he could be. This was the young man she had fallen in love with.

"There is still much to do." Godfrey's tone grew sober. "We must honor our dead, heal our wounds, and rebuild these lands we fought so hard to conquer. We are the new Northern Marches of Azgald. We are the northern shield of sacred Vindholm against the Five Clans. I ask everyone here to gather all the strength under our banner that we can. Our very lives depend on that strength."

The lords and knights present looked solemnly at Godfrey. The knights of Azgald were few while its enemies were many. The crusade had brought several stunning victories, but that glory was already beginning to fade.

"Trouble your hearts with these things no more today." Godfrey waved his hand. "Tomorrow's tasks will be waiting for us then. For now, let us eat!"

Elja and Thieda brought out more food and drink for the assembled lords and ladies, but it was somewhat meager even compared to Candac's dubbing ceremony. A few pipers began to play in the minstrel's gallery, and Madeline frowned as she noticed Roltar and Mauger's sudden absence from the chamber. She tugged on Thieda's sleeve as she refilled her goblet. Thieda leaned in.

"Is this all you've prepared?" Madeline whispered.

"Yes, my lady." Thieda pursed her lips.

"It's not a very generous display for our guests, is it?" Madeline furrowed her brow.

"I'm sorry, Lady Madeline." Thieda twitched nervously. "Winter is on our doorstep, and I thought it best to not overindulge while the hard months are still ahead."

"Don't be sorry." Madeline quickly dismissed Thieda's concerns with a soft gesture. "The last few months here have been rough. I just worry a more modest feast will be seen as a sign of weakness."

"We have endured a pretty bad siege." Thieda put a sympathetic hand on Madeline's shoulder. "It didn't end until just before the harvest, and we've had to dig pretty deep into our food stores just to survive. Everyone here understands what we've been through."

"I hope so." Madeline rubbed her temples.

The feast did not last long. However, even if the entertainment's modest scale made a bad impression on the guests, Madeline heard no complaints about it. These men were mostly Godfrey's closest warriors. They understood, Madeline assured herself. Her stomach did not mind the smaller meal at any rate after the Therismos Festival and Candac's knighting.

Soon, the guests began filing out of the great hall as evening approached. Madeline blinked in surprise at the darkness outside the window. The change was gradual, but every day was a little shorter and colder than the day before. Winter proper was almost here.

"You hardly touched your food," Godfrey prodded Walaric. "Are you all right?"

"What's wrong?" Madeline interjected.

"You need to tell them." Izold appeared out of a corner of the chamber with a grave expression written on his face. "No sense in delaying it any longer."

Godfrey, Sir Jordan, Elja, and Madeline all stood frozen in place. Their eyes were fixed on Walaric. What was he so afraid to tell them?

"I have to go." Walaric rose from the table.

"Go where?" Godfrey raised an eyebrow.

"To the Blighted Lands." Walaric shook nervously.

"Why would you speak such madness?" Elja set the pile of dirty dishes in her hands back on the table.

"Nera's ghost," Walaric explained. "I dreamed she left the castle and went to the Blighted Lands."

"I don't understand." Sir Jordan tilted his head. "Isn't that good? We're finally rid of her curse on Olso."

"No, we're not." Walaric shook his head. "I found one of Nera's journals we missed earlier in the library. There is a passage in it describing a deal she made with something called the Keeper of Souls. I think that pact is what is keeping her in the mortal sphere, even after all these exorcism attempts."

"But she's gone from here," Elja protested. "Let that be enough for us."

"Powerful necromancers dwell in the Blighted Lands." Walaric shook his head. "What if she stirs the dark powers that slumber there?"

"With ghouls gathering in the woods to the south, I'd say the undead are already fully awake." Godfrey frowned.

"Send me." Walaric gulped. "Send me after Nera to the Blighted Lands. I can't say anything for certain, but I feel that I need to go there and confront the Keeper of Souls as quickly as I can."

"Alone?" Elja asked.

"No." Izold stepped forward. "I will go with him. I have been there before. Grant us a small number of knights for this quest, and we will put an end to this matter once and for all."

"I can do better than that." Godfrey smiled ruefully. "I'll lead us to the Keeper of Souls myself."

"Lord Godfrey," Sir Jordan interjected. "You already promised Roltar to plead his case before the King at Vindholm. Let me lead the party to the Blighted Lands. I know the way. You do not."

"But this is more important," Godfrey huffed.

"We don't know that," Madeline countered. "We only have a dream and a journal entry to go on right now. You can't break a promise to your kin over that. Also, I need you back here for the wedding. Traveling to the Blighted Lands will take all winter. I can't have you gone for that long."

"I could fly Spathi…" Godfrey began.

"Godfrey." Walaric grabbed his friend by the shoulder. "Let me do this without you. This is *my* quest. I don't know what the Keeper of Souls is or what dangers it may bring, but I can find out without you. Don't delay your marriage any further on my account."

"The undead are dangerous." Godfrey creased his lips into a frown. "I couldn't…"

"You can't be everywhere at once, Godfrey." Madeline stood directly in front of him with her hands on her hips. "Izold and Jordan are going with Walaric. They know the way. Send Candac too so that he can prove his worth as a knight and Sir Paschal so that he may redeem his honor, but you be where you promised to be."

"I'll be where I promised to be." Godfrey slumped in his chair as if he had lost a great battle.

Chapter Four

The next morning came too soon for Godfrey. Dread filled the pit of his stomach from the moment he woke up. Blearily, he rummaged around his bedroom in the darkness. He dressed himself in his gambeson, trousers, and boots before donning his chainmail hauberk, coif, and mailed gloves.

It was his usual custom to prepare himself in the full panoply of war when he intended to leave the castle grounds at any point during the day. The world was dangerous. It was best to be ready for anything.

Grabbing his blue tabard, he frowned at the white griffin rampant emblazoned upon it. Sending others, especially Walaric, on an important quest while he stayed behind did not suit him well at all. He clenched his jaw. He would not stay behind long. He had to travel to Vindholm at the outset of winter with Roltar and Mauger to plead for Skasgun to be returned to House Hracour. It seemed trivial by comparison, but he had already promised he would do it.

"Being a duke is more than adventuring." Godfrey sighed at the heraldic griffin. "Sometimes our duties take us down more *mundane* paths."

After sliding the tabard over his head, he fixed his sword belt to his waist. His sheathed blade, secured to the belt by a leather frog, sagged against his side. Uriel, his magical sword, was a gift from the gods. With it, he had destroyed a vampire, a dragon, a demon-possessed grimoire, and countless other agents of evil. Why should Walaric's quest not be his, too?

Taking a deep breath, he scooped up his spangenhelm from its helmet stand on the table and set it atop his head. Next, he grabbed the guige of his shield and removed it from the hook that mounted it to the wall as he slept during the night. After slinging his shield onto his back, he caught a glimpse of himself in the mirror just as the morning's first light cracked through his window. He froze as he took note of the fierce expression his reflection bore. For someone who had already promised not to go on this quest, he sure looked determined to do so.

Scoffing, he adjusted the chin strap of his spangenhelm and left the room. His stomach grumbled, but he had to go to the chapel for the morning prayer service before he could eat. So much of life was about being where others expected him to be.

Entering the chapel, Godfrey assumed his usual spot in the front pew next to Madeline. She raised an eyebrow at him as he took his seat. Trying to ignore her, Godfrey focused on Walaric as he began chanting in the celestial tongue while swinging a censer filled with burning incense.

"Going somewhere this morning?" Madeline muttered under her breath.

"Not far," Godfrey murmured back.

"Father should be here today or tomorrow to discuss the wedding plans." Madeline pursed her lips. "You'd better not be going anywhere."

"I just wanted to see Walaric off after breakfast," Godfrey explained.

"Fine." Madeline sighed.

The prayer ended, and Walaric bade the congregation to rise. Godfrey, Madeline, and everyone else present complied. The priest began chanting another prayer in the holy tongue, and he paused briefly after each line so that the congregation could repeat it as they went.

At one point, Godfrey had the lines of this prayer translated for him, but that was years ago, and he had long since forgotten exactly what each word meant. The general ideas consisted of professing his faith and promising to act with honesty and virtue at all times. Though he generally felt these were already strengths of his, a twinge of guilt stirred as he recalled the long weeks he had spent moping after Turpin's death.

The second prayer ended, but no sooner had Godfrey finished his recitation than Walaric gestured for the congregation to kneel. Stiffly, Godfrey grunted. He bent his knees as he lowered himself onto the cold, hard floor in front of the altar, as Walaric led them in the third and last prayer of the morning.

Godfrey, likewise, had no more hope of remembering the finer details of this prayer than any of the others he had said or heard during the service. It had something to do with repentance and supplication, but that was little more than a safe guess Godfrey could have easily made based on the congregation's current attitude of kneeling before Walaric.

Godfrey's thoughts turned once more to the events of the siege. He had lost the Sun's blessing upon his sword after trying to avenge Turpin's death. The sortie had been in vain and only resulted in the needless deaths of more crusaders. Since then, he had repented, and Uriel sparkled as it had before, but he should have listened to his friends from the beginning.

The last prayer ended, and Godfrey shook this final thought from his mind as he stood. He *had* repented. There was no use dwelling on the past. No one spoke of his shame. He had to focus on the present and the future.

After breakfast, Godfrey, Madeline, and Walaric marched from the keep to Izold as he stood by the inner gate. Walaric carried one of the fine brass goblets from the chapel with him. In it was a deep pink wine. Godfrey's mind was so preoccupied with Walaric's impending journey that, by the time he thought to ask about the goblet of wine, he was too embarrassed to.

Meanwhile, Sir Paschal, Candac, and Jordan approached the gate from other parts of the courtyard. A light, powdery snow crunched beneath Spathi's feet as Godfrey led his griffin out of his pen by the reins. Nothing would grow again until spring.

Elja and Thieda also followed just behind Godfrey, Madeline, and Walaric. Elja probably came on account of Walaric and had convinced Thieda to come too. Her infatuation with the priest was fairly obvious to everyone at Olso by now.

"Too bad for both of them," Godfrey muttered under his breath.

Madeline gave Godfrey a quizzical look but said nothing. He pretended not to notice as they walked the last few paces to Izold, Candac, Paschal, and Jordan. There was nothing to say. They all knew what was ahead.

Izold stood next to his brown and white speckled stallion nearest to the gate. The creature's caparison of yellow and green matched the paladin's heraldry. The horse snorted. Its regal bearing put to shame all other steeds Godfrey had ever seen.

"This is Vielantiu." Izold patted his mount's side as the others came closer. "Where are the other horses?"

"I lost Moon Frost the same day Godfrey lost Baruch." Walaric lowered his eyes to the goblet of wine he clutched in his hands.

"Sir Garic lost his horse in the siege." Candac frowned. "He didn't have a spare to pass on to me."

"I haven't been able to afford a new steed for a while," Paschal sulked.

"Boreas was a timely gift from my father back at Pskov's Therismos Festival." Jordan gripped his mount's reins tighter as he took a defensive step closer to his steed. "But I'm afraid he can't bear all of us on this quest."

Everyone looked to Godfrey expectantly.

"I wish I had some to spare," Godfrey said. "We lost a lot in the siege, and most of the remaining horses now travel back to the Ostlands with their masters."

"Winter weather wasn't going to make traveling fast," Izold added, "with or without horses."

"So, it will take us a little longer to get to the Blighted Lands," Walaric quipped. "That's all right. The gods will provide for us what we cannot."

Godfrey smiled. Optimism was needed here. The journey would be perilous enough for them.

"Let us pray." Walaric bowed his head while raising his goblet aloft.

Godfrey looked at Madeline. She nodded before bowing her head. The others repeated the gesture.

"Loxias, Sol, Helios, or whatever other name the Sun wishes to be called this day," Walaric began, "hear my words. I feel inspired that I should pursue Nera's shade to the Blighted Lands. To what end, I do not know. All that I know is that I should lead these few with me to whatever fate you have in store for us."

Tensing as Walaric prayed, Godfrey opened his eyes and glanced at the priest's bowed head. His goblet glinted in the morning sun. It should have been Godfrey to go on this errand with Walaric. He had Uriel. He had a griffin.

"Bless us on our journey, o Sun," Walaric continued. "Protect us, your servants, from your hated foes, help us to discover the secrets of the Keeper of Souls, and accept this libation as a holy offering. Amen."

"Amen," Godfrey and the others chorused.

After opening his eyes, Walaric lifted his head and poured the wine out of the goblet onto the ground in front of him. The liquid stained the snow pink as it briefly melted before freezing again.

"Ice berry wine," Madeline noted. "Very expensive."

"Only the best to honor Helios." Walaric nodded as he handed the goblet to her.

"A little sour for my tastes," Godfrey muttered.

"You don't know a good thing when it's right in front of you." Madeline shook her head.

Godfrey frowned at the way she said that last statement. Was Madeline talking about more than just the wine? It was still too early for him to sort out any hidden meanings that may or may not have been in her words.

Izold and Jordan mounted their horses. Hurriedly, Godfrey jumped into Spathi's saddle. The inner gate creaked open, and Godfrey led his griffin through at a slow trot as Izold, Walaric, Paschal, Candac, and Jordan followed.

"Promise you'll come back," Elja called out.

Izold gave Walaric a stern gaze from atop Vielantiu.

"I promise I'll come back." Walaric's cheeks flushed red as he met Elja's gaze. "But not for you. I'm a priest. Remember that."

Pouting, Elja leaned into Thieda's side. Madeline and Thieda embraced her and whispered consolations he could not hear. Godfrey furrowed his brow as he briefly glanced between Elja and Walaric. The priest hid his face beneath his cloak's hood as they continued through the gate into the outer courtyard. It had to be done, Godfrey told himself.

Serfs doing their morning chores and footmen patrolling the grounds bade their farewells to Walaric's party as Godfrey led them to the outer gate. The mood was somber.

None at Olso had been to the Blighted Lands before, but all had a healthy fear of the undead.

After they had all passed through the outer gate, Godfrey led Spathi out a few paces farther before turning to the others. Izold's expression was determined, and Jordan's grim, but Candac and Walaric appeared less certain. Paschal refused to meet Godfrey's gaze, as though he were contemplating his certain doom.

"I could still lead you on this quest," Godfrey implored. "Let me help you with this."

"No." Walaric smiled ruefully.

"I don't understand." Godfrey clenched his fist around the hilt of his sheathed sword. "It seems wrong that one endowed such as I should not be involved with something so important."

There was so much more Godfrey wanted to say that he did not dare. Perhaps if it were just Walaric, he could have said what he really wanted to, but the presence of these others he did not know so well kept his mouth shut. If only he had time to confide in Walaric before this morning.

"I already told you." Walaric drew back the hood of his cloak and gestured to the others around him. "You are meant to go with Roltar. These men are meant to come with me. I prayed about each of these companions I have with me now, and I feel confident in this choice. The gods have their purposes. Have faith."

"Have faith," Godfrey repeated before looking at Jordan. "You know the way to the Blighted Lands?"

"Yes, Lord." Sir Jordan spurred his steed to the head of Walaric's party. "It's a long journey past the Eastern Marches, but I will take us there."

"And I have some familiarity with the area," Izold added. "Arktos has led me this far."

"I can ask for no better guides than Sir Jordan and the seven lights of the Northern Bear." Godfrey relaxed his grip on Uriel's hilt. "Very well. The gods be with you on this quest. May I see you all return safe soon."

With that, Godfrey spurred his griffin down the path. Spathi ran several paces before kicking off the ground. He flapped his wings hard and was soon flying above the fields in a wide circle.

Jordan led Walaric, Izold, and the others down the road east. Pensively, as Spathi continued to glide over the snowy fields and the men grew farther away, Godfrey watched pensively for a long while from the griffin's saddle. He had to have faith that the gods had their reasons. Could it really be something as trivial as already promising to take Roltar and Mauger to Vindholm that prevented him from journeying to the Blighted Lands with Walaric?

His cousin was nearly ever present in Olso's great hall; a silent if not constant reminder of the promise Godfrey had made. He wanted to help his kin. Allowing a noble house to dwindle into extinction was a fate he did not wish on anyone. Yet there was the wedding, seeing to the recovery of Kovdor after the siege, and now this business with the Keeper of Souls, whatever that was. There was so much to do already.

The only thing that really prevented Godfrey from going off to the Blighted Lands with Walaric was the uncertainty of what it was they needed to accomplish in the first place. Were he sure of the magnitude of the threat posed by the undead, the choice would be clear. However, the priest had shared few details about why he felt he should go, so it was hard for Godfrey to articulate a good reason for putting everything else aside in favor of this quest.

Once Walaric was finally out of sight, Godfrey determined to let Spathi do one more loop around the fields before retiring to the castle. His gaze wandered to the Wyrmwind Peaks up north. Somewhere out there were the elves of Farthest Thule. Surely, they could have helped. Would he ever be able to find them, or at least retrace his steps to Luka and the Watch Tower of Uvalin?

Godfrey sighed. Tyche had granted him the opportunity to come across one elf, and that was it. He and Madeline had hoped to find the fabled northern refuge of the elves in order to bring much-needed reinforcements to the crusade. Instead, he had found a single exile from Farthest Thule who had gifted him his griffin companion. Not that Godfrey begrudged such a magnificent gift. Spathi had proven not only a loyal friend but also instrumental in all of Godfrey's adventures since.

For several days after Walaric and the others left, Godfrey made excuses to spend much of his time out patrolling the skies with Spathi. Sister Vanya kept Madeline with her in the library most days, leaving him alone to entertain Roltar and Mauger. Mauger seemed more interested in winning either Elja's or Thieda's heart than anything else, but Roltar was persistent in reminding Godfrey of their pressing need to go to Vindholm. Since Godfrey could not make good on his promise until after finalizing the wedding plans with Madeline's father, it was just easier to avoid his cousin.

One morning, after many weary days patrolling the cold skies, Godfrey's eyes drifted to the fields near the castle. He frowned at several sets of footprints that broke up the otherwise undisturbed sheets of snow covering much of the ground. They led from Kolsmarden Forest beyond the farmers' fields to where the Nordsman dead from the siege had been buried and back. Several small holes had been dug into the mass grave, and a few bones jutted from the snow. Godfrey huffed contemptuously.

"We can do something about that, at least." Godfrey indicated the footprints to Spathi. "Come on."

The griffin tilted in the direction of the footprints and glided down to the snowy fields. Flaring his wings, Spathi landed just outside the forest's edge. After dismounting, Godfrey drew his sword and shield.

"Let's purge the ghouls from these lands once and for all." Godfrey gestured with his sparkling blade.

Creeping through the woods, Godfrey followed the footprints into Kolsmarden Forest with Spathi close behind. As the trees grew thick, the griffin kept his wings close to his flanks. It was not an ideal environment for a beast accustomed to open fields and high mountains, but even a magical sword was not enough comfort for Godfrey to face the ghouls alone.

A dark mist began to cover the ground as Godfrey and Spathi ventured deeper into the woods, and he soon lost track of the footprints he had been following. The cold bit his nose. It was unnaturally bitter, even for winter in Azgald.

"Don't be scared, Spathi." Godfrey's hand shook.

Memories flashed before him of some of his earliest combats as a squire only a few years ago. He had faced the undead before in Lortharain. Animated skeletons were unnerving, vampires were powerful, but zombies and ghouls were the worst.

He stopped in his tracks as he relived the vision of hordes of these repugnant creatures ripping apart still-living knights and footmen as they devoured their flesh. Godfrey and another squire about his age, Digoth, stood at the rear of a group of spearmen. The formation held as the men-at-arms plunged their spears into the oncoming horde, but soon gave way from the sheer press of zombies and ghouls before them. He could not look away as Digoth was pulled to the ground by a pack of these fetid creatures, yet he was powerless to stop it. It was not the screaming or the blood, but the pleading in Digoth's eyes that first made Godfrey's hand begin to shake in genuine terror.

His cousin, Fallard, and a group of other knights mounted on their horses soon swooped in from the flank and trampled over the horde, but it was far too late for what remained of Digoth. More knights, squires, and footmen fell around Godfrey, but he was rooted to the spot. He could not move or even think, much less draw his sword. Another squire, an older boy named Torold, sprang into action to save his fallen lord when he was dragged off his horse. Yet Godfrey could only stand in place, numb to all for the remainder of that battle.

The mists sustaining the undead began to dissipate. Godfrey was not sure how much time had passed, but a triumphant cry rose among the Ostmen that the necromancer controlling the undead army was destroyed. As the mists faded, the ghouls, zombies, and other undead horrors began to crumble to dust or scatter. It was over.

Torold was knighted that day for his bravery. His grateful lord withheld no honors. Fallard said nothing good or ill of Godfrey save some brief comment about holding his own well enough. Somehow, the intended commendation only made Godfrey's blood boil. Fallard did not really see what he had done, or rather, had failed to do. Why could he not save Digoth?

The mists Godfrey stood in now in Kolsmarden Forest reminded him too much of the mists back then. He shook his head and smirked at Spathi's curious amber eyes staring back at him. Taking a deep breath, Godfrey placed himself more firmly in the present. His days as a young squire faded into distant memory once again.

"I'm thinking too much about the past," Godfrey quietly confided. "At age fourteen, I was a lot more scared of the things we're about to face. But we have the gods' blessing, and we have a duty to Kovdor."

Spathi gave a soft chirp.

"We can't control what has already happened," Godfrey continued, "and we can't be everywhere at once, but we are here now. And here we can make a difference."

Taking several strides forward, Godfrey cautiously scanned the misty trees around him. Spathi followed just a few paces behind. Even with such a powerful creature at his back, Godfrey still trembled with each step.

Something caught Godfrey's foot. He stumbled face-first into the snow. When he looked behind him, his fears were soon dismissed. It was just a fallen branch in his path.

Before Godfrey could stand, Spathi's ears twitched. The griffin gave a low hiss. Godfrey's head swiveled. Shadowy creatures stalked around them from every side. The mists gave away only the vaguest forms of these creatures, but the sounds of their shuffling feet and bestial snarling hinted at large numbers all around them.

Frantically, Godfrey scanned the ground. Uriel had slipped from his grasp and was nowhere to be seen. A clawed hand swiped at him, but Godfrey blocked it with his shield. A pair of ghouls lunged at Spathi from either side, but the griffin's powerful talons made short work of them.

Spathi pounced on the ghoul reaching for Godfrey, allowing him to scramble onto his hands and knees. Finally, he caught a glimpse of the sparkling blade in the snow. With a grunt, he dove on top of it.

Another ghoul jumped at Godfrey from behind a tree, but he flashed his blade in front of it. Undead flesh sizzled as it made contact with the holy blade.

Squealing, the monster dropped with a searing gash across its chest. Godfrey turned about, searching for the next enemy. Spathi tore at a foul creature in front of him, but two more launched themselves at the griffin from behind. Yelling, Godfrey charged the snarling undead.

Swinging Uriel in a wide arc, Godfrey cleaved through one of the ghouls at Spathi's back. However, the other monster sank its teeth into the griffin's rear leg. Shrieking, Spathi whirled about and ripped the offending creature to shreds.

More ghouls emerged from the mists in every direction. Godfrey's heart raced. How many were there?

Godfrey bashed a monster with his shield. Desperately, he swung his sword at another. He cleaved through the ghoul's emaciated form before plunging his blade into the one he had just hit with his shield. Spathi, likewise, lashed out at every turn, dropping a hideous, cadaver-like monstrosity with every strike. Yet there was no end in sight to these creatures.

Something tugged at Godfrey's cloak. He jerked, and the fabric gave a long tear. Twisting on the spot, Godfrey found himself mere inches in front of the horrid maw of a sharp-toothed ghoul. Godfrey attempted to shove the creature away, but it still gripped his tattered cloak in its claws. It leaned in, snapping its jaws at Godfrey's face.

With a twang, an arrow struck the monster between its eyes. It reeled back, and Godfrey thrust his sword into the creature's neck. Another stroke of his sword, and he severed the ghoul's spine.

"My lord," Varin called out from the midst of the trees. "It's time to go, my lord!"

"I couldn't agree more," Godfrey answered. "Come on, Spathi. To Varin!"

Hacking and slashing, Godfrey and the griffin cut a path towards Varin. The ranger fired his bow at every target that came within sight, but the arrows, more often than not, stuck harmlessly into the ghouls' bodies. Wounds had to be both wide and deep to drop one of these vile things.

"This way!" Varin started running.

Godfrey knocked over one last ghoul with his shield and ran it through with Uriel's sizzling blade before racing to the ranger. Spathi bounded after them and soon fell in just behind Godfrey. Dozens of ghouls pursued.

Godfrey had no way of knowing how many gave chase, but his heart pounded in his chest too much for him to give it much thought. His legs pumped after Varin as he struggled to keep up. Spathi occasionally pounced on or swiped at a ghoul that got too close to Godfrey as they ran through the trees.

Eventually, the mists cleared ahead of them, and Godfrey could find no trace of their pursuers. Heedless, the ranger continued to run until they had passed well beyond the edge of the forest. His lungs burning, Godfrey sprinted until he almost collided with Varin in the middle of one of the empty fields closer to the fortress.

Godfrey and Varin collapsed on the icy ground. Godfrey's lungs burned. Varin was pale. Even Spathi's sides heaved with fatigue. However, the Sun stood bright over them in the late morning sky. They were safe now.

"Thank you," Godfrey managed between labored breaths. "I didn't realize how many there were in there."

"I don't know where they're coming from." Varin propped himself up on one of his elbows to face Godfrey. "But I would stay out of Kolsmarden Forest for now."

"What do you mean by 'stay out?'" Godfrey rolled over in Varin's direction. "I can't just let these things haunt my lands. I have a duty to Kovdor…"

"Zombies eagerly hunt the living, but ghouls prefer the taste of dead men's flesh and bones." The ranger stood. "They've mostly stuck to the forest, hiding in their mists. They only come out at night to find some moldering corpse in a shallow grave left over from the siege."

"Are they not a danger to us then?" Godfrey stood and sheathed his sword.

"I wouldn't go that far." Varin smiled humorlessly. "But we don't have the men to drive them out at the moment, and I think they'll move on to somewhere else once they've run out of bones to chew on here."

"That's not very comforting." Godfrey's gaze turned back to the woods. "I thought Walaric blessed these grounds three times over. Why are we still seeing ghouls here at all, Varin?"

"A powerful curse needs a powerful blessing to undo it, but more than that, I can't say." Varin shrugged. "Best we can hope for is they may start to cannibalize each other if they don't leave of their own accord."

"Ghouls eat each other?" Nausea filled the pit of Godfrey's stomach.

"Sometimes when they're desperate enough," Varin said. "Let's get back to the castle now. I came to get you because you've had a few more guests arrive, and none of them are too happy to see each other."

Spathi gave a low chirp.

"Can you tend to my griffin's wounds?" Godfrey asked. "I don't want ghoul rot setting in."

"Personally," Varin confessed, "I'd rather do that than face your guests."

A tall, broad-framed man with long, dark hair was sitting at the high table when Godfrey entered Olso's great hall. A white dragon was emblazoned on his red tabard. The House Drois coat of arms would have instantly told Godfrey this was Tancred, the duke of Pavik, even from a great distance. But, more importantly, this was Madeline's father.

Tancred had done much to try to sabotage Godfrey and Madeline's relationship at first. However, Godfrey eventually proved courageous enough in Tancred's eyes, and Madeline persisted in her preference for him over Conrad the Wolf. Eventually, the Duke agreed to let them marry.

Godfrey snorted at the idea of thinking of Tancred as *the Duke* any longer. He was a duke now, too. Kovdor was his realm, and he was Tancred's peer, theoretically, at least.

Madeline and Sister Vanya sat next to Tancred. While Godfrey's heart sang briefly at the sight of his beloved, Tancred's sneer instantly dampened whatever joy he felt a moment before. Godfrey could never really be happy in Tancred's presence.

While the sight of the duke of Pavik's cross face was familiar enough to Godfrey, he had to blink several times in befuddlement before he recognized the target of Tancred's withering gaze. At the other end of the high table sat a grizzled Silver Sun in his mid-forties. A web-like scar covered half of the thickly built man's face, and he carried a flanged mace on his belt.

This was Morgan the Bloodied, grand master of the Order of the Silver Sun. He returned Tancred's unpleasant sneer, and for good reason as far as Godfrey was concerned. Tancred had betrayed the crusade by demanding a ransom be paid to him in exchange for returning Epsberg to the Silver Suns after its capture. Whether this scheme was fueled by sheer opportunism or some older, unsettled grudge, Godfrey could not say. In either case, it was foiled only by Godfrey's personal intervention on Morgan's behalf.

Next to Morgan was a venerable, balding priest Godfrey had never seen before. The older man held his tongue, but his eyes narrowed suspiciously at the duke of Pavik. Did he have some personal grudge against Tancred as well, or was it by extension of some friendship with the grand master of the Silver Suns?

Not far from this tense scene, Roltar leaned against a wall in the corner. His posture was aloof, but his eyes followed Godfrey through the chamber with a predatory intensity. Godfrey pretended not to see his cousin. He already knew what *he* wanted.

The present company at the table said little, though Godfrey could guess at least some of the insults Tancred and Morgan would have liked to exchange under other circumstances. Tucking his spangenhelm under his arm, he cleared his throat as he approached. Everyone's focus shifted to him. Tancred and Morgan's mutual venom for each other did not fade when they turned to Godfrey, but Madeline relaxed a little, at least.

"You look like you took quite a beating," Madeline gasped as her eyes darted from his head to his feet.

"I'm fine." Godfrey cringed.

He took a deep breath. Madeline and the others exchanged skeptical glances. Stretching his arms wide, Godfrey grinned as he approached the guests. Madeline pursed her lips in response.

"Welcome," Godfrey said once he stood close enough to the high table for comfort. "Duke Tancred of Pavik, I've been expecting, but Morgan the Bloodied I was not. What brings you here, Grand Master?"

"Walaric wrote to me," Morgan explained. "He said you wanted to donate a fief to the Order."

"And some funds to build a castle on that fief." Godfrey scratched his chin as he recalled the penance Walaric had prescribed to him after he temporarily lost Uriel's blessing. "Sorry, I did not know he reached out to you about this already."

"He did when he informed me that he was going to be leaving Olso for a time and that a new priest was needed here." Morgan indicated the elderly man beside him. "May I introduce Father Edric?"

Godfrey bowed his head respectfully. He tried to conceal his frown at Father Edric but had little success. He knew Walaric would be gone for a while, and at least a short-term substitute would be required to fulfill the day-to-day religious duties at Olso. He cleared his throat again.

"You'll have to forgive me, Father Edric," Godfrey said. "Walaric did not discuss calling in a substitute with me. We haven't prepared a room for you."

"I'm not substituting for Father Walaric." Edric tilted his head. "I'm replacing him."

Godfrey's jaw dropped. Madeline bit her lip. Even Roltar raised an eyebrow at this.

"Father Walaric could be gone for some months on his journey to the Blighted Lands," Edric continued, "and there is no guarantee he will come back at all."

"He has the paladin, Izold, with him," Godfrey protested. "He said he had been to the Blighted Lands before. Surely, that counts for something."

"And three of Godfrey's knights are also part of that quest," Madeline added.

"I know Father Walaric is a friend of yours." Edric threw up a placating hand. "But few return from quests to the Blighted Lands. Entire crusades have been swallowed up by that cursed realm."

"Still," Tancred cut in. "Walaric would have done well to request a replacement from his direct superior, Bishop Manfred, rather than reaching out to the Silver Suns. He should have known better."

"He felt he needed to leave quickly," Godfrey answered. "He may have wanted to avoid the burden of writing too many letters in his haste. I care less about what order the priests of my realm come from than their ability to fulfill their duties."

"I'm also a priest of Helios," Edric added. "And you'll find that I can fulfill the necessary duties quite thoroughly. A far more experienced hand is required out here on the borders of the Five Clans. I will see the gods smile on Kovdor soon enough."

"Now, Walaric was doing a good enough job here." Godfrey bristled at Edric's last statement.

"The Nordsmen of Kovdor have accepted many doctrines of the Church." Edric tilted his head from one side to the other. "But Count Osvald still insists on keeping all of his wives and concubines. We cannot let that stand."

"How can I tell one of my subjects to divorce all but one of his wives?" Godfrey threw out his hands in exasperation. "None of us likes it, but can I give such a command in the first place? Walaric told me some of the old patriarchs in scripture had more than one wife."

"That was in ancient times." Edric waved dismissively. "The Church will continue to teach correct doctrines, and its subjects must obey."

Godfrey awkwardly shifted his gaze.

"The Church's will cannot be resisted, Father Edric," Tancred replied smoothly. "And, though you have much experience with holy things, I'm sure, you show yourself to be a novice to the Nordslands. Where did you come from before the Silver Suns sent you to us?"

"I came from Albionne before arriving at Helsirki last year," Edric confessed. "I spent sixteen years preaching at Ipswick before coming to the Nordslands."

"I thought that was a Cardigalian accent." Tancred smirked. "You'll find the Nordsmen do not give up all of their bad practices so easily. We don't want the few who are willing to work with us defecting back to the Clans at the first excuse we give them."

With a look of mild confusion written on his face, Edric glanced over at Morgan the Bloodied. The Grand Master nodded, apparently conceding Tancred's point. It made sense to Godfrey, at least.

"True enough," the old priest stammered. "We will work out some of these bad practices in time, I'm sure."

"I'll have someone show you around and prepare a room for you." Godfrey gestured to one of the footmen guarding the great hall's main entrance.

The footman led Father Edric out of the great hall towards the chapel. Madeline sighed as her gaze followed the old priest out of the chamber. Edric was no Walaric.

"Now, about your donation to the Order." Morgan raised an eyebrow at Godfrey.

"Yes," Godfrey agreed. "I was thinking an estate in Dovard or Upplad. Both counties border on the Clans."

"My brother Berig will be furious if you give part of his county over to the Silver Suns," Madeline cautioned.

"Upplad it is, then." Godfrey huffed. "Send word to Count Osvald that the Silver Suns will help fortify his realm against further Clan and orc incursions."

"Don't you believe Lord Osvald will feel slighted at having to surrender part of his fief?" Sister Vanya asked. "He will have some complaints once he realizes the Silver Suns will not be operating as his vassals."

"I'll lessen some of the Count's feudal obligations if he complains," Godfrey said to Sister Vanya, thinking of what his father might have done in a similar situation.

Morgan the Bloodied nodded at Godfrey.

"The dwarves down in the mint should have enough silver collected to pay for a suitable fortress." Godfrey turned back directly to Morgan. "Speak with my new overseer, Dachlann. He's the dwarf patriarch with the thick blonde beard."

"Upplad has better farmland than Dovard," Morgan noted. "A Silver Sun castle there will be of greater strategic value to the Order."

"I'm glad you approve." Godfrey and the Grand Master clasped each other's arm as they stood.

After this brief gesture, Morgan the Bloodied left the great hall with his footsteps echoing after him. Now it was just Madeline, Tancred, and Sister Vanya at the high table. Madeline gave Godfrey a worried glance.

"You know how much money it costs to build a new stone castle?" Madeline asked.

"There should be enough in the treasury." Godfrey frowned. "I checked earlier."

"Yes." Madeline gritted her teeth. "But we won't have anything left."

"Winter will be a little lean," Godfrey conceded. "But the dwarves are always mining. You said yourself that there is enough silver under us to support our children's children's children. We'll refill our coffers before too long, I think."

"I wouldn't have donated a fief to the Silver Suns if I were you." Tancred rolled his eyes. "That could've been a fortress, garrison, and vassal that all answered directly to you… But Kovdor's not my duchy, and I suppose you know what's best for your realm."

Godfrey's eyes darted around the room. He held back from saying anything about his penance in front of Tancred, Sister Vanya, or Roltar. They did not need to know anything more about that than they already did.

"Fortunate for you that it's the bride's family that traditionally bears the financial responsibility of a wedding." Tancred leaned forward in his seat.

"I'm glad we've finally come to that." Godfrey clenched his teeth.

Godfrey took his seat next to his betrothed. Clasping his hand, Madeline gave him an earnest look. Godfrey smiled back. They were allowed to be happy for a moment, at least. Ghouls, Nordsmen, and who should really be in charge of Skasgun could all wait.

"Winter will be too cold for most people to travel," Tancred began.

"So, let's hold the wedding on the first day of spring," Godfrey eagerly finished. "That will be Madeline's eighteenth birthday."

"Wonderful!" Madeline blushed.

"That will still be rough on Grandmother Annora and Aunt Moschia." Tancred scowled. "But I suppose we'll just have to find a way to bring them here."

"We need to also send invitations to Uncle Hilderic and Aunt Annina." Madeline began counting on her fingers as she rattled off names. "Oh, and don't forget Uncle Gerold or Aunt Collette."

Sister Vanya began to feverishly scribble down the list of names on a sheet of parchment with a quill that Godfrey only now took notice of. He had only the vaguest idea who most of these people were. Soon, his thoughts drifted towards High Warlord Alvir as Madeline and Tancred listed off several more names.

Roltar said something, but Godfrey was too deep in his own thoughts to care. Was the High Warlord preparing to strike out at Azgald again after recovering from his losses? Was he also having trouble with the undead? Might the Clan lords under Alvir be plotting a revolt after so many defeats? There was no way to know for certain. If he could send a spy to the Five Clans… Maybe Varin…

"And who else should we invite, Godfrey?" Madeline gently squeezed his hand.

Godfrey blinked several times. Sister Vanya's quill pensively hovered over the guest list as the old woman rolled her eyes at him. Who *should* he invite?

"Well." Godfrey tried to peek at the names already on the list. "There's my cousin, Fallard. He has estates in Tyrol back in Lortharain. We should send his invitation to Bres. A messenger will find him there during winter."

"Who else?" Madeline asked eagerly.

"Well, all of my knights here at the castle and my vassals throughout Kovdor should be there." Godfrey tensed his muscles. "King Lothar needs an invitation."

"They're already on the list." Madeline rapped her fingers across the table. "Is there anyone else back in Lortharain you want to invite?"

Godfrey paused for a long moment. He did not have much family in Bastogne anymore. There was no one else he was close to anyway.

"I can't think of anyone else right now." Godfrey shrugged in embarrassment. "My parents are dead, and so is Turpin. I think most of the people I care about are already here in Azgald."

"If you do think of anyone else, we can always send an invitation later." Madeline touched his shoulder.

"But think fast." Roltar stepped up to the high table. "Winter is coming, and we need to go to Vindholm now."

Chapter Five

Snow poured in heavy sheets for days on end as Walaric traveled along the road to Pskov with Izold, Jordan, Candac, and Paschal. The journey was slow. Though Izold and Jordan rode their horses for much of it, Candac, Walaric, and Paschal were obliged to make their way on foot. The snow and wind continued, no matter how much Walaric prayed for better weather.

The white flurries were so dense that Walaric could barely see past Sir Jordan on his dapple grey stallion at the head of the group. Walaric nodded in determination at the distant stone bridge barely visible ahead of them. There was a reason for all of this.

"Your horse is aptly named, Sir Jordan." Walaric trudged through the snow almost up to his knees. "But this blizzard makes me wonder if the god of the north wind is not displeased with how you treat his namesake."

"Boreas eats better than I most days," Jordan quipped. "He's as spoiled as they come."

"Perhaps the North Wind is chastising you for indulging him," Izold suggested. "A little hunger can help keep a man or steed sharp."

"Or thin, at any rate," Paschal muttered.

"Must you always be so glum?" Walaric asked.

"Berimund the Brash's humor did him no favors in the end." Paschal shot Walaric a dark look.

"You're just sore everyone thinks you're a coward after the way they found you at the end of the siege." Candac jeered at Paschal.

"Don't tempt me," Paschal glowered.

"I'm not trying to tempt you to do anything." Candac recoiled. "Don't get so upset. It doesn't matter what Vonig the Cold, Sir Berold, or Sigibald of Fulda says. You'll have plenty of opportunities to regain your honor on this quest."

Paschal's eyes narrowed dangerously.

"We have a long journey ahead of us." Walaric stepped in between Candac and Paschal. "Let's watch our tongues for now. Shall we?"

Paschal muttered something under his breath about Candac being an unproven whelp, but Walaric cleared his throat loudly to silence any reply Candac might have attempted. Walaric was clearly the youngest of the group, and he deferred to Izold or Jordan in most matters, but his office as a priest granted him some measure of authority. It was enough to stifle any further argument for now, at least.

Soon, the ancient bridge ahead of the group became more distinct as Walaric and his company drew nearer. Like the road and fields around them, much of it was covered in a thick layer of snow. However, the grey stone parapet jutted out on either side of the bridge as the dark waters babbled beneath its arches.

"That's the Mehlaus Bridge." Jordan pointed ahead. "We'll cross the Irelven River here and follow its southern bank through Bochsogen Forest."

"Impressive stonework." Candac whistled. "Did the elves make this bridge?"

"Dwarves." Jordan shook his head. "They always had better minds for sturdy things like bridges."

"Elves and dwarves worked together a lot during the Empire?" Walaric scrunched his nose as he tried to recall the little tutoring he had in history.

"Yes," Izold murmured, "but jealousy drove them apart in the years since then. Elves, dwarves, and men were all part of the Empire, but the elves were quick to remind the others who it all belonged to."

"So the legends say," Paschal added sardonically. "None of us were there to see it ourselves."

"Well, it does explain why we don't see men, elves, and dwarves all working together so much now, doesn't it?" Candac glanced sideways at Paschal as they walked. "There's no great council of oligarchs sending out decrees, dwarf masons carving cities out of the mountainsides, or gleaming bronze legions patrolling the roads these days."

Paschal huffed and turned his attention to the slow current of the Irelven as they crossed over the Mehlaus Bridge. It was not a particularly tall bridge. Walaric guessed the highest point was somewhere between ten and fifteen feet as he glanced over the edge of the parapet. It was a wide and sturdy bridge, though, and Walaric easily imagined whole armies crossing it back when it was first constructed.

"If only I could have beheld the glory of the days when this bridge was first built," Walaric mused.

"Everyone wishes to have lived in the days of their fathers," Izold scolded. "The past always seems nobler. Yet the gods have seen fit for us to live now."

"We have work to do," Walaric agreed. "They have given us this task and not our fathers or our children who have yet to be. Take comfort in that."

"Take comfort in that?" Paschal stopped in his tracks and turned directly towards Walaric. "What is this work we have been chosen for? Why is this quest so urgent that we must hasten to the Blighted Lands in the dead of winter but *not* with Lord Godfrey?"

Walaric swallowed a lump in his throat as he slowed to a halt. Candac's eyes were on him, too. Even Izold and Jordan stopped to glance behind them from their horses. Searching for the right words, he stammered. How could he say what he had to?

"Our quest is one of fact-finding." Walaric shook his head. "We need to find the Keeper of Souls and discover how to unbind Nera's shade from the mortal sphere."

Walaric cleared his throat. He twitched nervously. His words did not sound convincing, even to him.

"You are also here by Lord Godfrey's command," Walaric added. "We have a duty. I already explained that."

"Well, could you explain it some more?" Paschal pressed, taking a step closer to Walaric. "Because it sounds like we're going to just march headlong into the largest nest of undead in all the Nordslands without a plan."

Grimacing, Walaric closed his eyes and took a deep breath. Would Paschal be so obstinate the whole way? He opened his eyes and set his jaw.

"Well," Walaric began, "we know the undead are stirring throughout the Nordslands. Nera's ghost was haunting Olso Fortress, but is now making her way to the Blighted Lands. We have to find some answers there before things get worse for all of us."

"Can even Nera's ghost be enough to stir the undead like this?" Paschal crossed his arms and frowned.

"The Keeper of Souls will have the answers we need." Walaric ignored Paschal's question. "I have a good feeling about it."

"How can you trust your feelings so much on this?" Candac shifted his weight from one foot to the other. "Feelings are fickle. You're risking our lives on feelings? We don't even know what the Keeper of Souls is."

"I prayed about it," Walaric said after a pause. "I can only tell you I have faith that this is something we should do. I know it's not a lot to go on."

"Perhaps that's why Lord Godfrey didn't want to come and left it to the likes of us." Paschal rolled his eyes. "It doesn't matter to him if we all die in the wilderness."

"That's not true," Walaric protested. "You know he wanted to lead this quest."

"But what are we supposed to do when we get to the Blighted Lands?" Candac asked. "What can we do against the ghost of the Great Witch of the North?"

Biting his lip, Walaric looked into the eyes of each of his companions. He could not find the answer in any of their faces. With a sigh, he shrugged helplessly.

"Have faith." Izold turned Vielantiu towards Walaric and Paschal. "This quest is sanctioned by Lord Godfrey, and it's inspired by the gods. They will reveal more in time."

"See." Candac stuck his thumb in Izold's direction in a sarcastic gesture. "The paladin believes in our cause."

Paschal nodded, if only reluctantly. Paladins were few and far between these days, but they still held a reputation as divinely protected warriors. Any quest a paladin supported surely had the gods' favor.

"If no one objects," Jordan called out from near the far end of the bridge. "I say we get moving again before we are all buried in the snow."

Walaric, Izold, Paschal, and Candac rushed to catch up to Jordan at the end of Mehlaus Bridge. Izold had faith enough in this quest. Paschal's concerns seemed satisfied for the moment. However, doubt now crept into the back of Walaric's mind. He was so accustomed to doing what others told him to or finding the answer to his problems in some old dusty tome. Dangerous adventures in the dead of winter based on only vague impressions seemed madness now that Walaric was here.

After crossing the Mehlaus Bridge on the road to Pskov, Walaric's party stuck to the Irelven's southern bank as Jordan suggested. The northern side was still mostly Clan territory as far as any of them knew. A few more days passed as they traveled southeast along the Irelven River. The snowfall grew heavier, and thick sheets of ice began forming around the riverbanks.

Eventually, the skies grew clear, but a dense forest now stood before Walaric and his companions. A thick fog lazily hung amidst the tree trunks and swirled just above the icy surface of the river. Walaric's stomach sank at the foreboding sight.

"The Irelven will continue southeast through Bochsogen Forest," Sir Jordan explained as they drew near the dark, old trees. "Once we see Harlstad Bridge on the other side of the forest, we'll follow the road south to Epsberg and then the Blighted Lands."

Walaric shuddered at the menacing trees as the men marched closer to the woods. The faintest remnants of old paving stones cut a path along the Irelven through the woods in the few places they were not obscured by snow. However, the ancient trees of Bochsogen Forest itself had overgrown the vast majority of the great road Walaric imagined had once been there.

The mist grew thicker as they made their path along the riverbank. Paschal and Candac exchanged uneasy glances with Walaric, but Jordan and Izold pressed ahead on their horses without pause. Walaric swallowed hard.

Candac carried a sword and shield and wore a thick chainmail hauberk under his tabard. He also wore a spangenhelm similar to Godfrey's. Paschal was likewise armed and armored, though he carried an ax at his belt instead of a sword. Walaric, however, wore no armor and carried only the sword and shield he had used the night he fought against the ghouls with Izold.

"What's the matter?" Izold turned his head back.

Walaric looked at the sword at his belt. He had trained with it under Leon de Valois for some months and killed a cyclops with it during the final assault on Olso. With the gods' help, he would be ready for whatever came.

"Nothing." Walaric shook his head and leapt forward. "I'm coming."

Candac and Paschal bounded forward a few paces to catch up to Walaric, Izold, and Jordan. Soon, they were surrounded by the trees and mist. A soft burbling arose from the riverbank to Walaric's left as they crunched through the snow. Shivering at the nasty thought of falling into the Irelven, Walaric watched his feet carefully as he advanced along the foggy bank.

They walked without speaking a word for at least a few hours. Only the babbling Irelven and their muffled footsteps disturbed the slumbering forest. Walaric silently muttered a prayer to try to set his mind at ease, but to no avail. Did the gods even hear him?

"The fog should have lifted by now," Jordan murmured. "It's nearly midday."

"Most unnatural," Izold agreed.

"They say necromancers can enchant forests with obscuring mists so the rays of the Sun won't harm their undead thralls." Paschal gulped.

"Don't talk like that," Walaric snapped. "You'll put a jinx on us all."

"Undead in Bochsogen Forest would be pretty unusual." Jordan dismounted his horse and led it by the reins as they began crossing a narrow ledge near a dense thicket. "Lamassus prowl through Oblarv and tend to drive out the worst monsters."

"What is a lamassu?" Candac asked.

"It's a winged lion," Walaric answered, "just like on Sir Jordan's coat of arms."

"I don't know if I'd rather have to face zombies or winged lions," Paschal scoffed.

"Let's hope we don't find either today," Jordan said. "Bochsogen Forest is within the Duchy of Oblarv. It's my father's realm. I know it well enough. With the snow this thick, the lamassus won't be out much now, at least."

"Watch your step," Izold grunted at Walaric as he dismounted Vielantiu.

As he drew near the thicket, Izold fell in after Jordan's horse, Boreas, and Walaric deftly stepped behind Vielantiu. The horses twitched and swatted their tails. They were afraid. Something was off. Walaric prayed it was not what he feared it was.

Awkwardly, Candac and Paschal shuffled for a moment before Candac ended up directly behind Walaric, and Paschal, huffing, took the rear. Though no one said anything, Walaric had no doubt they all sensed the horses' fear. The group slowly continued in this order, single file, as they traversed the narrow ledge by the riverbank.

Holding his breath, Walaric concentrated on his steps. Gingerly, he skipped over a gnarled branch jutting from the misty bank. There were just a few paces left before they reached the end of the thicket.

Walaric's heart leapt as Candac cried out. The priest whirled to face where Candac had stood just a moment before. Panic written on his pale face, the young knight gripped the rim of the ledge. It was not a branch Walaric's foot had just narrowly missed a moment before, but the emaciated claw of a ghoul now wrapped around Candac's ankle. Only another heartbeat passed before the ghoul dragged him down screaming into the frigid water below.

Dumbfounded, Walaric and Paschal exchanged a brief, horrified glance. Coming to himself first, Paschal drew his ax and shield. Before Walaric could think of anything to say or do, Paschal splashed down into the water after Candac. It was too late.

More ghouls burst from the thicket as Izold and Jordan drew their weapons. Jordan's mace connected with the side of a monster's head, sending it careening down into the river with a splash. Another lunged at Izold, but the paladin raised his shield to deflect its raking claws.

Drawing his sword, Walaric tensed as a pale ghoul rushed him from the dark thicket. The creature reached out to his face with a bony, clawed hand. Batting the gnarled claws away with his shield, Walaric drove his sword into the ghoul's gut. The monster bit into Walaric's shoulder with its fetid, slimy maw.

Sharp pain ripped through Walaric as he cried out. He lost his grip on his sword as the monster wrapped one hand around his wrist while taking hold of the hilt of his weapon with the other. Falling to his knees, Walaric could do little but writhe in agony.

Leaping to the priest, Izold bashed the ghoul with his shield. It stumbled back a pace, still clutching Walaric's sword embedded in its gut. The paladin spared no time smashing in its skull with his war hammer as gore spattered against the faceplate of his helmet.

"On your feet," Izold urged Walaric as more ghouls gathered around them.

With the bite on his shoulder still throbbing, Walaric cringed as he stood. Wincing, he reached for the hilt of his sword, which was still planted in the remains of the ghoul next to him. Izold was already bounding towards the nearest undead as Jordan desperately swung his mace at an outstretched claw reaching for Boreas. The horses kicked and whinnied as the undead tore at them.

Walaric recoiled from the image of a ghoul's leering face and stretching claw rising from the riverbank. It swiped at his ankle, but he plunged his sword into its open mouth. Spewing dark ichor from its wound, the creature fell back into the murky water with a splash.

"Paschal," Walaric called out towards the river. "Candac! Where are you?"

No reply came but the groans of the undead, the struggles of Jordan, Izold, and the horses, and the splashing of more ghouls emerging from the riverbank. Walaric turned about at the sound of harsh braying. Tearing at his caparison, a trio of ghouls latched onto Boreas. Sir Jordan's horse kicked and reared, but the ghouls soon pushed him into the river.

Briefly, Boreas thrashed about in the river, but the ghouls soon dragged the barded horse under the murky water. Sir Jordan bawled at the sight. Weeping, he lashed out at the nearest monster. His mace struck it down and then smashed into a second and third ghoul.

With no enemies immediately before him, Jordan turned to dive into the Irelven. Just as he was about to leap, Izold blocked his path. He jostled to the side, but the paladin gripped his shoulder.

"It's too late," Izold bellowed. "You'll only drown in the river with Boreas."

Sobbing, Jordan dropped his mace and sank to the ground. Sweat dripping from his brow, Walaric breathed heavily as he glanced at his surroundings. There was only Jordan, Izold, Vielantiu, the Irelven, and Bochsogen Forest now. The ghouls were gone. Yet the mists persisted.

"Moon Frost and Baruch died in the Irelven too…" Walaric's voice trailed off as more splashing came from the riverbank below. "A cursed place for horses, indeed."

Walaric raised his sword and took a cautious step forward, but gasped when Paschal appeared under the ledge, dragging Candac out of the river. Both were drenched from head to toe. Their faces were pallid, and they were both coughing, sputtering, and gasping as they shivered.

"Help me." Paschal hoisted Candac to the others.

Walaric, Izold, and Jordan grabbed Candac under the arms and lifted him over the ledge. The gelid chainmail sleeves of his hauberk stung Walaric's fingers even through his gloves. Paschal clambered up after Candac and sprawled out on his back.

"When Vonig, Berold, and Sigibald call me craven, what are you going to tell them?" Paschal barked as he hit Candac's leg with a balled fist.

"I'm going to tell them how you jumped into the Irelven to save me from the ghouls," Candac sputtered.

"That's right," Paschal heaved. "You're going to tell them what a selfless hero I am. You're going to tell them the saints themselves turned green with envy at the sight."

"All right," Izold grunted, helping Candac to his feet. "Up. Both of you. We have wounds to tend to, and we need to change you out of those wet clothes before you freeze."

Still convulsing, Paschal extended his hand, and Walaric pulled him off the ground. Walaric flinched as fresh pain shot from the bite in his shoulder. Izold examined the wound curiously.

"The undead seem to have a particular taste for your flesh." The paladin frowned.

"It's not an honor I've aspired to." Walaric cringed.

"We'll need to clean it to prevent infection." Izold looked back at Vielantiu.

"Our only wine rations went down with Boreas' saddlebags into the Irelven." Jordan shook his head.

"We'll need to find somewhere to rest and resupply," Candac suggested.

"We can go to Kolarb Castle in the County of Valgo." Jordan rose to his feet. "Count Maurus is my kinsman and a friend to my father. It's a little out of the way, but it's closer than Epsberg or Skasgun on the other end of Bochsogen Forest. Who knows, maybe we can convince my cousins, Errit and Roemer, to join our quest."

"Should we not wait for Walaric to pray before giving them permission to join our quest?" Paschal sardonically raised an eyebrow.

"I don't think we have too much of a choice." Walaric grimaced, ignoring Paschal. "Prayers and determination might not be enough to make it through this cursed place after all."

Jordan led Walaric, Candac, Paschal, and Izold out of Bochsogen Forest in a nearly direct course southwest. The dark trees and mist were soon replaced by rolling hills and fields. However much Walaric may have opposed the idea of losing progress on their journey to the Blighted Lands, he liked the idea of leaving the ghouls behind more.

Sir Jordan said little as he led them through the cold, wind-swept hills of Valgo County. He wore a surly expression ever since he lost Boreas, and now Vielantiu was the only horse in the group. However, Walaric's focus remained largely on the barren landscape and the aching bite on his shoulder. If it became infected, the flesh might become necrotic, and then Walaric might turn into a ghoul. He cradled his aching shoulder at the thought.

Walaric's muted prayers that their journey would be swift were soon answered as they crested a large hill. Kolarb Castle was now directly ahead of them. It was a small square keep that sat atop a large mound of rock and earth amidst the meager farms and village it protected. Only a single stone wall encircled the keep, and only one tower stood at each corner of that wall. It was not nearly as impressive as Olso by Walaric's estimation. However, it was still more defensible than the wooden motte and bailey castles that could still be found guarding some of the poorer baronies.

A single yellow banner fluttered over the keep. A regal black lamassu passant occupied the middle of it. Momentarily forgetting the pain in his shoulder, Walaric cocked his head at the flag.

"Why does Count Maurus still bear the House Loridan coat of arms?" Walaric asked Sir Jordan at the head of the group.

"The Count wanted to maintain closer ties with my father, Duke Ivo," Sir Jordan explained, "so he chose to remain a part of House Loridan rather than found his own house when he was granted this fief. It may not be such a prestigious arrangement for my cousins, but they've not complained about it in all the years I've known them."

"So, you changed your heraldry and founded a new house to make a name for yourself?" Walaric glanced between the red lamassu against the white field on Jordan's shield and the black and yellow banner waving above the keep. "Is it just a matter of pride, or is there some bad history between you and your father?"

"Most lords invent their own coats of arms when they are given a new fief." Candac took a step closer to Walaric as they made their way down a road leading through the snow-covered farmers' fields. "It's more common for a noble to only keep his father's heraldry if he inherits his lands or serves in his household as a retainer."

"Like how you and Paschal wear Godfrey's heraldry because you're his retainers," Walaric said. "Now, Izold, you are of House Cretus…"

"I *was* of House Cretus." Izold leaned towards Walaric from Vielantiu's saddle. "I am a distant cousin of the late Duke Ulric, Godfrey's father, but when I swore my vows and became a paladin, I renounced all former allegiances, titles, and so on."

"So, the fleur-de-lis charge is only used by paladins so they won't be confused with knights of other houses," Walaric replied.

"Yes." Izold nodded as his steed plodded along. "Even knights who directly serve the Church are banned from wearing the fleur-de-lis unless they are true paladins."

Izold looked over the thatched-roof hovels as they drew near the village. Smoke billowed from the chimneys, but not a single person greeted Walaric and his party once they entered the village. No one wanted to be out in the cold if they could help it.

"Paladins are lone crusaders who vow to destroy evil, defend the weak, and serve justice wherever it is needed," Izold continued. "In return, the gods we swear our oaths to grant us divine protection, but our room and board must still be supplied by whoever is gracious enough to host us during our travels."

"Charlatans have taken advantage of people's generosity before," Paschal added.

"And that's partly why the military orders have become more popular in recent years." Izold grimaced.

"Why did you become a paladin and not join the Silver Suns or Knights of Saint Pelegius?" Walaric asked. "Isn't it better to pool your resources with people who embrace the same cause than to strike out on your own?"

"Paladins still have a purpose," Izold balked. "I can go where I'm needed in the moment. I don't need to spend my days wasting away in some barracks while waiting for my superiors to decide where I'm needed."

"Sounds almost like a black knight," Paschal noted. "No lords or lands. You just go wherever you desire, whenever you please."

"Hardly," Izold scoffed. "Black knights are mercenaries. They make no sacred oaths and care nothing for honor or piety. Black knights only serve themselves. I serve the constant light of Arktos."

"The Northern Bear leads none astray," Walaric cut in. "But how do you know where the gods need you?"

"Like you on this quest, Walaric, I often seek inspiration through prayers, omens, and dreams." Izold took on a sagely tone. "Sometimes I don't know if a decision was right until after I've shown my faith through right action. However, I've also found the world to be dangerous enough that any destination I set for myself is rarely wrong."

"Kolarb Castle may be the right place for a paladin after all." Sir Jordan frowned. "This place looks dreary even for winter in the Nordslands."

Though the snow had stopped some time ago, grey clouds had returned to the sky. A savage wind from the north dragged the clouds along overhead and cut through the warmth of Walaric's cloak as the men continued up the road. Walaric dared not say it, but he feared the god of the North Wind really was angry with them after Jordan lost Boreas to the ghouls. Nature gods were capricious and prone to foul tempers when slighted.

Only as Walaric and the others stopped outside of Kolarb's sealed gate did he hear a voice calling down to them. Twisting his head, Walaric soon spotted a sentinel atop the gatehouse. The guard was an older man clutching a spear in one hand while trying to keep his cloak wrapped about himself with the other.

"I said who goes there?" the guard shouted while shaking his spear at them.

"I am Sir Jordan, son of Duke Ivo," Jordan called back. "Let us in."

The guard gestured down to Jordan as if he could not hear his reply.

"I'm Errit and Roemer's second cousin," Jordan yelled over the howling gust. "Let them know I'm here."

With how loudly the wind roared around them, Walaric could barely understand what was said. The guard and Jordan made a few more attempts to talk, but their words were lost in the gale.

Visibly exasperated, Jordan unslung his shield from his back and pointed the heraldic charge up at the guard. Comprehension dawned on the old sentinel's face, and he shouted something to someone else behind the parapet out of Walaric's view. Finally, the gate creaked open.

To Walaric's surprise, it was not an armed guard in House Loridan's livery who met them in the courtyard once they walked through the gate, but a young woman about Walaric's age with blonde hair. She wore a heavy fur cloak and a brown dress that reminded Walaric too much of the Irelven's foul waters. At least the wind was not as loud in the courtyard.

"Jordan!" The young woman ran the last few paces to the knight before wrapping her arms around him. "It's been too long."

"Semke, how you've grown!" Sir Jordan returned her embrace. "Where's Roemer? I haven't seen your brother in almost as long as you."

The light in Semke's eyes faded as she pulled back from Jordan's embrace. She pursed her lips as if torn about how to respond. Confused, Walaric bit his lip as well. How quickly her countenance darkened at the mention of her brother's name.

"You'll have to ask Mother and Father about that." Semke shook her head.

Jordan opened his mouth to ask something else, but the young woman turned away from her cousin and now faced the rest of Walaric's group.

"Who are your friends?" The maiden's face brightened again just as quickly as it had fallen. "A priest, a mounted paladin, and two knights from a house I do not know. This is strange company to travel with."

"Everyone, this is Lady Semke, Count Maurus' daughter." Jordan beckoned to the others. "Allow me to introduce my companions. To start with, the priest you see before you is Father Walaric."

Walaric bowed his head.

"Forgive my impudence." The young woman blushed. "But you seem rather young for a priest."

"So I keep hearing." Walaric gritted his teeth.

"And the paladin accompanying us here is Izold, son of Kolen," Jordan continued.

"It's an honor, my lord." Semke curtsied.

"The honor is mine," Izold insisted as he dismounted his steed. "And this is Vielantiu."

"A noble stallion, indeed." Semke signaled to one of the few servants out in the courtyard. "We'll see that he is taken care of in the stables."

The stable hand, a young boy, maybe thirteen or fourteen years old, grabbed Vielantiu's reins before quickly leading the horse across the courtyard to the far end of the keep. Walaric could hardly blame the boy for rushing. Every day grew colder and shorter.

"And these two are Sir Paschal and Sir Candac." Jordan gestured to each in turn. "These knights serve as retainers to my lord, Godfrey de Bastogne."

"Oh, *Sir* Candac?" Semke removed the glove from her left hand and extended it to the young knight.

Blushing, Candac awkwardly grabbed her fingers and kissed the back of Semke's hand. Paschal clenched his jaw at the exchange. Walaric furrowed his brow in confusion. Normally, young maidens showed favor to knights in their prime. While Paschal could still be considered young, he had a few years on Candac, who, like Walaric, was only just filling out into manhood. Perhaps the scowl almost perpetually etched on Paschal's face was working against him.

"Well, come inside." Semke waved for them to follow her to the keep. "You must be freezing."

"We came from Bochsogen Forest." Candac bounded to keep pace with Semke. "We had to fend off a ghoul attack at the Irelven River."

"You must be very brave," the young woman said.

"Actually," Paschal corrected, "the ghouls dragged Candac straight into the river at the very beginning of their ambush. I had to dive into the Irelven and save him."

Candac stammered for something to say as Semke's eyes gleamed at Paschal as if seeing him for the first time.

"Walaric was bitten by one of the ghouls," Izold added. "We'll need someone to look at his shoulder and clean the wound as soon as we can."

"We have a physician." Semke opened the door to the keep as an urgent expression grew on her face. "I'll send for him right away."

Semke led them to the keep's great hall. The inside of Kolarb Castle itself was surprisingly empty, especially for winter. Only a couple of servants bustled past Walaric and his companions as they made their way to the largest chamber of the keep.

"This place is empty." Candac gasped as they finally entered the great hall.

Aside from an old maid tending the hearth, a young bard plucking lazily at his lyre in the minstrel's gallery, and a weathered couple sitting at the high table, Candac was right. Walaric fidgeted as he examined the aged lord and lady at the back of the chamber. Were they really so old, or had some stress aged them beyond their years?

Semke briefly introduced the pair at the high table as Count Maurus and Countess Sinne before excusing herself to find the physician on account of the wound to Walaric's shoulder. The bite still itched and burned, but the Count and

Countess' strained speech and tense movements completely distracted Walaric from his own pain.

"What troubles my lord?" Jordan asked at last.

The Count and Countess exchanged sullen glances.

"Why are my kinsmen's countenances so distraught?" Jordan pressed. "Why was only Semke at the gate to greet us? Where are Errit and Roemer? Where has everyone in Valgo County gone?"

"Didn't you hear?" Count Maurus' voice quivered. "We're all that's left."

"All that's left?" Walaric asked.

"Errit assembled an army and led it to Pskov when we were told the Clans were coming back to besiege the city," Maurus explained.

"But the Clans intercepted the army before it could reach Pskov," Sinne continued. "Lord Widemer's forces slaughtered my sons and everyone with them."

"This was while High Warlord Alvir was attacking Olso?" Jordan balled his fist. "A dark day indeed!"

Maurus nodded mutely.

"I'm sorry that such a misfortune should fall on your line." Jordan lowered his eyes to the floor. "Errit and Roemer were my friends."

Walaric exchanged a grimace with Paschal and Candac. He did not know much about the nuances of how noble houses conducted their affairs, but the loss of a son was always grievous. Worse yet, a county deprived of its manpower stood little chance against the Clans, undead, or whatever else might threaten the realm.

Chapter Six

Before dawn had quite cracked through her bedroom window, Madeline's eyes flashed open at the sound of small scurrying feet. Inky blackness filled the room, but more subtle tones of blue and grey slowly became distinguishable as her eyes adjusted to the predawn light. The sound of movement had ceased almost immediately after Madeline's eyes opened, but she knew what it was. She had heard mice scampering about her room for a few days now and had screamed when she thought she saw one on the bookshelf last night.

However, nothing came of it. The creature darted away the instant Madeline's cry pierced the night. With both Godfrey and Walaric gone, no one immediately came to her aid, and the mouse was long gone by the time Father Edric stumbled into her chambers with a pair of spearmen from the night watch.

With a sigh, Madeline glanced at the few dying embers still smoldering in the hearth. She might have tried to zap the mouse with a tiny ray of magical flame shot from her fingertips, but she worried she would miss and mistakenly light her books on fire instead. Her magic had improved much in the last few months, but she did not trust it quite enough to deal with small, agile rodents yet.

"I'll have to tell Godfrey to get us a cat," Madeline said aloud. "Then we'll see how boldly you mice prance around my room at night!"

Stretching, Madeline reluctantly pulled the covers off and sat up on the side of her bed. Her bare feet briefly touched the cold stone floor before finding her slippers. Shivering in her loose nightgown, she stumbled forward a couple of steps through her room to the armoire, where she kept her day clothes.

With a snap of her fingers, Madeline lit the candle next to the mirror on top of her drawers. Her parents had warned her about using her magic too much. Most men greatly feared magic, and accusations of witchcraft among the Ostmen were often answered by burning at the stake. However, Madeline had revealed her powers when Olso Fortress was first taken from the Clans, and now everyone in Azgald and all of the Clans knew. There was no sense in hiding anything now, even if Sister Vanya still quietly protested.

By the time Madeline had selected her dress from the armoire and thrown her nightgown on the bed, a soft knock came at the door. She glanced out the window. Rosy-fingered Dawn had already kissed the snowy mountains outside. Hurriedly, she tugged her deep red dress over her head and slipped her arms through the sleeves.

"Come in," Madeline called out.

The door creaked open, and Thieda marched into the chamber, followed by Elja. Thieda's arms were crossed, and her face was brooding. Elja slumped her shoulders as she dragged her feet into the room. The poor girl must have still been heartbroken over Walaric.

"You can't miss another one of Father Edric's prayer services." Thieda grabbed a hairbrush from Madeline's drawer. "We're already late."

"Sorry." Madeline grimaced as Thieda began brushing the knots out of her hair.

Elja grabbed the crumpled nightgown off Madeline's bed and tossed it into a basket with other dirty clothes destined for the washroom. Sluggishly, she began straightening out Madeline's pillows and blankets. Was there something she could say to comfort her?

"Trouble sleeping?" Elja glanced into Madeline's eyes through her reflection in the mirror as she finished with the bed. "I heard you scream last night."

"Mice." Madeline shuddered.

"We haven't seen anything in our room." Elja turned her gaze to Thieda. "Have we?"

The other handmaiden shook her head in agreement.

"All of the wedding invitations have been sent out." Thieda set the hairbrush down on the dresser where she had found it. "The dukes of Austlad, Gotlad, and Smalad were the last three we needed to write."

"They're not far," Madeline beamed as Elja began tying the bow on the back of her dress. "Not long now until the wedding. Can you believe it?"

"Very exciting." Elja rolled her eyes.

"Your day will come, Elja," Thieda said and rolled her eyes as she helped Madeline into her shoes. "Don't be jealous of Madeline and Godfrey."

"You're right." Elja blushed at Madeline's reproving stare. "I'm sorry."

"I know you liked Walaric." Madeline rubbed Elja's shoulder. "He was handsome and kind, but you know it could never work with a priest dedicated to the celestial gods. It's forbidden. It wasn't meant to be."

"I know," the young handmaiden sighed.

"It's worse that Walaric entertained this fantasy with you for so long," Thieda added. "He should have cut it off a while ago. What was he thinking?"

"I don't know." Elja's eyes grew moist. "I guess we were dreaming."

"Let's go back to something more pleasant," Thieda suggested. "The wedding?"

"Right," Elja agreed. "The wedding."

"Macsen the Elgunian should be coming to Olso," Madeline said. "Father already received his reply to our invitation we sent to Kalscony before the siege."

"He's a really good minstrel." Elja's face brightened up. "We heard him at Mendelpav a while ago."

"He's also a very expensive minstrel, if I remember right." Thieda pursed her lips thoughtfully. "But you get what you pay for. The duke of Pavik's not going to be too frugal about his only daughter's wedding."

Elja and Madeline sniggered. The handmaidens continued listing off guests and performers who had been invited to the wedding and how they felt about each. Some of the guests' names were met with excitement. Others sparked much less enthusiasm because they *had* to be invited for one reason or another. The more they talked about it, the more Madeline's stomach sank.

"Do you think I should really go through with it?" Madeline frowned at her reflection in the mirror. "After all, I'm still so young."

"Do you have a more handsome dragon-slayer in mind?" Thieda raised an eyebrow at Madeline's reflection.

"Or a more gallant knight?" Elja pantomimed swinging a sword and shield. "Besides, seventeen isn't that young. Go too many more years single, and folks will begin to wonder if there's something wrong."

Madeline stared at the emerald engagement ring on her finger. The jewel sparkled brilliantly. She had been so excited when Godfrey surprised her with it. Did she still feel just as giddy now?

"I'm sure your father could always write Conrad the Wolf." Thieda took on an ominous tone. "I'm sure he would be more than willing to take your hand still."

Elja and Thieda cackled hysterically at this last notion. Madeline giggled too. Of course, Godfrey was a fine young man. Who else would she rather be with?

"But Father still isn't pleased with Godfrey," Madeline conceded. "Father's approval means a lot."

"Remember." Elja stuck her finger up in the air. "Conrad the Wolf was your father's first choice. Maybe you shouldn't put too much stock in who he approves of."

"There's still time to see who else could be out there waiting for me." Madeline looked at the distant Wyrmwind Peaks outside her window. "Or discover more about myself before marriage and children tie me down forever."

"You could always wait for someone better to come along." Thieda placed her hands on her hips. "Or you could run off on an adventure like some legendary shieldmaiden. Just wait too long, though, and young, brave knights won't even notice you anymore. You see how many men are throwing themselves at Sister Vanya."

Madeline, Elja, and Thieda all chuckled at the mention of the old librarian.

"Oh, before I forget." Thieda unfolded a letter from the pouch on her belt. "Moric Cyclops Slayer is on his way."

"Moric Cyclops Slayer?" Madeline repeated. "What business does House de Toron have this far west?"

"He requested to meet Karl the Hammer here at Olso." Thieda scanned the letter. "It's a little closer to Moric than Karl's fief. He's bringing his sister, Alpia, with him."

"Alpia de Toron is said to be a real beauty." Elja raised an eyebrow. "Karl should count himself quite fortunate to have her brought to him like this."

"No one is bringing their brothers to Sister Vanya," Thieda said with a smirk.

"Men are lucky age doesn't curse them so." Elja blushed as she looked at her feet. "If anything, age and experience make them more attractive."

"No one said Tyche was fair." Thieda shook her head. "Come on. We need to get down to the chapel."

"Tyche is never fair." Madeline took one last glance at her beautiful dress and flowing dark hair in the mirror before toying with the emerald ring on her finger. "But sometimes Fate is kind."

Thieda opened the door and gestured for Elja and Madeline to go through it. Madeline blew out the candle on her dresser and followed Elja. If they were lucky, Father Edric would not even notice their late arrival.

"Alpia de Toron?" Madeline pursed her lips as they made their way to the stairs at the end of the hall. "Wasn't she betrothed to one of Count Maurus' sons?"

"I think the Count's son died in the Siege at Pskov or something like that." Elja shook her head.

"She moves on fast." Thieda briskly made her way down the stairs.

"You would think she might have spent a little more time mourning her betrothed's death." Madeline rushed to keep pace with Thieda.

"Would Alpia de Toron, the Beauty of the Bosvian Coast, notice if a single grain of sand disappeared into the sea?" Elja laughed as her shoes pounded against the cold stairs. "Maidens like her are so used to men's affection coming from every direction, they hardly notice when one man disappears."

"Yes, but Sir Errit was her *betrothed*." Madeline tilted her head from side to side as she thought back to when Godfrey and Conrad the Wolf were competing for her hand. "Still, I suppose it's nice to get so much attention once in a while."

"You've had a few other suitors before, too," Elja noted as they continued down the spiral stairs. "Conrad the Wolf was not actually your father's first choice."

"Yes," Madeline conceded, "but I was just a girl then, and those much older men were more interested in acquiring the Duchy of Pavik than they were in winning the heart of a damsel. It's more flattering to have men fighting over you for you and not your father's title."

"Well…" Thieda added as they reached the bottom of the stairs, "you're lucky to have Godfrey now. He's worth more than all those other suitors chasing Alpia."

"You're right." Madeline stopped at the bottom of the stairs. "That might be too much attention."

Light poured into the library from the eastern window as Madeline sat at a small desk between aisles of countless books. It was quiet. No. Reverent. The only sound to disturb the peaceful silence was the occasional rustling of a page as Madeline read through every tome about magic Sister Vanya would let her touch.

It was humbling to be surrounded by the works of so many great minds from ages past, preserved for future generations. Scholars, poets, saints, and so many others were all within Madeline's grasp. With Godfrey escorting Roltar and Mauger to Vindholm and Walaric off on his own quest, she found little to get in the way of her books. Yet the tranquility lasted only so long.

After a few days of going over Nera's old spell books and other scrolls and codices on the subject of magic, the words grew increasingly dense. There was no one to consult regarding what whole passages even meant. Maybe she was not translating certain words correctly, or the meanings had changed over time.

Stuck for perhaps the third or fourth time that morning, Madeline found herself absently staring off at the shelves as her thoughts wandered. A soft scraping sound against the wooden shelf brought her thoughts back to the present. Scanning the shelves for the source of the scratching, her eyes narrowed. Her heart jumped as a small, dark shape flitted between the books just in front of her.

Clenching her teeth, Madeline blinked several times and shuddered. The thing vanished just as suddenly as it had appeared. Now the mice were in the library too. It made sense more vermin would find their way into the castle as each day grew colder.

Letting out a tired sigh, Madeline relaxed only after she was sure the mouse was gone. She stood. Stretching, she marked her place in the tome with a crimson ribbon before closing it on the desk. She yawned. She needed a break.

Stretching again, Madeline pushed her seat back against the edge of the table. She wandered down the aisle and glanced at the titles of the books she passed on the tall shelves. They were old, musty, and fading. She had to stop and strain her eyes to read some of the titles on the spines of the oldest volumes.

Madeline did not care to stop long at any one book, though. Reading for pleasure was not too tempting after all of the studying she had been doing. If it were not so cold, she might have decided to go outside instead.

"There you are." Sister Vanya crept around the corner of the aisle behind Madeline. "I hope your studies are going well, Lady Madeline."

"Hardly." Madeline forced a smile. "Some of what I've been reading has given me a better understanding of magic, but other authors seem to think I already know things I don't. It can get confusing."

"One of my old tutors once said dense writing is a sign of dense thinking." Sister Vanya nodded sagely. "From what

I've read in these old wizards' grimoires, they seem more concerned about showing off what they know than teaching others how to learn their arts."

"So it would seem with Grith the Zemelian and Ouales' works, at least." Madeline sighed. "Would you be able to help me with some of these books?"

"I'm not a magician." Sister Vanya shook her head vigorously. "I couldn't help you understand these old tomes much. Besides, the Order of the Ivory Chalice has instructed me that these books are only supposed to be consulted under exceptional circumstances."

"You would risk getting in trouble with your order on my account?" Madeline blinked in disbelief.

"I have deemed you an exceptional circumstance." The librarian took on an imperious tone. "But I cannot teach you, and I still reserve the right to limit what you can dabble in. Magic always leads to trouble."

Madeline gave a small, uncertain smile. It was a concession. Not a big one, but a concession all the same.

"Are there any other books on magic I could read?" Madeline asked. "Perhaps I need to start on something easier before I can understand Artemios."

"I'll have to think on that," Sister Vanya replied tersely. "I will let you know if I find anything."

Madeline bit her lip at this response. The old librarian had previously tried to withhold all books on magical lore in Olso's library from her, but recently agreed to give her greater access. Was she holding out now? Did she really want to help, or was she purposely giving her material beyond her grasp, knowing she would fail to understand?

"I won't go looking for anything dangerous," Madeline said. "I promise."

"Let me check first," Sister Vanya insisted.

"Fine," Madeline reluctantly agreed.

With a brief nod, the librarian turned back in the direction she had come from and stalked away. Madeline shook her head. She hated being treated like a child, but she had to admit Sister Vanya was right to be cautious about spell books. Neither of them wanted something like *The Book of Elder Wisdom* to show up again. Still, the old woman had proven she could be jealous and spiteful to Madeline for no good reason at all.

Wandering down the aisle again, Madeline strolled towards the windows at the far wall. Like the rest of the windows throughout Olso Fortress, these were relatively small and narrow, leaving much of the library dark and damp, even when the morning sun was bright outside. A castle's primary function was that of defense, and much of the interior light came from candles and lamps spread throughout the chambers and corridors.

Soon, Madeline found herself staring down into the courtyard from the closest window. Spathi sat in his pen, gnawing at the remains of a speckled goat he must have picked out of the mountains on his morning flight. His powerful beak and claws shredded the goat's innards. Bones snapped as large chunks of meat went down Spathi's throat. Though the display was bloody, there was no denying the griffin was a magnificent creature.

Godfrey had left Spathi at Olso specifically so that Madeline could find him in a hurry if there was an emergency. She had ridden the griffin before but had never flown alone. Despite Godfrey giving plenty of encouraging words before he left, Madeline was still very unwilling to try riding him now. In her nightly prayers since Godfrey left, she always gave at least a short plea to the gods that she would not be put in a situation where she would have to fly Spathi by herself.

Before long, Madeline's thoughts turned to the upcoming wedding. Though winter had only barely begun in earnest, every day grew closer to the first day of spring. Would Madeline be ready? Could she go through with it?

She shook her head. Elja and Thieda were right. Godfrey was a brave, handsome young man. He said he loved her and had done much to prove it. He had rescued her from both Nera and *The Book of Elder Wisdom*, but these were extraordinary events. The mundane activities of day-to-day life in the castle proved far less thrilling, and opportunities for romance had lessened dramatically, overall, after Sister Vanya became her chaperone.

Brushing her hand against the bookshelves as she passed, Madeline began making her way towards the library's exit. She thought back to when she first saw Godfrey with the crusaders as they relieved the siege at Biorkon. He had charged headlong into a group of Nordsman berserkers, risking life and limb. Some would have called it foolhardy, but Godfrey went to such extremes out of a sense of duty to his men and the gods. Yes, there was no doubt about Godfrey's piety. He would make a good husband and father.

Soft footsteps pulled Madeline from her thoughts. As the sound drew nearer, she stopped in her tracks. Almost as soon as she did, Thieda emerged from a nearby aisle.

"Moric Cyclops Slayer and his sister are here," Thieda said. "Karl the Hammer won't be far behind."

"All right," Madeline replied.

"Elja is already getting something for them from the kitchen," Thieda added.

"You haven't noticed any mice in the kitchen or great hall?" Madeline pursed her lips thoughtfully.

"No," Thieda answered. "I haven't seen any in the pantry either. I've been watching for them since you first said you saw one in your room."

"That's good." Madeline sighed. "Let's just hope they don't spoil any of the food stores. It was already going to be a lean winter before guests started showing up."

"That's the last thing we need." Thieda's eyes went wide as if she could already see the rodents gnawing holes into the flour sacks in the pantry.

"Come on." Madeline gestured to the heavy oak doors at the library's exit. "It's time to meet this *Beauty of the Bosvian Coast.*"

For a moment, Madeline stood in stunned silence as Alpia de Toron and Moric Cyclops Slayer approached her, Thieda, and Elja from the great hall's entrance. Though Madeline guessed Alpia to be only a couple of years older than her, the dark-haired, brown-eyed maiden's figure was so elegant that she was almost sure it was Peitho, the love goddess, in disguise here to steal Godfrey from her. Elja and Thieda's dropped jaws suggested they agreed with Madeline's assessment.

Moric Cyclops Slayer, by contrast, was rather plain and approaching middle age. He wore the scars of an accomplished warrior, as one would expect of a man with an epithet like *cyclops slayer*, and there was nothing blatantly unattractive about him. Yet his younger sister clearly bore all the charm House de Toron had to offer their generation.

The man's most interesting quality was that, rather than carrying a one-handed sword and shield as most knights did, Moric carried a blade so long that its scabbard barely fit on his belt. Such an unwieldy greatsword could cleave a man in two with one swipe, Madeline was certain. On second thought, its intended targets were probably beasts similar to what gave Moric his sobriquet.

"You're Lady Madeline of House Drois, I presume," Moric grumbled with a polite bow.

"The same." Madeline extended her hand.

Moric kissed it. Alpia's head turned ever so slightly as she scanned the chamber. Madeline's stomach sank as she jealously guessed what she was searching for.

"And this is my sister, Alpia de Toron." Moric gestured to the Beauty of the Bosvian Coast.

"Charmed." Madeline curtsied.

"Likewise." Alpia repeated the gesture. "Is Godfrey de Bastogne, Duke of Kovdor, not here at Olso Fortress?"

"You will have to excuse my lord's absence." Madeline's jaw tightened. "He is away on business with his kin and could be gone all winter."

"That's a shame." Alpia's eyes gleamed. "I hear he is quite handsome."

"Indeed." Madeline clenched her teeth so hard that they began to hurt. "Our wedding is this spring."

"Oh?" Alpia gave a slight frown. "I'm sorry. I didn't receive an invitation."

"An embarrassing oversight, I assure you." Madeline took a measured breath before indicating the high table behind her. "Elja and Thieda have prepared a small meal for us. Would you care to sit down?"

"Yes." The alluring grin returned to Alpia's face as quickly as it had left. "Thank you."

Alpia, Moric, and Madeline found their seats at the high table as Elja and Thieda prepared their plates. Madeline bit her lip. The meal *was* small. A few rabbits Varin had caught this morning, some boiled turnips, and a pitcher of watered-down wine were all that Elja and Thieda had managed to prepare in time for their guests' arrival. It would have to do for now.

"I believe you and your brother have business with my lord's vassal, Karl." Madeline took a bite of rabbit.

"Yes, we do." Moric sipped his wine. "Thank you for hosting us on such short notice. I fear Bormheld County might be just a little too far for us to travel in this weather.

But don't worry. We won't forget your kindness. We will be more than happy to return the favor should you ever find yourself near Vorot."

"Karl the Hammer has proven both a fierce warrior and a loyal retainer to Godfrey since before he joined the crusade," Madeline explained. "Hosting you while on Karl's business is the least we could do."

Madeline took another bite of the rabbit on her plate. It was a bit gamey, but Elja had added enough salt and wild garlic to cover the worst of it. A few onions might have helped, but they had to make everything they had last through the winter.

"I'm so sorry to hear you have lost your betrothed at the Siege of Pskov." Madeline cut a slice of turnip with her knife before stabbing it with her fork. "You must be beside yourself with grief."

"Sir Errit's army was ambushed not long after they left Kolarb," Alpia corrected. "They never made it to Pskov. Only one knight returned to tell the tale."

"And what happened to him?" Elja blurted out.

Thieda shot Elja a dirty look, but Alpia ignored them both. She drained the last of the wine from her goblet but set it down with surprising grace for how much she had at once. Finally, she looked Elja straight in the eye.

"That knight left Kolarb in disgrace." Alpia's face grew dark. "I don't care to say more than that for now."

Madeline raised her eyebrow at the intensity of Alpia's last statement. Perhaps she mourned Errit's death after all. Either way, her purpose in meeting with Karl the Hammer seemed obvious enough.

"Vorot is pretty far from here," Madeline noted.

"We had been staying at Kolarb as Count Maurus' guests since before the war broke out between Azgald and the Five Clans," Moric explained. "The war made travel difficult, yet we decided it was best to leave Count Maurus after his son's funeral."

"So, you decided to travel farther west rather than back east through the Clans." Madeline nodded.

"In peacetime," Alpia said, "a man of Vorot can travel through the Clans by way of Zemel and Vasag and back without any trouble from the Nordsmen and avoid the orcish tribes altogether. But, during war, the Nordsmen remember Ostman blood is mixed in the Bosvian race, and our path through the Clans is shut."

"Meaning you would need to return to Vorot by sea," Madeline continued Alpia's thought, "but the Hydra Gulf is too treacherous in winter."

"So, we must winter here in Azgald and make the best of it," Alpia concluded.

"Couldn't Vorot help us in the war against the Clans since they don't like the Bosvians in the first place?" Elja wondered aloud.

"The Bosvians are a divided people." Moric shook his head. "Vorot is but one city, and its lordship has many claimants. House de Toron might be able to spare a few knights in time of need under the right treaty, but other houses are always scheming."

"Sounds like House de Toron is looking for outside help in claiming the lordship of Vorot." Madeline twirled her hair around her finger. "Is that not why Lady Alpia is accompanying you through Azgald, Lord Moric?"

"Such ambitions are far too grand for us." Alpia chuckled. "House de Toron could only dream of claiming the throne of Vorot."

Moric snorted in agreement.

"Now would probably not be a good time to be looking for recruits from the Duchy of Kovdor," Madeline insisted. "Leave such dreams and ambitions behind while you are here with us."

"Perish the thought that we are here to rob Azgald of her strength in some vain effort to seize control of Vorot." Moric laughed. "Imagine that, Alpia! And then, after we take Vorot, we march on Zemel and Vasag? Great Auk!"

"Why stop there?" Alpia's eyes gleamed. "Take Lubloin, and all the Bosvian people would be reunited. Who can say what we could accomplish after that?"

"Perhaps we could persuade the Knights of Saint Pelegius to hand Novod off to us at that point." Moric chuckled. "The gods know just as surely as we that they won't hold onto Tisgy long."

Alpia and Moric gave hearty laughs, but the joke was lost on Madeline. She glanced at Elja and Thieda, who could only shrug in reply. There was certainly more to Moric and Alpia than they wanted her to believe.

"Forgive me." Madeline frowned. "But what business do Moric Cyclops Slayer and Alpia de Toron, Beauty of the Bosvian Coast, have with Karl the Hammer, Count of Bormheld, if not something so ambitious as persuading him to help you seize Vorot?"

"Oh." Alpia looked at Madeline in surprise.

Moric's gaze focused on something distant behind the high table. An awkward silence followed. It lasted only for a short moment, but it was long enough.

"Isn't every young woman's desire to marry a strong knight who can provide for her children?" Alpia blushed. "And doesn't it behoove a young woman to do everything in her power to lay hold on the strongest knight she can?"

Madeline flushed for a moment but could not argue against Alpia's point. A few women like Madeline had the privilege of marrying for love. Some women married whom they could. Others married whom they were told to. Regardless of the circumstances, all wished to marry someone who could defend and provide for them. It was a dangerous world, especially for women.

The meal did not last long after that. Thieda showed Moric and Alpia to their rooms while Elja cleared away the dirty dishes. Satisfied, Madeline returned to her studies in the library once everything was in order.

Karl the Hammer arrived a few days later. Madeline had little interest in watching a courtship unfold between him and Alpia de Toron. However, Elja, Thieda, and the other women of the castle talked about it incessantly whenever they were around her. Sister Vanya was the only other lady who seemed immune to the gossip, but even she could not stop Elja and Thieda from interrupting Madeline's study.

"They are so in love!" Elja gushed over the table Madeline was studying at.

"Karl and Alpia are a perfect match," Thieda agreed.

"I never knew Karl could be so romantic," Elja continued. "Why, yesterday he showed up to the great hall with a dozen—"

"Ahem." Madeline cleared her throat. "We are still in the library, Elja."

"Oh, right." Elja lowered her voice. "So, anyway, Alpia had previously given Karl a token of affection, a scarlet cloak, and Karl didn't want to be outdone."

The volume of Elja's voice quickly grew back to being as loud as it was before as she continued recounting the precise details of Karl and Alpia's gift exchanges over the last three days. Madeline looked to Thieda for help, but the other handmaiden's eyes gleamed as the details of Elja's story unfolded. How could even Thieda get so wrapped up in such vapid triflings?

"Excuse me, just a moment." Madeline closed the book in her hands and stood. "You'll have to fill me in on the rest when I come back."

"Don't you want to hear what Alpia said next?" Thieda furrowed her brow at Madeline.

"A little later," Madeline insisted. "I just need to lie down for a little bit."

Soon, Elja and Thieda became completely engrossed in the details of what Alpia's reply was to whatever Karl said after giving her a ruby pendant yesterday. Madeline was fairly certain they neither noticed nor cared that she took the heavy tome she had been studying with her out of the library. She needed to make some progress in her studies, and none of what they were saying would help.

With a huff, Madeline climbed the spiral stairs. She continued past the fourth floor, where her bed chambers were. She did not want Elja and Thieda finding her there, however good their intentions.

Finally, she stopped at the top level of the southern tower. It was colder here than in other parts of the keep, but it was also quieter. Most of the footmen and archers still at Olso Fortress preferred to billet in the less drafty portions of the castle now that winter was here, and most other servants already had rooms on the second floor.

With a heavy thud, Madeline set her book on a table near the window. She sat and opened the tome where she had left off before Elja and Thieda met her in the library. She adjusted the position of her chair and the table so the pages of her book could catch the most daylight possible. Then she screamed and fell out of her chair.

A sharp pain ran up and down her spine as Madeline's seat met the hard stone floor. Scrambling, she jumped up and pressed her back against the wall as she looked at her overturned chair and table. There it was.

Standing in the center of the open book on the floor was a brown mouse with a white underside. Madeline gawked in disbelief. Yes, it was standing on its hind legs in the middle of the book.

"Careful now," the rodent squeaked. "That was a nasty fall, my lady."

"What?" Madeline's jaw hung open incredulously. "I didn't know… What… How can you…?"

Madeline stumbled over her words for a minute. No coherent thought could leave her mouth. A dozen questions wanted to fly from her lips all at once. The mouse crossed his forelegs in a gesture that Madeline could not interpret as anything but patience wearing thin.

"Snap out of it, Lady Madeline." The furry creature shook his head. "You're not making sense."

"I'm not making sense?" Madeline stammered. "You're a talking mouse!"

"Oh, yes." The rodent twitched his whiskers. "Sorry, Lady Madeline. Where are my manners? I'm Sir Fravash. At your service, my dear."

Fravash made a flourish as he tilted his head to her. Madeline blushed, but knowing the mouse's name hardly settled her unease. There were still so many questions.

"*Sir* Fravash?" Madeline asked.

"An honorific bestowed upon me by the elves of Farthest Thule some time ago," the mouse explained.

"And you know my name?" Madeline took a tentative step closer to the rodent. "How?"

"I first heard it from Lady Nera here in this castle." Fravash tapped his foot emphatically.

Madeline shivered at the mention of the name of the Great Witch of the North.

"Oh, don't worry." Fravash scurried closer to Madeline, off the pages of the book she had dropped on the floor. "I'm no friend of Lady Nera's or any of her kind. Glad to be rid of that foul thing, if you ask me."

"Well, I'm glad you're no friend of Nera's." Madeline squatted to examine Fravash more closely. "But, if you don't mind my asking, what are you?"

"What do you mean?" Fravash looked himself up and down. "Have you not seen a mouse before?"

"Of course I have!" Madeline scolded. "But mice don't normally talk. You know this."

The mouse rubbed his whiskers in apparent agitation. Briefly, he squinted. Should Madeline be amused at this odd behavior, or was it a trick meant to lower her guard?

"Young damsels like you always get caught up in such details." Fravash scratched his ear. "I suppose you could call me a guardian spirit if you're looking for an explanation beyond my physical form."

"I see." Madeline rose and took a step back. "And what do you want with me?"

The mouse stood on his hind legs in silence for a moment. His small pink paws quivered near his face as his dark eyes gleamed in the reflected light from the window. Frowning, Madeline took another cautious step back.

"I asked, 'What do you want with me?'" Madeline crossed her arms.

"Forgive me, my lady, but that has been a fairly difficult question to answer until recently." Fravash scampered closer to Madeline.

The mouse pantomimed a scooping motion with one of his forepaws. Madeline hesitated, but Fravash repeated the signal. Reluctantly, she lowered her hand until the back of it touched the cold floor.

The mouse jumped into Madeline's hand. Though she was ready for this, she still had to bite back a squeal. Rodents were filthy, disease-ridden vermin, no matter how cute they may appear.

Madeline rose to her full height again with Fravash in hand as he clutched to her thumb with his forepaws. She gave a small smile as his whiskers trembled. He was not that filthy after all.

"I've been watching you since you first entered Olso Fortress' keep, Lady Madeline," Fravash explained. "I saw you first as a prisoner here, then as a lady of this castle.

Always intelligent, curious, and kind, you were, but not without faults too large to ignore."

Madeline took a breath as if about to protest, but then released it as she thought better than to interrupt.

"I would have revealed myself to you earlier," the mouse continued, "but then you took hold of *The Book of Elder Wisdom*. A nasty piece of devilry that was. When that spell book got hold of you, I thought you were lost."

"I still don't understand." Madeline shook her head.

"I have spent some time observing you, testing you, and, finally, judging you." Fravash sniffed Madeline's palm.

"Did you put that cursed spell book in my room?" Madeline cried. "Do you know what that almost did to me?"

"Stars above, I did no such thing!" Fravash stamped his foot. "But magic draws magic to it. *The Book of Elder Wisdom* got to you before I did, and I could not risk exposure to the monsters that gnawed at the mortal sphere from the pages within. Only once it was destroyed, and I knew the danger had passed, could I approach you and offer my humble services."

"To help me learn magic?" Madeline's heart raced.

"Indeed." Fravash gestured to the book on the floor. "I'm here to help you learn magic."

The creature clambered up Madeline's sleeve and rested on her shoulder. She reached down for the spell book before placing it on the table. Then, she grabbed her chair by the leg and set it upright again.

"So, you're a spell familiar?" Madeline asked. "I thought those had to be summoned in a ritual."

"*The Book of Elder Wisdom* often dealt in half-truths," Fravash muttered. "But it was not above outright lies."

Madeline swallowed. Now that the ordeal was behind her, she could see plenty of instances where that was true. The only question was whether she should trust this rodent so easily, given her experience.

"All right." Madeline sat in her chair facing the open spell book. "Help me understand what Grith the Zemelian is trying to say here."

The mouse turned and squinted down at the words on the page. Madeline bit her lip nervously. What would Fravash have to say about all of this?

"This is what you've been reading?" Fravash tilted his head at the book.

"It's what Sister Vanya gave me," Madeline said.

Fravash squeaked in contempt.

"She also gave me Artemios, Ouales, and a little Laskaris to read," Madeline added.

"No offense, Lady Madeline, but those elvish wizards are far too advanced for you right now." Fravash shook his head. "And even Grith the Zemelian was writing in an age when certain fundamentals about spell casting were still common knowledge."

"So, Sister Vanya was setting me up for failure." Madeline gritted her teeth.

"Hardly." Fravash squeaked. "Sister Vanya is a librarian, not a witch or sorceress. She doesn't understand enough about magic to know where to really start teaching you."

"Well, what books should we start with?" Madeline crossed her arms. "I was thinking these grimoires were a little too hard to start with."

"I think, before we get too deep into any of these mages," Fravash began, "a little more practical experience would do you some good."

"What did you have in mind?" Madeline smirked.

"I think the time has come for you to construct your first magic staff." The mouse wagged his tail.

Chapter Seven

A wolf howled somewhere out in the black night. Dark, heavy clouds covered the moon and stars. Godfrey's only source of illumination was the crackling fire he, Roltar, and Mauger huddled around. Silently, he prayed the wolves would not grow bold enough to attack the camp. The horses snorted from just outside the light of the fire. They did not seem to care about wolves, at least.

Mauger's horse was a dark brown steed he called Nova, while Roltar's blue dun stallion was named Gaspard. When they had briefly stopped at Pskov a few days ago, Godfrey had bought a young chestnut colt named Dash in the hopes that it would help speed up the rest of their journey to Vindholm. The results were less than favorable.

"I think I'll give Dash to Vonig the Cold or Sigibald of Fulda after I get back to Olso." Godfrey rubbed his hands over the fire. "My knights are in need of horses."

"He is a stubborn one." Mauger tilted his head in the direction of the steeds. "Are you sure you just don't want to break him in?"

"I had to put a lot of time and energy into breaking Spathi in," Godfrey confessed. "I don't know if I want to break in a horse now, right after doing the same for a griffin. I have a wedding to get ready for."

"Breaking in a horse does take time," Roltar agreed, "but we still have a while before we reach Vindholm. I think you'll have Dash broken in soon enough."

"I was hoping all three of us on horseback would speed that up." Godfrey sighed at the campfire. "But Dash has been harder to work with than I had hoped."

"The snow's deep," Roltar noted. "The horses are just as cold as we are. You can't treat them like mere tools."

"You're right." Godfrey gave a small smile. "But there are worthy knights in my household who deserve recognition. Sigibald of Fulda saved my life during the siege at Olso. I think he deserves a new horse."

"Your knights need to be honored for their service," Roltar agreed. "You'll find gifts like that can go a long way."

"Now if we could just convince Boreas to ease up on all this snow," Godfrey muttered. "Are winters always this bad in the Nordslands?"

Roltar and Mauger chuckled but said nothing in reply. The three of them ate salted beef and hard biscuits as they shivered on the logs they sat on. There had been little game to catch in the midst of the near-constant snowstorms, and Godfrey had run out of cheese after the first few days.

"Perhaps you won't ever get used to it so long as you have a warm castle to go back to," Mauger said and grinned after tossing the gristly remains of a strip of meat beyond the light of the campfire.

"Where have you been staying all this time?" Godfrey narrowed his eyes. "You're no black knight living in exile. You're too well-groomed to have spent your whole life out in the woods."

Mauger huffed. Godfrey did not really mean to insult him. There was a lot to like about his kinsman, but he also had little tolerance for jealousy these days.

"We have a few small estates in and around Vindholm," Mauger confessed, "but we are in exile as long as Skasgun is out of reach. We have nothing as cozy as Olso Fortress to call home."

"House Hracour was once the head of the Duchy of Stormsud with Skasgun at its center," Roltar explained, "but the realm's glory faded after generations of bitter losses. The constant assaults from Azgald's enemies proved too much for my fathers to bear."

Godfrey's attention began drifting. He cared about helping out his cousin as much as he could, but he had heard all this before. There was nothing to do but put on a serious expression and agree that it was all so unjust.

"King Wymund eventually rescinded the title of duke from our house and made Skasgun subservient to Pskov." Roltar pointed an accusing finger at the fire.

"Who is King Wymund?" Godfrey interrupted at the sound of the new name that had popped into the narrative.

"Wymund was the last King of Azgald," Mauger answered with what sounded like strained patience. "He was King Lothar's elder brother."

"Why haven't I heard of him before?" Godfrey raised an eyebrow.

"King Wymund interfered too much in local affairs." Roltar gave a dark look. "Few were sad to learn of his untimely death four years ago."

"I see." Godfrey nodded in understanding. "So, Wymund stripped Uncle Badian of his title when he should have been a duke?"

"No." Roltar shook his head. "He never gave him the title he deserved in the first place. When my father... your uncle, Badian, inherited Skasgun, King Wymund declared what remained of the Duchy of Stormsud was to be reformed as a county under Duke Ivo of Oblarv."

Godfrey frowned.

"But the county was dissolved when the Clans razed Skasgun," Roltar continued. "If we can regain Skasgun, then maybe we can reform Stormsud as an independent lordship. With some hard work, we can see it recognized as a duchy again soon enough."

"That's very ambitious." Godfrey whistled. "You hope to gain an independent lordship out of our petition at Vindholm? What would Lothar gain?"

"I have the right connections in King Lothar's court." Roltar grimaced. "It's not as far-fetched a scheme as you might think."

"You had a duchy of your own carved out of nothing." Mauger furrowed his brow at Godfrey.

"That's true," Godfrey conceded.

"Have faith, cousin." Roltar gave a deep sigh. "Faith in better things to come is all that keeps us moving through the chaos of the spinning cosmos."

The three sat in silence for a long moment. Godfrey took a swig from his waterskin. It had initially been filled with ice berry wine, a sour yet expensive treat, but Godfrey soon ran out as days on the road turned into weeks. Now it was filled with water from whatever streams they could find that had not frozen over.

"I'm going to turn in for the night." Roltar stretched. "We still have more than a week until we reach Helsirki at this rate, and another twelve days after that before we make it to sacred Vindholm."

Godfrey gave a humorless smile. Vindholm *was* sacred, but their errand was hardly holy. Or was it? Did the gods not care about justice in this world? Walaric might have had a good answer to that question if he were here.

Roltar stood, stretched again, and made his way to his tent. Godfrey's eyes followed his cousin, but they soon came to rest on Mauger, who stared at him from across the blazing logs. Unsure what to make of Mauger's expression, Godfrey began rummaging through his satchel as if in search of more food.

Another wolf's cry pierced the black night. It was soon answered by more howling from farther off. Frowning, Godfrey looked at the hilt of his sword.

"Do they not have wolves in Bastogne?" Mauger's eyes glowed bright in the light of the fire.

"Of course they do," Godfrey scoffed.

"Dire wolves and wargs, too?" Mauger raised an eyebrow at Godfrey.

Godfrey made no reply. These kinds of monsters could be found in every climate he knew of, from scorching desert to frigid tundra. What was Mauger getting at?

"See," Mauger continued, "there is a special breed of dire wolf here in the Nordslands called an amarok. It's very dangerous. Have you heard of it?"

"I don't believe so." Pensively, Godfrey bit his lip. "Orcs in the Black Iron Mountains have trained wargs for riding, and I've seen dire wolves in the Kol Woods. They're tough beasts I'd rather not have to deal with on a cold winter's night in the middle of nowhere."

"Like the hellhounds that guard the Abyss, they say amaroks thirst for men's souls." Mauger folded his hands in his lap. "If one eats you here out in the wilderness, your spirit won't go on to the celestial kingdoms. There will just be nothing. Can you imagine that? No afterlife. Just an eternity of nothing."

"Do you think those are amaroks out there?" Godfrey gestured to the shadows.

"Hard to say." Mauger shrugged. "The cry of a wolf and a dire wolf are easily mistaken for one another at this distance, and a dire wolf and an amarok look and sound a lot alike until you get close enough to see the fire in the amarok's eyes. By then, it's too late. If you see an amarok, you can either fight or run for your life."

"I take it you've seen an amarok up close then?" Godfrey crossed his arms.

"It was the final quest given to me before being dubbed a knight," Mauger replied. "If I had to do it again, I'd rather face your vampire than my amarok."

"The vampire I fought wasn't exactly easy," Godfrey countered. "It nearly killed me."

"Aye." Mauger nodded. "We both survived our trials, but I still think back to mine even now. If I had died the night I faced that amarok, it would have been the end of my father's line, and I would not have even been able to greet him or my mother in the afterlife."

"How did your mother die?" Godfrey bit his lip.

"She left us in the travail of childbirth." Mauger stared deep into the campfire. "My younger sister, within her womb, did not survive either."

"I'm sorry." Godfrey shook his head. "Tyche can be cruel. I had older brothers and sisters not survive childhood. I don't really remember them, though. I was the youngest."

"Father refused to remarry after Mother's death." Mauger's gaze turned to Godfrey again. "After she died, he focused all his efforts on regaining Skasgun. Our house has become all but extinct without our ancestral home."

"That's why rebuilding House Hracour is so important to him?" Godfrey mused. "He wants power?"

"That's why rebuilding House Hracour is so important to *us*," Mauger corrected. "Everyone wants to control their own destinies. Do you want to spend your whole life simply doing what others tell you to?"

Godfrey held back a retort. He was out here in the snow weeks away from Olso precisely because Roltar and Mauger wanted him to be. Slowly, he opened his mouth.

"We all have to perform our duties," Godfrey answered at last. "We have a duty to the gods, our lords, our vassals… our kindred; no man worthy of his station can run from his duty."

"It has been House Hracour's duty to protect the realm of Stormsud since the very foundation of the Kingdom of Azgald." Mauger clenched his fist. "It should not fall to another. It all comes back to Skasgun. We need to reclaim our birthright. There is no future for us without it."

Godfrey paused. Both of his parents were dead. His cousin, Fallard, was still alive as far as he knew, but Godfrey no longer had brothers or sisters to carry on Ulric's legacy should he fall. Could he die in peace, knowing he was all but the last of House Cretus?

"I think I understand," Godfrey said after another long pause. "But if you've been spending so much time trying to win back your birthright, how did you allow Skasgun to fall into Davin's hands in the first place?"

"As I said, House Hracour is not nearly as mighty as it once was." Mauger shook his head. "Our allies are few. Some are influential, but they are few. King Lothar tasked my father and me with Vindholm's defense while he and Conrad the Wolf retook Skasgun."

"Conrad the Wolf is a very difficult man to work with." Godfrey shook his head. "I don't know if he would have handed Skasgun over to you even if you could have been with the crusaders there."

"A fair point." Mauger nodded. "His reputation is bad even here in the Nordslands."

"I was surprised even High Warlord Alvir knew of him," Godfrey added. "If you get Skasgun back, aren't you worried you might lose it to the Clans again? It seems that Stormsud is going to be hard to hold onto."

"The whole Kingdom of Azgald is hard to hold onto." Mauger gave a sad smile. "That's why all of these crusades have been called, right? Some say if our kings were more righteous, our knights would win more battles against the Clans. Others say that if the nobles would just unite under the King or give more of our lands to the Silver Suns, then our troubles would all disappear."

Mauger spat into the fire. It hissed so briefly that Godfrey would not have been sure he had done anything at all were he not watching. His contempt was understandable. Everyone had opinions about circumstances they did not have to live through.

"Let's first worry about getting Stormsud into the right hands again," Mauger continued. "Then we'll worry about how to hold onto it."

"Right." Godfrey frowned.

Mauger and Godfrey said nothing for a while. Godfrey shifted uncomfortably on the log he sat on. Could he find a way to speak his mind without angering his kinsman?

He let out a heavy sigh. He hoped to play some part in restoring Skasgun to Roltar and Mauger, but the contesting claim was legitimate. House Hracour had not occupied Skasgun for many years, and Davin of House Talhout was there now. Yet he promised to help his kin, and such promises were sacred. His duty was to his family.

Gradually, the campfire smoldered down to glowing coals. Stifling a yawn, Godfrey stretched. He rose to his feet and began walking to his tent, but Mauger remained sitting where he was. The heir of House Hracour stared into the crackling embers with his shoulders hunched as if all of his ancestors back to Louis the Blue were chastising him for not taking possession of Skasgun sooner.

A shrill whine startled Godfrey awake. His tent was shrouded in blackness as he fumbled out of his bedroll. Something had upset the horses. Scrambling, he pulled his boots on in the dark.

Godfrey froze in place. Harsh Nordsman voices called out from Roltar's side of the camp. Hastily, Godfrey drew his sword from its scabbard. Even before dawn, Uriel's blade gave the faintest sparkle.

Rushing out his tent door just as the predawn light began to illuminate the sky, Godfrey found a Nordsman blade already poised at his neck. He stopped as his eyes bulged at the weapon. He dared not move a muscle for fear of the enemy's sword slicing through his exposed neck.

On the other end of the blade was a gruff Clan warrior sitting atop a barded steed. It was not as large or muscular as the horses used by the Ostmen, but the Nordsman steed's hair was long and thick. Winters, undoubtedly, were less of a problem for Clan stallions.

More Nordsman cavalry moved about the camp. Their horses' saddlebags were laden with goods. How much innocent blood had been shed in exchange for these treasures they carried?

"Raiders." Godfrey seethed.

He shivered. He had not taken the time to don his armor or grab his shield before leaving his tent. He did not even have his cloak. He wore only his tunic, boots, and trousers. His only means of attack or defense was his sword held with white-knuckled fury at his hip.

There were almost a dozen Nordsman cavaliers in the camp. They were fully armed and armored. The oldest of their number held Roltar at spear point from atop his charger while another Clan warrior restrained his cousin. Roltar was likewise dressed in the full panoply of war, but his sword was still in its scabbard.

Mauger, like Godfrey, had only his sword for protection and wore little more than his night clothes, and was held hostage by another pair of Nordsmen. He, too, must have been awakened by the noise and rushed out of his tent without thinking.

"As I was saying." The oldest Nordsman turned his attention between Roltar, Mauger, and Godfrey. "Hand over all of your possessions, and we won't kill you."

Godfrey silently cursed as his eyes darted among the Nordsmen. Three against eleven were poor odds. Something was familiar about the markings on their shields, but they were not Clan Black Dragon warriors. Godfrey did not know enough about the Clans to say which one was represented by the great tusked beast adorning their weapons and armor.

The oldest Nordsman's eyes narrowed on Godfrey's sword. Surprise dawned on his face. However, the moment soon passed, and he sneered at Godfrey.

"Well." The older Nordsman turned his steed to face him. "How vulnerable we are this morning, Godfrey de Bastogne. Tizyr smiles on me today."

"You know me?" Godfrey gritted his teeth.

"I should think all the Clans know you by now, Godfrey de Bastogne." The man laughed harshly. "But I am disappointed you don't remember me."

Though the older Nordsman's accent was thick, it was easy enough for Godfrey to understand his speech. He fidgeted, but the Clan warrior next to him pressed his blade against Godfrey's throat. His eyes narrowed on the image of the red tusked beast with the long trunk of a nose on the warriors' yellow shields. Where did he last see that heraldry?

"You were at the siege of Olso." Godfrey defiantly set his jaw. "I can say, at the least, I've killed enough of your kin in recent days."

Mauger and Roltar's eyes went wide. Godfrey was tempting Tyche with his bravado, but he was not about to go quietly if they were all about to be killed anyway. Perhaps Loxias would show him a way out.

"I am Lord Storolf of Clan Behemoth." The man's horse stepped within striking distance of Godfrey. "I was at Olso Fortress with High Warlord Alvir during the siege."

"I'm surprised you had this many men left after that," Godfrey spat.

Storolf's face contorted with rage. Godfrey had taken it too far. The Clan Lord aimed his spear directly between Godfrey's eyes.

"The High Warlord will reward me handsomely when I bring him your head," Storolf snarled.

The old warrior had pulled back his spear for the death strike when a defiant yell rang out from Mauger's side of the camp. Storolf turned in the direction of the noise with a confused expression as a dark grey steed trampled one of Mauger's captors. Godfrey's jaw dropped. Atop the stallion that had thundered into camp sat the black knight from the joust at Pskov's Therismos Festival.

The black knight swung his spiked war hammer in a wide arc, which connected with the head of Mauger's other captor. The Clan warrior crumpled to the ground as his crimson blood stained the snow next to where he lay. Without even the slightest pause, the black knight moved to engage the next raider.

The Nordsman nearest Godfrey pulled back his sword in a defensive posture at this unexpected attack. Seeing his chance, Godfrey swung Uriel at Storolf's horse. The poor beast whinnied in anguish as it threw Storolf from the saddle. The warrior nearest Godfrey swiped at him with his blade, but he leapt to the side.

Grunting, Roltar broke free of his captor, and the two were soon wrestling in the snow. Another raider leapt off his horse in an apparent attempt to help pin Roltar to the ground, but Mauger rushed to his father and skewered the Nordsman. With a cry, the wounded raider fell face-first into the smouldering ashes of last night's campfire.

The horseman nearest Godfrey slashed at him with repeated downward strokes. He parried the first few strikes but had to stop himself from raising his bare left arm to block the next attack. Narrowly avoiding the sharp Clan steel, he twisted out of the way at the last moment. He was unaccustomed to fighting without his shield, and it had nearly cost him his arm.

Bellowing, the black knight charged the horseman attacking Godfrey. He swung his war hammer, and the rider fell from his steed with a thud. Godfrey nodded in thanks, but the black knight's great helm obscured any sign that he had acknowledged the gesture.

As his father rolled in the snow with the Nordsman now on top of him, Mauger grasped the enemy by the shoulder. He ripped the Clan warrior off Roltar with one hand and plunged his sword into the enemy with the other. Now the odds were decidedly in Godfrey's favor.

Shouting something in the Nordsman tongue, the rest of the Clan horsemen spurred their steeds away as fast as they could manage. Storolf rose to flee, but Godfrey held the tip of Uriel's blade to his neck.

"Ransom." Storolf swallowed hard as he dropped the mace he had been holding. "Ransom me."

"It seems Tizyr is not with you today after all." Godfrey huffed. "You were about to kill me and send my head to High Warlord Alvir. Why should I spare you?"

The Clan Lord's expression was stone. Sweat dripping from his brow, Godfrey turned to Mauger, Roltar, and, finally, the black knight. Though Godfrey asked the question, they all knew what honor demanded.

"We will ransom you," the black knight answered.

"Under the condition that you will end these raids," Godfrey added. "You have some audacity coming this deep into Azgald for plunder."

"Oblarv and Kovdor are weak right now." Storolf smiled humorlessly. "There was no better time."

Godfrey clenched his jaw. Storolf was right. Pskov was virtually emptied of its knights by the time Godfrey had visited, and now there were no crusaders to help garrison the burg. Were opportunistic Clan warriors likewise raiding Kovdor even now?

"Your men left rather quickly." Roltar gestured in the direction the other Nordsmen had fled to. "Clan Behemoth has grown soft since the last time I dealt with your kind."

"They will be punished upon my return to Sigtun," Storolf reassured him. "Now, about the ransom…"

"Before that, one more matter," Godfrey insisted. "What is High Warlord Alvir up to? Is he planning another attack? How many soldiers does he have left?"

"I'm under no obligation to answer you, Godfrey de Bastogne." Storolf snorted. "You should have asked me those questions before agreeing to ransom me."

Biting his lip, Godfrey knew Storolf was right. He could not go back on his word and slay his captive now. Chivalry demanded better of him. The gods were watching, and Godfrey did not have the heart to kill him anyway.

"I'll take him to Pskov and send word to Sigtun that Storolf of Clan Behemoth is to be ransomed for fifty gold talents," the black knight answered. "Half will be delivered to Olso Fortress, and the other half I will keep."

"So, that's your fee for rescuing us." Mauger raised an eyebrow.

"Do not take it lightly," the black knight sneered. "You would all be dead without me. Allow me this fee so that I may continue as I will."

"Who are you?" Godfrey asked. "Surely, exile is not preferable to whatever home you left. Kovdor sorely needs knights of your abilities. If you but share your name, I can offer you a place in the halls of Olso Fortress."

The black knight stared at Godfrey without saying anything for a moment. A shadowy face lurked behind his helmet's narrow vision slits, but Godfrey could see nothing beyond the cold steel. He shifted uncomfortably.

"To whom might I tell the bards I owe my life?" Godfrey asked one more time. "Do you hide a great shame, or do enemies pursue you at every turn?"

"I am the black knight," he responded as if his words were heavy iron. "I will give no other name now or as long as I bear this burden, and I will bend the knee to no lord so long as I am called the black knight."

Godfrey nodded. A mixture of pity and curiosity stirred in his bowels. There were no more answers to be had from either Storolf or the black knight today.

Chapter Eight

Darkness crept through the windows of Kolarb's great hall as evening settled in. The burning hearth crackled in the center of the chamber as Semke and a few other maidens close to her age sang and danced around it. A minstrel accompanied the beautiful young womens' tune on his lute, providing an eerie melody.

Walaric rolled his shoulder as he sat with Izold, Jordan, Paschal, and Candac at the high table with Count Maurus and Countess Sinne. The bite to his shoulder had been dressed by the Count's physician and blessed by his priest, but Walaric still winced every time he thought back to the Irelven. On more than one night at Kolarb, he had woken up in a cold sweat after having some nightmare about ghouls leaping from the mists covering Bochsogen Forest. That was over now. The bite was healing.

Not many others were in the great hall tonight. A few aged retainers occupied some of the outermost feasting tables, but the somber old men had little life in them. Like Olso, there was too much emptiness.

"I hear the mists have spread all over the Irelven now." Paschal shot Izold a worried glance. "It won't be long before they overcome Bochsogen Forest, and then it could spread to Valgo County!"

"Be quiet," Izold hissed. "Fearing what *may* come will neither stop nor hinder it. For now, enjoy the music."

"Only these walls remain," Maurus muttered as Semke and her friends continued their song, apparently unaware of the darker conversation taking place before them. "I have no sons left to send forth against the evils outside of Kolarb Castle."

"We will find the answers we need." Walaric looked the Count and Countess in the eye. "The more I see of what threatens Azgald, the more certain I am of the quest before me. Have faith."

"Let's hope you're right." Countess Sinne leaned into her husband's shoulder. "The world is growing too dangerous for people to wander about without the gods' blessing. What will happen if all the young and strong disappear before the old and tired are laid in our graves?"

Walaric swallowed hard at the thought.

"Nordsmen, orcs, undead; it's all too much for one count," Maurus sighed. "If only my fathers were here with us now. They were true knights of Azgald. They could have driven back the scourge."

Paschal grimaced awkwardly before burying his face in his mug of ale. Was saving Candac's life not a great enough deed to restore his honor, or did the memory of his shame need time to fade? Walaric could not say.

"My lord." Candac cleared his throat. "Semke is a very lovely maiden. Perhaps we could speak after I return from our journey?"

"Candac!" Walaric gasped.

Jordan and Izold glared at the younger knight, but Semke and her friends continued with their singing and dancing, still oblivious to the conversation. They were young, but not so young that talks of courtship, betrothals, and marriage arrangements should surprise any of them. Walaric shook his head.

"Lord Godfrey just knighted you," Walaric scolded. "We need you at Kovdor."

Candac made no reply, but his gaze turned to Semke just long enough for Walaric to notice. She and her friends were very attractive and good singers, too. Perhaps they were more beautiful than Elja or Thieda back at Olso, now that Walaric was really looking. Then again, Walaric might think differently if Elja were in the midst of the dancing maidens.

"Ha!" Maurus' laugh made Candac flinch. "I needed something funny to brighten my spirits tonight."

Candac slumped his shoulders and frowned.

"Give yourself a few more years, boy." Maurus patted Candac on the back. "Win some accolades, estates, and a title or two—maybe even a small bag of gold—and then we might talk about your prospects with my daughter."

"I don't see many other suitors here tonight," Candac quipped. "And the lances in your armory grow duller by the day."

Maurus chuckled. The Countess gave him an earnest look as she squeezed his hand. He sighed before turning back to the young knight.

"I like you." The Count winked. "Come back from your quest alive and whole, and we may have something to talk about in the future."

"For now," Izold brooded, "focus on the work."

Paschal had watched the whole exchange between Candac and Maurus with a sullen expression, but Walaric said nothing in reply. These kinds of discussions were well beyond Walaric's expertise, aside from what little he had seen of Godfrey's talks with Madeline's father about their upcoming wedding. He wanted to say something meaningful to Paschal but had no idea what that might be. Courting beautiful damsels and negotiating with their fathers was not something Bishop Clovis ever taught Walaric about.

"Perhaps I can introduce you to Mabel and her father." Jordan leaned close to Paschal's ear as he indicated one of the darker-haired maidens dancing beside Semke. "She is Sir

Garic's youngest daughter, and he is fairly eager to see her married off soon."

Walaric winced at the mention of the name Sir Garic. Paschal and Candac did too. The Count's aging retainer bore little resemblance to Candac's deceased master of the same name. Yet Walaric still could not help but think back to the empty seat at Vonig the Cold's table where Candac, Sir Garic, and Sir Taran used to dine every meal.

"Everything changes," Walaric muttered to himself. "Nothing stands still."

"By all means," Paschal said to Jordan after quickly regaining his composure. "It would be a great favor to me."

Semke's song soon ended, and the maidens retired to the feasting tables. A couple of the girls followed Semke to the high table, where Walaric sat, while the rest scattered to join their kin at other tables. Rising from his seat, Sir Jordan gestured for Paschal to follow him to Sir Garic's table, where Mabel now sat. Walaric smiled. There was some hope.

As everyone settled in their seats, the minstrel abandoned his lute in favor of a recorder. The tune he played was similar to one Walaric heard Godfrey practicing back at Olso late at night. *The Light Within*, he thought it was called. He never asked Godfrey about it. On the few occasions he had stumbled upon him practicing, his friend's face grew a deep shade of pink as he hurriedly tried to hide the instrument. Perhaps it was too embarrassing for him to share a talent that was not yet perfected.

The minstrel played a few more songs on his recorder as the fire in the hearth sputtered into cold ashes. However, a different kind of spark flew between Candac and Semke's eyes, though Maurus' stern gaze prevented their conversation from getting too carried away. Slowly, the older members of the Count's household began leaving for their bed chambers.

"I'm Terrwyn." A curly-haired maiden plopped into the spot at the high table directly in front of Walaric.

"*Father* Walaric." The priest stiffened.

"I know." Terrwyn gave a sly smile. "Guests at Kolarb Castle are rare enough that everyone here knows your name by now."

"I don't think we'll be here for much longer." Walaric gulped. "As soon as the snow lets up…"

"We're entering the middle of winter." Terrwyn's smile grew wider, revealing glimmering white teeth in the middle of her freckled face. "We could be trapped here for weeks on end."

Terrwyn's dark curly hair cascaded down the sides of her face. Her eyes sparkled like sapphires set in snowy fields. Did Godfrey's heart pound at the sight of Madeline as Walaric's now did for Terrwyn?

"Try some of my mother's ale." The gorgeous maiden slid a tankard across the table to Walaric. "Flur the Blevin's brewery is said to be the best in Valgo County."

"No, thanks." Walaric raised a hand in protest. "I think I need to get to bed now."

"So soon?" Terrwyn pouted.

Walaric cleared his throat. Izold was talking with an aged retainer at the far end of the great hall. Sir Jordan, Paschal, and Candac were nowhere to be seen. The Count and Countess had already left the high table and were making their way out of the chamber.

"I'm afraid so." Walaric rose from his chair.

"Have I done something to offend my lord?" Terrwyn clasped his hand.

"No!" Walaric immediately shot back.

"Do you find me unattractive?" She frowned.

"No." Walaric vigorously shook his head. "Quite the opposite, I'm afraid."

The young maiden's face was pleading, desperate. Walaric ground his teeth. He gazed down at her hands folded around his.

The signet ring Bishop Clovis gave him when he was first ordained a priest irritated his finger. First Elja. Now this. Why did she have to pick him?

"I—" Walaric glanced from one end of the chamber to the other. "I have vows to uphold."

The pleading in Terrwyn's eyes turned into some fierce anger that shook Walaric's core. He could hardly recall ever making a young woman so upset. Then again, he had hardly interacted with many so closely outside of Madeline and Elja. Madeline was spoken for, and Elja should never have been counted in Walaric's future in the first place, so far as he was concerned.

"My father is the same priest who blessed your wound the night you arrived here," Terrwyn scoffed. "It's the biggest secret everyone at Kolarb knows. Well, maybe the second biggest… But don't talk to me about upholding vows. I know what a man's vow means."

Stammering, Walaric could think of nothing to say. Terrwyn's father, a priest Walaric had met only a little while ago, was guilty of a grave sin, but had he repented, or did he continue to surrender to temptation even now? Did he try to hide his transgression from his bishop, or had he atoned and now needed to live with the shame of his past actions?

Walaric could not even remember the other priest's name at the moment. He knew far too little of the particulars concerning Terrwyn's father. What could he possibly say about this?

"No one wants me." Terrwyn released Walaric's hand as she wiped a tear from her eye. "Oh, sure, men will look at me the way all men do, but no one really wants *me*. No knight or prince wants to sully their line by marrying the illegitimate daughter of a priest. I thought you would be kind, at least. Maybe you would understand."

"And you wanted me…" Walaric began to adjust the gleaming band around his finger.

"To take me away from here to wherever you're going," Terrwyn finished the thought. "Olso, Vindholm, Cardigal—doesn't matter. I just need to escape my father, make a new past, and start over. There's been enough destruction round about. No one will question a beautiful maiden like me seeking a new home."

"We're going on a dangerous quest." Walaric gulped. "No handsome knights or warm hearths await you there. The journey is too perilous. We can't take you."

"But you do find me attractive?" Terrwyn batted her eyes at Walaric.

"Very." Walaric blushed.

Walaric gasped and immediately looked away. He should not have said that. He could imagine the shock on Bishop Clovis' face all the way back at Vosg. Even going this far with a young woman was dangerous territory. Sterner bishops or priests might have insisted Walaric was in need of confession if they had overheard this exchange. He had to leave.

"Try some of my mother's ale." Terrwyn nudged the tankard a little closer to Walaric. "They really do say it is the best in Valgo County."

Walaric took one last look across the chamber before glancing down at the frothy golden liquid before him. Izold was also no longer in the great hall. Reluctantly, Walaric resumed his seat.

"I don't know how I can help you." Walaric took a tentative sip of the ale. "We won't be here long."

"For now." The grin returned to Terrwyn's face. "Let's just talk. That's all I need tonight."

"All right." Walaric took a long swig of ale from Terrwyn's tankard. "This is really good."

"Thanks." Terrwyn giggled.

"You said your parentage was the second biggest secret everyone at Kolarb knew." Walaric wiped away a film of malty ale from his lip with his sleeve. "What's the biggest secret everyone here knows?"

"Yes." Terrwyn nodded after a moment. "Yes, we can talk about that. Let's start with this: What do you know about Count Maurus' dead sons?"

Panting, Nera stumbled through the shadows. She fell forward, her hands and knees splashing into a murky puddle in front of her. Though the water was exquisitely cold, she rose to her feet and started running again without taking the slightest pause to dry herself. She had to keep going.

In the distance, something howled beyond a rocky outcropping behind her. Everything in the twilight world between the living and the dead was bleak. There were no plants or animals—at least nothing living she would recognize. There was no warmth. No Sun. No Moon.

All that surrounded Nera was grey rocks, shadows, and mist. A black covering filled the sky like a starless night. Color barely existed here.

Time was meaningless in this realm of endless wandering. Had it been a week, a month, or a year since Nera was finally forced to flee that priest's abjurations at Olso Fortress? She could not say.

Occasionally, Nera found a small stream or pool filled with icy cold water as she strayed about this desolate land. On even rarer occasions, she spied some hideous phantom lurking in the darkness or drifting aimlessly a few feet above the hazy plains. It was all so surreal. Until the hellhounds caught her scent.

More howling made Nera's heart pound faster in her chest than she thought possible. Without a physical body, she could not tire in the sense that she knew before now, but she still knew fear, and her movements eventually grew slower over time. As her pace grew sluggish, the howls mixed with braying and barking. They were close.

A black wolf-like creature leapt in front of Nera, barring her way forward. A thin layer of tiny hot glowing embers fell from its sooty fur as it landed on all four paws. She turned, but two more hellhounds blocked her retreat. With glistening yellow fangs, all three beasts snarled as they surrounded her.

"The hunt is over, witch," the hellhound in front of Nera growled. "The Abyss calls for you now."

"Nurlg." Nera gasped at the lead hellhound. "My death has not been avenged. I still have work in the mortal sphere. Give me time."

"You will not find success." Fire gleamed in Nurlg's eyes. "Tyche has decreed your doom. You will either descend through the well at Vardsa with us, or we will consume your spirit here."

"How can Fate declare my doom already?" Nera sneered. "I made a bargain with the Keeper of Souls. We signed a pact in blood at Mirtys. He was supposed to stay Tyche's hand."

"Your husband has forgotten you, and your goblins have died." The hellhound flicked his tail impatiently. "You have nothing left to bind you to the mortal sphere but impotent rage and an empty promise. Now that you have been cast out of Olso Fortress, you can only diminish in strength and form."

Gritting her teeth, Nera balled her fists.

"Come and see." Nurlg tilted his head towards a small puddle behind him.

The scent of brimstone grew unmistakable as Nera drew nearer to the hellhound. She bent over her reflection in the water. She was no longer the beautiful, terrifying Great Witch of the North. All that remained of her once full, dark hair was a few silvery wisps. Her once fair skin was now withered and dry. A clawed skeletal creature with empty eye sockets stared back at her now.

Nera wailed bitterly. How could her form have wasted so much? Was this why Alvir had abandoned her in death? Her hatred for him simmered. He would suffer in this life or the next, whenever she saw him next.

She looked at her bony, clawed hands. There was no way to repair the damage. Even the strongest necromancy could only preserve her current form at best. There was no recovering her youth and beauty ever again. Eventually, she would deteriorate into one of the wandering phantoms of this twilight realm if left here long enough, unless…

"Grant me but one boon, Nurlg," Nera pleaded.

"I will hear it." The hellhound sat on his haunches.

"Allow me to continue to the city of Mirtys in the Blighted Lands," she said. "Let me speak with the necromancers there. Athanatos, god of undeath, grows restless and will surely keep me on as his thrall if I may be given the chance to propitiate his oracles."

Nurlg snorted and shook his head. He stood on all four legs and began ambling towards Nera, licking his jaws. The other two hellhounds began circling her and snapped at the fringes of her tattered dress. Nurlg bared his fangs.

"I still have much to offer," Nera screeched. "Do not underestimate me!"

The witch produced a ball of flame in the palm of her hand and hurled it at Nurlg. The hellhounds paused as the magical fire hit the ground in front of their leader. It vanished just as quickly as it had appeared, but all three hellhounds remained motionless for a moment. Wagging his tail, Nurlg sniffed the spot.

"You still have magic." Nurlg's eyes met Nera's. "This changes the odds in your favor. We will tell this news to

Tyche. Yoan may wish to refashion you into some minor demon or devil."

"I will petition Athanatos, not Yoan," Nera insisted. "I still have work among the mortals."

"As you wish." Nurlg lowered his head. "But Yoan will be displeased. If you fail to impress the Deathless One, then we shall come for you again."

"You forget the Blighted Lands are a sanctuary to the spirits of the damned," Nera corrected. "You cannot touch me there. And don't forget I still have the Keeper of Souls' promise binding me to the mortal world."

Nurlg huffed.

"Athanatos will hear me." Nera gestured towards the Blighted Lands. "It was my runestone that Alvir erected, which first stirred him from his slumber."

"Athanatos cares for runestones but not destroyed idols." Nurlg snorted. "There has been much death in the Nordslands as of late, and it makes the Deathless One thirst. There are forces at work far greater than a shade's spite."

"Don't speak to me of the long winter." Nera twitched. "I know the lore of Ragnarok."

"If we come for you again, we will not leave empty-handed," Nurlg snarled before turning back in the direction he had come from.

The other hellhounds followed Nurlg into the darkness. Shadow gradually obscured their forms. Soon, only faint embers trailing from their fur pierced the black.

"Hellhounds always get their prey," Nurlg called over his shoulder. "Not even the Blighted Lands can protect you forever. We will find a way or make one."

Eventually, the embers faded away, though the scent of brimstone remained. Nera sighed in relief. Once she was sure the hellhounds were gone, she rose a few feet off the ground and allowed herself to drift in the wind. It was heading towards the Blighted Lands and would convey her there quickly enough.

Gripping his blanket, Walaric shot up from his bed in a cold sweat. His breath was short. His heart pounded.

He blinked several times, expecting to see Nera's ghost standing beside him in the darkness. After no such apparition appeared, he released his hold on his blanket. It was just a dream.

"Or was it a vision?" Walaric asked aloud as he tried to piece the details back together in his mind. "Mirtys. The Great Witch of the North is going to Mirtys."

Sleep had fled from Walaric's eyes entirely. After slipping out of his night clothes, he quickly dressed for the day and began packing his things away. They needed to go.

Once he had packed up all his things, Walaric found himself rapping his fist against Izold's door across the hallway. After a few moments of impatient knocking, the oak door creaked open. Bleary-eyed, the paladin gazed down at Walaric, but his expression soon regained the fierce sobriety he was known for.

"What is it?" Izold scowled.

"Where is Mirtys?" Walaric asked.

"Mirtys?" Izold repeated. "That's a necropolis in the Blighted Lands. It's the heart of the realm of the damned."

"Right," Walaric said. "I thought as much. But where *in* the Blighted Lands is it?"

"It's at the northern end of the Dovern Highlands," Izold answered. "I suppose you ask because that's where we're going now?"

"That's where Nera's ghost is heading." Walaric grimaced. "She'll be there soon."

"How soon?" Izold raised an eyebrow.

"How fast does a crow fly?" Walaric cringed. "I don't know, but we can no longer winter here in Kolarb. We need to leave now."

"We will need to cross almost the entire breadth of the Blighted Lands to reach Mirtys." Izold's jaw tightened. "Even I shudder to think of the horrors we will face."

"If that is the road the gods would have us walk, then it is the road we must walk." Walaric gulped.

By dawn, Walaric, Izold, Jordan, Candac, and Paschal were all trudging through the deep snow with Kolarb Castle far behind them. The grey clouds hung low overhead, and an icy wind howled in Walaric's ears. No one wanted to be out in this weather.

"How fast can a ghost fly?" Paschal wondered aloud.

"Faster than a crow." Candac shrugged.

"How do you know?" Paschal shook his head.

"They have… powers." Candac looked at Walaric as if seeking clarification or approval.

"There is much about the afterlife and spirits we don't understand," Walaric replied. "Sages have studied and catalogued what they could, but there is a lot of disagreement and speculation. Some things cannot be revealed while we are bound to these mortal bodies."

"Well, I'm not so eager to find out that I'm willing to give up this mortal body yet." Paschal looked back towards the distant Kolarb Castle.

"Don't worry," Candac jibed. "I'm sure Mabel will still be waiting for you when we get back. She wasn't so pretty that a more handsome knight will sweep her off her feet while we're away."

Glowering, Paschal turned a deep shade of red. Some knights took great offense at insults hurled at their ladies, but that was far more common with those who spent significant time in courtly life, from what Walaric had seen. Warriors out on the border marches had far more practical concerns to worry about. At any rate, Paschal had already regained his composure.

"You were pretty bold about your own intentions regarding Count Maurus' daughter last night." Paschal shook his head at Candac as they continued pressing through the snow.

"Tyche favors the bold," Candac answered as he quickly averted his eyes.

Walaric also blushed as he thought back to Terrwyn. Nothing romantic had actually happened. He had certainly entertained more thoughts than he should have, but a quiet conversation and a tankard of ale was the end of it. Kolarb and all its secrets were behind him.

"It will be nine days through the woods at this rate." Sir Jordan pointed to the dark tree line ahead. "We can turn south and resupply at Narlstad or go directly east to Epsberg. It will take us longer to find a place to rest, but Epsberg puts us closer to the Blighted Lands, so I suggest we follow that course."

"Haste seems most prudent now," Izold agreed.

"I stayed in Narlstad's infirmary for several weeks after getting paralyzed by a cyclops," Walaric said. "The castellan, Marshal Horvath, will treat us well if we stop there, but I agree that haste is more important than hospitality now."

The smile on Walaric's face faded as he considered the shadowy tree line before them. The woods were generally an unwelcoming sight filled with mystery and danger, but the possibility of undead lurking amidst the treacherous branches and brambles forced Walaric's jaw to clench. If only there were another way.

"What's the name of that forest there?" Walaric pointed to the trees.

"This is still Bochsogen Forest," Jordan answered. "It extends south and east of the Irelven for several days."

Walaric gulped. He brushed his hand against where the ghoul had bitten him. It had healed a while ago now, but the memory lingered.

"It would take more than a fortnight to go around," Jordan answered the question in Walaric's eyes. "I don't think you want to add any more days to our journey; we don't have to right now."

"Word is that the mists are only around the Irelven," Candac added. "We should be fine going through the southern part of the woods to Epsberg."

"Oh, I remember Epsberg." Walaric cringed. "No great memories of that place either."

"Epsberg is under the Silver Suns' control now," Paschal reassured him. "I'm sure they don't hold anything against us anymore."

"Lord Godfrey did help them win Epsberg back from Tancred and Conrad, after all." Candac crossed his arms. "They should be grateful to us."

"Let's hope the Silver Suns see it that way." Walaric set his jaw as they drew nearer to the woods.

The next four days traveling through Bochsogen Forest proved just as cold and arduous as Walaric had come to expect of any journey through the Nordslands. He was numb, his clothes were filthy, but he kept his complaints to himself. Walaric expected Jordan and Izold to meet these hardships with rigid stoicism, but even Paschal and Candac's responses to the poor weather were fairly muted.

At one point, there were signs of an old satyr camp that Jordan said looked recently abandoned. Walaric did not mind that, but the sound of wolves howling for their first three consecutive nights in Bochsogen Forest gave him the distinct impression they were being followed. Then, by the fourth night, the wolves grew silent, and that somehow bothered him more than when they were trailing the camp.

"Wolves are fiercely territorial," Jordan explained when Walaric brought this up over breakfast on their fifth day in the woods, "but they usually don't follow people once we leave their homes."

"Or maybe they stopped following us because we're about to come across something worse." Paschal took his seat next to the fire. "There are supposed to be winged lions here in Oblarv. We are still in the Duchy of Oblarv, right?"

"I wouldn't worry about lamassus here." Jordan waved his hand over his bowl of porridge. "They usually stay farther north than this."

Walaric looked down at his own bowl of porridge. A large pot over the fire was filled with more. It was blander than he would have liked, but it was the one warm meal he had to look forward to in the forest. Most game animals were harder to find during the winter, which meant the men had to eat more dry foods they were carrying with them.

On the far side of the camp, Izold fed his horse from a bag of grain. Vielantiu was the last steed they had, and he served as more of a pack animal than a riding horse at this point. Jordan frowned as Izold approached the campfire with an empty bowl.

"You might want to leave your horse at Epsberg when we get there," Jordan suggested. "Vielantiu is a noble stallion, but he's not hastening our journey. I'd hate to see any harm come to him once we enter more hostile realms."

"No." Izold furrowed his brow as he filled his bowl from the pot over the fire. "I understand your concern. Boreas was a great loss, sired from a noble lineage, but Vielantiu goes wherever I go. Only death will part us."

Jordan nodded solemnly. Candac and Paschal did too. Ironically, it was only after many of the crusaders began losing their horses in battle that Walaric began to notice how much knights valued their steeds. Some openly wept at their losses. Others, like Sir Jordan, carried their burdens quietly, but the change in demeanor could still be felt.

Once breakfast had ended, Walaric doused the flames, and the others began tearing down their tents. There was no use in lingering out in the cold. They still had at least a few days before they reached Epsberg.

The sky was bright for the first time in several days as Walaric and his party continued on a nearly straight eastern path. For a little while, Walaric had given up on praying to Helios that the weather would improve. The cloudy North Wind prevailed in the struggle between Boreas and Helios for many days, but the rays of the Sun now chastised Walaric's faithlessness.

The others' moods noticeably improved as well throughout the morning as they happily chattered through their trek. After the midday meal, Izold started singing an old Gothian marching song once they resumed traveling. None of the others knew it at first, but Walaric soon picked up on the lyrics, and Jordan and Candac joined in not long after. Even Paschal's normal gloom eventually yielded to the occasion, and they all sang the chorus together.

They continued singing for some time; however, Walaric's heart jumped into his throat as the sight of mist hugging the tree trunks ahead came into view. The old Gothian marching song came to an abrupt halt. Vielantiu whinnied nervously, and Izold patted his steed's face. Everyone stood frozen in place.

"We should go around," Walaric quietly urged.

"Agreed." Jordan clenched his jaw. "No need to continue this way."

For a moment, all eyes fell on Izold. Sternly gazing into the mist ahead, the paladin said nothing at first. His expression was unreadable beneath his steel great helm.

"South to Narlstad then?" Candac whispered.

"South to Narlstad." Izold nodded.

Letting out a long, steamy breath, Walaric relaxed his shoulders. Jordan turned and began leading the way south. Candac jogged a few paces to catch up, and Izold slowly guided his horse after them. However, Paschal crossed his arms and remained where he stood.

"I thought paladins were supposed to welcome these kinds of challenges," Paschal quipped. "Is there not a great evil in there we must destroy?"

Izold halted Vielantiu and turned back to face Paschal. Jordan and Candac also stopped and turned. Unsure how Izold might respond to this veiled accusation of cowardice, Walaric held his breath.

"The difference between bravery and rashness is prudence," Izold slowly answered. "A great evil does lie waiting in that haze, but we cannot needlessly throw our lives away in some vain effort to eradicate every ghoul and zombie in the Nordslands."

Apparently still unsatisfied, Paschal shook his head.

"Will you go in there alone?" Izold asked. "We are pursuing the source of this madness with all diligence. Let us pray that it will be enough to cleanse the land of this vile curse."

With that, Izold turned his horse back towards Jordan and urged Vielantiu south. Jordan and Candac resumed their march, leaving just Walaric and Paschal. His feet firmly planted as he gazed into the mist, the young knight ignored Walaric as the priest took a few tentative steps through the crisp snow.

"Why do you linger?" Walaric asked after a moment. "There's nothing for us here."

"They called me a coward." Paschal's grip grew tight around the handle of the ax on his belt. "They called *me* a coward after I was wounded in the siege. I didn't want to stop fighting, but I couldn't go on. Do you understand? I didn't have the strength…"

With an awkward grimace, Walaric shifted on his feet. He was sure this was the reason for Paschal's outburst at Izold, but he was previously told to let the warriors settle their own affairs regarding martial pride. Now he had to say something, but what?

"I was sure I was going to die there." Paschal's voice grew agitated. "I felt my strength leaving me in that filthy bed of straw as I bled out. But what could I have done?"

Walaric's jaw opened and closed, but he thought it better not to speak yet. Paschal's frustrations had been boiling under the surface for weeks on end. Sometimes it was better to listen before offering a solution.

"Now Izold tells us we can just go around these undead monsters because he doesn't find it convenient," Paschal spat. "Who is the real coward here?"

Silently, Walaric prayed Loxias, Truth Giver would reveal the words he needed in this moment. He had not thought much about what it meant to be a chivalrous knight, when to fight, or when to flee, until now. He had only a few brief experiences in combat to relate. May they be enough.

"All I can say about courage is that I think it means doing the right thing no matter what." Walaric looked into the fog ahead. "I don't know exactly what's through that mist, but it's probably only death for us. There are too few of us to come out victorious. And there's no good reason to throw ourselves at death right now."

At last, Paschal turned to meet Walaric's gaze.

"I remember when Alvir's men broke through Olso's walls that night," Walaric continued. "Some of us fought. Some of us ran. Most of us didn't have a choice, but some did choose to fight—to buy the rest of us time—when they could have run."

Quivering, Paschal nodded.

"I don't think it's fair of the others to judge your actions that night." Walaric placed a hand on Paschal's shoulder.

"You did what you had to do to live. It was no different than barricading yourself in one of the towers or falling back to the keep."

"Then why do they judge me so harshly?" Paschal's eyes grew fierce.

"I think you judge yourself most harshly." Walaric grimaced. "No one here thinks you are a coward. Give yourself time. Your valor will be given the chance to shine through once more."

"Then no one will sing a shameful song about me?" Paschal snorted.

"Lord Godfrey does like to say that a lot." Walaric smiled. "Cheldric had his struggles, too, in that song."

Chapter Nine

Elja wrinkled her nose in disgust as she ran her hand through her hair. Thieda crossed her arms and looked expectantly at Madeline, but did not say anything. Rolling her eyes, she turned away from her friends and gazed out her bedroom window. There was always some drama that needed to be discussed.

"I think you need to tell Karl and Alpia to take their courtship somewhere else," Elja insisted as she leaned against Madeline's bookshelf.

"They're our guests." Madeline shook her head as she rose from the chair next to her table. "I'm not throwing them out in the middle of winter."

"They're overstaying their welcome," Elja said. "Our pantry grows bare while Alpia insists that every meal be a feast. Moric Cyclops Slayer is a man of great wealth. They can manage, if you tell them to go."

Madeline bit her lip. Karl the Hammer was loyal to Godfrey, but few men could not be bought by something. Moric had wealth. Alpia had beauty. Better to keep them all at Olso, where she could make sure Karl did not get whisked away to Vorot without them knowing.

"Thieda?" Madeline looked at her other friend, who was staring into the hearth. "What do you think? Is House de Toron being unreasonable in their requests?"

"I think Elja is jealous of the Beauty of the Bosvian Coast." Thieda's gaze bored into the other handmaiden. "But they do have voracious appetites for just two guests."

"I think you may be right," Madeline agreed. "Elja, you're still young and as beautiful as any knight could hope to marry. Don't try to compete with Alpia. None of us can."

"That's easy enough for you to say," Elja huffed.

"You need to get over Walaric." Thieda stepped away from the hearth. "He's been gone for a while now, and he may not come back."

"Don't say that," Elja moped.

"I know you prefer forbidden fruit." Madeline smirked. "But there are other men here in the castle *not* pledged to the celestial gods."

"Like Evroul!" Thieda squealed.

"The blacksmith's apprentice?" Elja furrowed her brow. "No, thanks! I can go without all the soot."

Thieda and Madeline giggled for a moment as Elja blushed. Poor Elja had always been so concerned about finding the right man. If only she knew how to choose one.

"Sir Magnus and Berold are both unmarried." Madeline raised an eyebrow. "I've seen the way they look at you. It would not take much for you to put your charms on one of those two."

"Or Sir Halinard," Thieda quipped. "I hear he's recently widowed."

"Sir Halinard?" Elja wrinkled her nose again.

"What about Vonig?" Madeline suggested.

"Vonig the Cold?" Elja's eyes lit up.

"He's spoken for," Thieda quickly answered.

"By who?" Madeline raised an eyebrow as Elja's countenance fell once again.

For a moment, there was silence. Though Thieda's mouth remained shut, every passing second only confirmed what

Madeline had initially guessed. Only one damsel at Olso could truly be a good match for Vonig the Cold.

"By me." Thieda cast her eyes to the floor.

"And you didn't tell us?" Madeline gasped. "How long have you been seeing each other?"

"A while," Thieda confessed, "since we first arrived here in Kovdor."

Elja's jaw hung open. Madeline's mind raced as she tried to think of any past clues that might have given away Thieda and Vonig's secret romance. Too much of her time had been spent under the watchful eye of Sister Vanya for her to notice, but apparently, Elja was just as surprised by this revelation.

"We didn't want to announce anything with your wedding so close," Thieda explained. "It's your big day coming up, and we didn't want to diminish it."

"All this time shut up in the castle was bound to make more than one couple fall in love." Madeline twirled her hair around her finger. "I'm happy for you."

"You're serious about Vonig?" Elja stammered.

"We've spoken to Father Edric," Thieda answered, "but we weren't going to say anything to anyone else until after the wedding."

"Vonig the Cold and Thieda." Madeline pursed her lips. "I can see it. You two would get along well enough."

"At least it seems easy enough to catch a private moment without Sister Vanya following your every move." Elja brushed her hair out of her face.

"I'll have to request the Order of the Ivory Chalice send us a few more librarians." Madeline gazed sternly at Elja. "That will put us all on a more even footing."

"No, please don't!" Elja giggled. "I might never find love if I have an old sister following me around everywhere I go. One Sister Vanya is enough for all of us."

Madeline laughed at the idea of several nuns following them around the castle. Elja and Thieda joined in. However, Madeline soon grew more serious. Why was she the only young woman in Olso Fortress with a chaperone? Did no one care about Elja and Thieda's purity, or were Elja, Thieda, and Madeline all supposed to watch each other?

"Are you ladies done with all this vapid gossip yet?" Fravash hopped up onto the table next to Madeline. "Lady Madeline and I have a lot of work to do."

Elja and Thieda shrieked at the sight of the rodent standing on its hind legs. Madeline had only noticed him as he first spoke up, but she immediately jumped between her friends and Fravash. Hoping to prevent any unfortunate accidents as they panicked, she vigorously waved her arms at Elja and Thieda.

"It's all right," Madeline cried. "It's all right! He's a friend. Calm down."

"A friend?" Thieda's eyes bulged.

"A talking rat?" Elja squeaked.

"Mouse," Fravash corrected. "I'm a talking mouse, but, yes, a friend too."

"Elja, Thieda." Madeline pointed from the young ladies to the diminutive spell familiar. "This is Fravash. He's here to help me."

Elja and Thieda's initial terror moderated down to timid glances over Madeline's shoulder. Madeline lowered her arms and nodded encouragingly. Stepping to the side, she gestured to Fravash again.

"Help with what?" Thieda's eyes narrowed.

"We're gathering materials to construct a magic staff for Madeline," Fravash answered. "We already acquired a handful of sapphire dust from that old dwarf patriarch, Dachlann, down in the mines. We can get the ox flesh from the butcher. The vial of unicorn—"

"Does Sister Vanya know you have a talking mouse in your room?" Thieda interrupted.

"How rude!" Fravash crossed his arms.

"No." Madeline's face grew hot. "I wanted to wait a little bit. You know how Sister Vanya would feel."

"Yes." Thieda's eyes went wide. "She'd tell you to get rid of it. That thing could be dangerous!"

"I'm not an *it*, and I'm right here!" Fravash stamped his foot. "Don't talk about me as if I'm not right in front of you, you ill-mannered, brash, ignorant, young damsel. I'm a very distinguished spell familiar, I'll have you know. I have received some of the highest honors among the wizarding kind. You can't just—"

"You don't know what this thing is really trying to get you to do." Thieda wagged her finger at Madeline. "Remember how much trouble *The Book of Elder Wisdom* caused for us. I don't want us to get in trouble again."

Thieda was about to say more, but no sounds would form in her mouth. With trembling hands, she grasped at her throat. Madeline and Elja looked down at Fravash as he leered at Thieda.

"I am Fravash the Bright." The mouse stood up to his full height. "I am an honorary knight of Farthest Thule. I composed *The Ways of Uzul*. The angel, Yael, allowed me to taste the fruit of the Golden Tree and live. I don't need to manipulate Madeline to get anything I want. Now put your fears aside. All right, young Thieda?"

Apparently still unable to speak, Thieda replied with a meek nod. Fravash blinked twice, and an unseen force released its grip on her tongue. Thieda drew in a deep breath, but seemed unharmed.

"As I was saying." Fravash cleared his throat. "We'll need wood to fashion the staff from. Elm or ash; something pure. Thieda, can you speak with one of the carpenters for us?

Have him make a wooden rod that equals Lady Madeline's height exactly. Understood?"

"I can do that," Thieda answered with a timid frown.

"It needs to have a hole drilled through the top, no wider than her finger and twice as long," Fravash continued. "We're going to need to insert a powerful magical artifact into the staff to increase its potency. Madeline, do you have an affinity towards any particular magical beast?"

"Not particularly." Madeline glanced out the window again. "Well, there is Spathi."

"The griffin is a noble choice," Fravash conceded, "but I don't think he's right for *your* staff. Is there a magical creature that *you* are particularly drawn to?"

"I will need to think about that." Madeline frowned. "House Drois has some famous dragon-slayers in our lineage. Maybe that's something we can work with?"

"Dragons!" Fravash snapped his finger. "What did you do with Vozzab's body after he was slain?"

"Lord Godfrey carries one of the dragon's horns on his belt," Elja answered excitedly. "The rest of Vozzab's remains were returned to the cavern he slumbered in at the bottom of the silver mine."

"We can work with that." Fravash stroked his chin. "Maybe not for the core, but there are other uses for dragons. If we can grind a tooth or scale down into powder, we can use that as a very potent ingredient for the potion we will need to infuse the staff with. Elja, will you go down into the mine to retrieve a scale?"

"Not alone!" Elja protested.

"Vozzab is dead," Madeline countered. "He can't hurt you. But, Fravash, will we not offend Yoan by further defiling the corpse of her son?"

"Yoan is always offended by followers of the light." The rodent chuckled. "If Godfrey already carries one of the dragon's horns, things can't be made any worse for you."

"But Lord Godfrey carries a sword blessed by Helios himself," Thieda said. "He has special protections against the instruments of evil."

"Don't worry about Yoan's influence here anymore," Fravash squeaked. "Nera's shade has left us, and there are no remnants of her malice left in Olso. Elja, I will go down to Vozzab's remains in the mine with you."

"Thanks." Elja gave an uncertain smile.

"Lady Madeline, do you know the source of your magic?" The mouse twitched his whiskers. "That is going to be the key to making the most powerful staff we can."

"I always assumed it was a gift from Loxias or some other god." Madeline shrugged. "How can I find out?"

"Sometimes a mage's powers will imitate the source from whence they came." Fravash rubbed his nose. "Fire could mean one of your ancestors communed with a dragon, and that was carried through your family's blood. Invisibility, though, that's a tough one."

"Madeline can turn invisible?" Elja and Thieda gasped at the same time.

"Fravash!" Madeline gave the mouse a scornful look. "I hadn't told anyone about that."

"Didn't you?" Fravash flattened his ears.

"Oh, well, I did tell Godfrey," Madeline corrected herself. "But he's the only one who knew."

"You always keep secrets from us!" Elja cried.

"Did you ever spy on us?" Thieda asked darkly.

"I'm sorry." Madeline cringed. "It was for my own protection. I never spied on either of you, I swear it. I didn't want you to know in case I ever had to escape the clutches of kidnappers or some monster. I didn't want anyone to know I could just slip away unseen."

"And yet you told Godfrey," Thieda pointed out.

"Godfrey was the first person I told many things." Madeline threw out her hands in exasperation.

"Well, when you're in love…" Elja conceded.

"Right." Fravash sighed. "Now about the source of your magical abilities…"

"I don't know where they came from," Madeline admitted. "I was born with them as far as I know. Mother and Father never had any powers that they spoke of."

"What about other members of your family?" Fravash pressed. "An uncle or aunt? Grandparents? Sometimes, magical gifts may skip a generation or two for reasons no one can comprehend."

"None have had any as far as I know." Madeline shrugged. "Remember, magic is looked down on here in Azgald. I was told to keep my powers hidden for all of my life until I couldn't keep them a secret anymore. People accused me of witchcraft when they found out."

"Oh, yes." Fravash sighed. "Men are so fearful of things they can't control. The dwarves are also fearful and guard their magic through endless ritual, but the elves don't carry nearly as many superstitions about the arcane arts."

Madeline looked down at Fravash curiously.

"Now that your secret is out." The mouse gestured to the room at large. "I suggest you consult some of your extended family, privately. The core of your staff will need an appropriate artifact."

"I can write Aunt Collette," Madeline answered after a moment's thought. "She is one of the Queen's ladies in waiting at Vindholm."

"That's a good start." Fravash nodded enthusiastically. "Write her as soon as you can."

"What about this?" Elja pulled a book from Madeline's shelf.

Madeline took the musty tome from Elja's hand. The fading title on the spine read *The Histories of House Vred*. Slowly, she flipped through the pages. What secrets could it reveal?

"This is about my mother's family." Madeline closed the book after scanning through a few pages. "Maybe there is something in here that could help us learn more."

"Study it." Fravash nodded earnestly. "That's our best lead so far."

Several days passed. Many of the material components had been gathered for the staff in Madeline's room, and a large kettle had been set over her hearth where the contents of the potion brewed. Fravash had shown Madeline how to make it, but there was little variance from what *The Book of Elder Wisdom* had previously divulged to her. At least the demon-possessed tome had been honest about a few things.

There was no use in hiding what Madeline was attempting. Soon, everyone in Olso Fortress knew she was trying to create a magic staff. No one openly opposed her efforts, but many of the household servants and armed retainers gave her more space than usual as she went down the corridors or entered the various chambers she needed to go to in the course of her day. The old fear of witches was alive and well.

Nervously, Madeline adjusted her wimple as she made her way up to the library after breakfast. She did not typically wear wimples, but they were becoming more popular among the noble ladies of Azgald. There were not many other women for Madeline to impress at Olso aside from Lady Alpia, but the wimple served her purposes.

Madeline walked up the steps of the spiral staircase at a brisk pace. Fravash softly squeaked as he clung to the inside of the wimple's thick cloth. Cringing, Madeline slowed her ascent.

"Do we have to travel like this?" Fravash whispered in Madeline's ear. "This is highly undignified!"

"We can't keep the staff a secret," Madeline replied, "but I don't want to reveal your presence yet. One thing at a time for the simple folk of Olso Fortress."

"If you insist," the familiar squeaked.

"I do," Madeline huffed as she neared the third-floor landing. "Now hush. I don't want people thinking I've gone mad and started talking to myself."

Fravash chirped. Stopping briefly at the third-floor landing, Madeline bit her lip. Was the familiar upset? She could not dwell on it too long. She had to get to the library with Fravash undetected.

Resuming a faster pace, Madeline made her way down the corridor to the library. The mouse gripped the inside of her wimple more tightly but did not vocalize any complaints. Soon, she found the old librarian at her desk, poring over a large codex.

"You're late," Sister Vanya noted without looking up from her book. "Do I need to start escorting you from the moment you wake up to when you go to bed again?"

"No, Sister Vanya." Madeline shook her head. "I'm sorry. I'll try to be quicker next time."

"Good." Sister Vanya flipped the page in her book. "Punctuality is important for any leader worthy of respect. Now tell me about this sorcerous business you have going on in your room before you get on with your chores. You're making a magic staff, but you don't have any grimoires to aid you in its construction?"

"That's right." Madeline swallowed hard. "The books you gave me weren't much help."

"Then how do you know what to do?" Sister Vanya squinted at Madeline.

She stammered as she searched for the right words. Could she claim inspiration from the gods? Would the nun believe her if she said it was revealed to her in a dream?

Then, Madeline's heart froze as Fravash slid down her wimple. With her jaw clenched, the librarian's eyes followed the mouse as he scurried down Madeline's sleeve before leaping onto Sister Vanya's desk. Madeline could do nothing but stare in abject horror as the mouse stood upright. She told him not to do this earlier. What was Fravash thinking?

"You!" Sister Vanya hissed. "I *thought* it was you, Fravash. I told you not to come to my library again. What are you doing here now?"

"That was the library at Sudvall." Fravash raised a finger. "This is clearly the library at Olso Fortress. You can't ban me from every library you happen to be at."

"I can and I—" Sister Vanya began.

"Wait!" Madeline's jaw hung open. "You two know each other?"

"Fravash is a menace." Sister Vanya wagged her finger. "He was always trying to get into forbidden lore even after I expressly told him he could not. I had him banned from Sudvall's library years ago."

"That's some gratitude you show for the author of *The Ways of Uzul.*" Fravash twitched. "You know, I could have the elves of Farthest Thule collect that book for me and keep it in their library. *They* appreciate the nature of my research, at least."

"What are you doing here, Fravash?" Sister Vanya's nostrils flared as she forcefully set her book on the desk.

"I'm trying to help Lady Madeline mature into a proper sorceress." The familiar gestured to Madeline. "There are many opportunities to get this wrong, and I don't believe you have the insight needed to train her further."

"*I* don't have the insight?" Sister Vanya raised an eyebrow. "I would like to see you do better! When was the last time you took on a student?"

"At least none of my pupils ever communed with possessed spell books." Fravash pointed to the librarian.

Silently, Sister Vanya fumed. Madeline averted her eyes as her cheeks grew hot with embarrassment. Her head still spun at so many unexpected turns in this conversation, but she desired no reminders about *The Book of Elder Wisdom*.

"Remember why we came here, Fravash," Madeline pleaded. "I didn't want you to start a fight with Sister Vanya. In fact, I didn't want her to know you were here at all."

"My apologies, Lady Madeline." Fravash bowed his head. "Sister Vanya, we'll pick up this discussion later."

The librarian's eyes narrowed at Madeline.

"We think my magical abilities may be tied to something that happened to one of my ancestors." Madeline cleared her throat. "I've been studying *Histories of House Vred*, and there are a few vague references to *fiery blood*, but I don't know if it's talking about magic. Could you help me find something in the library about my father's side, House Drois, or more about my mother's house?"

"Genealogy is a far less dangerous topic." Sister Vanya nodded. "Let me see what I can find for you."

The librarian rose from her seat. She took a few tentative steps towards the bookshelves. However, she quickly turned to face Fravash.

"Remember, you're still not allowed in the forbidden archives, even if this isn't Sudvall's library." The old woman pointed a bony finger at Fravash.

"Sister Vanya, I thought we were past this now," the mouse protested.

"Make sure he stays with you." Sister Vanya turned her gaze to Madeline. "There is some lore the Ivory Chalice has deemed even Fravash the Bright should not delve into too deeply, for his own sanity."

Madeline briefly nodded before the old librarian stepped off into the midst of the rows of bookshelves that filled the library. With Sister Vanya out of sight, Madeline turned to Fravash. His whiskers twitched.

"You didn't tell me you knew Sister Vanya." Madeline crossed her arms.

"It didn't seem important until now," Fravash confessed, "but, yes, we have a history of sorts. I do much of my research in libraries."

"What does a spell familiar need to research?" Madeline tilted her head down at Fravash.

"I am also a student of magic," he answered. "In our craft, there are few true masters. We must all learn through continuous practice and study."

"But you're a spirit with innate magical gifts." Madeline frowned. "I thought it all would've come to you naturally. Is that not true?"

"I am not susceptible to death by natural causes, disease, or hunger," Fravash explained. "Magic sustains my life force, and it flows through me, but I must learn and grow as all other beings must to reach their full potential. I just have far more time to hone these gifts than mortals do."

"I see," Madeline answered. "How long have you been alive, then?"

"I have memories of the orcs' first fathers and when men first sharpened steel." Fravash's gaze grew distant. "I knew elves who could remember when dragons were new. Time grows meaningless after one has seen so much."

"Then why do you need to study?" Madeline pursed her lips. "If you've been alive since before the Empire, then what could you learn from wizards who weren't even born until after its fall?"

"I have to admit the spell casters of later ages have less to teach me than their fathers did." Fravash twitched his whiskers. "But how can I know that if I'm unwilling to read what they've written? Wisdom can often come from unexpected sources."

"Is that why you tried to break into the forbidden archives at Sudvall?" Madeline asked.

"I didn't just try." Fravash smirked.

"And you weren't afraid dark powers would corrupt you?" Madeline gasped. "What if you had come across something like *The Book of Elder Wisdom*?"

Fravash paused. His gaze met Madeline's. The smirk on the mouse's face quickly disappeared.

"The risk is always there." He sighed. "Even an angel can fall from grace or descend into madness. It's important to recognize the signs of corruption early."

"Why risk it at all?" Madeline asked. "The Order of the Ivory Chalice certainly doesn't want us to."

"Take no offense, Lady Madeline, but men are weak," Fravash explained. "Oh, they can do great and mighty things too, but if a hedge is not set up around their law, they can fall prey to the worst evils imaginable."

"I've heard sermons about this at church," Madeline added. "The dark gods and celestial gods battle most fiercely for the souls of men out of all the races because we are the most easily persuaded."

"I don't know if I would reduce it to a simple contest of free will," Fravash corrected. "The race of men is a race of passion as much as it is potential. The orcs and goblins are not wholly predisposed towards evil, but those who show the slightest mercy or kindness to any but their nearest kin rarely survive long."

"I've wondered about that since Izold came to Olso and took Walaric and the others with him," Madeline confessed. "I haven't read or seen much of dwarves or elves worshipping the dark gods, but you will find almost no paladins in their numbers either."

"That's right," Fravash agreed. "Men are more willing than any other race to take up a cause beyond mere kinship. It is a strength, but it must be tempered."

"That's a lot to think about." Madeline sighed.

"In time, you will mature," Fravash insisted. "Power is tempting, but I think you can still learn control. When you are ready, I will teach you everything I know."

Madeline pondered Fravash's words for a long moment. Soon, Sister Vanya returned with a few large tomes. There were not as many as Madeline might have expected, given how long she was gone, but they were thick and heavy. It would be plenty for Madeline to sort through for the time being.

"Fravash." The old librarian turned to the mouse sitting on Madeline's shoulder after leading them to a table near one of the library's windows. "You have my permission to stay, but only as long as you are serving Lady Madeline. Is that understood?"

"For the last time," Fravash answered, "I'm not trying to steal your forbidden lore."

"Madeline," Sister Vanya continued, "These books are not to leave the library. Return them to my desk once you've finished. Good luck."

"Thanks." Madeline smiled awkwardly as the librarian left them alone.

"Did you ever write your aunt at Vindholm?" Fravash asked after Madeline sat in one of the chairs at the table. "I'd be very interested in what she has to say about any connections to magic your family might have."

"I wrote Aunt Collette, but I don't expect to hear back from her any time soon." Madeline began leafing through the pages of the book on top of the stack Sister Vanya had left behind. "Godfrey will probably be back before I get her letter."

"It is the middle of winter." Fravash put his paw on the frosty glass window pane next to their table.

Madeline spent hours reading through the first book in her pile. The yellowed pages recounted the names and deeds of many ancestors she was already familiar with, though the details of their stories varied from what she had been told earlier in life. Who remembered these stories about House Drois correctly? Her father, her grandmother, or whoever compiled this tome?

Fravash also had a book laid out for him on the opposite side of the table from which Madeline sat. He scurried across the pages as he turned from one to the next. Madeline could not help but smile at the comical sight.

Soon, her focus drifted between the books, Fravash, and the snowy courtyard outside the keep. Spathi landed in his pen with a mangled and bloody musimon in his claws. Madeline only recognized the griffin's victim because of its two sets of horns. She should have him groomed soon.

"Aha!" Fravash cried.

"What?" Madeline's head whipped back to the mouse. "What is it?"

"Here's something!" He pointed down at the page he was standing on. "I can't believe I didn't see the connection before. It's so obvious!"

"What's so obvious?" Madeline stood and peered at the paragraph Fravash was still gesticulating at.

"Here it talks about your maternal grandmother, Chloe de Rode," the mouse explained. "The details are vague, but it says your grandmother was hurt in the wilderness as a small child. A phoenix heard her cries, and she was healed by its touch!"

"A phoenix?" Madeline's mind raced.

"That's why your fire can both heal flesh and consume it at your command." The familiar stamped his foot in triumph. "You have phoenix fire!"

"Phoenix fire!" Madeline took a deep breath. "And the invisibility? Is that phoenix magic, too?"

"Let me think." Fravash scratched his nose. "Some older breeds of phoenix were more than just fiery raptors that could be reborn from the ashes of their own immolation. Some could also cast spells in their own right."

"So, you don't really know?" Madeline frowned.

"No," Fravash admitted, "but, as I said earlier, there are a lot of strange things about magic not even the gods know. However, I'm very confident the phoenix is our answer. Chloe de Rode was touched by a phoenix, and her power now lives in you."

"Great." Madeline clapped. "That explains a lot, even if we still don't have all the answers. Now what do we do?"

"We get a phoenix feather for the core of your staff," Fravash answered.

"Where do we get a phoenix feather?" Madeline wondered.

"From Farthest Thule," Fravash answered quickly. "The elves keep a phoenix in the heart of their city. Its magic is what allows them to dwell so far north."

"And how do we get to Farthest Thule?" Madeline could hardly believe the prospect of going to the elusive realm. "The city is hidden."

"You forget that I'm an honorary knight of Farthest Thule." Fravash gestured to himself. "The elves will allow me to pass through the wards that protect their realm."

"But *how* do we get there?" Madeline asked. "It's the middle of winter, and we need to go farther north?"

Fravash tapped the glass as he pointed out the window. Madeline's heart sank as she gazed upon Spathi. The griffin knew the way. They had to fly.

Chapter Ten

Vindholm's outer wall and towers jutted from the large snowy hill it sat atop like a shining beacon. The earthworks surrounding the outer wall were only slightly less noticeable thanks to the depth of the snow covering them. Beyond the earthworks, Godfrey, Roltar, and Mauger rode their horses along the road to the northern gatehouse.

Godfrey's gaze was immediately drawn to the Temple of Spes near the citadel of the high city beyond the inner wall. It was a majestic and ancient structure. Nothing but the best would do to glorify the celestial gods.

He frowned as he looked at Roltar and Mauger. It was not worship that brought them to this sacred city but the business of his kin. Perhaps he could still find a moment to visit the Temple of Spes or some of the other sacred sites now that he was no longer on crusade.

"You had a vision at the Temple of Helios and Luna?" Mauger gestured to one of the two other temples in the city. "What was that like?"

"It was at the Temple of Spes," Godfrey corrected.

"But it was Loxias who gave you the revelation?" Mauger furrowed his brow.

"Yes." Godfrey nodded. "In the Temple of Spes."

Mauger pursed his lips.

"It's hard to describe." Godfrey looked back at the temple. "It was like being in a dream, but I remember the details much more clearly. I didn't know what any of it really meant until after it had already come to pass."

"Word of your vision spread throughout the city almost overnight," Roltar added. "That was my first indication you were here in Azgald at all. Did you have any more dreams or visions after that?"

"No." Godfrey shook his head. "And I'm glad I didn't. Not everyone believed me. Some thought I was lying or had made a pact with witches and devils."

"Don't you think your vision helped you slay the dragon and secure Olso Fortress?" Mauger asked.

"It's hard to say." Godfrey bit his lip. "For a while, it seemed like the revelation raised more questions than it answered. I didn't know the dragon was Vozzab. I thought it was a symbol for something else, and I kept second-guessing my decisions all the way until I got to Olso."

"You don't think you would have done anything differently if you were not touched by Loxias?" Mauger pressed. "That sounds ungrateful."

"Well, Loxias did bless my sword," Godfrey confessed. "I'm very grateful for that. I guess the vision was also some comfort as I went to face Vozzab. I felt Loxias had led me to that moment, and it gave me the courage I needed to do what I had to."

"Courage is often in short supply when facing a real terror." Mauger snorted. "I suppose it's easy enough to draw upon extra reserves when you have the gods' favor."

Godfrey clenched his jaw. This was not the first time he sensed Mauger's jealousy boiling just beneath the surface as of late. What could he possibly say in his defense?

"We'll go straight to the King." Roltar gestured to the gate as they drew nearer. "He spends much of his time in the citadel during the winter."

The three proceeded through the massive stone gatehouse atop their steeds. Every eye followed Godfrey as they made their way through the winding streets of the outer city. Hushed whispers spoke his name or that of his sword, Uriel, as they passed by both commoner and noble.

"They know your coat of arms at sacred Vindholm now." Mauger's eyes grew dark.

"Which is to our advantage," Roltar cut in. "King Lothar would be foolish to refuse a request coming from someone of Godfrey's reputation."

"Let's hope so." Godfrey blinked up at the citadel.

Soon, Roltar, Godfrey, and Mauger passed through the inner gatehouse. The high city was less crowded, and the buildings were more impressive. Godfrey quickly identified the goldsmith's guild, the jewel cutter's guild, and a few of the other more refined trades among them.

Second in grandeur only to the Temple of Spes itself was King Lothar's citadel at the very center of Vindholm. The fortress was plainer and more recently constructed than the temple it stood next to. However, no expense had been spared in adorning the structure with stone walls, towers, battlements, and other defensive features sure to give pause to any potential attacker.

After they entered the citadel's gate, Mauger and Roltar relinquished the reins of their steeds to stable hands ready to receive their guests in the courtyard. Godfrey, likewise, gave Dash's reins to a young boy as the Duke dismounted his horse. The boy looked up at his face with gleaming eyes as he took the leather straps from his hand.

"Godfrey de Bastogne!" The boy's eyes bulged.

With a chuckle, he nodded in reply.

"And that's Uriel, the blade you slew Vozzab with!" The stable hand pointed to the sword in Godfrey's scabbard. "Where is your griffin? Is this Baruch?"

"This is Dash." Godfrey patted the horse's saddle with a grimace. "Baruch fell into the Irelven."

"Oh." The boy cast his eyes to the ground. "A dark day, my lord. Sorry for your loss."

"Indeed," Godfrey agreed. "Be careful with this one. He hasn't been broken in yet."

"Yes, sire." The stable hand vigorously nodded.

With that, Godfrey turned from the young man and joined Roltar and Mauger as they ascended the stairs to the citadel's entrance. Mauger said nothing, but Godfrey sensed the jealousy still burning within him. What could he say?

"One day, your deeds will inspire young squires like that, Mauger." Godfrey gestured over his shoulder.

Mauger broke his stride for a fraction of a second. Godfrey bit his tongue as a dark look passed over his kinsman's face. It was subtle enough that, if he had not been watching closely, Godfrey would not have noticed. He cringed. That was not the right thing to say.

Godfrey said nothing else as he, Roltar, and Mauger ventured into the citadel's great hall. Finely crafted woodwork decorated much of the interior. Trophies and the banners of Azgald's greater houses hung from the walls. The servants' apparel was no less cultivated. None could doubt this was the hall of a king.

"Roltar of House Hracour arrives with his son, Mauger, and Godfrey de Bastogne, Duke of Kovdor," a herald bellowed after the chamber doors swung open.

King Lothar looked up at Godfrey from the high table at the far end of the great hall. His armored retainers, dressed in the same white surcoats and tabards with red dragons emblazoned upon them that the King wore, parted to give Lothar a better view of his guests, who now strode through the chamber.

Sitting next to Lothar was a young blonde woman. Her skin was fair, and her eyes were a deep shade of blue. A golden bejeweled crown rested atop her head.

"Noela the Sornian?" Godfrey whispered to Roltar as they passed the room's hearth.

"The same," his cousin quickly answered.

Once they reached the high table, Godfrey, Roltar, and Mauger all bowed before King Lothar. After a moment, the King bade them to rise. A warm smile creased his face.

"Welcome, friends," Lothar said.

"Thank you for granting us an audience," Roltar answered.

"It is an unexpected pleasure to see you at this time of year, Roltar." The King gestured for them to take their seats at the high table once they were past the hearth. "And Duke Godfrey, I did not expect to see you here with your wedding to Madeline of House Drois so close at hand."

"The pleasure is ours," Godfrey insisted. "A few weeks ago, I might have also been as surprised to find myself here as you are. But I am kin to House Hracour, and important business brings us here to Vindholm."

"Isn't it always something important?" Lothar sighed. "Well, state your business, and I will do what seems right in my eyes and that of the council."

Godfrey smiled nervously.

"My lord." Roltar bowed his head. "Skasgun has been returned to the Kingdom of Azgald thanks to the might of your arm and the timely aid of the crusaders who came from the Ostlands. However, there is still more to do before justice is truly served."

"I know what you would say." Lothar waved his hand. "Skasgun is the ancestral home of House Hracour, but another has laid claim to it now."

Roltar gave Godfrey an expectant look. Swallowing hard, Godfrey turned his attention to the King. What difference could he make?

"Sire," Godfrey began. "Louis the Blue founded Skasgun. House Hracour's claim is as old as the Kingdom of Azgald itself. If Stormsud does not belong to House Hracour, who can lay claim to anything in Azgald? Surely, another estate can satisfy Lord Davin?"

"And who would yield a fief that would satisfy Lord Davin?" Noela spoke up for the first time. "Should we confiscate Biorkon from the Silver Suns or Kalscony from Baron Oksar? Would you be willing to give up part of Kovdor, Lord Godfrey?"

Godfrey flushed with embarrassment but kept silent. He understood well that Davin could not simply be removed without compensation, but this was Roltar's argument he was obliged to make. It should be his cousin talking to Lothar, not him.

"Davin of House Talhout fought beside Conrad the Wolf and me at Skasgun," the King added. "He earned his reward through right of conquest. Where was House Hracour as we retook Skasgun from the Clans?"

"May I remind the King that we were guarding sacred Vindholm at his command, my lord," Mauger added with a bowed head. "Were it not for that request, I would have been the first to scale the walls of Skasgun."

The King crossed his arms and leaned back in his chair. Clearly, he had forgotten that detail until now. This complicated the matter more than Godfrey had anticipated.

"So it was." Lothar's expression softened as he stroked his beard.

The King exchanged a glance with the Queen and his nearest retainers. So much was said in the subtleties of their facial expressions and body language. Godfrey was sure he missed much of the nuance.

"A matter like this cannot be judged lightly or quickly," Noela added smoothly. "Allow us three days to discuss this in council, and then the King shall return his answer to you."

Godfrey frowned. It was not a *no*, but it was not a *yes* either. Mauger shook his head in silence while Roltar's face remained unreadable.

"We eagerly await your decision," Roltar said at last. "May the King's justice prevail in this matter."

Roltar gave a subtle nod to Godfrey. He fully understood what his cousin meant by that, at least. The King's *justice* would naturally align with whatever arguments Godfrey, veteran crusader, dragon-slayer, and champion of the gods, made. It did not matter what his exact arguments were, so long as he made it known that he wanted Skasgun returned to House Hracour.

"You are welcome to stay at the citadel in the meantime," Noela offered.

"One more item should be brought to your attention before we are dismissed." Godfrey raised his finger.

"Go on," Lothar urged.

"We were attacked by Nordsman raiders on our way here," Godfrey explained. "The Clans are still a threat, and I believe it unwise to leave them alone for too long. They are still bold enough to encroach upon our lands, and it is only a matter of time before they recover their strength."

"Lord Godfrey," the King began. "You haven't been here long. You are still new to the Nordslands, so your ignorance on this matter is forgivable."

"Ignorance?" Godfrey's eyes narrowed.

"The Clans are always raiding Azgald," Lothar explained. "It's in their nature. Treaties may be signed with their leaders, but small bands of marauders, roving Amazons, and their ilk are nearly impossible to restrain."

"High Warlord Alvir will honor no truce." Godfrey shook his head. "He will plot. He will scheme. And he will strike where we least expect it."

"Right now, we have more urgent concerns." The King's jaw tightened. "Roltar and his son do not represent the only house seeking to press old claims."

Godfrey clenched his fists. Even a knight of his reputation had limits to what he might expect his king to agree to. Asking Lothar to lead an offensive into the Five Clans' territory would simply be too much. He grimaced. He would have to continue to build up Kovdor's strength and prepare for such an eventuality without the King's support.

"We look forward to speaking with you again in three days, my liege." Roltar bowed his head again.

Roltar swiveled about and made for the great hall's exit. Subtly, he gestured for Godfrey and Mauger to follow. As Godfrey turned after his cousin, his eyes briefly locked with the Queen's. Her gaze was cold and calculating, as if she were trying to decide which of Godfrey's ribs she would slide a dagger between.

Shivering as he turned his back to Noela, Godfrey hurried after Roltar. The guards opened the great hall's doors for Godfrey and his kin, and a servant showed them to a guest chamber up on the second floor.

"Try not to overwhelm the King with too many concerns next time you speak with him." Roltar shut the guest room's door behind him. "Asking for Skasgun to be returned to our family is a large enough favor."

"Do you think he's really going to grant that fief back to you?" Godfrey crossed his arms as he leaned against the wall. "It sounds like there is a lot on Lothar's mind already."

"The King was not the only one listening to us in that chamber." Roltar raised an eyebrow. "Your position can do much to sway the council's opinion, even if your arguments were ineloquent. Just try not to grow too overbearing with unnecessary distractions."

"The Queen hardly seemed persuaded." Godfrey tilted his head in uncertainty. "Who else mattered in that room?"

"Queen Noela the Sornian is a wild fox," Roltar explained. "She can say one thing in the great hall and another in her private chambers."

"She looked like she wanted to murder me." Godfrey swallowed hard.

"After King Wymund's untimely death, the Queen discovered a plot to kill Lothar," Roltar explained. "His own chamberlain was the culprit; a man who had served House Brogile since King Lothar's father was young."

"Who was the King's chamberlain?" Godfrey's jaw dropped. "Who could betray the royal family like that?"

"By decree, that chamberlain's name is not to be spoken in all of Vindholm forevermore," Mauger warned. "Such was the King's sorrow at learning of his betrayal."

"What happened when the plot was discovered?" Godfrey bit his lip.

"Word is that King Lothar wished to extend mercy." Roltar gazed into the hearth. "However, Noela claimed that the chamberlain was also responsible for murdering Wymund. With such a damning conviction, he was thrown in the dungeon and executed immediately."

"Did the chamberlain really murder King Wymund?" Godfrey asked. "A lot of this seems to hinge on the Queen's testimony. Could she have been mistaken?"

"The evidence seemed convincing at the time." Roltar shook his head. "It's hard to say in retrospect. There are still some who believe King Lothar's brother simply fell victim to an unfortunate hunting accident."

Godfrey frowned. Power turned men mad. The envy of power made men worse. His thoughts turned back to King Wilhelm in Lortharain and the injustices he had suffered at his hands. Part of him still wished to go back to Bastogne and liberate his home.

"Many held grudges against King Wymund," Roltar continued. "Even your betrothed's father, Tancred, was said to have uttered a threat against him in a moment of rage."

"I have difficulty imagining Duke Tancred threatening a king." Godfrey's eyes went wide. "He can get angry, but he's not a fool."

"Duke Tancred was younger back then." Roltar sighed. "But regardless of whether Wymund was murdered, few truly grieved his death. Noela's cunning was sufficient to prevent Lothar from meeting the same fate, and for that, we give thanks to the gods."

"Lothar seems like a more honorable king than his brother or Wilhelm back home, at any rate." Godfrey shifted his weight from one foot to the other as his gaze turned to the chamber door. "Speaking of Tancred, one of his sisters is among Queen Noela's ladies-in-waiting. I should make sure she received her wedding invitation while I'm here."

"Do what you must." Roltar gestured to the door. "We have time. For now, I will do what I can to influence the King's council in our favor."

"What will you be doing, Mauger?" Godfrey wondered aloud.

"Nothing important." Mauger rolled his eyes. "It seems Tyche would have me live in other men's shadows."

Madeline's aunt walked with Godfrey through the citadel's courtyard. Their heavy cloaks hung loosely over their shoulders as they progressed across the icy path. The shrubs and trees decorating the garden were bereft of foliage, but snow clung to twigs and branches in its place.

Collette was no longer a young woman, about forty years old by Godfrey's estimation, but her resemblance to Madeline was uncanny. He suspected, in time, Madeline would grow to resemble her aunt even more.

"No, I'm not Tancred's sister," Collette said. "I'm from House Vred. I'm Lissette's sister; Madeline's mother."

"Oh, right." Godfrey blushed. "Sorry. There are so many people I've met and have been told about as we have been getting ready for the wedding. It's hard to remember how everyone is related."

"That will come in time." Collette waved her hand. "Thank you for the invitation. I will be more than happy to attend the wedding. I wouldn't miss it for anything. Madeline has grown up so fast."

"We'll be happy to see you there." Godfrey smiled. "Now, the twins, Arius and Berig, have a different mother than Madeline? I don't think she was invited."

"Her name is Sennin." Collette frowned.

"And Tancred had an affair with her?" Godfrey awkwardly looked at his feet as they walked.

"Oh, no!" Collette shook her head. "Nothing like that. Sennin and Tancred *were* married."

"Is that so?" Godfrey's jaw dropped.

"Tancred had two brothers," Collette explained. "The older was named Euric, and he was going to inherit the Duchy of Pavik. Tancred's younger brother is Hilderic, and he joined the Silver Suns."

Godfrey cringed at the sound of the name Euric. It was a common enough name among Ostmen, but he had not forgotten his father's knight who also bore that name. Would Sir Euric have remained with Godfrey at Kovdor had he not died at Epsberg, or would he have returned home to Bastogne with Rodair and the others?

"Right." Godfrey nodded. "I heard Uncle Hilderic can't come because of his obligations to the Order."

"Yes." Collette paused for a moment as a forlorn look crossed her face. "At any rate, Tancred's parents didn't care very much if he married a commoner at the time, but when his older brother died, Hilderic had already made his vows. Then it mattered a lot who Tancred was married to."

"So, they made Tancred annul his marriage to Arius and Berig's mother?" Godfrey furrowed his brow. "That's why they're always so hostile."

"Tancred was heartbroken." Collette stopped in front of a small stone statue set between two trees next to the path. "I don't know if he ever truly loved my sister."

Godfrey pondered the alabaster figure before them as he read the inscription on the pedestal. *Peitho,* it read. She was said to be the most beautiful of all the goddesses and the most persuasive. She often worked with Tyche for both the good and ill of man.

On the opposite side of the path, another statue was set between two more trees. The inscription on this figure's pedestal read *Bia.* She was Peitho's sister and was said to rely on force when words failed.

"Lissette was always jealous." A tear rolled down Collette's cheek. "She could never take Sennin's place in Tancred's heart. He didn't deserve my sister. Even after everything she did for him…"

Collette's voice trailed off as she frowned bitterly. Godfrey crossed his arms and nodded politely. He was never sure what to say when people began divulging far more of their personal histories than he had asked for.

"He seems to love Madeline, at least." Godfrey shrugged. "I have to admit, I've had a lot of disagreements with Tancred, but I don't doubt he tries to do what he thinks is best for her."

"Yes," Collette agreed. "He may have been a terrible husband to Lissette, but he is a good father."

"What happened to Madeline's mother?" Godfrey asked. "She never spoke much of her."

"She died a while ago." Collette's eyes grew misty once again. "It was the Grey Pox; very slow and painful. Madeline couldn't have been more than eight or ten years old when it happened. Poor thing."

"My mother died just before I left on crusade." Godfrey nodded soberly. "I grieved for weeks."

"You still miss home?" Collette asked.

"I do." Godfrey frowned.

"I see it in your eyes." She gave a humorless smile. "Do you ever think about going back to Bastogne?"

"How can I?" Godfrey sighed as he gestured to the citadel. "I'm now the Duke of Kovdor. I have responsibilities here. I'm getting ready to marry Madeline, and my cousin is dragging me around Azgald in the middle of winter trying to reclaim Skasgun."

"Others will always seek to pull you in the direction they want." Collette wrapped her arms around herself as she started walking down the path again. "But don't forget you have a duty to yourself as well as your lord and kin."

"A duty to *myself?*" Godfrey repeated as he followed her. "What do you mean?"

"If you don't take care of your own needs and wants, you'll break." Collette nodded to herself. "Most men need constant reminders of their duty to their lords, vassals, and so on. I don't think you have a problem with that. You look like a young man who would sacrifice anything and everything for the right cause."

"I sacrificed Bastogne for the crusade." Godfrey tightened his jaw. "If I ever do go back, I'm sure King Wilhelm will not be pleased. But the gods were mindful of me and gave me Kovdor in its stead."

"Do you wonder about the people you left behind back home?" Collette paused again as she met Godfrey's gaze.

"How do you suppose King Wilhelm is treating those who were loyal to your father?"

"I haven't thought a lot about it lately," Godfrey confessed. "I received some letters from home a while ago, but I've also been busy here. Kovdor and Azgald are where my duty lies today."

"But you are still Godfrey de Bastogne," Collette reminded him. "An appellation like that isn't given to just anyone. You carry part of Bastogne with you wherever you go and whoever you serve."

"I don't know if King Lothar sees it that way." Godfrey shook his head.

"You don't have to have all the answers today." Collette raised her hand in a placating gesture. "But give these ideas some thought as you sort out where you really want to be and what you really want to do."

"I will," Godfrey promised.

After leaving Collette back at the citadel, it did not take Godfrey long to find himself at the Temple of Spes. Now that he was not as pressed for time and he was alone, he focused his gaze on the details of the temple's frieze as he slowly ascended the steps cut into the podium. It depicted Helios, Selene, and a host of other celestial gods and goddesses attended by angels at a great feast. The temple was a place of feasting, he had been taught. The sacrifices that took place were feasts to the gods, but the worshippers were also supposed to spiritually feast as they pondered the gods' will for their own lives.

As Godfrey entered the temple, the sentinels bowed their heads to him. The irony was not lost on Godfrey. The last time he had seen the temple guards, they had taken him prisoner in the belief that some evil spirit had possessed him as he prophesied. The priests would have tortured him on the spot had Turpin not intervened.

Godfrey's stomach sank. His thoughts dwelled less on the deceased chaplain these days, but when they did, all the pain of his loss returned. He stopped for a moment to rub the tears from his eyes before continuing to the altar.

One of the priests greeted Godfrey with a bow. It was one of the men who had escorted Godfrey to the dungeon on the night of his vision. He clenched his jaw at the unexpected sight.

Clearing his throat, Godfrey produced a large silver coin from his satchel. It sparkled brightly in his hand as he placed it in the priest's open palm. The cleric pursed his lips.

"It hardly seems right that I should take a coin from someone of your reputation, Lord Godfrey." The priest weighed the silver in his hand. "It's not every day our temple gets a visit from a dragon-slayer."

"I don't see how I can offer a sacrifice if you won't exchange my silver for a trio of doves." Godfrey crossed his arms. "It's newly minted from Olso's mines. Take it."

"Of course." The cleric put the silver in his coin pouch. "I meant no offense. I'll get the doves right away."

The priest turned to a storage room behind the altar, but stopped after taking just a few steps. As his face contorted into a painful grimace, he turned to Godfrey again. His mouth opened and closed a couple of times.

"I hope we can forget about that awkward business last time you were here," the priest said at last.

"Think nothing of it." Godfrey sighed.

There was more Godfrey wanted to say, but he held his tongue. It would do no good to bring up the past. The only reasonable thing was to move on.

"Can I do anything else for you while you are here to worship?" the priest asked.

"I would like to consult an oracle." Godfrey rubbed his face. "There are worries weighing heavily on my mind."

"I understand." The priest bowed his head again. "Please wait here while I go tell High Priest Throst."

With that, the cleric left. Godfrey's eyes turned to the statues of Tzuk and Lihi that oversaw the central altar in the chamber. The twin angels were depicted in tall plumed helmets and scale mail armor. They also carried large round shields and spears. It was the fashion of the arms and armor of the elves during the Imperial Age. He cringed at the thought of how much had been lost since the Empire fell.

After he had stewed in his thoughts for some time, the repugnant stench of incense drifted from some other part of the temple to Godfrey's nose. He gagged. Most people liked the smell of the various spices and herbs that burned in the sacred incense, but Godfrey could never understand what they enjoyed about the thick smoke.

Soon, the priest Godfrey had spoken with returned, followed by High Priest Throst. The High Priest was an elderly man dressed in expensive robes. His regal bearing spoke of connections to high nobility. In fact, there were many physical similarities between the High Priest and the members of House Brogile now that Godfrey thought about it. It would make sense to Godfrey that Throst was related to King Lothar in some way.

After removing his spangenhelm and lowering his coif, Godfrey knelt in front of the altar as all supplicants were required to. Solemnly, the priests prepared Godfrey's sacrifice. To his surprise, High Priest Throst himself slew the doves with his knife and lit the fire on the wood beneath them upon the altar. Quizzically, Godfrey stared at Throst.

"It is customary for the High Priest to *preside* over the sacrifice rather than offer it himself," Godfrey said.

"Suffer me to honor you now in reconciliation for past deeds," Throst replied. "Vozzab's destruction at your hand through your blessed blade deserves no less an honor."

Smoke billowed from the burning sacrifice to the ceiling. The flames licked the bodies of the doves as their meat roasted amidst the glowing coals. Godfrey may have been gifted a magical sword by Loxias himself, but that did not mean he could neglect the obeisance owed to the divine.

"I seek an oracle." Godfrey bowed his head again. "There is much on my mind concerning Kovdor, Bastogne, the Clans, and a lot of other important matters. I hardly know where to begin."

"Start at the beginning." Throst nodded sagely.

"Very well." Godfrey swallowed as the scent of the burnt dove meat began to make his mouth water. "I am here with my cousin Roltar of House Hracour and his son, Mauger. They are trying to convince King Lothar to return an old estate to them, and I'm worried that this is pulling me away from more important things."

"What is more important than helping your kin find the justice they seek?" The High Priest raised an eyebrow.

"I was supposed to be preparing for my wedding to Madeline of House Drois on the first day of spring," Godfrey explained. "I worry that she thinks I'm abandoning her on this errand. Meanwhile, my friend, Walaric, departed with some of my knights to the Blighted Lands chasing the shade of the Great Witch of the North. Worse still, the Clans have not ceased to cause trouble, and I fear they may attack Azgald again soon."

"Heavy is the burden of leadership." Throst sighed.

"What am I doing here when so much is at stake in other places?" Godfrey threw out his hands. "Who controls Skasgun Fortress seems so petty by comparison."

The High Priest closed his eyes. Godfrey took a deep breath. So much of his life was doing what other people wanted. He needed to know what the gods wanted.

"Come back tomorrow." Throst opened his eyes as he answered at last.

"Tomorrow?" Godfrey cringed.

"Fasting and prayer are required here," the High Priest responded. "You cannot expect a revelation concerning something so great without putting in any effort on your part. Come back tomorrow."

"But what about my vision last time I was here?" Godfrey countered. "I wasn't fasting then."

"But you were on crusade," Throst answered. "That armed pilgrimage prepared you to receive the word of Loxias directly. Now that the crusade is over, you need to do more to ready your mind and spirit."

"Right." Godfrey frowned as he stood. "I will be back tomorrow. King Lothar will have ruled on Skasgun by the day after that. Then I'll need to know where the gods want me after that has been decided."

"I can only promise to deliver the gods' message to you," the High Priest warned. "It is up to you to decipher their words' meaning."

"I understand." Godfrey sighed.

Godfrey's stomach gurgled as he turned away from High Priest Throst and began walking to the temple's exit. As his footfalls echoed off the stone floor, he placed his helmet back on top of his head. He had not eaten since breakfast, and it was growing late in the afternoon. Now he had to fast until at least tomorrow morning, *if* the High Priest would see him that soon.

Though the Sun was still bright outside, it was far lower in the sky than Godfrey had expected. The days were still growing shorter. As he descended the temple's stairs, he considered visiting some of Vindholm's other sacred sites. There were two other temples close by, and a few sacred springs and groves were scattered throughout the city. However, a bitterly cold breeze bit through Godfrey's cloak, and he returned to the citadel instead.

As Godfrey entered the citadel's great hall, the evening meal was just being brought out. Savory venison, rabbit, and pork steamed from the platters as servants brought them to the long feasting tables. Several pitchers of ale and wine were also set in the middle of each table. Godfrey's stomach grumbled once again. He would have to ignore the food.

At the head of the high table sat Lothar and Noela, and their closest kin and friends filled the other chairs around them. The chamber was so crowded with guests, retainers, entertainers, and others whose business Godfrey could not readily distinguish, that Roltar and Mauger had to sit at one of the lower tables. If Vindholm had suffered at all during the Clans' invasion of Azgald, it did not appear to have faced anything nearly as bad as Olso.

Godfrey waved briefly at Mauger as he caught his eye, but he continued along the outskirts of the chamber near the wall, where he hoped to attract less attention. Mauger brooded as Godfrey passed the table his kin sat at. However, after having just committed to a fast, Godfrey thought better than to join Roltar and Mauger. The temptation to fill his rumbling belly was too great, and the King and Queen were busy enough seeing to the needs of other guests. He would not be missed.

Soon Godfrey found himself in the guest room he had been shown to earlier that day. Though it was growing dark, he did not expect Roltar or Mauger to enter the bedroom any time soon. Royal feasts had a reputation for lasting well into the night.

With little else to do, Godfrey changed into his night clothes and knelt beside his bed in prayer. Silently, he begged Loxias for a clear understanding of what to do next. He felt little comfort that night.

Darkness still filled the bed chamber as Godfrey arose the next day. The cold bit his nose as he fumbled to get his day clothes on. Roltar and Mauger still slept in the beds next to his. He had not heard them come in last night. They must have stayed at the feast until the very end.

After finally dressing, Godfrey made his way through the citadel back to the Temple of Spes in the early predawn light. There, the priests offered a bull for the morning sacrifice just as the dawn broke. Godfrey bowed in reverence as the clerics performed their duty. High Priest Throst stood behind the others as they completed their rites, but he soon caught Godfrey's eye among the worshippers who had gathered at the temple. The ceremony soon ended, and Godfrey made his way to the High Priest.

"I'm surprised King Lothar isn't here for the morning sacrifice," Godfrey noted as he approached Throst.

"The King and Queen visit from time to time," the High Priest explained, "but Archbishop Lopt resides at the citadel, and he ministers to House Brogile there most mornings the King is at Vindholm."

"I see." Godfrey pursed his lips. "Are you ready to deliver my oracle?"

"Yes." Throst gravely folded his hands. "I thought you might come early today. This way, please."

The High Priest led Godfrey to an anteroom at the back of the main sanctum, beyond the stairs that descended into the dungeon. It was a small chamber filled with books and scrolls. A single window at the wall opposite where Godfrey and Throst entered provided the only light in the otherwise dim chamber.

After grabbing a scroll from one of the shelves, Throst unfurled it at a heavy wooden lectern that occupied the center of the chamber. He scowled at it for a moment before looking up at Godfrey. Awkwardly, Godfrey swallowed as the High Priest met his gaze.

"You seek great things, man of greatest deeds." The old man began reading from the scroll. "Whose arm has been tested by iron and his faith by fire. But fear not, Bastognian.

Trust in your blood, and you will see your home and the farthest ends of Aestas."

His jaw hanging open, Godfrey stood dumbfounded. He tried piecing the words together in his mind again. What did trusting his blood have to do with seeing the farthest ends of Aestas? He frowned, then tightened his jaw. This whole prophecy seemed less than useful.

"Thanks," Godfrey said uncertainly.

"It's the best translation I could write in the time given." Throst rolled up the scroll and pursed his lips. "I consulted the augers concerning the portents. I watched the skies myself for a time."

"As you said yesterday." Godfrey shrugged with a defeated sigh. "Knowledge of the gods' will has to be worked for. I guess it's up to me to figure out what the oracle means."

"That's right," Throst agreed with a sad smile. "Sometimes I am granted certain insights into these prophecies and oracles, but I must remember that I am just the messenger, and the message is for you."

The High Priest emphatically placed the scroll in Godfrey's hand. Godfrey unrolled it, read the words written on the parchment a few times, and rolled it back up. Shaking his head, he held the scroll out to Throst. He was not about to gain any more insight from it now.

"Will you need it back?" Godfrey asked.

"A copy has already been placed in the archives." The High Priest shook his head.

"All right then." Godfrey nodded as he put the scroll in his satchel. "I suppose there is nothing for me to do now but press on in faith."

"Be of good cheer, my lord," Throst said as Godfrey began marching to the exit. "The gods are mindful of you. I believe they are guiding your steps even now."

"How do you know?" Godfrey turned back to the High Priest. "That prophecy didn't really tell me anything."

"Do not discount that oracle so lightly." Throst raised a warning finger. "I will admit it may be difficult to interpret that one, but significant omens accompanied it. Take the time to study it, ponder it, and act on your impressions. The gods will bless you in the end."

"Right." Godfrey cast his eyes to his feet. "I meant no offense. I just wish the path forward were clearer."

"More will be revealed in time," Throst assured him.

"I hope so," Godfrey sighed. "Walaric thought it was important for me to accompany Roltar here."

"Your duty to your kin is an important one," the High Priest agreed. "If you intend to stay in Azgald for long, you need to know who you can depend on, and others need to know who can depend on you."

"I have no arguments against that." Godfrey frowned as he placed his hand on his satchel. "But I wanted to know if I should stay in Azgald or return to Lortharain. The oracle didn't say anything about that."

"Didn't it?" Throst raised an eyebrow.

Godfrey pursed his lips. So much about these prophecies was indirect. If only the gods would speak more plainly to simple mortals.

"It did say I would see my home and the farthest ends of the world if I trusted in my blood," Godfrey recalled. "But where is my home now? Bastogne was home, but I am the duke of Kovdor now."

"Search your heart, and you will know," Throst insisted. "Time reveals all."

Chapter Eleven

Marshal Horvath's black cloak fluttered in the wind as he marched through Narlstad's outer gate. Horvath was tall and broad by Ostman standards, yet he was dwarfed by the scale of Narlstad's fortifications. His steely gaze melted into a broad grin as Walaric jumped to the front of the party before him and waved at the Silver Sun castellan. After days of hard travel, Horvath was a welcome sight.

"Back so soon?" Horvath embraced Walaric. "I thought you would still be at Olso Fortress after repelling High Warlord Alvir's siege. It's a bad winter."

"My stride has regained its vigor." Walaric returned the gesture. "No cyclops attack could keep me down. I've been walking just fine for a few months now."

"Praise Iatrus, Physician," Horvath answered after releasing Walaric from his embrace. "Those were some long weeks you spent in Narlstad's infirmary."

"Amen." Walaric made a pious sign towards the morning sun. "And amen."

"Now." Horvath's expression grew serious as his gaze shifted to Walaric's companions. "What brings you here with a paladin, two of Lord Godfrey's knights, and a son of House Loridan?"

"A brief stop only, I'm afraid," Walaric answered.

"We are on a quest to the Blighted Lands and need provisions," Izold elaborated. "Our destination is Mirtys, and we need any news you can give of happenings in the East, no matter how insignificant it may seem."

"That quest will be perilous," Horvath grumbled. "What madness drives you to such an awful place?"

"We are pursuing the shade of the Great Witch of the North," Walaric answered with what he hoped was determination in his voice. "Our task is to put her to rest."

"Even in death, Lady Nera still haunts the Nordslands…" Horvath's gaze grew distant for a moment. "We can sell you provisions at a reasonable price, but I do not recommend traveling directly through the Blighted Lands to Mirtys."

"The undead are growing too strong?" Paschal shifted his weight from one foot to the other.

"Nothing is safe past Epsberg." Horvath shook his head. "Perhaps Nera's ghost is stirring the undead. You will be swarmed by zombies or worse long before you reach the Blighted Lands proper."

"That doesn't bode well." Sir Jordan cringed. "What route do you recommend?"

"And what plans do you have to stop the undead plague from spreading farther?" Candac asked.

"We are gathering what forces we can." The Castellan spread his arms wide. "But the Order's resources aren't limitless. We lost a lot of good men in the crusade against the Clans. It will take time to rebuild our strength."

"We may not have time." Paschal crossed his arms. "What is Morgan the Bloodied doing now? Shouldn't *he* be organizing a response to this threat?"

"He is still negotiating the location of a new fortress to be constructed in Upplad, last I heard." Horvath frowned. "Count Osvald welcomes the Silver Suns' protection, but House Rime Wyrm is less keen to surrender enough land to facilitate its defense."

Paschal rolled his eyes.

"Have faith." Walaric nudged Paschal. "Who is to say our quest will not reverse the evils unfolding before us?"

"We have been in touch with our brethren of the Knights of Saint Pelegius," Horvath added. "They may be able to apply some pressure to the Blighted Lands' eastern borders before long."

"That's wishful thinking," Jordan muttered.

"We must remain optimistic in trying times." Izold frowned. "Do not give in to despair. The gods are mindful of their servants."

"I'd recommend your party travel south through Azgald's Eastern Marches after resupplying here." The Castellan tilted his head back to Sir Jordan. "One of the crusaders, Raymond of Wrehst, has had great success in bringing peace to that part of the realm. From there, take the road to Sval and then go north through the Dovern Highlands. That's your safest path to Mirtys."

"That will take a lot longer," Jordan murmured.

"But it's the only road to Mirtys I would travel with fewer than ten thousand men," Horvath countered.

"If you believe that to be the best path, I will take it." Walaric grimaced.

"I agree." Candac nodded. "There's no use in taking the fastest road if it only leads to death."

"It's the only road to Mirtys you have now," Horvath reassured them.

"So be it," Izold concurred.

"We'll spend the night here if you can lodge us." Jordan looked between Walaric and Horvath. "But we should head out by first light tomorrow."

After they had considerably lightened their bags of coins from Olso's mint in exchange for food, drink, and other supplies, Castellan Horvath led Walaric's party to the great hall in Narlstad's main keep. A monk poured some wine into unadorned goblets for the guests before silently disappearing into the dark alcove from whence he came. Not long after that, Horvath made his excuses to attend to other duties in the castle before he also left the chamber.

"No food?" Candac frowned at the pitcher of wine left behind by the Silver Sun monk.

"It's not their way to provide feasts for guests unless prompted by a festival or other holiday," Sir Jordan answered. "The Silver Suns are strict to observe a plain warrior's diet with few exceptions, but don't worry. They will share their evening meal with us at dusk."

Candac's stomach gurgled, but he took a large gulp of wine from his goblet without further complaint. For a while, Walaric was content to listen to the Silver Sun brethren chanting from a nearby chapel during one of their services as he warmed his feet at the hearth. He took comfort in the familiar hymns. He had heard them many times before at the orphanage at Vosg.

Soon, Paschal fell asleep at the long table they sat at. He had drunk too much wine too quickly, and Walaric was almost surprised not to see him vomit. Izold and Jordan murmured to themselves about the path ahead, but Walaric was too exhausted to pay much attention. The troubles to come would be upon them soon enough.

Izold and Jordan eventually stood and took their conversation out of the great hall. Walaric looked at Candac. The young knight gazed into the flames of the hearth in cheerless contemplation. Gritting his teeth, Walaric scooted nearer to him on the bench they sat on.

"What's wrong?" Walaric prodded.

"It all seems so pointless." Candac shook his head. "Haven't you been listening to Sir Jordan and Izold talking about all the danger ahead? Can we really make a difference? Can we even make it to Mirtys?"

"How can you speak like that?" Walaric flinched. "You came all the way from Bastogne on crusade, fought at Biorkon, Epsberg, and Olso, and put down the goblin rebellion in the mine."

"I only watched Sir Garic do most of the fighting until the last siege," Candac scoffed. "I'm barely considered a man. I heard what Arius and Berig were saying before the dubbing ceremony. Lord Godfrey was desperate for more knights, and I'm the most expendable. That's why I'm here."

"Don't listen to the twins." Walaric shook his head. "Those two are venomous vipers. You have proven your valor more than once."

Slowly, Candac nodded in agreement.

"If experience were the most important thing, I would have asked Godfrey to give me Vonig the Cold or Sigibald of Fulda," Walaric continued. "You saved my life down in the mine when the goblins attacked. The gods have a plan for you. That's why you're here."

"What is that plan?" Candac raised an eyebrow.

Walaric was silent for a long moment. Some things seemed clear. Others not so much.

"For now, we see through a glass darkly." Walaric shrugged. "Now we know in part; but then we shall know perfectly after the trial of our faith."

"It always comes down to faith?" Candac sighed.

"Always." Walaric frowned.

"Faith didn't save Sir Garic at the end of the siege." Candac frowned. "It didn't stop Turpin from being sacrificed by the Clans."

"I think Sir Paschal's gloom is starting to rub off on you." Walaric patted Candac's shoulder. "Turpin and Garic are now in the celestial courts, where all the faithful go."

"That much is certain." Candac's gaze shifted to somewhere deep in the blazing hearth.

Walaric cleared his throat but was unsure what else to say. None of them wanted to take the longer route to Mirtys in the middle of winter, but walking straight into the jaws of death was even less appealing. They would continue. They each understood their duty.

The evening meal passed without incident and was only remarkable to Walaric because of the company they ate with. The food was bland. The wine and ale were watered down. The Silver Suns exemplified all the austerity their order was known for. Yet they were incredible storytellers.

Marshal Horvath and the other veteran Silver Suns spent the evening exchanging tales of exotic lands, strange peoples, and terrifying monsters. To Walaric's surprise, many had held postings in the distant Estlands and Sudlands before losses forced their transfer to the Nordslands. War was everywhere, and peace fleeting. Despite these hardships, the Silver Suns still spoke of a lasting victory to come in this life or the next.

By dawn, Narlstad was already far behind Walaric and his companions. Sir Jordan insisted there was no good road leading directly from Narlstad to Laht, so they would have to cut across country until they reached the Narewd River. With luck, they could find a good crossing without needing to follow the river back north to Odsha.

"We have clear skies, at least." Candac shivered as they trudged through the icy fields. "No ghouls will be ambushing us out here."

"Boreas has taken pity on us," Walaric agreed. "I burned a sacrifice before we left."

"Nature gods are always so capricious." Paschal rolled his eyes. "Why not appeal to Helios instead?"

"I pray to Helios every day," Walaric answered. "It hurts nothing to ask a boon of another god, too."

A full week passed, traveling through the snow and ice. The wet, bitter cold began to bite Walaric's toes through his boots, but the skies remained clear and the wind mild. Walaric's sacrifice at Narlstad was worth something, at least.

"I recognize where we are." Jordan pointed to some gentle hills in the distance as the men pressed through the snow. "We should be reaching the Narewd River early tomorrow. Once we cross the Narewd, we should find the road to Laht easily enough."

"We'll want to set up camp," Paschal grumbled. "Dusk will be upon us soon."

"No," Walaric protested. "Let's keep going to the river if we can. I'm eager to get back on the road."

"The roads haven't been much better than traveling across the countryside." Candac shivered. "We don't need to press any harder than we already are."

"Getting caught in the dark could be very bad for us," Izold added. "Are you sure you want to wait to set up camp until we reach the river?"

"I think we are almost to the Narewd." Jordan glowered at Walaric's questioning gaze.

Walaric gave a humorless smile. He understood the need to make camp before it got too dark, but progress in the wilderness had been so slow. He wanted all of that behind him as soon as possible.

With a nod, Sir Jordan continued to lead the way up the hills. Groaning, Paschal, and Candac followed Walaric, Izold, and Jordan. The incline was not very steep, but Walaric slipped on the snow, ice, and mud more than once. The others did not fare much better. Izold led Vielantiu by the reins on foot rather than risk falling from the saddle.

At last, they reached the top of the largest hill, and the Narewd River was visible below. The dark, babbling waters flowed nearly straight south as far as Walaric could see. He frowned as he scanned for a good place to cross.

"Let's not risk it today." Jordan put his hand on Walaric's shoulder. "We made great time, but it's getting too dark. We'll find a place to ford in the morning."

"We are past time to set up camp," Izold agreed.

"All right," Walaric sighed.

Sunset came too quickly to properly set up tents, obliging Walaric and his companions to lay out their bedrolls under the stars. Candac and Paschal gave Walaric dark looks as they spread out their bedrolls on the opposite side of the fire from him. It would be a cold night.

For a long time, Walaric gazed at the tiny stars dotting the night sky. His companions had started snoring hours ago, but Walaric lay restless. From the bright beacons in the endless skies, the gods looked down on him. What plan did they have for him? For Candac? The others?

Before long, something rustled in the bushes beyond the light of the campfire. Tensing, Walaric held his breath. Whatever it was stirred again.

Holding his breath for a long moment, he got up on his hands and knees and strained his eyes in the direction of the defoliated bushes. The shadows concealed all but the vaguest form of some figure clambering up the hill. Or was it nothing at all?

Hastily, Walaric stood and drew his sword from its scabbard by his bedroll. His heart pounding in his chest, he crept towards the bushes. He could not reveal himself to the creature sneaking towards the camp too soon.

Walaric's eyes slowly adjusted to the darkness beyond the glow of the campfire. A gaunt, cloaked figure made its way towards him. He clenched his teeth. What sort of undead monstrosity was this?

The creature stiffened as its gaze fell on Walaric. It rose to its full height as his hands tightened against the grip of his sword. His jaw fell as the creature lowered the hood of its cloak, revealing a bright, freckled face.

"Terrwyn!" Walaric gasped, dropping his sword. "Of all the foul creatures of the Abyss, you were the one I expected least to see stalking to our camp!"

"A pleasure to see you too, *Father* Walaric." Terrwyn's sapphire eyes gleamed.

"You followed us all the way from Kolarb Castle?" Walaric pointed back in the direction they had marched from. "That was weeks ago."

"You left early that morning," Terrwyn pouted. "You promised to take me with you."

"I made no such promise!" Walaric furrowed his brow as he retrieved his sword from the ground. "Where in all of Aestas did you get that idea?"

"Perhaps Mother's ale made you forget that part of the night." Terrwyn gave a sly smile.

"Why didn't you join us at Narlstad?" Walaric tilted his head at the young maiden. "Have you been out in the wilderness all this time?"

"I only now caught up with you." Terrwyn gestured in the direction she had come from. "At any rate, I'm here now. You'll just have to take me the rest of the way."

"Don't you understand where we're going?" Walaric blinked. "What about your mother? You want to break her heart by running off like this?"

"She knows I had to leave for a better future." Terrwyn's eyes grew misty. "She understands."

Walaric looked Terrwyn up and down. The faint glow of the campfire revealed a fine traveling gown under her cloak. The fabric was royal blue with a golden hem. Delicate lace adorned the neck. It was not so ornate to be impractical for a long journey, but it did make a statement about the prestige of the wearer.

"Dare I ask where you got that dress?" Walaric raised his eyebrow. "I would think such garments were well beyond the means of a brewer's daughter, even if her mother does make the finest ale in Valgo County."

"It's best not to ask." Terrwyn blushed. "Call it a parting gift from an otherwise negligent father if you have to call it anything."

"Terrwyn." Walaric stamped his foot. "We're going to Mirtys in the Blighted Lands. Didn't anyone tell you? You can't follow us there. It's too dangerous."

"Mirtys?" The maiden gulped. "You said you were on a dangerous quest, but I didn't hear anyone say anything about the Blighted Lands."

Walaric nodded grimly.

"Why would you want to go there?" Terrwyn shook her head. "You're too handsome for an early grave."

"Our quest is to put the shade of the Great Witch of the North to rest," Walaric explained. "I don't know how we're going to do it, but we have to try."

"The Great Witch of the North." Terrwyn fidgeted. "We were told she died in the crusade months ago, but some said a sorceress of her power couldn't really be killed."

"She is dead," Walaric reassured her, "but the rest isn't so simple. She made some sort of pact with a being called the Keeper of Souls, and I think it may have the answers we need."

"I see." Terrwyn fidgeted in apparent discomfort.

"Do you still want to come with us?" Walaric stuck the tip of his sword into the ground and leaned against the hilt. "I do remember telling you there would be no handsome knights or warm hearths where we're going."

For a moment, the maiden made no reply. Her lips were pursed as she looked up at the stars. At last, a long, steamy breath escaped her mouth.

"I came this far." Terrwyn crossed her arms as she locked eyes with Walaric.

Terrwyn held out her hand. His heart pounding in his chest, Walaric gulped as he looked her up and down. She was the most beautiful maiden he had ever seen. If the celestial gods above intended them to be apart, they certainly were not making it easy on him now. Taking the maiden's hand, Walaric led her to the campfire.

A surprised yelp startled Walaric awake the next morning. His eyes flashed open to greet the dawn as he took in his surroundings. Paschal stood over the bedroll next to Walaric's. Comprehension slowly dawned on his face as he met Terrwyn's eyes poking out from it.

"You were at Kolarb." Paschal shot an accusing glance between Walaric and Terrwyn as they sat up next to each other. "How did you get here?"

"What's going on?" Candac yawned as he shook himself out of his bedroll on the other side of the smoldering remains of the campfire. "Walaric, you've got some nerve bringing a damsel along."

"I didn't bring anyone along!" Walaric's face flushed. "She followed us here."

"Explain yourself, Walaric." Izold approached and crossed his arms as his eyes narrowed on the maiden sitting beside the priest.

Unsure where to begin, Walaric stammered for a moment. Izold and Paschal scowled while Candac shook his head. Jordan, by contrast, barely contained his sniggering. How he saw any humor in this, Walaric did not know.

"I'm Lady Terrwyn." The maiden stood.

Walaric raised an eyebrow at the appellation *Lady* Terrwyn. Her father may have come from a noble line, as the clergy usually did, but illegitimate children rarely inherited titles. Walaric rose to his feet and pursed his lips at her. Now it made sense why she wore the expensive traveling gown.

"Your priest offered to escort me to Laht while we were at Kolarb Castle," Terrwyn continued, "but he neglected to inform the rest of you before leaving. I caught up with your party late last night."

"Not that I would ever neglect my duty to escort a fair young noblewoman through dangerous country," Candac began, "but if you made it all the way from Kolarb to here, I'd hardly think you needed us to escort you the rest of the way to wherever you wanted to go."

"I have urgent business from my father at Laht," Terrwyn answered swiftly. "I need to get there with or without an escort."

"It's a miracle some beast didn't devour you in the night, traveling alone all this time." Candac whistled. "Shame on Walaric for forgetting his promise."

Walaric clenched his jaw. He was as certain he did not promise anything to Terrwyn as he could be. She had no business at Laht from her father. Then again, she spoke with such confidence that he began to question if he did have too much to drink that night. It was reputed to be the best ale in Valgo County, after all.

Jordan raised an eyebrow at Terrwyn before focusing his attention on Walaric. Perhaps he suspected something amiss about her story. His kin ruled Kolarb and the lands surrounding it. He would have heard of a *Lady* Terrwyn if there was one, especially if she was so beautiful. Yet a fine traveling gown such as hers was hard to come by.

"I don't know how I could've forgotten such an agreement." Walaric held out his hands apologetically. "Some jinx must have come over me. Forgive me for such foolishness, Lady Terrwyn."

"Laht is on the way," Jordan said at last. "It should take us about a week from here if the road is better than the countryside we've seen so far."

"If." Paschal frowned.

Izold gave Walaric a cold glare. He shifted uncomfortably as the paladin's gaze bored into him. Walaric had not done anything wrong. He remembered no agreement with Terrwyn, yet he would honor it at her insistence. He had no reason to feel any shame outside of being caught lying beside her just now. Even that was circumstantial. They had slept in separate bedrolls, after all.

Still, Walaric clenched his jaw as he wondered if he should call out Terrwyn's deception. She was no noblewoman, but there did not seem to be any immediate harm in playing along. She fancied him and he her. That was good enough for now.

"Let's eat breakfast and break camp," Izold grumbled. "Lady Terrwyn, I trust you will have no trouble keeping up with us from here?"

"No trouble at all," Terrwyn replied and smirked.

Walaric could hardly focus on breakfast. His gaze continually drifted to Terrwyn, who sat beside him. She smiled and winked at him every time she caught his eye. Walaric blushed as he struggled to remember his vows. Did she really come all this way for him?

Paschal and Candac occasionally shot Walaric a jealous glance, but he ignored them. He did not do anything wrong, he reminded himself. Now that Terrwyn was here, they had to at least take her to Laht.

Izold quietly grumbled to himself but said nothing directly to him or Terrwyn. Walaric cringed as he thought back to what the paladin had told him about Elja. Was Walaric making the same mistake now that he had previously made with Madeline's handmaiden?

Only Sir Jordan's bemused expression broke the intensity of his other comrades' withering stares. He obviously saw some spark between Terrwyn and Walaric. Dare he indulge? What of Elja back at Olso Fortress? Could Walaric return home with another maiden after rejecting Elja on account of his vows to the celestial gods?

Walaric shook his head. He had not the slightest inkling what Terrwyn's real plans were or how much they involved him. He had to focus on his quest, not her schemes. His palms grew sweaty. What a mess.

After breakfast, they quickly broke camp and began searching the Narewd's banks for a good place to cross. Walaric frowned at the fast-moving current in front of him. Downstream was slower but filled with ice, while upstream was too deep for comfort.

"Which way?" Paschal groaned.

"North will force us away from Laht, so I suggest we look for a better crossing farther downstream." Jordan pointed towards the ice forming on the banks.

"Agreed." Izold nodded.

Jordan led the way south along the Narewd's bank, and Candac, Paschal, and Izold followed closely. Walaric fell in beside Terrwyn at the rear of the group. For a long moment, he struggled to find the right words to say.

"What are you really doing here?" Walaric asked Terrwyn after he was sure the others were distracted in their own conversations.

"I want to go with you." She winced. "Didn't I already make that apparent enough?"

"How far?" Walaric furrowed his brow. "You're not going to the Blighted Lands."

"I told your friends Laht." Terrwyn pursed her lips. "That will be far enough, I think."

Now Walaric winced. He should have been glad to hear the words. It would be less complicated that way. Still, his stomach sank.

"What will you do after reaching Laht?" Walaric asked. "You're not going to wait for me there, are you?"

"Don't tempt Fate." Terrwyn winked. "Remember, you have vows to uphold. Don't become my father."

"There are other vows I could take that would allow for a special dispensation," Walaric explained. "After this quest, Bishop Manfred may see fit to elect me as an exorcist. They are permitted to have families."

"Don't get too far ahead of yourself, *Father* Walaric." Terrwyn giggled.

"You're right." Walaric cleared his throat. "But when this quest is over, I'll be sure to find you at Laht."

"What changed?" Terrwyn asked. "At Kolarb, you wanted nothing to do with me."

"Back there, you reminded me of someone," Walaric confessed. "She would flirt with me. She was beautiful, but I thought she only chased me because she knew it was a dream that could not be realized. You're different."

"Dreams are hard to understand." Terrwyn's gaze drifted down the bank as they walked. "We know they're not real, but still we chase. Don't you think she wanted her dream to come true?"

"I'm not sure." Walaric sighed. "We were under siege at Olso. Things were bleak, and we all wanted to take comfort in what we could. It was a dream for me too."

"Try not to read too much into dreams." Terrwyn's voice took on a warning tone.

"Have I offended you?" Walaric could not help but appreciate the irony of asking Terrwyn this after she asked him the same thing not long ago.

"No." The glimmer in Terrwyn's eyes returned just as quickly as it had faded. "The future is just uncertain.

Sometimes we miss the opportunities before us while waiting for something else."

Attempting to decipher Terrwyn's meaning, Walaric bit his lip, but his thoughts soon turned to the others as they stopped ahead of them. Izold and Jordan were pointing downstream as Candac and Paschal joined in their discussion. Walaric strained his ears as he jogged forward a few paces to catch up.

"This might be the best place we've found to ford so far." Jordan gestured to the bank ahead of him.

"We can't spend all morning looking for the perfect crossing," Candac added.

"What if we go back to where we set up camp?" Paschal turned his gaze upstream. "The water was deeper, but the current was slower."

"Let's not waste time," Izold argued. "The flow of the river may have changed before we reach there again."

Without waiting for the others, the paladin splashed as he began leading his horse across the Narewd. The waters went only about halfway up to his knees, and his slow, careful steps gave Walaric some confidence. Jordan and Candac soon followed Izold.

"We'll see if the gods have a sense of humor." Paschal rolled his eyes at Walaric before wading into the icy river. "Say a kind word to Helios on my behalf if I fall downstream, will you?"

Walaric chuckled but nodded. Though his first few steps were tentative, Paschal soon caught up with Candac. Jordan and Izold were now several yards across.

"I don't have any dry clothes or boots to change into," Terrwyn sulked at the Narewd.

"You should've said something," Walaric scolded. "You could've ridden Vielantiu."

"Let's call the paladin back," Terrwyn suggested.

"No," Walaric disagreed. "It's too early in the morning to tempt Tyche. There are enough hazards fording a river once on a winter's day. "

"Then carry me." Terrwyn crossed her arms.

"What?" Walaric blinked.

"You heard me," Terrwyn insisted. "Carry me across the river. It's not that far. Izold and Jordan are almost to the other side now."

Before Walaric could protest, Terrwyn wrapped her arms around the back of his neck and jumped into his grasp. He wobbled awkwardly as he tried to maintain his balance. After steadying himself, he took a few short steps to the water. Her grip was tight, and his shield pressed into his back. The others were too preoccupied with their own crossings to give Walaric's precarious position much heed.

"Let go of the guige," Walaric gasped.

"The what?" Terrwyn clasped Walaric tighter as he struggled to find his footing.

"The guige," Walaric rasped through gritted teeth and bulging eyes. "It's the leather strap hanging from the back of my shield. You're choking me with it."

Terrwyn loosened her grip around Walaric's neck, and his shield fell back into place. He coughed as he took several deep breaths. At last, the coughing subsided, and Walaric waded into the Narewd River.

"Be careful." Terrwyn kissed Walaric's cheek as he took his first step into the water.

Walaric's heart pounded in his chest. His head was light. Was this how Godfrey had felt the first time Madeline kissed him?

He took several adventurous strides forward. He was a new creature, not the scrawny, unsure orphan who had the priesthood thrust upon him to please his betters, but a man who could conquer the wilderness to protect his beloved.

Then, he nearly slipped on a stone at a sharp angle. Reality deflated his fantasy in an instant.

Walaric regained his balance, and his next steps were far shorter. The stones in the riverbed were slippery and difficult to see in the murky water. His arms strained under the weight of the maiden he held as high as he could above the water's surface. Terrwyn's grip around his neck also began to tighten again as they progressed across the river. Sweat beaded around his forehead.

The water drew up past Walaric's knees. He struggled not to loosen his grip around Terrwyn's waist and legs. With every laborious step, he muttered a silent prayer that he would not fall and get carried away in the current. She was not heavy, but he was no athlete.

Finally, they reached the opposite bank. Walaric's aching arms gave way and released Terrwyn just as she let go of his neck. Panting, he collapsed on the bank.

"Well done, Walaric," Jordan said with a smirk. "Perhaps you have the heart of a true knight, after all."

"We must hurry and make a fire to dry our clothes," Izold warned. "Cold, wet clothes will sap the heat from our bodies faster than a ghoul's touch."

"We spent all morning looking for a place to cross the river, and now we need to stop again?" Terrwyn placed her hands on her hips.

"I'm afraid so, my lady." Izold shrugged.

"You'll never catch Nera at this rate," she muttered.

Silently, Walaric groaned in agreement.

After two more days, they found the road to Laht. It was not much better than traveling over the countryside, but it signaled progress. At least there were fewer brambles to get stuck in along the way.

"Bless Tyche, looks like an inn!" Candac cried as he pointed out what appeared to be a large house on the side of the path ahead. "Three days on the road to Laht, and finally we get our first look at civilization."

A sign above the door confirmed Candac's suspicion. Carved into the wood was what appeared to be the profile of a green turkey with its head drawn back to the sky. While noble houses usually chose proud symbols for their coats of arms, odd emblems such as this were a sure indication of a man's business establishment.

Walaric grinned. The others cheered at the sight. Vielantiu snorted at the appearance of a stable next to the inn. Even Izold sighed in relief as his eye caught the inn's chimney billowing smoke into the late afternoon sky.

"We'll rest there tonight," Jordan said.

"There will be no arguments from me about that," Paschal answered.

"I think this is the first inn I've seen outside of a city or town since we entered the Nordslands." Candac gave the large house a skewed look. "Why aren't there more along the roads in Azgald?"

"War has ravaged these lands for too long." Jordan shook his head. "You must be very brave to build a home for yourself outside of the protection of city walls."

With the thought of hot food and drink filling his mind, Walaric pressed down the road. A warm bed surely awaited him by the hearth. Maybe a bard's song in the main hall, too, if he was fortunate enough.

As they drew nearer, the inn's door swung open. A portly man waved to Walaric and his companions, urging them inside. Without hesitation, they rushed to oblige.

"Ah, travelers!" the portly man greeted them as he ushered Terrwyn through the rough oak door. "Welcome! Welcome! What a pleasant New Year's Eve surprise, having all of you show up at my door."

"Is it the Kalends Feast already?" Walaric frowned as he made his way past the threshold. "Helios, curse me. I should have known, but one day just blends into another while traveling for so long."

"You have been on the road a while." The man took Vielantiu's reins as Izold dismounted his stallion. "I can see the cold has gone straight to your bones. I'm Keird, and welcome to the Verdant Turkey."

Walaric chuckled at the inn's amusing name.

"We'll need two rooms for the night." Izold produced a few silver coins from his pouch. "And a stable for my horse."

"Of course, sire." Keird bowed his head. "Dinner is on the house for my lord, paladin, and his noble company."

"We are grateful for your kindness." Izold returned the gesture.

"Nevyn," Keird called over his shoulder. "Take this horse out to the stable, and tell Tosha to get the other roast out of the oven."

A young man, a little older than Walaric, shouted something in reply. He did not understand it amidst the din of the inn's other patrons in the main hall. There were not many other travelers at the Verdant Turkey, but most of them were boisterous from what Walaric could see. A crackling fire, the aroma of savory beef, and a mug of ale were sure to cure the gloom of Azgald in winter.

Terrwyn had already found a spot at one of the booths against the far wall, and Walaric bustled past the tables in the center to reach her. Candac and Jordan also found their way to Terrwyn's booth while Izold and Paschal were obligated to sit at a nearby table.

Soon, Keird came with a mug of ale for each of them. After everyone had their drinks in hand, the innkeeper left with the promise of returning with roast beef. Walaric's stomach grumbled after the retreating form of the portly innkeeper.

"Who are they?" Terrwyn pointed to a trio of armored warriors at the other end of the hall.

Walaric turned his head. The warriors wore heavy chainmail, and their black surcoats were crossed with white saltires. At the center of the saltires, black down-turned swords were outlined in white.

"Those men are from the crusade." Candac's voice rose in excitement. "They're from House Wrehst. Those are Duke Raymond's knights."

"Duke Raymond?" Terrwyn frowned.

"Raymond of Wrehst was one of the Gothian crusaders," Walaric explained. "His men were given the task of capturing Laht while we took Epsberg."

"So, Raymond of Wrehst decided to stay behind like Lord Godfrey did," Terrwyn deduced.

"At the Council of Biorkon," Walaric spoke slowly as he tried to recall the details, "we agreed that the Silver Suns didn't have enough men to hold all the Eastern Marches. Raymond of Wrehst volunteered to garrison Laht until his forces could be relieved."

"Don't you suppose some Azgaldian lord will get upset and press his claim on Laht before the Silver Suns can consolidate their hold on the Eastern Marches?" Terrwyn asked.

"Lord Godfrey did not join our quest precisely because he was asked to help resolve just such a dispute over at Skasgun," Jordan answered.

"They've spotted us." Terrwyn gestured towards the House Wrehst knights as they rose from their table.

"Good evening, my lady." The lead knight tilted his head at Terrwyn. "What an auspicious day seeing such a fair maiden at the Verdant Turkey on New Year's Eve."

"I am Terrwyn of House Zemel." The maiden extended her hand over the table. "Father Walaric and his company are escorting me to Laht."

"I am Sir Ervig." The lead knight kissed her hand. "And these are my companions, Veduco and Atharid."

"Charmed." Terrwyn bowed her head.

Walaric cringed. Terrwyn lied far too easily for his liking. However, Candac and Jordan absently smiled at the exchange, oblivious to her fabrication.

"These are Godfrey de Bastogne's men." Ervig indicated Candac and Paschal over at the next table. "You came from Kovdor?"

"No," Walaric cut off Terrwyn before she could respond. "We met in Valgo. Our quest happens to take us through Laht before we proceed to the Blighted Lands."

"The Blighted Lands?" Ervig's gaze turned to Izold over at the next table. "So, that's why a paladin travels with you. Take heed. Do not let the relative safety of the road to Laht deceive you. Raymond of Wrehst drove out the Nordsmen in Azgald's Eastern Marches between Odsha and Mirborg, but House Laht's patrols do not extend to the petty kingdoms farther east."

"Odsha to Mirborg is still a lot of ground." Jordan's eyes grew wide. "I didn't think Lord Raymond brought that many crusaders with him."

"House Laht?" Terrwyn asked. "I was told you were from House Wrehst."

"Trouble back in Gothia saw my lord bring most of his family here once Laht was secure," the knight Ervig called Veduco answered. "Lord Raymond emptied Wrehst's treasury to purchase Laht and Odsha from the Silver Suns, much to the chagrin of his half-brother. Lord Raymond broke ties with Gothia, formed House Laht, and you are now in the Duchy of Taivalski. Not all of us have had the means to change our heraldry yet to reflect this new arrangement."

"Is this an independent lordship?" Candac's eyes gaped wide.

"No." Ervig chuckled. "Lord Raymond serves King Lothar now. He turned over his estates in Gothia to his half-brother, Sisbert, as part of the exchange for Taivalski."

"I'm sure King Lothar appreciates having so many crusaders settle in Azgald." Jordan rolled his eyes.

"Your own lord did the same." Veduco pointed a finger at Jordan. "The King may be reluctant to surrender lands and titles to crusaders from foreign kingdoms, but it weakens the power of the local lords. As long as the likes of Lord Godfrey and Lord Raymond are loyal to the King, the arrangement works in his favor."

"I wonder what Lord Davin over at Skasgun will do if Godfrey is able to help House Hracour reclaim that fortress," Walaric added. "I don't trust Conrad the Wolf or anyone he would leave in a position of authority."

"Power struggles can get messy." Terrwyn shrugged.

"Sorry to interrupt." Keird bustled over to their booth with a steaming roast and more mugs of ale. "But it seemed your faces were turning a little too dark for New Year's Eve, and the beef is ready. Drink your ale. Celebrate!"

"You're right," Walaric answered as Keird set the platter in front of them. "Too long has our attention dwelled on heavy subjects. We're overdue for a little merriment."

"Happy New Year!" Terrwyn raised her mug.

"Happy New Year!" Ervig toasted Terrwyn after taking a mug of ale from the innkeeper.

"Happy New Year!" the others chorused as they took their mugs and repeated the gesture.

"Excuse us." Ervig nodded to Terrwyn before gesturing to Veduco and Atharid. "Perhaps we'll see you at Laht. Be safe until then."

With that, the knights of House Laht left. Walaric took a long sip of ale. The frothy drink might not have been as good as Flur the Blevin's malty brew back in Valgo County, but anything was better than nothing after weeks of exhausting travel in the bitter cold. He silently praised the gods as he swallowed a large gulp and forgot his troubles.

Chapter Twelve

ew Year's Eve was upon Madeline before she had even realized it. Not only were all of the castle's servants invited to the Kalends Feast, but all of the villagers outside the walls had been called into the keep's great hall for the celebration as well. Soon, many of the common folk crowded the chamber. The air was thick with their raucous songs, chatter, and dancing.

"More of the serfs decided to stay in their homes than come," Madeline explained to Alpia de Toron as they sat at the high table, "but tradition holds that Azgaldian lords and ladies always invite everyone the castle protects to the major holidays and festivals."

"Bosvian tradition demands the same courtesy," Alpia replied. "Our ways are not so different from yours."

"It's a good thing Azgaldian tradition also has the villagers bring some of their own food to the Kalends Feast," Thieda quipped as she took an empty tray from the table. "Otherwise, we might not have had enough for breakfast tomorrow morning."

Madeline frowned at Thieda as she hurried off to the kitchen with her dirty dishes. The handmaiden knew better, but Alpia ignored the barb. Still, Thieda's point was keenly felt whenever Madeline looked in the pantry.

The room settled as Father Edric stepped up beside the hearth to give a traditional New Year's sermon. There was nothing remarkable about it as far as Madeline was concerned. Speeches about renewing covenants with the gods and striving to improve oneself from one year to the next were just a formality before the guests tired themselves out with far too much eating and drinking.

Once Father Edric found his place back at the high table after his speech, the festivities resumed in earnest. Pipers played prancing melodies from the minstrel's gallery. Farmers laughed at each other's jokes. Children ran from one end of the chamber to the other as they played their chaotic games. Everything was as it should be.

Evroul, the blacksmith's apprentice, danced in the middle of the great hall with one of the carpenters' daughters among other young folk. Karl the Hammer wooed Alpia from the other end of the high table with sweet nothings. Madeline turned her gaze to the dark window and gloom outside. Where was Godfrey?

Arius and Berig took large gulps of wine from their goblets as they sat at the opposite end of the high table from Alpia and Karl. Madeline rolled her eyes. They could have just as easily stayed at their own estates.

"Enjoying yourselves?" Madeline wrinkled her nose at the twins. "Try not to get too drunk tonight."

There were other people Madeline would rather have talked to, but none readily appeared at the high table. Most of the young bachelor knights competed for the attention of the few eligible maidens in the chamber. At least Elja was included among them.

"New Year's is a time to be with family," Berig commented and smirked at Madeline.

"What would a Kalends Feast be without our sister?" Arius pouted. "We would have been so lonely celebrating in Trondhelm without you."

"We even turned down an invitation from Leon de Valois to celebrate with him in Mosjen," Berig added. "You mean the world to us. Besides, Father insisted we check in on you, so blame him we had to come."

"Where is that old nun who usually hovers over your shoulder?" Arius looked up and down the chamber.

"Sister Vanya is in her room next to the library," Madeline answered. "She doesn't care much for feasts that go late into the night, and when she saw you two enter the great hall, she used it as an excuse to turn in early."

"Charming." Berig snorted.

"What is this we're hearing about a magic staff?" Arius raised an eyebrow. "Do you plan on burning down the castle with it?"

"Careful, Arius." Berig raised a warning hand. "She might turn you into a toad if you provoke her enough."

Madeline huffed. The twins' insolence quickly grew tiresome. If only she could turn them into toads, at least for long enough to prove a point.

"The staff's construction goes very well," Madeline said. "You're fortunate I respect Father enough not to turn you into toads."

"Now, that's not fair, threatening to turn me into a toad too." Berig crossed his arms. "I was coming to my dear sister's defense. But, of course, she wouldn't appreciate it."

"And what would Lady Madeline do with a magic staff?" Arius pressed. "Berig and I were completely unaware you had such powers until you came here to Olso."

"Does it surprise you that Father would keep secrets from us?" Berig frowned into his wine goblet.

"Father?" Arius shook his head. "No. But Madeline? I thought she was always too innocent and pure to harbor such dark secrets."

"Father must have put her up to it." Berig waved his hand as if swatting at an invisible fly in front of his face. "We all know she would do anything he told her to."

"That's not fair," Madeline hissed. "You know it was for my own protection. We all know how most Azgaldians feel about magicians."

"How long has it been since the last witch burning?" Berig raised an eyebrow.

"Azgald has certainly become a place where you should fear being accused of witchcraft." Madeline clenched her teeth. "Try spending a day in my shoes."

"You're under the King's protection now," Arius cut in. "You don't have any room to complain."

"That doesn't mean much when the King is all the way in Vindholm," Madeline countered.

"Pavik isn't far," Arius replied.

"Trondhelm is closer," Berig prodded his brother.

"And what of Dovard?" Arius scowled at Berig.

"Dovard will answer any plea for help that Trondhelm does." Berig furrowed his brow. "I'm shocked you would doubt my loyalty."

Madeline winced. She could hardly imagine calling on Trondhelm or Dovard for help. Though the twins had only intermittently been a part of her life, they understood the family dynamics well enough. Not only did they enjoy getting under her skin, but they knew just how to do it, too.

"The magic staff will help me grow my powers and channel them more effectively," Madeline answered. "Now that it's common knowledge that I'm a sorceress, it's important that I become the most powerful spell caster I can be. Don't you agree?"

"We certainly don't want any harm coming to you." Arius exchanged a nervous glance with Berig. "But how do you know how to construct a magic staff?"

"My ways are beyond your understanding." Madeline cocked an eyebrow. "It would be too much for me to explain to your feeble minds."

Though what she said was not entirely true, Madeline still did not want to reveal Fravash to anyone she did not have to. He was unusual if not entirely beyond the twins' understanding. Her explanation would be enough for now.

"Oh, come off it!" Berig laughed.

After a moment's hesitation, Arius laughed too.

"She has all those books in the library." Berig pointed to the great hall's exit. "She's reading old grimoires to teach her how to make the staff."

"Oh, of course!" Arius rolled his eyes. "Don't try to scare us with all that sorceress talk."

"Try not to be fooled so easily," Madeline jibed.

The party continued well into the night. Without many young noblewomen to flirt with, the twins eventually made their excuses to retire to their guest chambers after they had drained their goblets of the last of Olso's ice berry wine. Slowly, others followed their examples and staggered out of the great hall in pairs or small groups.

"How much longer is this going to take?" Fravash twitched his whiskers as he stood on Madeline's leg.

"I told you not to be here!" Madeline blinked incredulously. "What if someone sees you?"

Nervously, Madeline glanced from one end of the high table to the other. Karl the Hammer and Alpia de Toron had disappeared, leaving Moric Cyclops Slayer dozing on the far end by himself. Father Edric's attention drifted somewhere between the dancing around the hearth and the edge of sleep, too. No one noticed the mouse that had appeared in Madeline's lap.

"Mice and rats are everywhere." Fravash waved his paw dismissively. "I chose this form specifically to not arouse suspicion."

"Well, you saw how well that worked with Elja and Thieda earlier," Madeline countered.

"Yes, yes," Fravash sighed. "I will try to stay out of sight. Now, how much longer will this celebration last?"

"It's tradition that the Kalends Feast goes until dawn, and I'm the host." Madeline pointed to herself.

"Well, that's a stupid tradition," the mouse replied. "Half of your Ostman kin are falling asleep, and the Nordsmen aren't far behind. Only your dwarf servants seem to have the stamina to stay up all night."

Madeline looked out over the celebrants. Fravash was right. Dachlann and some of the other dwarves from the mine were deep in a heavy drinking contest at one of the tables near the great hall's entrance. Erikur, one of the Nordsman serfs, sat in the midst of the dwarves and held down his liquor well enough. However, most of the other human guests were beginning to show signs of fatigue if they had not already left or fallen asleep where they were.

"First, you wouldn't leave for Farthest Thule because you were waiting for Lord Godfrey to come back." Fravash tapped his foot. "Then, you wouldn't go because of the Kalends Feast…"

"I shouldn't leave without telling Godfrey." Madeline shook her head. "He should be back soon."

"He left you here all alone," Fravash answered.

"His family asked for help." Madeline crossed her arms. "Godfrey didn't want to go."

"Lord Godfrey wanted to go with Walaric." Fravash gave Madeline a sideways look. "Even if House Hracour hadn't gotten involved, you would still be here alone now."

"We've just worked so hard for this wedding to happen," Madeline began.

"And it's still not until the first day of spring," Fravash interrupted. "You have months until then. Godfrey probably still won't be back from Vindholm for a little while. I thought you would see this as the perfect opportunity to go to Farthest Thule."

"I suppose it is." Madeline bit her lip.

"What are you afraid of, Lady Madeline?" Fravash's eyes gleamed. "What's stopping you from making the most incredible decision of your life?"

"I'm afraid to fly." Madeline averted her eyes. "I know it seems silly."

"But you've grown so much," the mouse exclaimed. "You're already a great sorceress. You're maturing into a fine young lady. I know the journey is far, and the elves can be enigmatic and aloof, but—"

"No." Madeline shook her head. "That's not what I'm talking about. I mean flying Spathi."

"The griffin?" Fravash blinked several times. "Why? You've done it before."

"Yes, but only with Godfrey," Madeline clarified.

"Well." Fravash cleared his throat. "I suggest you get over that fear pretty quickly, if you want to get that phoenix feather. There's no other way we'll reach Farthest Thule this winter. Understand?"

"Yes." Madeline swallowed hard.

"Good." The mouse nodded. "We won't leave tomorrow since you'll need time to recover from all this nonsense, but we should make ready for the next day."

"All right," Madeline reluctantly agreed.

"Enjoy the rest of the feast then." The mouse scampered off Madeline's lap before disappearing into some dark corner of the chamber.

As the night wore on, the pipers' songs grew sluggish. The dancing had all but stopped, and only Dachlann remained upright among all the dwarves and men who had competed in their drinking contest. Madeline's turning stomach kept her eyelids from growing too heavy. If Godfrey came back fast enough, she would not have to fly Spathi alone.

By the time dawn's first light crept through the great hall's windows, fatigue had nearly made Madeline's eyelids too heavy to keep open. Those few hardy enough to still be awake rose to their feet and raised their goblets to the dawn. Madeline's feet wobbled ever so slightly as she rose next to Father Edric, who yawned as if he had just awoken from a restful night's sleep.

"With the New Year comes a new beginning." Father Edric held his jeweled goblet aloft for all to see. "May the dawn ending the Kalends Feast end the evils that have pursued this company over the last year, and may it also bring to pass the joys we pursue in the present."

"Amen," Madeline and the others still awake echoed before draining their goblets, mugs, and tankards.

With that, Madeline fell back into her chair. She did not care if she fell asleep at the table in front of everyone. Fravash was right. The Kalends Feast was a stupid tradition. Her eyelids closed, and she drifted off for a long time.

Several days flew by faster than Madeline could count them. Karl the Hammer eventually went back to Bormheld with Alpia and Moric. They had decided to brave the elements and venture to Karl's estates, and Madeline could say or do little to persuade them to stay longer.

By contrast, Arius and Berig would not leave, no matter how much Madeline hinted that the twins had overstayed their welcome. It was as perplexing as it was annoying. Did they not have business in Trondhelm and Dovard to attend to?

"I want to see you finish making this magic staff of yours," Arius insisted over breakfast one day.

Madeline's stomach sank. Arius watched her with an expectant look. Berig watched her with a spoonful of porridge hovering close to his mouth. She still needed to get the phoenix feather, and the twins would no more approve of such an adventure than Sister Vanya would. What excuse could she make to the twins?

"You can't." Madeline shook her head as she wrapped a piece of bacon around her fork.

"Why is that?" Arius leaned over the table.

"It's too dangerous," Madeline answered.

"Dangerous?" Sister Vanya raised an eyebrow as she leaned in from Madeline's other side.

Father Edric also paused over his sausage and scrambled eggs. Madeline cringed. Dangerous was the wrong idea. That would only make them all more afraid. What could she say to get out of this?

"Not dangerous," Madeline corrected. "Not exactly. Forgive me. I misspoke. Really, it's just going to take a while to finish. I need time and concentration. I can't focus on my work with you and Berig here."

The twins scoffed. Father Edric exchanged an uneasy glance with Sister Vanya. Madeline grimaced at them. The old librarian only begrudgingly approved of Madeline's arcane studies. The new priest, however, had not spoken much to Madeline on the subject. She clenched her teeth at what could lie behind his veneer of soft-spoken axioms and uninspiring conventional sermons.

"We're good enough at entertaining ourselves until you're ready," Arius replied smoothly.

"Though there are more women at Dovard." Berig rolled his eyes. "They could be far more entertaining than anything we can do for ourselves."

Father Edric rapped his fingers across the table. Berig flinched as the old priest leered at him. Edric's stance on appropriate table conversation was clear enough, even if his opinions on Madeline's magic studies remained a mystery.

Berig withered under the old priest's stare. He had crossed a line. His face turning red, he stammered something incoherent that might have passed for an apology before excusing himself from the high table. Chuckling, Arius pushed his chair back from the table and followed Berig out of the great hall.

"And I thought those two were such well-mannered young men." Disapprovingly, Sister Vanya clicked her tongue as the twins left.

"The Kalends Feast must have made them restless," Father Edric suggested as his gaze returned to his eggs.

"Don't let first impressions fool you." Madeline scraped the last of her breakfast into her mouth with her fork. "The twins have always been crass bullies. I wouldn't let them stay any longer than good etiquette permits, and good etiquette is wearing thin."

Soon, Varin entered the great hall. Melting snow squelched from the ranger's boots as he carried a trio of strangled geese over the cloak on his back. He stopped just in front of the high table.

"A good catch this morning," Father Edric beamed.

"All too rare these days," Varin muttered.

"Why is that?" Madeline grimaced.

"The ghouls." Varin shuddered. "They're scaring all of the wild game from the forests."

"That's dark news for the middle of winter," Edric sighed. "Game like those geese is hard enough to come across this time of year already."

"What can we do?" Madeline asked.

"Not much, I'm afraid." The ranger shook his head. "Lord Godfrey tried to clear them out before he left, but there are too many for one man."

"Send Sir Magnus and some of the other knights to get rid of them," Sister Vanya suggested.

"We have only about a dozen knights left here after the siege." Madeline shifted uncomfortably in her chair. "It's too risky. We can't afford to lose even one more right now."

Silently, the old librarian brooded.

"Any other ideas?" Madeline looked to the others at the high table.

"We could ask the Silver Suns for help." Father Edric took a bite of his eggs.

"Construction of their new fortress in Upplad will not begin until the spring," Madeline countered. "Their presence in Kovdor will be very limited until then."

"I'll warn the other hunters to be careful for the present." Varin's gaze turned cold. "We'll keep avoiding Kolsmarden Forest the best we can. Fortunately, the ghouls haven't ventured very far from there for the most part."

Varin walked past the high table back to the kitchen. There, Thieda and Elja would clean the geese and cook them for dinner that night. Any catch like Varin's helped stretch out the castle's food stores. Such bounties were, unfortunately, too rare this winter.

"We should encourage Sigibald of Fulda and Sir Eozen to engage in a little more falconry," Madeline said between bites of a small, hard biscuit. "That may give us a few hares or quail."

"Segeric and Corbus recently acquired falcons, too," Father Edric added.

"Make it a contest." Madeline brightened at the prospect. "Since Arius and Berig need entertainment, make sure they participate, too. The first to bring in more than a dozen quails and a dozen rabbits before the end of the week gets one of Vozzab's claws."

"His claws?" Sister Vanya swallowed hard.

"Ask Dachlann to fashion a pendant necklace from one of the dragon's claws." Madeline turned to Father Edric. "He's not afraid of an old skeleton down in the mines. Tell him he can use all the silver he needs from our reserves."

"We don't have much silver left in the treasury," Father Edric warned. "We're still recovering from the large donation we made to the Silver Suns."

"Then we can impress upon the knights' minds just how special this dragon claw pendant will be," Madeline replied. "We need to motivate the knights to hunt, and we can't eat the gold and silver sitting in the treasury."

With that, Madeline gulped down the last of the milk from her cup and pushed her chair back. She stood, wiped her mouth on her napkin, and set it on top of her plate.

"Don't forget," Sister Vanya called out as Madeline made for the great hall's exit. "I need you in the library after lunch, so don't spend all day in your room."

"I won't," Madeline reassured her.

Huffing, she made her way up the spiral stairs. However, she made it up only to the second floor before she stopped and gasped at the small figure standing on the windowsill. Fravash crossed his arms as he met her eyes.

"It's been two weeks since the Kalends Feast." Fravash impatiently tapped his foot. "We can't accomplish much more on this staff until we get that phoenix feather."

"I know." Madeline bit her lip. "But Arius and Berig won't leave the castle. I don't want them telling Father I've disappeared. He'll be furious."

"Your father will understand when he sees what we will accomplish," Fravash countered. "Kovdor will be the safest duchy in all of Azgald once we fully unlock the secret to your powers. Mark my words."

"I see your point," Madeline slowly agreed.

"You do want this, right?" Fravash pressed.

"Of course," Madeline replied. "I want to grow my powers more than anything else right now."

"Then let's delay no longer," Fravash insisted.

Madeline looked past Fravash out the window for a long moment. Spathi lay napping in his pen. There were no other excuses to make. It was time.

"I should tell Elja and Thieda, at least." Madeline glanced back down the stairwell.

"I already wrote them a letter on your behalf," Fravash answered. "I left it in a place easy enough for them to find. I told them that Vonig the Cold should be in charge until your return. He's the best choice for a castellan. Don't you agree, my lady?"

"I think so." Madeline fidgeted. "But I haven't ever discussed it with him. What about food and other supplies?"

"I already put them in the stables next to the griffin's pen." Fravash nodded towards the window. "You have a tent, winter bedroll, and two weeks of trail rations waiting for you down there."

"You already…" Madeline's voice trailed off. "How could such a small mouse do all that in the time it took me to go to the morning prayer service and eat breakfast?"

"Magic can make a great many tasks far easier once you know how to really use it." The rodent's eyes gleamed. "All you need to do is grab a warm cloak, and we can be on our way to Farthest Thule."

"Farthest Thule!" Madeline's heart jumped.

"Did you honestly forget that's where we're going?" Fravash chortled.

"Almost," Madeline confessed. "I've been so preoccupied with the obstacles to leaving."

"Keep your mind on the goal." The mouse's tail twitched. "Don't focus on what stands in your way."

Farthest Thule, the hidden northern city of the elves, had long evaded Azgaldian explorers attempting to establish contact. Godfrey and Madeline had previously tried to find the fabled city, but that effort failed before it could hardly begin. Only one Ostman had ever succeeded in reaching Farthest Thule as far as Madeline knew, and that was long ago. Myths and legends had spread in the years since about its riches, elegance, and people, especially concerning magic.

"Let's hurry then." Madeline scooped Fravash out of the windowsill.

With Fravash hanging off her shoulder, the young sorceress ran the rest of the way up the stairs to her bed chambers. She forgot all about the twins, Father Edric, Sister Vanya, and her duties as the lady of Olso Fortress. Even Godfrey and the wedding were only vague concerns to be put off until later. Only the thought of her father's disappointed face gave Madeline any pause as she reached for the door handle to her bedroom.

"We're really going to Farthest Thule?" Madeline tilted her head to the mouse on her shoulder.

"I can take you there," Fravash promised. "Don't worry about anything else. Your family, friends, and all the weight of your responsibilities will be waiting for you when you come home again."

"All right." Madeline tugged on the door handle.

Once inside, she grabbed her cloak from the closet. The mouse hopped onto her bed before she threw the heavy woolen garment over her shoulders. Next to Fravash on the bed lay the pieces of the partially assembled staff.

"Is it safe to leave here?" Madeline picked up one of the staff's silver end caps. "We already infused the shaft with that dragon scale potion a while ago."

"No, we can't leave it here." Fravash shook his head. "We can't risk losing or damaging the phoenix's feather on the way back to Olso. We need to take the staff to Farthest Thule to complete its construction. The elves will be able to help us there."

"I'm glad you think they'll be willing to help with this," Madeline said. "But they go to such great lengths to separate themselves from the affairs of men. Are you sure I will be welcome there?"

"Magic is a currency the elves have in greater abundance than most," Fravash explained. "They are willing to share it for the greater good."

"If only they would take a broader view of the greater good regarding the defense of Azgald," Madeline countered. "Elvish crafts, magic, and griffin knights could do much to uplift the kingdom."

"The elves are a fading race," Fravash answered as if having anticipated Madeline's response. "Their resources aren't unlimited. Though one of their kind may live a thousand years, each death is viewed as an irreplaceable loss. And every year, fewer elves walk the mortal sphere."

"It sounds like their sense of self-preservation keeps them from doing much good in the world." Madeline picked up the shaft of her staff and began twisting the end cap on.

"We are in the age of men." Fravash climbed back onto Madeline's shoulder. "Luka gifted Lord Godfrey a griffin to defeat Vozzab, but he could do no more. Godfrey had to slay the dragon."

"I see." Madeline began walking back to the bed chamber's door.

"Do not judge the elves too harshly," Fravash insisted. "They still know right from wrong. However, most of them would prefer to work indirectly towards the greater good of Aestas."

Madeline threw her hood up over her head and held her breath. She glanced in the mirror. Not only was she invisible, but the mouse on her shoulder was, too.

Quickly, she slid down the stairs back to the ground level. She was able to do most of this while invisible and caught the attention of few servants or armed retainers as she made her way to the keep's exit. However, one of Godfrey's knights, Berold, stood directly in front of the large oak door leading outside. Fravash scurried under Madeline's hood as she slowly released her breath.

"Oh, Lady Madeline!" Berold gasped as Madeline walked towards the knight from a dark alcove. "Forgive me. I didn't see you there."

"It's no worry." Madeline smiled at Berold as the young knight stood stiff at attention. "Can you let me through the door?"

"Of course, my lady." Berold swiftly stepped to the side before opening the keep's door for Madeline. "Father Edric just announced the falconry contest. Will you be presenting the prize to the winner?"

Playfully smirking, Madeline passed Berold without further answer. It was not fear of her magic that she sensed, but rather the sort of timidity most young men felt around beautiful women. That was a welcome change, at least.

Once Berold closed the door behind her, Madeline took a few steps out into the inner courtyard. The grounds were largely empty. No one caught her eye, at least.

Holding her breath, Madeline crossed to Spathi's pen invisible. She exhaled loudly only after unlatching the door to the stables and entering.

Crocus the Entillan's and Halinard's horses greeted Madeline with friendly snorts, but the stables were otherwise empty. Squeaking, Fravash pointed to the provisions he had laid next to the griffin's pen. Madeline set her staff against the wall and reached down for the supplies. She carefully packed them into Spathi's saddlebags. Everything was ready.

With all preparations now complete, Madeline took a decisive step towards Spathi. The griffin lay curled up in a bed of straw next to the stable's wall. However, her heart leapt in her throat, and she jumped as a shadowy figure appeared in the doorway leading to the pen.

"Oh!" Madeline exclaimed. "Varin, it's you. You frightened me."

"Curious that I should find Lady Madeline's footprints in the snow without Lady Madeline to accompany them," Varin muttered as he glanced at Spathi's saddle in her hands. "I thought I was going mad, but, then again, there's plenty of madness around here already."

Unsure how to respond, Madeline furrowed her brow. There were times when Varin seemed to be little more than a grizzled woodsman; someone hardened by the capricious forests into a callous, brooding man. At other times, Varin seemed a little more broken.

"Take that mouse on your shoulder." Varin's gaze shifted to Fravash. "It always follows you. Always watches you. Most unnatural."

"Oh." Madeline flushed as she turned to Fravash. "Varin, this is Fravash the Bright. He has been helping me construct the magic staff."

"At your service, Master Varin." Fravash bowed.

"You would be a magic mouse, wouldn't you, Fravash the Bright?" Varin cackled. "And, no, it's just Varin. I'm not a master of anything but my bow."

Uneasily, Madeline chuckled. Thieda and Elja screamed when they first heard Fravash speak. Sister Vanya might have, too, had she not been such an educated woman who had previously dealt with him. Varin had just a strong enough touch of madness to accept talking mice by virtue of simply hearing it.

"So, where are you taking Spathi?" Varin asked.

"Farthest Thule," Madeline confessed.

"You tried that before." Varin tilted his head with an uncertain expression.

"Without my help," Fravash added. "It's about a five-day journey from here, if we fly by griffin. Farthest Thule is near the edge of the Great Ice."

"Sounds promising." Varin nodded.

"You're not going to try to stop me?" Madeline asked. "Aren't you upset?"

"It's not my business to tell a noblewoman what she can and cannot do." Varin shrugged.

"You won't tell the others?" Madeline gripped the saddle tightly.

"I doubt they'll have the opportunity to ask." Varin grimaced. "I'm taking the other rangers farther afield on a hunting expedition. The ghouls haven't infested the lands too far west of us yet. We'll be gone for a few days. With Tyche's help, we'll bring back something good."

Varin took the saddle from Madeline's hands and whistled to Spathi. The griffin's ears perked up, and Varin produced a strip of salted meat from one of his pouches. Spathi's beak snatched it in one sharp motion before Varin began harnessing the saddle around the creature's flanks.

By the time Madeline retrieved her staff and returned to Spathi's pen, the ranger had finished his work. Varin handed the reins to the young sorceress. She extended her fingers but froze before she could grasp the reins.

"You've come this far." Fravash nudged Madeline encouragingly. "Don't be afraid."

"You're a resourceful young woman," the ranger added. "I have no doubt you'll make it back here whole. Maybe you'll come back strong enough to rid Kovdor of these ghouls."

"You're right." Madeline grasped Spathi's reins with her free hand. "This isn't just for me. This is for all of us. If Walaric can't put Nera's shade to rest and stop the undead incursions, I'll need to be strong enough to drive the ghouls back from here myself."

"That's what I've been trying to tell you," Fravash agreed. "Don't worry about Sister Vanya, the twins, or your father. This is for the good of the realm."

"For Kovdor." Madeline straddled Spathi's saddle.

The griffin hopped over the fence to his pen, ran a few paces, and kicked off the ground. Madeline's stomach lurched as Spathi soared over the inner gatehouse and then the towers of the outer curtain wall. Varin was now just a tiny figure waving from far below.

"To the Wyrmwind Peaks!" Fravash clutched the side of Madeline's hood. "Brace yourself. It's going to get a lot colder from here!"

Chapter Thirteen

Godfrey aimlessly wandered through the drafty corridors of Vindholm's citadel with Mauger. Three days awaiting the King's judgment concerning the transfer of Skasgun back to House Hracour had turned into weeks of inaction. Godfrey clenched his teeth harder with each passing day. The growing tension in Mauger's face was not lost on him either.

Other nobles came and went with *their* urgent business in the interim. The Kalends Feast also came and went, but no summons came for Roltar. Godfrey balled his fist every time he thought about just how long he had been away from Kovdor. This whole affair should have been settled long ago.

"A hasty ruling will not be in our favor." Mauger shook his head when Godfrey made these complaints known. "Father is working with some of the King's advisors. If we are patient, Tyche will reward us."

"Perhaps King Lothar's lack of a straight answer *is* his answer." Godfrey rolled his eyes as they walked through the darkening passageway. "Can you really imagine the King of Azgald forcibly removing Lord Davin from Skasgun? There would be an uproar."

"It's the home of my forefathers." Mauger's expression soured. "I have to believe justice will prevail."

"There is plenty of injustice in this world." Godfrey's lip curled into a frown.

"That shouldn't keep us from trying." Mauger stopped in his tracks. "I thought you would know that better than most people in Azgald."

"You're right." Godfrey stopped a pace ahead of him. "But there are a lot of other problems that also need attention. The undead are growing restless. The Clans are still raiding. I wonder if my time is best spent here. Roltar seems to know how to handle this without me."

Godfrey held his tongue when he thought to say something about Madeline or the wedding. She had not written a single letter to him since he had arrived. Though being away from his betrothed made his stomach sink, he did not want to appear selfish. He had a duty to his kin. There was still time to work out the wedding's details.

"On the contrary." Mauger started walking again. "Your mere presence at Vindholm helps our efforts. You're the only living dragon-slayer in all of Azgald. Your opinion matters at King Lothar's court."

"I suppose that's true." Godfrey sighed as he fell in beside Mauger.

More than one lord had toasted Godfrey's health during their evening meals at Vindholm. So many pages, squires, and commoners had stopped to gawk at him that he began to not notice as much. There was no denying his reputation meant more now than ever.

"I hope we get our answer soon," Godfrey added. "Waiting is the most painful part."

"You have no idea." A scowl darkened Mauger's face. "I've waited my whole life for this answer."

Godfrey bit his lip. Just as he thought he had made some improvement in his relationship with Mauger over the last few weeks, all of the jealousy and resentment came back in an instant. Like his father, Mauger could only be satisfied when he had Stormsud returned to House Hracour.

"Do you have plans for after Skasgun is returned to your house?" Godfrey cleared his throat.

"I haven't thought much past accomplishing the goal at hand," Mauger confessed.

"Perhaps you could speak with Isbeil of House Perch," Godfrey suggested. "She's kin to some of the Ogleddish crusaders who just left after the Therismos Festival. She is very beautiful and in need of a husband."

"Are you blind?" Mauger's face grew even darker. "I've seen her attending Lothar's court since we arrived. Lady Isbeil only has eyes for you."

"Me?" Godfrey blushed.

"You are an unmarried duke." Mauger's pace slowed as he gestured to him.

"I'm engaged to Madeline of House Drois." Godfrey creased his brow. "We are supposed to be married on the first day of spring."

"But you are still unmarried as of now," Mauger countered. "You have the land. You have the title. Olso sits on top of a rich silver mine. Knights will begin flocking to your banner by spring at the latest. It should hardly surprise you that more than one woman thinks herself in competition with your beloved."

"Right." Godfrey frowned, remembering the other maidens he had been introduced to since he acquired the duchy of Kovdor.

Mauger glowered. Every word he spoke in Godfrey's favor also served as a point of attack. Why should it not be him receiving so much attention from lords and ladies? Why did he not deserve to have the fortune of ruling over a newly formed duchy atop a rich silver mine? How could Tyche be so cruel to his line?

Godfrey shifted an uncomfortable pace away from Mauger as they neared the landing of a spiral staircase. All he had ever done was his duty to his lords and the gods. Why

Mauger received fewer apparent blessings was beyond his ability to say.

"I'll see you later." Godfrey abruptly turned to the stairs. "Get a good meal and some rest."

Mauger grumbled something indistinct in farewell as Godfrey began to climb the stairs. Vindholm's citadel was vast, and it was easy for Godfrey to lose himself in the many chambers and corridors he had not fully explored yet. He did not care much about where he ended up as long as it was somewhere away from Mauger. After clambering up the stairs for a short while, the task proved easy enough.

Eventually, he found himself in one of the citadel's lesser halls. It was occupied by several of King Lothar's other guests idling away the chilly winter evening. Some gathered around the hearth, reading by the light of the fire, while others played chess or other board games at tables near the walls. Between the two groups, the majority of the lords and ladies present sat at long tables enjoying food, drink, and useless gossip.

Godfrey scoffed as the words *black knight* came up at more than one table. Ever since he had arrived at Vindholm's citadel, rumors flew concerning who the mysterious knight was and where he was going next. Some said he was a disgraced crusader seeking atonement. Others said he was one of Count Maurus' sons, back from the dead. No one could know for certain.

A trio of young maidens gathered around Arthur of House Drechov as he showed off the stag's horns fastened to his great helm. He had recounted the story of how he had earned the title *Victor of the Great Hunt* on at least a few other occasions since Godfrey's arrival at the citadel. However, the impressionable, young maidens did not seem to get tired of it, from what Godfrey could see.

Lady Isbeil of House Perch joked with the Duchess of Smalad. A few other noblewomen from both near and far mingled freely in the chamber. More than one tried to catch Godfrey's eye, and he blushed in reply as he recalled Mauger's words about other women competing with Madeline for his attention. Godfrey pressed his lips together. Did Madeline deserve such attention?

"Godfrey de Bastogne?" An armored man in a blue tabard emblazoned with a golden frost lion approached him as he entered the chamber.

"Yes?" Godfrey replied warily.

"I am Hugo of House Merrich." The knight bowed.

Godfrey studied the man as he returned the gesture. Hugo was blonde and had green eyes. He was four or five years older than Godfrey, and a little shorter than him, but not below average height. After a moment, Godfrey recognized his heraldry.

"You're one of the Duke of Gotlad's sons?" Godfrey asked. "I believe I met your father at Biorkon when the crusade first reached Azgald."

"That's right." Hugo nodded with an encouraging smile. "My father, Duke Sigurd, spoke very well of you after meeting the crusaders at Biorkon. It is a real honor to finally see you in the flesh."

Godfrey attempted to conceal the grimace crawling across his face. Hugo was not the first to approach him with honeyed words like these. It did not take any of them long to reveal their true purpose and ask a favor of him.

"How can I be of service?" Godfrey's jaw tightened.

Hugo gestured for Godfrey to sit with him at a nearby table, and he complied. The knight produced a pair of tin mugs and filled them with ale from a pitcher on the table. With a broad smile, Hugo passed Godfrey one of the frothy mugs.

Even after both men found their seats, Godfrey's muscles remained tight. The knight's small talk did little to set him at ease. Hugo's voice was too smooth and his compliments too well-practiced for him not to want something of Godfrey. He was like a viper waiting in the grass. Tentatively, Godfrey took a sip of ale from his mug.

"House Merrich has long befriended House Hracour," Hugo began after taking a long swig of ale from his own mug. "I can speak with my father about lending his support to Roltar's claim on Skasgun."

"That would be quite the boon." Godfrey raised an eyebrow. "I'm sure you're aware that King Lothar still has not given a final ruling on House Hracour's petition."

"It's only natural that what is discussed in the King's private council has a way of reaching the ears of those willing to pay the right price." Hugo tapped his finger against the tin mug in his hand. "There is just one problem with me talking to my father on your behalf. Otherwise—you see—I would have spoken with him already."

Godfrey leaned forward and crossed his arms over the table. There was always a catch. How much would this boon cost him, if it could really be called a boon at all?

"Go on," Godfrey answered as neutrally as he could.

"You see." Hugo made a sweeping gesture across the table. "My father recently granted me an estate within Gotlad – a modest county, really – however, my brothers openly resent this arrangement since I am the youngest, and I fear they may try to persuade Father to rescind my fief. I can't hold any sway in my father's court without land and a proper title."

"This sounds like a family affair." Godfrey shrugged sympathetically. "I'm not sure how I can help."

"But it's not dissimilar from what you're asking of King Lothar," Hugo pressed. "Speak with my father – no – write a letter to Gotlad saying he needs to ignore my brothers and honor the inheritance I have received. Then, I will tell King Lothar House Merrich backs House Hracour's claim to

Skasgun. Then Yolanda, the Duchess of Smalad, agreed that she would—"

"I'm not sure if I should really get involved in this." Godfrey ran his hand through his hair. "I don't know your father or brothers. I've never even been to Gotlad."

For a brief moment, Hugo's mouth hung open. However, his jaw tightened as some new arithmetic appeared to work itself out behind his scheming gaze. A wicked grin curled his lips as he leaned in closer to Godfrey.

"I could introduce you to my sister, Elna, should you decide to visit Gotlad," Hugo whispered with practiced intensity. "Or I could arrange for us to visit Kovdor, if you'd prefer. She is young and quite beautiful. Many a brave knight is seeking her hand."

"I am already engaged to Madeline of House Drois." Godfrey shook his head. "You're not the first to underestimate my commitment to her."

"Of course, you're committed." Hugo snapped his fingers. "She's Duke Tancred's daughter, beautiful in her own way and has frightful talents, I'm told."

Godfrey took a breath, but Hugo continued before he could get a word in.

"We need to make sure that any potential match is not only exceptionally beautiful but also powerful." Hugo took another sip of ale. "Perhaps I can arrange a meeting between you and Aethling Lili of Cobh?"

"Cobh?" Godfrey pursed his lips. "Where is that? Brogue? You're sorely mistaken if you think I'm going there any time soon."

"Brogue may be the Isle of a Dozen Kingdoms, but Lili of Cobh is a genuine princess as lovely as they come," Hugo reassured him.

"Thanks, but no." Godfrey wrinkled his nose before setting his mug of ale down on the table.

"You would turn down the opportunity to favor a Broguish aethling?" Hugo's eyes went wide. "Lili of Cobh is the fairest princess on that whole island."

"I'm sure she is." Godfrey rose from his chair. "But I don't care if Lili of Cobh is a Broguish aethling, a Sornian princess, or an elvish queen. I'm marrying Madeline on the first day of spring. I'm sure your county in Gotlad is safe."

A mix of unpleasant emotions crossed Hugo's face. Lurching from side to side, he stammered. He could offer nothing else to Godfrey.

"You'll regret not making friends with me." Ale spilled from Hugo's mug as he forcefully set it down and rose from his chair, too. "I know people."

Dismissively, Godfrey waved at Hugo and began making his way to the chamber's far exit. Too many minor lords thought Godfrey could give far more than he really could, and offers like Hugo's amounted to little more than fool's gold. Perhaps coming to Vindholm was a mistake.

Lady Isbeil smiled as she caught Godfrey's eye, but he pretended not to see her as he marched across the hall. Then a dwarf in merchant's clothing gestured to Godfrey, but he walked right past him. He did not care for any of their games right now.

Godfrey sighed as he pushed open the wide oak doors. The corridor before him was dark with only a few dim candles to light the way. His father had faced petitioners similar to Hugo of House Merrich back at Fuetoile Keep more often than he cared to keep track of. Perhaps it was just one of the costs of being in a position of power.

His footsteps echoing off the walls, Godfrey made his way through the shadowy passageway as he brooded. Ghostly statues resting in umbral alcoves lined both sides of the corridor. Each represented some long-dead king Godfrey was sure must have also felt the heavy burden of responsibility during his reign.

Metal scraped against metal. Godfrey raised his eyebrows as he was torn from his thoughts. Drawing Uriel, he spun just in time to deflect a dark figure's blade.

The soft glow of Uriel's holy light revealed a cloaked man before Godfrey. The assassin brought his sword down on him again with a downward slash, but he jumped away. Godfrey's armor and shield were in his room. His only defenses were his blade and agility.

The assassin's face was partly obscured by his hood. Godfrey strained his eyes as he failed to recognize him in the darkness. The man lunged at him again.

"Who sent you?" Godfrey clenched his jaw as he parried the strike.

The dark man replied with another thrust. Godfrey parried the attack, but the assassin's blade still grazed his shoulder. As the cold steel cut into him, Godfrey seethed and jumped a step back.

The cloaked figure struck again. Fuming, Godfrey batted away the attacker's weapon and offered an immediate riposte. The assassin fell back into the shadows, but Godfrey surged forward with a wide slash. As if expecting this response, the mysterious attacker weaved around Godfrey's blade and bashed him with the pommel of his sword.

Crying out, Godfrey fell to the ground. Blood trickled down his forehead. The assassin stabbed, but Godfrey rolled out of the way.

His head still throbbed, but Godfrey slashed at the attacker's legs. Cursing, the man jumped aside. Springing to his feet, Godfrey thrust Uriel but only caught the edge of his pine green cloak. The garment ripped as the assassin scrambled away.

"What's that?" someone called out from down the corridor. "Hello? Who's there?"

At least two or three pairs of feet rushed to Godfrey from the direction he had come. He ran after the assassin a few paces but only met an empty alcove in the dim light. Gnashing his teeth, Godfrey stamped his foot against the floor. The assassin had escaped.

"Lord Godfrey?" a woman called from down the corridor as she and two armored warriors approached him.

"Lady Isbeil." Godfrey blinked as he recognized the maiden flanked by her two knights. "House Perch comes to the rescue, not a moment too soon."

"We heard a struggle." Isbeil examined Godfrey's aching head wound with a small oil lamp in one hand before putting a dry cloth to it with the other. "What happened?"

"There was an assassin." Godfrey pointed in the direction in which the cloaked man had fled. "He tried to kill me."

After exchanging a glance with Lady Isbeil, the two House Perch knights raced down the corridor. Godfrey clenched his jaw. They would not find him. No doubt the mysterious attacker was long gone by now.

"Who would want to kill you?" Isbeil removed the blood-stained cloth from Godfrey's head. "You are so noble and pure, my lord."

"High Warlord Alvir." Godfrey's hand trembled.

Godfrey bit back his next statement about the Clans. Did Hugo of House Merrich not say that Godfrey would regret spurning his offer only a little while ago? How many others had he inadvertently offended during his short stay as King Lothar's guest?

"I pray not!" Isbeil gasped. "To think that the Clans could reach this deep into Azgald."

"I did not see him all that well." Godfrey sheathed his sword. "It could have been anyone. His blade looked like the craft of Ostmen. That's all I can say for certain."

"We did not see anyone else in the corridor," one of Isbeil's knights panted as he ambled back. "Sir Peadar went to alert the King's guard."

"Thank you, Sir Ealan." Isbeil nodded.

Lady Isbeil's gaze returned to Godfrey. There was a longing in her eyes. She was a year or two older than Godfrey, but only just.

"If only I were a little quicker." Godfrey swallowed awkwardly before averting his gaze. "I could have got the assassin before he fled."

"You're safe now." Isbeil caressed Godfrey's head wound once more with the cloth in her hand. "That's what is important."

Godfrey swallowed. Lady Isbeil had been trying to gain his attention since the Therismos Festival back at Pskov. She desired him, and something about that made Godfrey want her, too. He frowned. Did she really want him, or did she want to be the duchess of Kovdor?

Isbeil's fingers slid down Godfrey's neck, but he recoiled from her touch. A sad look crossed her face as she let her hand fall to her side. Godfrey's stomach turned. She knew he was engaged to Madeline. Why tempt him so?

"Is something wrong, my lord?" Isbeil asked.

"I cannot—" Godfrey started.

Tensing, Godfrey turned to the sound of footsteps echoing down the hallway. Lady Isbeil held her breath and clutched his arm. He ignored her as he gripped Uriel's hilt. After a moment, one of the House Perch knights came into view. Godfrey sighed in relief.

"King Lothar has been alerted," Sir Peadar announced as he staggered back down the passageway. "Every room and corridor is being checked. I'll escort Lord Godfrey to his chambers, if it pleases my lord."

"My lady, we must get you to your room," the other knight insisted. "None of the King's guests are safe."

Isbeil gazed deep into Godfrey's eyes before Sir Ealan pulled her away with a tug on her shoulder. Reluctantly, she released the grip on his arm. Godfrey frowned at the longing in her eyes.

"Farewell, my lord," Isbeil called back as Sir Ealan led her down the hallway. "Rest that weary head of yours."

A sharp pain ran down Godfrey's back as he waved farewell. The cut on his shoulder was still fresh. Tilting his head, he tried to examine it in the poor lighting. At least it was not bad enough for Lady Isbeil to have noticed.

With sword drawn, Sir Peadar cautiously led the way down the corridors to Godfrey's chamber. After a moment's hesitation, Godfrey drew Uriel as he followed the House Perch knight. Part of him believed the unknown assassin was long gone. The rest of him did not care to risk getting ambushed a second time in one evening.

Godfrey frowned at Sir Peadar's heraldry. His shield and surcoat depicted a red tyger set against a white saltire amidst a green field. It was very much like the other Ogleddish knights' coats of arms he had seen.

"You weren't with Torcul of Cumbria on the crusade?" Godfrey asked the knight.

"No," Peadar replied. "My duties kept me at Perch. Lady Isbeil decided to visit her aunt and go on pilgrimage to Vindholm only after the fighting had ended."

"I see." Godfrey's eyes shifted from one corner of the passageway to the other as they neared a set of stairs. "Is that all Lady Isbeil intends while she is here?"

"It is not my place to say, Lord Godfrey." Sir Peadar took a cautious step down the stairs ahead of him. "But her intentions should be obvious enough."

Godfrey swallowed hard as he followed the knight down the stairs. He had promised himself to Madeline. He should not entertain thoughts of seeing another. What good could come of that?

"You're sure the sword was of Ostman make?" Roltar locked eyes with Godfrey as they stood in front of the hearth. "What else did you see?"

"I can't say much else." Godfrey furrowed his brow. "He was tall. He had a short beard. He wore a green cloak, and his tunic was grey. I couldn't see much of his face, and his tunic might have been blue if it wasn't grey. The passageway was too dark to say much with certainty."

"Clan warriors prize the superior craftsmanship of Azgaldian blades," Mauger added from across the chamber. "Possessing an Ostman blade doesn't mean this assassin wasn't a Nordsman."

"We have too little evidence to accuse anyone." Roltar glowered. "The King's guards found nothing. All we're left with is wild speculation."

"Who else could gain from my death?" Godfrey stared into the crackling fire.

"Lord Davin has his supporters in Lothar's court," Roltar grumbled. "More wish Skasgun to remain in his hands than I initially thought."

"That doesn't bode well for us," Godfrey moaned. "How much longer until we receive King Lothar's ruling?"

"Not long." Roltar's gaze shifted out the bed chamber window. "For better or worse, it sounds like the King's councilors have largely decided what they want."

"King Wilhelm also doesn't like you, Godfrey." Mauger gestured excitedly. "Do you think he could have sent the killer?"

"What do I have to do with Lortharain anymore?" Godfrey threw out his hands.

"Bastogne is still your home," Roltar countered. "You have a claim even if you don't press it."

"I gave that up when King Lothar dubbed me Duke of Kovdor." Godfrey clenched his jaw.

"King Wilhelm might not know that." Mauger grimaced. "He is said to be a paranoid man."

"It's all still speculation." Godfrey snorted. "For all we know, the black knight could be behind this."

A hard knock came at the door.

"Yes?" Roltar called out.

The door creaked open. One of the King's retainers entered. All the King's men wore their full panoply since news of the attempt on Godfrey's life got out.

"News about the assassin?" Godfrey took a step towards the door.

"No." The retainer shook his head. "I came to announce King Lothar has reached his decision regarding Lord Roltar's case. He is to be summoned to the throne room after breakfast tomorrow morning."

"So soon?" Roltar glowered.

Godfrey bowed his head in dismay.

"King Lothar has reason to believe the assassination attempt on Duke Godfrey this evening was motivated by House Hracour's case against Lord Davin," the armored knight explained. "The King decided to expedite his decision for Lord Godfrey's safety."

"Thank you." Roltar nodded grimly. "Tell the King we will be there."

The retainer bowed and closed the door behind him as he left. Mauger, Godfrey, and Roltar exchanged a glance. Though Mauger and Roltar grimaced, Godfrey sighed in relief. Tomorrow, this would be over.

"I don't know if I had enough time to persuade Lord Fulrad of our cause," Roltar said.

"I don't know if you were ever going to convince the King's chamberlain, Father." Mauger shook his head. "Fulrad has never cared for our house."

"But Chancellor Evrard is an ally we can count on," Roltar countered.

"Who else?" Godfrey frowned.

"Constable Magneric needed a hefty bribe," Roltar continued, "but he said he would speak in our favor. Sir Durand keeps his opinion closely guarded, as usual. Thidrec de Istad is against us, though I cannot say why. Chaplain Morvred also remains against us."

"Morvred is against us?" Mauger's jaw tightened. "Why? He has supported us before."

"Other parties must have proven more persuasive this time," Roltar answered darkly.

"And the Queen?" Godfrey asked. "What are her feelings on the matter?"

"Queen Noela has been hard to reach," Roltar confessed. "But you've made a good impression on some of her ladies in waiting, Godfrey."

"Madeline's aunt?" Godfrey guessed.

"Lady Collette is one of the more prominent voices in our favor." Roltar nodded. "Some foreign guests, such as Lady Isbeil, have also spoken very highly of you."

Godfrey blushed. Lady Isbeil's support was not exactly what he wanted to hear about right now. Getting too close to her would be a mistake, and owing her something would be worse. He had to be true to Madeline.

"So, two councilors are for us and two against." Mauger scratched his head in agitation. "A few may be undecided, but we can't count on them to come to our aid in this hour. Maybe the Queen's handmaidens will tilt the scales towards us, if Tyche wills it."

"That is our best hope at the moment," Roltar agreed. "Offer prayers to Fate and Persuasion before going to sleep tonight. Nothing else can be done until morning."

Roltar, Mauger, and Godfrey entered Lothar's throne room as the herald announced their presence. The stone floor was bitterly cold, and the hearth's flame did little to warm the morning air. Godfrey's stomach sank at the sight of the King and his councilors.

Lothar sat on his throne, and Noela the Sornian sat on hers beside him. The King leaned to his side as, even now, the Queen whispered something urgently in his ear. The other councilors flanked either side. Their expressions were stony.

Roltar, Mauger, and Godfrey stopped in the center of the chamber. Mauger stood rigid as if his entire future hung in the balance. Godfrey scoffed as he reminded himself, indeed, it did.

Roltar remained cool, if not unusually aloof, for the occasion. His thoughts must have all been focused inward. Godfrey tried his best to maintain a stoic demeanor, but his thoughts were already beginning to stray to his return journey to Kovdor. He had done his duty. He would set out for Olso at the soonest opportunity.

"Roltar of House Hracour." The King unfurled a sheet of parchment. "I, King Lothar, have heard your request to transfer Skasgun and the realm of Stormsud out of the hands of Lord Davin. After careful consideration, I have denied this request."

Mauger grunted. Roltar clenched his fist. With clenched teeth, Godfrey nodded. This outcome was not unexpected.

"While House Hracour's claim to its ancestral home is significant," Lothar continued, "Conrad the Wolf won this realm from the Five Clans by right of conquest. This fief was then passed on to Conrad's kinsman, Davin, legally and in good faith. According to ancient custom, the King of Azgald cannot dispossess Davin of House Talhout, a vassal of the King and a subject of the Azgaldian throne, of any of his estates without due cause."

"Forgive me, your grace." Mauger's voice rose. "But we waited all this time for that?"

"Son." Roltar raised a warning hand.

"This is outrageous!" Mauger shook his head. "House Hracour stood ready to defend Vindholm at the King's request. We were going to march on Skasgun with the crusaders until we received that command. If we had been allowed to go with them and planted *our* banner upon Skasgun's citadel, no one would have challenged our right to our own home."

Godfrey cringed. Mauger raised some good points, but the law was on Lord Davin's side. There was nothing that could be done about any of it. Fighting against this judgment served no purpose that Godfrey could see.

"Watch your tone in front of the King." Roltarraised his hand in a warning gesture.

Mauger took a deep breath, but the fire was still in his eyes. Lothar's retainers glared at the young knight. While Mauger fumed, Roltar's eyes lit up.

"My lord," Roltar addressed Lothar. "You said *the King* cannot dispossess Lord Davin of Skasgun."

"Correct." Lothar nodded.

"In that case," Roltar continued, "let it be known at the King's court that I challenge Lord Davin for the right to rule Skasgun by trial of personal combat. The King's grace is not required to exercise this custom."

Lothar's retainers murmured.

"Such a trial should not be allowed after my lord has already ruled on this matter." One of Lothar's retainers stood between the King and Roltar. "This would undermine my lord's authority."

"It is House Hracour's right to make this request," another councilor insisted. "Skasgun was built by Louis the Blue. Stormsud is their home. We must honor the request for a trial by combat."

"Since I make this request for a trial by combat to regain my ancestral lands without the assistance of my lord, the King," Roltar continued, "I further request that, should I win this trial, Skasgun will owe no feudal obligations to the Duchy of Oblarv, but the realm of Stormsud should be recognized as in former days."

"Absurd!" a third retainer shouted. "House Hracour does not have the men to reform the Duchy of Stormsud."

"Should Skasgun return to my hands under the proposed circumstances," Roltar countered, "House Hracour will relocate all of its strength to that realm, and I will relinquish all other estates to King Lothar in exchange for Stormsud's recognition as an independent lordship."

Lothar's men began talking excitedly to each other. Impressed, Godfrey raised an eyebrow at his cousin. Even Mauger's countenance brightened at the prospect. After exchanging a few words with his men and then the Queen, Lothar gestured for silence.

"Let it be known that the King of Azgald recognizes House Hracour's challenge for Skasgun through trial by combat," Lothar announced as his chancellor began to scribble furiously on a fresh sheet of parchment. "Should Roltar prove successful in his bid, Stormsud shall be recognized as a lordship independent of all laws but the King's and shall owe no feudal obligations to any lord but the King of Azgald."

"My lord is most wise and just." Roltar bowed.

"Thank you, King Lothar." Tears welled in Mauger's eyes. "May I never question the King's intent again."

"Duke Godfrey." After sealing the document with crimson wax, the chancellor handed Godfrey the parchment he had just finished writing on. "You are hereby charged with delivering this message to Davin of House Talhout on behalf of King Lothar and ensuring the trial by combat is conducted according to time-honored tradition."

Godfrey's hand shook as he grasped the parchment. It would take weeks to travel from Vindholm to Skasgun. He still had a wedding to prepare for. What would Madeline have to say about all this?

"Yes, my lord." Godfrey clenched his jaw.

Chapter Fourteen

Crunching his boots through Laht's icy streets, Walaric shifted his gaze from one building to the next. Most doors were closed and windows shuttered. Only the occasional peasant or craftsman braved the cold for the briefest moments as they scurried from homes to shops or guild halls and back. Walaric had little hope of finding Terrwyn out in weather like this.

"Where could she have gone?" Walaric muttered.

"Didn't she say she was here on her father's business?" Jordan indicated the inner walls encircling Laht's high city. "Did you try looking there?"

"I guess I could try." Walaric frowned. "Terrwyn spent most of the first three days with us here in the outer city, and I thought she would wait for us to leave before engaging in much business."

"Hurry," Jordan urged. "The others will be waiting for us at the outer gate by midday."

"I won't be long," Walaric insisted.

"There is a great deal about Lady Terrwyn's story that does not make sense in retrospect." Jordan grabbed Walaric by the arm before he could make his way to the inner gatehouse. "Perhaps it is best that you just let her go without saying goodbye."

"She disappeared from the inn this morning without saying a word." Walaric shook his head. "Something might have happened. I have to make sure she is all right."

"I know it's more than that." Jordan met Walaric's eyes before letting go of his sleeve. "Just be careful."

"Have you ever been in love?" Walaric gulped.

"Me?" Jordan scoffed. "Only once. Fifth-born sons of dukes do not attract beautiful women the way their older brothers usually do."

"I'm sorry to hear that," Walaric answered.

"Don't be too sorry." Jordan shook his head. "She was a schemer, and I was glad to see through her web of deception before it was too late."

"I see." Walaric blinked uncertainly. "Well, you're one of Godfrey's barons now. Maybe Peitho will begin to smile on you soon."

"Go find your maiden." Jordan gave a rueful smile.

With a nod, Walaric set off.

Climbing the hill to Laht's high city proved arduous. The patches of ice on the streets were thick. Gasping, Walaric slipped.

Throwing his hands in front of him did little to soften the blow as Walaric's chin struck the ground. He grunted and blinked away the tears as he got to his feet. Gingerly, he felt his bruised chin with his hand. At least it was not bleeding.

His chin throbbing in pain, Walaric proceeded up the hill more cautiously. Some of the ice was covered in snow, and Walaric could not avoid stepping on all of it. Even taking smaller steps more slowly could not prevent his feet from slipping more than once.

Finally, Walaric reached the inner wall's gatehouse. The ground was relatively level, and he took more confident strides through the open gate as a pair of sentries watched with bemused expressions. Walaric lowered his eyes as he passed, pretending not to see the guards.

"The way down is worse," one of the soldiers called after Walaric. "We'd hate to see you fall again."

Flushing with embarrassment, Walaric continued through the gate without responding. The homes and shops of the high city were larger and less crowded than those in the lower city. However, even with fewer options to choose from, finding Terrwyn would still be difficult.

First, Walaric scoured the nearest taverns and inns. The occupants huddling around blazing hearths offered few clues concerning Terrwyn's whereabouts. Walaric could hardly blame them for their brusque, unhelpful grunts. Most city dwellers were concerned with little outside of staying warm and fed during the harsh winter months.

Next, he explored some of the finer craftsmen's shops. Terrwyn had tried to pass herself off as a noblewoman in Walaric's company. Perhaps she was looking for some additional adornment to complete her disguise.

To his dismay, the shopkeepers proved no more helpful to Walaric than the tavern patrons. Most of the nobles he had seen at Laht were of Ostman stock. However, the commoners were a mixed bunch, and unless Walaric was imagining things, the Nordsmen among them appeared disdainful if not hostile. Could they be trusted to give Walaric a fair account of who they had seen that morning?

Finally, Walaric approached the citadel. The morning hours had quickly fled. If he did not find Terrwyn here, he would have to leave without even knowing where she was.

"Greetings." Walaric revealed the bronze four-pointed star pendant hanging from his neck to the sentries guarding the citadel's gate. "I am Father Walaric. Will you let a servant of Helios warm himself in your halls?"

With a respectful nod, the sentinels parted for Walaric. The guards might have more thoroughly scrutinized another stranger approaching the citadel, but Walaric's pendant and golden signet ring easily identified him as a member of the clergy. Too many tales of gods taking vengeance on behalf of scorned clerics filled Ostman mythology to be ignored under normal circumstances.

Inside the citadel's great hall, various lords and ladies whom Walaric did not recognize filled the chamber. Some petitioned Raymond of Wrehst with requests too unimportant to warrant ceasing the music playing from the minstrel's gallery. Others entertained themselves with poetry, songs, games, and all the other forms of amusement aristocrats could be expected to enjoy inside the chambers of a mighty lord's citadel on a cold winter's day.

No one stopped to greet or question Walaric. His simple habit was worn and stained from weeks of questing. His sword and shield were scratched and dull. Only his amulet and signet ring denoted his vocation. Most probably assumed he was a traveling cleric seeking little more than a free meal and a warm hearth at the local nobility's expense.

Walaric searched their faces as he mingled among the citadel's guests. Raymond of Wrehst's attention was focused on one of his knights arguing with a brutish creature before him, not that Walaric expected the Duke to recognize him. Though the other being also wore armor and a surcoat displaying Raymond's livery, small tusks protruded from his snout-like maw. A wave of nausea surged through Walaric's gut to his throat as he beheld the beast's misshapen face.

"Half-orc." Walaric swallowed before turning his gaze to another part of the chamber. "I suppose everyone needs to make compromises."

Soon, Walaric's eyes fell on Terrwyn. Her face was bright as she laughed and sang at one of the feasting tables in the far corner. Her hair shimmered like the stars at midnight. Walaric's heart stopped. Her arm was around one of Raymond's knights.

Walaric bit his tongue so hard that it bled before he gained the sense to stop. The man Terrwyn wrapped her arm around was muscular and handsome. His jaw was square and his golden hair dashing. A faint scar running across his chin spoke of fell deeds, while his sharp eyes spoke of cunning bravery. Walaric could not hope to compete with such a knight.

As the knight began recounting some tale of his heroic exploits, Terrwyn looked into his eyes with a desire Walaric previously believed she had only for him. How could she leave him just like that? Did their time together mean nothing?

Hot tears blurring his vision, Walaric stormed towards the chamber's exit. Only then did Terrwyn briefly frown as her gaze fell upon him, but Walaric was too furious to stop. Bounding out of the great hall, he huffed as his body shook all over.

Let her have her charming knight, Walaric silently fumed. Let her live a lie with that fool too blind to see past Terrwyn's sapphire eyes and delicate freckles. Maybe she could maintain her deception for a while, but eventually, everyone in Raymond's court would learn she was an imposter. Then, she would be the fool.

Ten days passed as Walaric, Izold, Jordan, Paschal, and Candac traveled on the road east to Sval. The clouds were grey and the winds cold. Walaric prayed less, and he frowned more often than not.

Walaric said nothing of Terrwyn, and no one asked. He cringed every time he thought of her. He should have known better. The Church warned against priests allowing their heartstrings to be pulled by fair maidens, and so did Izold. It should not have been.

"We are approaching Tivelden Forest." Jordan pointed to a large group of pine trees on either side of the road. "This is a cursed realm. We must be exceedingly cautious as we pass through."

"The mists return." Candac pointed to the creeping fog hanging about the tree trunks.

"We could not avoid this evil forever," Izold grumbled. "Take courage, Sir Candac."

"If the gods will it." Candac gulped.

"Beyond the Tivelden lies Sval," Jordan explained. "I've never been there. It's one of a few petty kingdoms that broke away from Azgald about seventy-five years ago, after Loic the Pretender was removed from the throne."

"You can hardly call a single city and its surrounding hinterland a kingdom." Paschal rolled his eyes. "What do you think Lord Godfrey would do if I wore a crown and locked myself in the stables back at Olso? Could I be called king of the straw beds?"

"We'd call you mad if nothing else," Candac quipped.

Walaric and Candac briefly chuckled.

"We'll hear none of that once we reach Sval," Jordan cautioned. "It is said that King Rivold guards his title as jealously as a troll guards stolen gold."

Three more days passed following the road through the woods. The ominous mist grew thicker with every step, and Walaric's unease only grew with it. Eventually, he remembered prayer. He could trust little else outside of the weapons he and his companions bore in the menacing silence of Tivelden Forest.

"What's that?" Izold stopped his horse as something rustled in the brush nearby.

Walaric's mind turned from his mute supplication to the present. After days of deathly silence while traveling through Tivelden Forest, something finally stirred on the side of the road. Did Walaric dare to step closer?

"Ambush!" Jordan shouted as several dark figures charged at them from either side of the road.

Walaric instinctively drew his sword as a group of wailing, gaunt men ran at him. They brandished crude knives and wore no armor he could see beneath their dark grey cowls and robes. The blood drained from Walaric's face. Insanity gleamed in their eyes.

Swinging his sword in a wide arc, Walaric downed two of the madmen at once. Another rushed Walaric from behind, but Paschal hacked into him with his ax.

Izold smashed the face of one attacker with his war hammer and slammed a second with his shield as he approached from the other side. A third attacker slipped under the swing of Izold's war hammer and stuck his knife into the paladin's leg. Izold cried out in anguish. There were too many madmen to keep track of.

Jordan turned and swung his mace at the robed lunatic who was cackling with glee as he twisted the knife in Izold's leg. Bone crunched as Jordan's mace made contact with the man's neck, and he fell to the ground, sputtering blood. More rushed forward to take their gasping comrade's place.

Candac slashed through the chest of one of the attackers, but another tackled him to the ground from behind. Walaric lunged at the howling man straddling Candac and skewered him with his blade. Dropping his knife in the snow, the madman barked some curse in a dark tongue Walaric did not recognize, then keeled over.

Walaric stretched out his hand, and Candac took it before leaping to his feet. Walaric jolted as more crazed men roared with fury. They threw themselves at Walaric and his friends, heedless of the danger to themselves.

"Why are they doing this?" Paschal shouted as his ax tore into the shoulder of another dark-robed figure. "What foul spirits overtake them?"

"They must be some sort of cultists." Jordan turned one of the madmen's knives away with his shield. "Brigands would have run by now."

Maybe ten or fifteen of the dark figures had fallen around Walaric's party. Some were missing limbs. Others had deep gashes running across their bodies or were contorted with broken bones. Blood stained the snow crimson, but that did not slow the attackers. Only an unholy fury could drive these haggard wretches forward.

A cultist slashed at Walaric's face with his knife. Walaric leapt back, but the blade still sliced his cheek. He gasped and fell back another step. Hissing something in the dark tongue of his brethren between his rotting teeth, the madman thrust his blade at Walaric.

Candac slammed his shield into the cultist in front of Walaric before the grim figure could jab his knife into his comrade's face. The wailing madman stumbled to the ground, and Candac drove his blade through him. Walaric frowned as genuine terror petrified the cultist before Candac slashed open his neck.

Jordan struck down a cultist with his mace, and Vielantiu shattered a cowled man's teeth with a powerful kick. Izold brought his war hammer down atop a madman's head, and Paschal hacked into an attacker's chest. Walaric turned to the assailant charging at him and bashed the jabbering maniac with the pommel of his sword. Then all fell silent once again.

"That's it?" Paschal huffed as he scanned the tree line on either side of the road.

"None of them ran away." Candac sheathed his sword. "They fought to the last man."

"Madness," Jordan grunted as he began wrapping Izold's leg in a bandage.

Izold grimaced but made no complaint. His wound was small and only a little worse than the cut on Walaric's face. Gingerly, Walaric touched the laceration. Blood was already scabbing over it.

Walaric surveyed the fallen cultists around him. Most were dead. A few writhed in agony, barely clinging to life.

"Who sent you?" Walaric put the tip of his sword to the neck of the cultist he had bashed with his sword pommel a moment ago.

The cultist lay face-up in the snow. Blood trickled from the corner of his mouth. He coughed and gurgled but made no other reply.

"Who do you serve?" Walaric prodded.

"My master is Gardesh the Pale." The cultist's eyes grew distant. "And his master is Athanatos."

"Gardesh the Pale is a lich." Jordan took a step towards Walaric. "He has been haunting these woods since at least the last great eclipse more than two decades ago."

"Why would mortals serve the undead?" Candac furrowed his brow as he glared at the dying cultist.

"You don't see the vision," the madman sputtered. "Immortality awaits the faithful. The rest of you perish at the dawn of Ragnarok."

"Enough of this nonsense." Paschal spat on the ground. "Run him through, and be done with it."

"Gardesh the Pale will raise my bones." The cultist coughed. "The final victory belongs to Athanatos."

Shaking his head, Walaric pressed his blade through the cultist's throat. What little light was left in the crazed man's eyes faded. Only then was the madness gone. He was just the corpse of an emaciated old man now.

"News of a lich roaming Tivelden Forest does not bode well for us." Izold rode Vielantiu forward a pace to join the others. "If he is not sequestered in some dungeon, and he is prowling about in the open, odds are he is hunting for fresh victims."

"Why would a lich hunt us?" Candac shivered.

"Not us in particular," Walaric clarified. "Liches are scheming necromancers that always seek to expand their power by creating more undead thralls."

"They might try to turn you into a zombie or ghoul," Paschal added. "Maybe something worse."

"Let's continue." Izold winced as he shifted in Vielantiu's saddle. "There's no sense in lingering here."

"Wait." Walaric raised his hand. "If the necromancer returns, he'll reanimate these cultists as undead. We'd better burn the bodies before we go, just to be sure."

"Fair point," Jordan agreed.

Another three days passed with the men marching through the Tivelden Forest. The road grew narrower in parts and almost entirely overgrown by trees, brambles, and bushes in others. Walaric took extra time to bless their campsite each night with what little holy water he had on him. It was not an unwarranted ritual. More than once, Walaric awoke in the dead of night to hear something prowling through the trees just beyond the light of the campfire.

"Seven days in Tivelden," Paschal murmured as they pushed their way through some particularly thick brambles.

"We're almost out." Walaric ripped his cloak free from a prickly branch.

"That's right," Jordan added. "It's only one more day until we're out of the woods. Take heart!"

Vielantiu snorted ahead of Walaric as Izold, mounted atop his steed, led the way. The horse caught the worst of the briers in his caparison as he broke the path open for the rest of them. Still others snagged at his legs and tail. If anyone had room to complain, it was Vielantiu.

Before long, Walaric and his companions cleared the brambles, and the icy road widened again. This brought less comfort to Walaric than it might have otherwise. The mists were thicker than ever.

Vielantiu's ears perked up at some indistinct sound ahead. Izold stopped his horse. Walaric held his breath as he strained his ears. Everyone drew their weapons with grim determination on their faces. None of them had forgotten Gardesh the Pale's cultists.

Soon, the sounds ahead grew more distinct. Muffled hoof beats clopped through the snow. Walaric froze. They all exchanged fearful glances. Was it a death knight or perhaps Gardesh the Pale riding some nightmare steed?

The hooves stopped. Walaric sniffled as the cold bit his nose. A horse snorted, but Walaric could not see through the mist. He swallowed.

"Hail!" Izold called out.

"Hail," someone repeated through the fog.

Walaric sighed in relief. It was not the rasping whispers of some foul death knight, a lich, or some other undead horror. It was a man's voice. A living man's voice with an Ogleddish accent not unlike Torcul of Cumbria or Izold's. If only it would prove to be that very crusader.

A mounted knight emerged from the mist a few paces ahead of the paladin's. He clutched a lance in one hand and his shield in the other. Just behind him, a small group of foot sergeants followed. Though they were all ashen-faced with cold and fatigue, Walaric's heart leapt as he recognized their black and white heraldry. They were members of the Silver Suns.

Sighing, Walaric put away his weapons, as did his friends. It was a cause for celebration to see other people in the woods. So much of Tivelden Forest featured little more than dreaded mists in the day and shambling monsters lurking just beyond the light of the campfire at night.

"The gods have heard our prayers." The knight of the Silver Suns took a long, weary breath as he slung his shield over his back. "They sent a paladin to help us in our hour of need."

The Silver Sun sergeants beat their spears against their shields in applause, and a few modest cheers followed. Paschal and Candac scowled as Walaric exchanged a glance with them. What *help* was required?

"I am Izold, son of Kolen." The paladin nodded. "With me are Father Walaric, Sir Jordan, Candac, and Paschal. We are on a quest to put the shade of the Great Witch of the North to rest. How might we aid the brothers of the Silver Suns today?"

"I am Fionn of Cromant." The Silver Sun knight removed the great helm from his head. "Gardesh the Pale has been raiding Sval's hinterland, killing innocents, and raising their corpses for his undead army. His cult spreads through the Tivelden Forest with alarming speed. The Order has tasked me with finding the lich's lair and destroying his phylactery."

"Phylactery?" Candac asked.

"A phylactery is a tiny magical scroll that contains a lich's spirit," Walaric explained. "It's usually contained in an amulet or some other piece of jewelry the lich wears to keep it safe. If you destroy a lich's body but not its phylactery, the monster will reform in a matter of days."

"You've studied the undead quite thoroughly, Father." Fionn gave a wan smile.

"It was my specialty when I was an acolyte back at Vosg," Walaric added. "It's what qualifies me to lead this quest against Nera's ghost."

"We request that you and your present company assist us in destroying the lich before you leave Tivelden Forest." Fionn's lip curled into a frown. "I started this endeavor with twenty sergeants. You see what Gardesh the Pale has reduced us to."

The Silver Sun indicated his men. There were only six foot sergeants in total. Like Fionn, their tabards were ripped, and claw marks scratched the paint on their shields. Their eyes were hollow as if they had seen horrors they dared not speak of.

"We found the lich's lair," Fionn continued. "It's in the ruins of an old castle overgrown with trees. You only need to follow us and strike true when the time comes."

"We've already encountered some of Gardesh's cultists." Candac gestured back in the direction they had come from.

"We were fortunate to have found no other signs of Gardesh the Pale on the road," Paschal added.

"Far worse creatures lurk in that dungeon." The Silver Sun's face grew dark as his gaze drifted to a small path off the main road.

"Was time not of the essence in our quest to the Blighted Lands?" Candac turned to Walaric.

"Yes." Walaric clenched his teeth.

Izold exchanged a glance with Walaric. Then he looked to Paschal, the Silver Sun warriors, and the others. Was this detour urgent enough?

"We must answer the call for aid," Paschal urged.

Walaric's jaw dropped. Sullen Paschal, who spent so much of their journey embittered by his undeserved reputation for cowardice at the siege of Olso, was the last person Walaric thought would say this. What had changed?

"Of course," Izold agreed. "My paladin vows dictate I must answer the call to such a noble request."

"A lich's evil will only grow if left unchecked." Jordan grimaced. "Could it be that Nera's passage to the Blighted Lands stirred Gardesh the Pale from his slumber?"

"Let no one sing a shameful song about me," Candac chimed in. "If the people of Sval and the Silver Suns need us, we should not shirk such a great task."

"It's settled then," Fionn answered. "The Silver Suns are forever in your debt."

Fionn of Cromant led the way down a small trail that branched off the main road. Their path veered north, so far as Walaric could tell. Though the mists could grow no thicker, the rot in the vegetation spread from just a few unsightly blemishes in the trees here and there to crumbling holes in nearly every trunk. Walaric could hardly imagine the cold getting any worse than what an Azgaldian winter naturally provided, yet he shivered as if naked in the frigid air. The telltale signs of undead taint were all around them.

Eventually, a few blocks of stone jutted from the ground in their path amidst the trees. They were heavily eroded, but their rectangular shapes suggested that, long ago, they had been cut by living hands. Fionn dismounted his stallion, and Izold followed suit.

"We leave the horses here." Fionn secured his steed's reins to a fallen log before setting his lance aside. "We venture underground next."

Fionn put his helmet back on and grabbed a torch from his horse's saddlebag. His boots crunched a few paces through the snowy trees. More broken stones littered the ground, partly obscured by the snow. Walaric hopped over the log and marched just behind Izold and Jordan. Candac, Paschal, and the Silver Sun sergeants were only another pace or two behind them.

A crumbling stone tower and wall section gave Walaric a sense of what might have stood here years, decades, or even centuries ago, but there was little left now. Soon, they were greeted by a yawning staircase that descended into a dark pit. How far down it went, Walaric could not say. Nor did he desire to find out.

"You know the lich is here?" Jordan asked.

"We know he's not in the tower." Fionn lit his torch. "We searched there first. Gardesh the Pale is hiding in the dungeon below. I lost some of my best men down there, but a few hours before finding you."

"You lost some of your best men to what, exactly?" Walaric gulped.

"Ghouls, zombies…" Fionn shook his head. "I'm sure at least a few animated skeletons are creeping about. Hard to tell what all the terrible things are down there with only a few torches to light the way for us."

"What are we waiting for?" Paschal glowered.

"If Tyche smiles on us, there aren't many more undead left in this dungeon." Fionn began descending the stairs. "We destroyed many abominations the first time we came down here, but we were forced to withdraw before we could explore all of the passages and chambers. Whatever the case, we know the lich is still down there somewhere."

"Arktos guide me." Izold pressed down the stairs after Fionn. "Will this blasted fog finally lift once we destroy Gardesh the Pale?"

"It's impossible to say," Fionn confessed. "The fog started several weeks ago. It covers Tivelden Forest, and it spills from the Dovern Highlands. Wherever the undead are, the mists precede them."

"The undead hate the Sun." Walaric followed Izold. "Potent necromancy is causing this fog. It aids their spread across the whole Nordslands."

"So it would seem," Fionn agreed.

Fionn continued down the stairs with his sword in one hand and the lit torch in the other, but his shield was still slung over his back. Walaric nodded at the voided four-pointed star emblazoned upon the Silver Sun's shield. The celestial gods were with them on this errand.

Izold and Walaric followed next, then Paschal and Candac descended the steps amidst the Silver Sun foot sergeants. The stairs were steep and crooked. The darkness and snow did nothing to help Walaric find his footing.

Walaric drew his sword and shield, and soon everyone had a weapon in one hand and a torch or shield in the other. Everyone who had a helmet was also wearing one now. A grim silence fell over Walaric and the others as the passage darkened around them. Perhaps this was what descending to the Abyss was like for the damned.

Before long, the stairs ended, and Walaric and the others found themselves in a shadowy, damp chamber. The walls and floor were carved of stone, and only the few torches among the men provided any light. Walaric looked at Fionn expectantly.

"There are several passages and chambers like this we haven't fully explored," Fionn whispered. "Some were part of the original castle's dungeon, but other parts seem to be later additions."

"Could Gardesh's cultists have dug them?" Izold strained his eyes, looking down one of the corridors.

"It's possible," Fionn admitted, "but we've seen only undead down here."

"Which way?" Candac asked.

"Follow me." Fionn gestured to a set of open wooden doors at the far end of the room.

"Wait." Walaric frowned. "A prayer, first, before we go farther into this cursed place. It may prove our most valuable defense in this dungeon."

"Of course." Fionn bowed his head.

The others followed suit. Walaric glanced from one end of the chamber to the other. How could one describe what pure evil felt like?

"I call upon Helios." Walaric held his star pendant overhead. "Loxias, Iatrus Physician, Sol, and whatever other names the Sun wishes to be known by this day. I also call upon the Moon, Arktos, the stars, and all the rest of the celestial gods by all the names they are known by on Aestas and in the firmament above."

Walaric gulped.

"Help us," he continued. "Help us cleanse this foul place of the great evil that plagues it. Help us find Gardesh the Pale and destroy him. Grant us victory, even if the cost is high, even if it is our very lives. Amen."

"Amen," the others chorused.

"I'd rather it not cost our very lives, thanks." Candac sulked. "I still have more to do after this. With luck, there's a maiden waiting for me back at Kolarb."

Paschal cleared his throat.

"And Paschal, too," Candac added.

"So say we all," Walaric agreed.

Walaric and the others stepped cautiously. Any shadow could hide a gnarled claw ready to grab. Any crevice could contain some foul hunter ready to pounce.

Stepping into the next chamber, Walaric grimaced at the sight of several broken skeletons littering the floor. Dismembered bony limbs still clutched rusting blades, and pockmarked kettle helmets sat atop cracked skulls. In one corner, a freshly slain corpse in Silver Sun garb lay with its hands folded across its chest.

"Brother Porthos." Fionn indicated the fallen Silver Sun. "We destroyed several skeletons in this chamber. Fortunately, it looks like none have risen again since we were last here."

Walaric nodded grimly. Brother Porthos deserved a proper burial, but that might need to wait until after Gardesh the Pale had been dealt with. Until then, they needed to press on.

They passed through another stone chamber much like the first two. More shattered bones of deceased warriors littered the floor. More Silver Sun corpses rested in the corner of the room.

Eventually, they came to a corridor carved from rough-hewn rock. It descended deeper than what the torchlight could illuminate from Walaric's vantage point. His teeth chattered from the chill in the air.

"It gets far more dangerous from here." Fionn grimaced. "Watch your backs."

The walls were slick with glistening water. It dripped down the tunnel floor until the passage opened into a wide cavern. The torches reflected the still surface of a deep pool at the far end of the cave.

"What is this place?" Jordan squinted.

"The torchlight doesn't reach the far walls," Candac murmured with a hint of fear in his voice.

"There are other tunnels carved from the rock to our left and right." Fionn gestured. "But there is a door ahead of us by the pool we weren't able to reach last time we came down here. I'm far more interested in what's beyond that."

"Lead on," Izold urged.

They pressed farther into the cave. The dim torchlight barely penetrated the darkness. Water dripping from stalactites onto stalagmites echoed from some shadowy corner Walaric could not place. At last, they were close enough to the water for Walaric to peer into its depths.

With a gasp, he flinched. At the bottom of the pool, a corpse gazed back at Walaric. Only a crude loincloth remained of whatever clothes it had in life. Its rotting face was frozen in a disgusting rictus. Its unseeing eyes were glazed white.

The corpse moved, and Walaric yelped. More corpses beneath the pool's surface, Walaric just now noticed, stirred. His heart pounded as they began clambering from the water.

"They're all around us!" Paschal cried.

Moaning zombies shambled towards them from almost every direction. Their grasping arms reached for them. Walaric's eyes flitted from one unseeing face to another. Brother Porthos and the other recently killed Silver Suns were among the numberless horde.

"Necromancy is afoot," Walaric hissed.

"Stand close!" Fionn warned. "Shield wall. Form a circle. Form a circle!"

Walaric and the others needed no convincing to comply. They stood shoulder to shoulder in a tight defensive ring. Izold smashed a zombie's head with his war hammer, and Paschal chopped a cadaverous arm with his ax. Candac bashed a monster with his shield, and Sir Jordan finished it with a blow from his flanged mace.

Fionn's sword hacked through a pair of zombies with ease, but his sergeants' spears got stuck in the chests and guts of the undead as the unthinking monsters instinctively grabbed the shafts of the weapons embedded in their bodies. Walaric clenched his teeth at a sudden realization. Spears were designed to pierce, not slash. Against monsters that could not feel pain, these weapons would not do.

Brother Porthos' unfeeling hands tugged on one of the sergeants' spear shafts as he attempted to dislodge it from his chest. The sergeant screamed as gnawing teeth and grasping claws found his arms and legs. It soon ended in one agonizing outburst as the sergeant was torn apart under the weight of ripping hands.

Some of the spearmen's strikes found their marks in the zombies' heads. Those wounds instantly dropped the undead, while similar punctures across other parts of the body were ignored. Walaric silently cursed. The greatest difficulty was getting enough spear thrusts to hit their heads.

Walaric slashed at a zombie. Its putrid ichor spilled over his habit. He slashed again in a wide arc. Barely containing his bile, Walaric retched. The work was grisly.

Another spearman cried out as he was severed from his place at Walaric's side. Before Walaric could respond, the zombies were already tearing flesh from bone. There was nothing he could do to help. They could only tighten their circle in hopes of preventing more deaths.

A zombie grasped Walaric's habit. Its cold, filthy hand found the chain of his pendant as Walaric recoiled. To Walaric's shock, the monster's hand sizzled as his bronze star pendant slipped into its grasp.

"Of course!" Walaric shouted.

The zombie's hand withered into a mere husk after touching the holy symbol of the celestial gods. A moment later, it fell to the ground. Finally, the zombie's remains crumbled to ash.

"I rebuke thee!" Walaric quickly sheathed his sword and held his pendant aloft. "By Helios' light, I rebuke thee, foul creatures of Hell!"

The zombies faltered and then fell back a pace from Walaric's pendant. Walaric gulped. It was only a pace, but it was enough to halt their attack for the moment.

"What's going on?" Paschal shifted uneasily as the zombies withdrew another pace. "Why do they cease?"

Huffing, the Silver Suns and Walaric's companions exchanged uneasy glances. They were pale and covered in gore and bile. They were also still severely outnumbered.

"The dark magic sustaining zombies cannot stand against the power of the divine," Walaric answered between heavy breaths. "My amulet is not just a symbol of the priesthood; it's been consecrated."

"Can it push them back any farther?" Candac heaved.

"I've never done this before," Walaric panted while still holding his pendant overhead. "I wasn't even sure if it would work at all."

"A miracle?" Paschal scoffed.

"I told you faith matters," Walaric beamed. "Our prayers have been answered."

"I've seen this once before in the Estlands," Izold quickly explained. "Walaric, the undead will not attack us only as long as they can see your star. If you put it away, they'll immediately swarm us again."

Walaric looked about. There were still dozens of zombies surrounding them. He raised his eyebrow. Cut into the cave wall near the pool sat a heavy set of iron doors.

"Let's go that way." Walaric gestured to the doors. "Fionn said he wanted to see what was back there."

"We don't know what's in there," Paschal scolded Walaric. "There could be more undead."

"It can't be any worse than what we're seeing right here," Fionn countered.

Maintaining their circle, Walaric and the others tepidly marched to the doors. The zombies before them shuffled away with painful groans and sobs, and they now had a clear path to whatever lay behind the doors. Walaric silently gave thanks to Helios. He had also not been sure if that would work.

To Walaric's dismay, while the zombies in their path yielded to their approach, the monsters behind them moved up, maintaining the circle around them. Walaric gulped. They were almost there.

"Open the doors," Walaric said. "Run in, and then bar them as soon as I'm inside."

"I'm still not sure about this," Paschal objected.

"It can't be worse than fifty zombies," Jordan replied. "You'd rather stay out here with them?"

"Pray it's not worse," Fionn muttered.

As soon as the doors were in arm's reach, Izold tugged on one of the heavy ring handles. It scraped in protest, but the door did not budge. The agitating noise stirred the zombies a step closer.

"Locked?" one of the spearmen asked.

"I don't think so," Izold grunted as he pulled again.

"I think they like the noise less than Walaric's star." Paschal gripped his ax tightly.

The handle grated against the door as Izold pulled on it a third time, but it still did not give way. The zombies pressed forward. One reached for Candac, but he lopped its arm off with his sword. More putrid hands reached out.

Jordan's mace swung, and the sergeants' spears jabbed. Walaric let go of his pendant and grabbed his sword hilt. He swiped at a zombie's jaw and sent its head rolling back into the dark pool with a splash.

"Violence and courage are needed now!" Walaric cried as he slashed the animated remains of Brother Porthos. "Valiant men, stand your ground!"

Izold slammed the door with his shoulder to no effect. Another spearman fell, screaming. Fionn, Walaric, and Candac desperately slashed with their swords. Paschal hacked away with his ax, and Jordan smashed open a zombie's skull with his mace. The three remaining sergeants thrust their spears, but the zombies had all but pressed the men's backs to the door.

"It's rusted together," the paladin exclaimed.

"Break it open!" Jordan answered.

The zombies pressed in closer. Their stench was unbearable. If they got any closer, Walaric and his friends would be overwhelmed. With a resounding clang, Izold struck the doors with his war hammer. He hit them again and again until the rust broke free from the iron doors. Finally, he kicked them open with a mighty yell.

"In we go!" Izold bellowed.

A Silver Sun spearman slipped on the wet rock as he turned to the open door. Rotting hands grasped his ankles and dragged him into their midst. He screamed as he struggled to break free, but the horde pressed in. Walaric cringed. There was no saving him.

Fionn was the first through the doors after Izold. His two remaining sergeants followed next. Walaric jumped through the doorway immediately after the last sergeant.

Candac turned to face the door, but a zombie snatched his cloak. Paschal bashed the creature with his shield and shoved

Candac through the portal. Now surrounded, Paschal tried to hack his way through the foul monsters, but they tugged and pulled from every side. A moment later, he was on the ground, crying out as the zombies piled on top of him.

"We have to help!" Walaric wailed.

"It's too late." Fionn slammed the doors shut with Izold's help. "We can't do anything for him."

"May no one sing a shameful song about him." Candac shivered amidst Paschal's cries.

His lip quivering, Walaric nodded.

The sergeants braced the doors shut with their spears as Paschal's agonized screams were cut short on the other side. The undead horde banged against the door, but it held for the moment, at least.

Walaric glanced around the dark chamber that he and the others found themselves in. Izold and Candac overturned a moldering table and shoved it against the entrance. Fionn and his sergeants also began piling furniture against the iron doors in a makeshift barricade as Jordan began examining a cut to his ankle with one of the torches.

Shaking, Walaric sheathed his sword and put his hand to his face. He gulped. He looked at his comrades in disbelief. Paschal was gone. They could not bring him back.

"You are not invited to my library," a cold voice hissed from the shadows.

Walaric squinted. Bookshelves did, in fact, line the walls of the room, and a few other tables and chairs that had not been thrown onto the barricade were arranged on the floor. It was a library so far as Walaric could see. What ancient lore was kept in those books?

From the far side of the chamber, a pale, skeletal figure emerged from a shadowy anteroom. He wore dull, ancient scholar's robes and a tall, pointed hat with a wide brim. Red pinprick lights gleamed from his skull's eye sockets. Leaning against a gnarled staff, the creature hobbled forward a few paces.

"You've been making all this noise and disturbing my studies." The creature aimed its staff at Izold.

"Gardesh the Pale?" Walaric asked, eyeing the creature's bleached bones.

"I won't tolerate this intrusion!" The monster turned on Walaric. "Gardesh the Pale is ruled only by Athanatos."

A dark eldritch blast of energy leapt from the lich's staff. Candac pushed Walaric to the side and stood right where the priest had been a second before. Candac shrieked as his flesh withered and fell as a dry husk.

"I rebuke thee!" Walaric held his star pendant aloft with tears streaming down his face. "I rebuke thee, lich!"

"That won't work against me in my own lair." Gardesh cackled. "Observe my power and glory!"

The lich shot another bolt of blackened necrotic energy from his staff, and one of the Silver Sun sergeants fell to the ground just as Candac had. Crying out, Walaric unsheathed his sword and charged. Fionn's last remaining sergeant picked up Candac's sword and also charged. Roaring, Izold, Jordan, and Fionn followed.

The lich drew a sword of his own with frightening speed and parried Walaric's overhead strike. Jordan swung with his mace, but Gardesh deflected it with his staff. Izold swung his war hammer, cracking loose one of the lich's ribs. The lich replied by immediately thrusting the end of his staff into Izold's face. The paladin hit the ground hard.

Gardesh skewered the last sergeant with his venerable blade. Fionn severed the lich's sword arm with a yell, and Gardesh wailed with such unearthly horror that Walaric fell back a step. However, the lich turned its fury against the Silver Sun with another necrotic blast. Fionn fell in stoic silence, as if accepting this horrid end.

As the undead monstrosity reveled in the destruction, Jordan bashed Gardesh in the head with his mace. The creature's skull cracked, and Jordan swung again. The lich fell, but Jordan continued to strike until only shattered fragments remained of Gardesh the Pale's skull.

"Walaric." Izold groaned as he got to his feet. "Where is its phylactery?"

Walaric searched Gardesh's body in the dim light. A thin gold chain hung around the stump of the creature's neck. A few emeralds encrusted the tip of its staff. Nothing stood out. Where was it?

Finally, Walaric's eyes fell on the lich's severed arm. A small signet ring glinted in the dim light around its bony finger. After sheathing his sword once again, Walaric ripped the ring off its hand. A metal box was built into the piece of jewelry, so tiny that Walaric would not have noticed had he not been looking for such a subtle thing.

"This is it." Walaric held the golden band up to Izold's face. "The magic scrolls stored inside this ring are Gardesh's phylactery."

Izold scrutinized the ring for a short moment. Walaric set it on one of the tables. Bellowing, the paladin smashed it with his war hammer. The sound of metal striking metal rang out.

An oily puff of rancid smoke emanated from the cracks in the jewelry before it disintegrated. The zombies stopped pounding on the door for the first time since the sergeants barred them shut. Only Walaric, Izold, and Jordan stirred now.

"Why do they do this?" Walaric shook his head at all the deceased. "What evil drives the undead to commit such abominations?"

"They lust for power above all else," Izold answered. "Necromancers believe themselves to be above the natural order. They don't care who they hurt along the way."

"Candac and Paschal." Walaric shook his head.

"They're at peace now," Izold answered. "They died warrior's deaths in the name of the celestial gods. No further harm can come to them."

"We have to keep going," Walaric sobbed. "But I don't want to."

"Death and loss are risks in every quest." Izold gave a weary sigh. "The key to putting Nera's shade to rest lies in Mirtys. *You* have to confront the Keeper of Souls to make this happen. No one else can."

"I know." Walaric sniffed. "I know."

"This anteroom leads to another passage," Jordan called out from the spot from which Gardesh had entered the room. "This explains how the lich could go to the surface while those doors were rusted shut."

"Should we go find out?" Izold asked Walaric.

"No." Walaric shook his head. "Let's go back the way we came. We have seen too much sorrow here already."

Chapter Fifteen

ive days passed as Madeline flew Spathi north through the Wyrmwind Peaks. The cold bit her face, the wind howled in her ears, but the view was majestic. The grandeur of the Wyrmwind Peaks' towering mountains could only truly be appreciated from the back of a griffin.

The higher they flew, the colder it grew. Madeline quickly discovered that if she went too high, the prevailing winds became too strong for Spathi to handle. Best to stay relatively close to the peaks.

Madeline squinted at the faint movements she spotted from Spathi's back as they flew over the heights. A herd of musimon leapt from rocky outcropping to outcropping. In pursuit, a great white feathered beast reminiscent of a large bear lumbered across the slopes.

Thick claws extended from the beast's four legs, and a dark, hooked beak snapped after the slowest goat-like creatures. The chase lasted only a minute or so. Finally, a spray of crimson gushed from one of the musimon as it bleated in terror.

"Owlbear?" Madeline pointed down to the beast feasting on its struggling prey.

"Looks like it." Fravash gulped. "Don't get caught by one of those out in the open."

"I'll try not to." Madeline frowned at the gory mess the owlbear left behind as they passed overhead.

Because of the difficulty Spathi had flying in the cold air currents, Fravash suggested they make camp on the mountain slopes each night. That way, the griffin would not need to expend so much effort climbing above the peaks every day. It made pitching Madeline's tent more difficult, and it was harder to find a good spot to lay her bedroll, but she eventually became accustomed to sleeping at odd angles.

Madeline drifted in and out of sleep as she lay in her tent. Restful was the last word she would use to describe any of her experiences outdoors. She stirred in her bedroll as Fravash tapped her face. She blinked several times and stretched. Sitting up, she frowned. It was still dark.

"Good morning," Fravash said.

"It's not morning yet." Madeline stifled a yawn.

"Oh, but it is," Fravash insisted.

"Then where is the Sun?" Madeline peeled off her bedroll. "It's a poor joke, waking me up this early."

"This is no joke, Lady Madeline." The mouse shook his head. "We are so far north that the Sun's light does not fully reach here for part of winter."

"Is it some kind of magic?" Madeline wondered. "Is it a part of the elves' defenses to deter travelers from finding Farthest Thule?"

"No." The mouse chuckled. "It's not magic at all in this case, though, rest assured, they do use some magic to defend Farthest Thule."

He paused and cleared his throat.

"Aestas is round, correct?" the mouse asked.

"Of course." Madeline nodded. "You can see the sails of ships dip below the horizon as they go out to sea. Ancient philosophers measured shadows to figure out the world's circumference. Everyone knows it's round."

"Well, the world spins," Fravash explained. "That gives us night and day, but it's tilted, and it also wobbles."

"It spins and wobbles?" Shaking her head, Madeline raised an eyebrow. "No. Helios orbits Aestas. You've got it backwards."

"How do you explain seasons, then?" Fravash crossed his arms.

"It's because of the shorter and longer days." Madeline shrugged.

"Well, yes, that's part of it." Fravash twitched his whiskers. "But why are there longer and shorter days to begin with? Hmm?"

"The Sun moves at different speeds, and its path changes through the year." Madeline bit her lip. "Isn't that what happens?"

"Not at all, Lady Madeline." Fravash pointed above his head. "Aestas orbits the Sun."

Madeline twisted her hair around her finger as she thought about the Moon and stars in the night sky, their regular motions, and everything she had ever read about those things. She shook her head. Fravash was extremely intelligent, but even the smartest people could have some eccentric ideas.

"Are you sure?" Madeline cocked an eyebrow. "It doesn't feel like we're spinning."

"Trust me." Fravash pointed his finger at Madeline. "Seasons, the retrograde motion of certain stars, and everything else in the sky are all best explained by Aestas spinning through the cosmos with Helios at its center."

"Helios is a powerful god." Madeline rubbed her forehead as she considered this. "But I don't know if he's the center of the cosmos."

"It's ultimately why you won't see the Sun when we reach Farthest Thule," Fravash said.

"If you insist," Madeline mumbled. "How much longer until we reach Farthest Thule?"

"Prevailing winds have been against us," Fravash muttered. "With about three hundred miles behind us, I'd say we have a little less than a day or so left at this rate."

"I can't argue with those numbers." She smirked.

Madeline dressed in her heaviest cloak, put away her bedroll, and took down the tent. A faint light glowed in the east; she could just make it out from the mountainside where they made their camp. It was as if Dawn would crest over the horizon with her rosy fingers at any moment, but it did not come, no matter how long Madeline watched for it. Fravash was right. They had only a strange twilight to illuminate their path in this frigid realm.

In the valley below, a herd of six huge, furry beasts trudged through the snow. Madeline gasped at their long, curled tusks and trunk-like noses. What could sustain such large creatures in this harsh, freezing climate?

"Clan Behemoth uses that animal in its heraldry." Madeline gestured to the hulking monsters.

"Yes, that's right." Fravash nodded. "You may call them behemoths, but, in the Nordsman tongue, they're called mammoths."

"I didn't know they were real." Madeline crossed her arms. "Scholars always talked about them being long-extinct beasts from the age of myth."

"The behemoth used to be far more plentiful in these parts," Fravash explained, "but the Nordsmen nearly hunted them to extinction in generations past. You're fortunate to see as many in one place as you do now."

"They seem to be having an easier time this far north than any of us." Madeline glanced at Spathi.

The griffin lay curled under a thick woolen sheet on a rocky outcropping without much snow. It was growing too cold for his feathers alone to be sufficient insulation.

Madeline held a strip of salted pork in one hand and snapped her fingers with the other. Spathi's ears perked at the noise. The griffin slid the blanket off his head, turned to Madeline, and began sniffing the air.

"Come here," Madeline sang as Spathi's eyes narrowed on the strip of pork. "Food, Spathi."

The griffin shook himself out from under the blanket and trotted to Madeline a few paces. Spathi snatched the meat with a speed that still made her recoil the instant the food was out of her hand. Though his accuracy never wavered, Madeline bit her lip as she thought of potential missing fingers or worse.

Madeline, likewise, ate a strip of salted pork for breakfast while Fravash contented himself with a few small crumbs of hard cheese. Once that was done, Madeline packed the last of their provisions into Spathi's saddlebags. Then, she harnessed the griffin in his saddle. Last, she grabbed her staff and mounted Spathi, with the spell familiar securely gripping her cloak near the shoulder.

"It's time," Madeline urged the griffin. "You know the way from here."

Spathi kicked off the icy mountain slope. He flew for what Madeline guessed was all morning, though the Sun never fully rose. Helios continued to hide his face just below the horizon, but Madeline suspected he still tracked west.

Eventually, the majesty of the Wyrmwind Peaks gave way to smaller foothills and then large sheets of ice as far as the eye could see. Madeline's heart sank. There was nothing but barren, frozen wasteland.

"This is the Great Ice," Fravash explained over the whistling wind. "You're almost on top of the world. You're the first human to see this place since Talorc the Paladin more than half a century ago. Come to think of it, you're the first woman ever to see this place."

"How thrilling." Madeline clenched her teeth. "Fravash, there's nothing up here. Let's go back."

"Go back?" the mouse stammered. "Are you mad? We're almost to Farthest Thule."

"All I see is frozen waste and darkness." Madeline wept. "This is a cursed realm. I'm cold. There's nothing here. Spathi, take us back."

"No." Fravash tugged on Madeline's ear. "Trust me. We're almost there. You'll see."

Spathi flared his wings and began descending towards the Great Ice. Before long, a pair of armored figures on barded warhorses came into view. Curiosity overtook Madeline's fear as the pair of cavaliers gestured for the griffin to land. To Madeline's surprise, Spathi complied, but a few feet in front of the mounted figures.

The steeds had the appearance of white horses. They wore bronze scale barding with thick padding underneath, but little else to protect them from the cold. The riders also wore bronze scale mail, heavy round shields, and tall plumed helmets, but their cloaks and tunics did not appear especially well-adapted to the cold.

"Who are you?" Madeline's mouth gaped.

"I am Trophnus," one of the riders said before indicating the other with his lance. "This is Mygdon."

The two riders removed their helmets, revealing smooth faces, long golden hair, and pointed ears.

"You're elves from Farthest Thule?" Madeline swallowed. "I was beginning to think it was all a myth."

"No." Mygdon laughed. "Farthest Thule is quite real, as are the cataphracts who patrol her borders."

"Cataphracts?" Madeline raised an eyebrow.

"You would call us knights, I believe." Trophnus set his jaw. "We don't welcome uninvited guests to our realm."

"This is Farthest Thule?" Madeline asked incredulously. "Say it isn't so."

"You are close," Trophnus confessed. "Any traveler wishing to go to Farthest Thule must first see the Great Ice before he can reach the true path."

Trophnus stopped to examine Spathi more closely. The elf squinted before running his hand through the griffin's feathers. Spathi replied with a soft chirp.

"Could this be one of Luka's griffins?" Trophnus turned to Mygdon.

"Luka always had a soft spot for mankind." Smiling ruefully, Mygdon shook his head.

"Had we not stopped you, I'm sure your griffin would have circled back south and turned the right way." Trophnus shifted his gaze back to Madeline. "The true path to our city is not easily reached by the uninitiated, but your griffin seemed to know it."

"But we had to see who this griffin conveyed before we allowed you to roam freely through our lands," Mygdon added. "It is not our custom to allow any outsiders access to the golden city of Vathepoli."

"Vathepoli…" Madeline struggled to pronounce the name aloud. "That is—"

"Our name for what you call Farthest Thule," Trophnus interrupted. "We've answered enough of your questions. Now you must tell us who you are and how you've made it this far before we see you away from here."

"I'm—" Madeline started.

"Sir Fravash the Bright!" Mygdon pointed to the mouse as the diminutive creature waved from Madeline's shoulder. "You evasive scoundrel, it's been ages!"

"You brought this child here?" Trophnus gave a disapproving look. "You know better."

"Child?" Madeline grumbled under her breath.

"Yes, I know better." Fravash bowed. "Forgive our intrusion, but you must understand, this is the only place I knew that I could turn to for help."

"What do you need help with?" Mygdon's eyes brightened. "Name it."

"Mygdon, don't forget your place," Trophnus warned. "This child is an outsider, even if Fravash is an honorary cataphract."

"Fravash the Bright is a friend of Vathepoli," Mygdon insisted. "We should hear him."

"Madeline of House Drois has the gift," Fravash explained. "I am tutoring her the best I can, but there is only so much she can learn among men. I ask that she be granted an audience before Anistemi."

"The phoenix?" Trophnus raised an eyebrow. "Impossible! No one from the race of men has ever communed with Anistemi."

"Trophnus." Mygdon put his hand on his companion's shoulder. "I believe it is you who is forgetting your place now. This petition must be taken to the Queen. Our law states that *any* friend who requests access to the phoenix must be heard. Anistemi will ultimately decide who she will or won't see."

"Very well," Trophnus agreed. "We shall take you to Vathepolito petition the Queen."

"My thanks, noble elves." Madeline bowed her head.

Farthest Thule sat deep in a valley amongst a part of the Wyrmwind Peaks. Madeline was certain she had passed over on Spathi's back earlier that morning. Only then had there been no city sitting in the valley. At least, Madeline thought there was no city there.

Farthest Thule's outer walls stood high above the snowy banks that surrounded them. The white stone was so polished that Madeline might have mistaken it for glistening snow, too, had the shape of crenelated parapets and towers not been so distinct. The craftsmanship was so fine, magic was the only explanation she would accept.

After Trophnus briefly waved to the sentinels at the outer gate, the dark wooden doors slid open with only the faintest groaning of the chains and pulleys that moved them. The elvish cataphracts led their horses by the reins through the gate, and Madeline urged Spathi through on foot. Then her jaw dropped.

Farthest Thule was grand in every sense of the word Madeline could think of. White stone covered every surface where vibrant evergreens did not grow. Gilded columns lined immaculate streets lit by softly glowing lamps. The statuary was so lifelike, Madeline at first believed them to be the petrified victims of a gorgon's gaze.

"It's warm here," Madeline marveled at how light the snow cover was within the city as an elvish stable hand took Spathi by the reins. "Not so warm that I want to take off my cloak, but it's a lot warmer than I expected it should be this far north in winter."

"The phoenix emits a powerful aura that keeps all within Farthest Thule's walls comfortable throughout the year," Fravash explained as Spathi and the cataphracts' horses were led away to the stables. "Elvish food sustains Vathepoli's denizens longer than normal meat and grain, so they can survive the harsh winters with less farming."

They walked down the street for a long while. There was not a single hovel or peasant as far as Madeline observed. Were there no poor among the elves?

"If conditions are so prosperous, why are there so few people here?" Madeline turned to Trophnus as he and Mygdon escorted them to the high city.

Despite the grandeur of the wide streets and tall buildings in good repair, few elves were out and about. Some lone figures or couples in regal dress gracefully strolled down the colonnades, made idle chatter up in balconies, or tended small, blooming flower beds. However, Madeline suspected Farthest Thule had been initially built to support a much larger population.

"We still live on the edge of the Great Ice," Mygdon answered slowly after Trophnus averted his gaze. "And families have never been a strong priority for the elves. Most of our kin died with the Empire, and we take solace in our art, music, and other crafts."

Madeline glanced at a pair of dark-haired elves dressed in fine robes walking the opposite way down the street. While they lacked nothing in material comforts, she could see a touch of melancholy etched on their pale faces. Almost every other elf Madeline had come close enough to see in detail also bore the same grief in his or her eyes. Not every aspect of Farthest Thule was so enviable after all.

"But you maintain your youth and vigor for centuries." Madeline bit her lip. "Could your women not bear you hundreds of sons and daughters in that time? Why choose to suffer on the brink of extinction while living in such opulence?"

"Opulence?" Trophnus clenched his jaw. "It is not our way to bring children into this world so lightly."

Madeline wished to say more, but stopped herself after seeing the pain in the elf's eyes. Mygdon scowled and looked away. What secrets hid behind those sea-green eyes?

"I think it's best to let the subject drop." Fravash shook his head at Madeline. "Elves live a thousand years but bear only a few children in all that time. We must leave it at that, you see?"

With a frown, she complied.

Soon, they approached the inner wall's gate to the high city. It resembled Olso Fortress' gates in some ways, though this structure bore little scarring from countless years of war or hostile elements. It was surely hundreds, if not thousands, of years old, yet it had the appearance of freshly carved stone.

Once they had passed through the inner wall's gate, Trophnus and Mygdon escorted Madeline and Fravash through the high city to the Queen's palace without saying much else. Fountains, gardens, and groves decorated much of this area in addition to all the other finery that could be found elsewhere in Farthest Thule. Madeline hardly thought it possible to be so impressed after what she had seen upon initially entering the city.

The Queen's palace sat in the heart of Vathepoli's high city like a crown jewel. In fact, many bright jewels did adorn the tops of gilded marble columns. If Farthest Thule was opulent, the palace was almost garish. *Almost garish*, Madeline thought. While the decorations were far more ornate than anything Madeline had ever seen, the elegance of elvish architecture helped it all seem *natural.*

A pair of heavily armored guards with spears barred the doors to the palace as Trophnus and Mygdon led Madeline and Fravash to them. They bore similar arms and wore armor like what the cataphracts wore, only it was somewhat more ornate and polished to a mirror shine.

"Who do you bring to us, Mygdon?" one of the guards asked. "Should you not be patrolling the Great Ice with the other cataphracts of the Winter Watch?"

"I bring to you Madeline of House Drois," Mygdon answered. "She is a friend of Fravash the Bright."

"Fravash the Bright requests Madeline be given an audience before Queen Kypris." Trophnus indicated the mouse that had not left Madeline's shoulder since they entered Farthest Thule. "We were obliged to escort them here."

"That is a grave request," the guard replied, "but we cannot ignore the petition of an elf friend in need."

"Enter," the other guard answered as they yielded the palace gate.

Mygdon and Trophnus led Madeline into the palace through an anteroom into a large hall, which she guessed was meant for receiving visitors. Polished floors reflected the glowing lamps set in the wall's alcoves. Gold and jewels decorated almost every surface.

"This is where we part ways." Trophnus frowned after directing Madeline to the very center of the chamber.

"We must return to our patrol," Mygdon explained.

"Surely, there is nothing out on the Great Ice," Madeline scoffed. "What could possibly survive out there?"

"Occasionally," Trophnus started, "a great beast can be found roaming out there. Our enemies also know that going to the Great Ice is the easiest way to find the true path to Vathepoli."

"We found you there, if nothing else." Mygdon curled his lip into a smile so subtle that Madeline almost missed it.

"Thank you for seeing us this far." Madeline curtsied to the cataphracts.

"Farewell and good luck, Lady Madeline." Trophnus nodded in reply. "Until we meet again."

"Come back soon, Fravash," Mygdon implored. "Next time, make sure you're not on urgent business. We should really enjoy having you stay awhile."

After a deep bow, the two elvish cataphracts marched out of the palace the way they had entered. Their footsteps grew quieter before finally deadening completely. A profound silence followed.

Madeline tapped the end of her staff against the floor. Though soft, the noise echoed through the hall. Did anyone even live in this place?

"All this splendor and hardly anyone to appreciate it." Madeline pursed her lips at the vaulted ceiling overhead.

"The age of the elves ended long ago," Fravash whispered. "But do not speak of it openly to them. They are a proud race, and they are slower to confess their demise than others."

"Even if Godfrey and I could've reached here to ask for help during the crusade, they would not have been able to give it to us." Madeline sighed.

"Numbers aren't everything," Fravash corrected. "House Fabii sent three hundred and six of its warriors to aid Talorc the Paladin during the crusade he took part in. They alone were able to relieve the siege at Lubloin, such is their skill at war."

"Three hundred elves relieved the Siege of Lubloin?" Madeline furrowed her brow.

"It cost the lives of every one of those warriors." An elf in a fine tunic crossed the hall to meet Madeline. "House Fabii is now extinct because of that battle. Their homes lie empty, and few remain to honor their tombs."

"I'm sorry." Madeline gritted her teeth.

"Why should you be sorry?" the elvish man scoffed. "You never knew anyone from House Fabii. Dust is all that has filled their halls since before you were born."

"It's still a tragedy." Madeline gripped her staff tightly. "And it obviously brings you quite a bit of sorrow some fifty years later, so you'll have to forgive me for trying to sympathize."

"We don't need your pity." The elf shook his head in a way that betrayed the falseness of his words. "The Queen will see you now. This way."

The Queen's Hall was no less elegant than any other chamber in the palace Madeline had seen so far. Much of the furniture was fashioned from fine, creamy timber. Gilded ivory and marble covered most other surfaces, and sparkling sapphires, emeralds, and rubies accentuated the columns. However, Madeline's awe at the sights diminished the more of it she took in.

On a raised dais, Queen Kypris sat on her bejeweled throne, beckoning Madeline into the chamber. Her alabaster skin was completely unblemished. On top of her head rested a silver tiara that had the appearance of a laurel wreath, more so than anything Madeline had seen crafted by mortal smiths. Her braided hair flowed over her shoulders like an auburn waterfall. Her deep blue dress shimmered like the night sky. Even the perfectly white teeth set in her smile had an ethereal quality Madeline could not hope to match. Alpia de Toron, the Beauty of the Bosvian Coast, was but a shadow compared to the Queen of Farthest Thule.

Beside the Queen's seat sat a somewhat larger but empty throne. Madeline had heard nothing about a king of this realm, but she dared not ask about it now. There was enough sorrow here.

"Welcome, Fravash the Bright." Queen Kypris gestured to the mouse on Madeline's shoulder. "It has been far too long since you have graced our realm."

Fravash jumped down from Madeline's cloak and took a bow in the middle of the hall. Madeline twisted a strand of her hair. What had he done to earn so much respect from the elves while they barely acknowledged her presence?

"My queen." Fravash raised his head. "My travels have taken me far and wide, and I am only grateful to find your hearth as welcoming as ever."

"What brings you to Vathepoli in such an inhospitable season?" Kypris asked.

"May I introduce Lady Madeline of House Drois?" Fravash turned to her.

"It is a pleasure to meet your majesty." Madeline curtsied. "Thank you for allowing me here."

Queen Kypris briefly nodded at Madeline before her attention returned to Fravash.

"She has the gift of magic flowing through her veins," the rodent continued. "I have taken it upon myself to instruct her in the arcane arts, but our resources among the race of men are limited."

The Queen nodded with a sympathetic smile.

"We have constructed the magic staff you see Lady Madeline carrying, but it does not have an appropriate core." Fravash gestured. "I suggested we come here to rectify this problem of ours."

"Let me see what you have made." Kypris extended her hand to Madeline.

With a bow, Madeline handed her staff over to the Queen. She ran her hand down the smooth length of the staff while inspecting every detail with her imperious gaze. Madeline tensed. Queen Kypris' mannerisms reminded her too much of Sister Vanya.

"It is a crude device." Kypris handed the staff back to Madeline. "But it has been infused with dragon essence. It should be sufficient for your purposes."

"Crude?" Madeline muttered.

She bit her lip. She did not mean to speak the thought aloud, but the Queen's insult surprised her. Her magic staff was her most refined possession. Its construction called for the highest level of craftsmanship available in all of Kovdor. It would be harder to find something more exquisite in all of Azgald. Then again, compared to the beauty of Farthest Thule, crude might not have been an inaccurate description of her staff.

The Queen rose from her throne and grabbed Madeline's free hand. Shocked, Madeline clenched her jaw. Examining Madeline's wrist, the elf tilted her head.

"So, you do have the gift." Kypris' amethyst eyes met Madeline's. "Your magic comes from the touch of a phoenix, does it not?"

Though the elves' eyes all sparkled with brilliant colors, there was some faintly old quality about them. It was almost as if Madeline were looking into Grandmother Annora's eyes rather than those of a fey creature of unearthly youth and beauty. They were ancient beings that bore the cares of many men's lifetimes. There was intelligence behind the Queen's eyes, but weariness too.

"That's what we suspect," Madeline confessed. "How did you know?"

"Elvish eyes can see much that the eyes of men are too dull to notice." The Queen's gaze turned hard. "So, you wish to commune with Anistemi?"

"We believe one of her feathers will make a suitable core for Madeline's staff," Fravash interjected.

"A phoenix's feather could temper the staff's dragon essence into something more suitable to human needs." Queen Kypris' expression softened. "I'm glad you thought of that, Fravash. I would have been worried if too much of this staff's character was shaped by dragons."

"Will you allow us to speak with Anistemi?" Madeline implored.

"She is the only phoenix I know of in all the Nordslands," Fravash added.

"Anistemi has not been well for many seasons." Kypris curled her lip into a frown. "We must consult with the guardians of the grove before you may see her."

"The guardians of the grove?" Madeline asked.

"They are the special caretakers of Farthest Thule's phoenix," Fravash explained. "They are the most renowned lore masters regarding phoenixes in all of Aestas, expert handlers, and fierce warriors."

"And they say the phoenix is sick?" Madeline asked. "What happens if Anistemi dies?"

"If the phoenix left us forever?" Kypris grimaced. "Life in Vathepoli would not be possible without Anistemi. The valley's crops would fail. We could not weave strands of her feathers into our clothing to protect us from the winter's biting chill. Our whole way of life would perish."

"And that's why the guardians of the grove must also be warriors." Madeline raised an eyebrow. "They protect her from anyone who would want to destroy Farthest Thule."

"That is right," Kypris replied. "Come. Let us see."

Fravash clambered up Madeline's cloak until he once again rested on her shoulder. Queen Kypris led the way out of the throne room. To Madeline's surprise, no royal guards escorted them into the next chamber. Though unarmed, the Queen appeared free to move about as she pleased without fear, even in mixed company. Fravash the Bright must have been truly respected among the elves.

Soon, the Queen led them to a courtyard in the center of the palace. Ivy climbed the walls, statues mounted to plinths stood sentinel at intervals, and mosaics and fountains decorated what ground was not filled with plants.

After taking but a few steps into the courtyard, Madeline jumped at the appearance of two pairs of warriors emerging from the shadows on either side of her. They wore bronze scale mail like all the other elf warriors Madeline had seen thus far, though their helmets were round rather than conical, and their shields were oblong and taller than their counterparts' in other parts of the city.

"My queen brings strangers to the grove," the lead guardian hissed as she stepped forward with a hand on the hilt of her sheathed sword. "They are not welcome."

Madeline gasped. One of the guardians of the grove was a female warrior. Nothing would ever shock her again after today's revelations.

"Stand down, Baucis." Kypris waved her hand. "I am not compelled to lead them here."

"The guardians of the grove answer to Anistemi, not the Queen." Baucis sneered. "You must consult me *before* bringing outsiders to the grove. Do not overstep your authority again."

Madeline's shoulders tensed at the exchange. The two bickered like old rivals repeating the same argument for the hundredth time. Clearly, Queen Kypris was not free to go anywhere she wished, after all.

"Your dedication to the grove is commendable, but I do not seek to overthrow your order." Kypris' expression hardened. "Fravash the Bright has brought this human child to speak with the phoenix."

Baucis' eyes darted over Madeline and Fravash. Her frown intensified. Madeline gulped.

"What is this rod you carry?" Baucis asked.

"It is a magic staff," Kypris answered before Madeline could reply to the question. "It is not dangerous. I inspected it myself."

"I asked the girl," Baucis growled.

"It's not complete." Madeline extended her staff for Baucis to examine. "We came to ask the phoenix for one of her feathers. If she were willing to gift us one, that would serve as the core of my staff."

Baucis exchanged a silent glance with the other guardians around them. Shaking heads and grimaces abounded. Madeline clenched her jaw. She knew their answer already, but she had not come all this way to be denied. There had to be some argument she could make.

"She is not well," Baucis insisted. "Even Fravash the Bright cannot cheer her. Anistemi needs rest."

"Will she recover?" Fravash asked.

Baucis' violet eyes grew misty. The guardian of the grove's shoulders slumped. However, it was just an instant before she snapped out of her momentary lapse, and she returned to being the rigid soldier barely able to contain her contempt for the grove's trespassers.

"No," Baucis answered at last. "The phoenix is dying. This night shall be her last."

"What?" Madeline blurted out.

"Anistemi has lived a long life, and after seven hundred and fifty-three years, it is finally time for her to close her eyes for good." Baucis gestured to the hedge behind her. "A phoenix normally lives only for half a millennium. She is long overdue."

As she turned her attention to the faint glow behind the hedge, Madeline's stomach sank to the furthest depths she could comprehend. What did this mean for her staff? More importantly, what did this mean for Farthest Thule?

"What will happen to the city?" Madeline asked. "Can your people handle what is to come?"

"Of course we can," Baucis scoffed. "We have been preparing for some time now."

"And you're so calm about it all." Madeline's jaw hung open. "Where will you go?"

"We're not going anywhere," Baucis snapped.

Another guardian of the grove emerged from the hedge. He whispered in Baucis' pointed ear. Grunting, she nodded in reply.

"It is time," Baucis announced. "Your majesty, it is your honor to oversee Anistemi's passing. Fravash the Bright, as an elf friend, is also permitted to bear witness. We will also grant the human child the right to witness the phoenix's passing as an honored guest."

"Thank you," Madeline stammered, too curious to see the phoenix to feel insulted at being repeatedly called a child by the elves.

The guardians of the grove escorted Madeline, Fravash, and Kypris beyond the hedge to a wide clearing. There, a great bird almost as large as Spathi lay sprawled across the ground. Its feathers were mostly a dull orange; however, some red and yellow feathers gave it a fiery appearance. While its plumage might have been vibrant some time ago, now it was old and faded.

No grass or other plants grew in the clearing. A wave of heat singed Madeline's face when she approached, and she took a reflexive step back. Not even the dozen or so guardians of the grove present stood any closer than Madeline dared.

"Anistemi," Kypris called out, "your eyes are dull, but your ears are still sharp. Hear the words of your queen."

The phoenix turned her head on her long neck towards the Queen. She cooed weakly. Madeline grimaced. May she never grow so old and frail.

"You have served Vathepoli these many centuries with dignity and honor," Kypris continued. "You have given us a home and a life in the Wyrmwind Peaks when no other refuge could hold us. Through your strength, we have bested trolls, Nordsmen, and all other foes who sought to plunder our riches and devour our flesh."

Kypris glanced at Baucis, Fravash, and then everyone else in the clearing. Beneath the calm surface of her face, a stormy sea boiled. The phoenix was more than a mythical bird. She was a friend.

"I release you from your service to Vathepoli," the Queen concluded. "Go to your mothers and your mothers' mothers in the sky. Be at peace."

Resting her head on the ground, Anistemi closed her eyes. A crackling noise started beneath her legs, and soon, voracious flames began to lick her wings and tail. A moment later, her whole body was ablaze.

Madeline squealed. Her heart pounded in her chest. However, it was all over in less than a minute.

Only a pile of blackened ash remained of Anistemi. The sweet aroma of cooked meat was overwhelmed by the stench of burnt feathers and less pleasant things. The face of every elf was sullen. Madeline swallowed. It was a bitter moment to behold.

"What now?" Madeline asked as the clearing began to cool. "How will they survive without the phoenix?"

"Hush." Fravash raised a finger to his mouth. "You'll see. Just watch."

A guardian of the grove wearing thick leather gloves stepped forward. He sifted through the ash. Then, Madeline's mouth dropped as he lifted a bright coppery, speckled egg from the phoenix's ashes.

"Anistemi is dead." The guardian held the egg aloft for all to see. "She lives on through her daughter, Anistemi."

"So it shall be," the other elves chorused as one.

"The egg will take a few days to hatch." Baucis turned to Madeline. "From there, she will mature in a matter of weeks. I will ask her if she is willing to commune with you once she is ready."

"That's what happens to a phoenix when it dies?" Madeline scowled. "So, Farthest Thule was never in any danger? What was all that about preparing for the phoenix's death if she was just going to be reborn in that egg immediately after?"

"Vathepoli is in danger." Kypris pointed up to the snowflakes falling from the black sky. "Even as we speak, the city grows colder. Gardens will die. Fountains will freeze. We will need to stay inside until Anistemi's magic grows strong enough to protect us again."

"And Vathepoli is no longer concealed to prying eyes," Baucis added. "Should our enemies stumble across our city, they would see it. We do not have enough warriors to fully man the battlements."

"For now, we'll make ourselves at home," Fravash replied. "Madeline is used to damp, cold castles."

Chapter Sixteen

Just beyond the hill, Godfrey, Roltar, and Mauger crested on their steeds, the Irelven River lazily meandered to the southeast. To the west, the dark trees of Bochsogen Forest were covered in a thick mist near the river. The water was deep and icy. The only safe crossing was an ancient stone bridge that cut across the Irelven.

"That's Harlstad Bridge." Roltar gestured down the road. "Everything on the north side is Stormsud."

"We're finally home," Mauger sighed. "Twenty days' journey from Vindholm, and we're home at last."

"Not yet." Godfrey pointed to a figure emerging from the mist on the far side of the bridge.

As they rode their stallions down the hill, the figure standing in their path grew more distinct. He held a drawn war hammer in one hand and a shield in the other. Fine chainmail gleamed over his body, and his face was covered by a heavy great helm. Godfrey's heart sank. The warrior's black tabard and shield bore no heraldic charge.

"The black knight," Godfrey murmured.

They dismounted their horses at the bridge. The black knight gripped his war hammer tightly as they approached. Clearly, he intended to block their crossing.

"What are you doing here?" Roltar asked as they neared the black knight. "I thought you would have preferred to winter in some warm inn with expensive wine and a good woman rather than bleak Harlstad Bridge."

The black knight made no reply.

"Surely, you did not go through twenty-five gold talents already," Mauger jested. "Or could Clan Behemoth not afford Lord Storolf's ransom?"

"You need not worry about my money," the black knight tersely assured them. "I am here of my own accord."

"Let us pass." Roltar's tone grew stern. "We have no quarrel with you, black knight."

"Lord Davin has asked that I protect this bridge." The black knight shook his head. "None shall pass."

"The King recognizes Roltar has issued a trial by combat to Lord Davin." Godfrey produced the sealed scroll from his satchel. "This was placed in my hand by the King's chancellor, Evrard. You must let us pass."

"I see no decree in your hand, Godfrey de Bastogne," the black knight insisted. "None shall pass."

Godfrey clenched his jaw. No meaningful reprimand could be made against the black knight since no one knew his true identity. Perhaps Davin of House Talhout had sought out the black knight's services precisely because he was not honor-bound to obey any lord's commands.

"I have been charged with delivering this message to Lord Davin." Godfrey waved the scroll in front of the black knight's face.

"I have been charged to not see it." The black knight smacked the scroll out of Godfrey's hand with his shield. "None shall pass."

Godfrey's hand throbbed. His rage boiled. This insult could not go unanswered.

"I challenge you," Godfrey spat. "Right here and now, black knight."

Godfrey drew his sword, but the black knight was already swinging his war hammer at him. He leapt out of the way, but the black knight swung again. Godfrey blocked with his shield as the war hammer gave a heavy thump across its steel surface.

Roltar and Mauger tensed but held their positions. Once a challenge was issued, they could not interfere. Honor demanded that this fight would be between just Godfrey and the black knight.

Leaping forward, Godfrey thrust Uriel at his foe. The enemy turned Godfrey's blade away with his shield. Blessed by Loxias or not, he still needed to land a hit against his enemy for the sword to do anything.

The black knight bashed him across the face with his shield. Blood trickled from the corner of Godfrey's lip. His head spinning, he fell to one knee. Gasping, he brought his shield up just in time to block what would have otherwise been a fatal hammer blow to the head. That was far too close.

Glimpsing a narrow opportunity, Godfrey stuck his blade into the enemy's side. Crying out, the black knight fell back a step. Mauger cheered. Panting, the black knight clutched his crimson wound. Wiping the blood from his mouth, Godfrey rose to his feet.

"Stand aside," Godfrey heaved. "You're bested."

"Hardly!" The black knight surged forward.

Roaring, he slammed Godfrey to the ground. He rolled out of the way as the black knight's war hammer struck the icy bridge. Godfrey tried to rise but slipped. Simultaneously, Mauger and Roltar cursed. Godfrey kicked out at the black knight, who also slipped on the ice.

Godfrey stood first. He slashed at his foe. Grunting, the black knight dodged and clambered to his feet against the bridge's parapet.

The black knight struck Godfrey's shield with his war hammer. The force of the blow rippled through his whole arm. Before he could react, the black knight bashed Godfrey across the chin with his shield. Godfrey gave a pained yelp before stumbling back a pace.

The enemy lunged at Godfrey, but he anticipated the move. Slashing in a low arc, he gashed the black knight across the leg. Bellowing, the black knight stumbled on the ice once more.

"Yield." Godfrey spat blood. "You fought well. Now yield the challenge."

"I yield for no one." The black knight staggered to face him. "I am the black knight."

With a yell, the warrior flew at Godfrey. Side-stepping the attack, Godfrey pounded the back of the black knight's head with the pommel of his sword. He skidded across the snow face-first before coming to a halt. Groaning, he feebly attempted to rise but collapsed in the effort. Too much of his blood stained the snow and ice.

"Tie him up." Godfrey coughed. "He'll ride on Dash the rest of the way to Skasgun."

"No," Roltar recoiled. "You should kill him. It's your right to kill him after defeating him in such a duel."

"The black knight fought with honor." Godfrey sheathed Uriel. "It is also my prerogative to extend mercy to a worthy adversary."

"What is to stop him from trying to loosen his bonds and kill us when he comes to?" Mauger asked. "His pay depends on us not reaching Skasgun."

"That is true," Godfrey admitted. "But he did his duty, even if it was only in the service of coin. He saved our lives before. We will take him to Skasgun, where his wounds may be treated. We owe him this mercy."

Mauger looked at his father expectantly.

"So be it," Roltar muttered.

The black knight painfully grunted as Mauger bound his wrists behind his back with strong cords before bandaging his wounds. For a moment, Godfrey pondered the half-conscious man beneath his great helm. It would be too easy to lift it and see who was underneath the cold steel. Godfrey sighed. He would not take away the little dignity his captive had left.

Together, Godfrey, Mauger, and Roltar lifted him into Dash's saddle. The horse snorted in what Godfrey could only interpret as contempt. Dash was still hardly willing to let Godfrey ride him. Placing another in the saddle was asking a lot.

Taking in a sharp breath, Godfrey cast his gaze on the scroll of parchment the black knight had smacked out of his hand. It lay in the snow on the bridge, a bit wet around the edges but otherwise unharmed. Godfrey snatched it up and put it in his satchel. Forgetting that would be inexcusable.

The black knight slumped and moaned in the saddle as Godfrey led Dash by the reins across Harlstad Bridge. Roltar rode a few paces ahead and Mauger a few paces behind in case the black knight attempted an escape. They would take no chances.

Once across the bridge, Mauger dismounted his steed. Godfrey and Roltar paused. Mauger knelt and grabbed a fistful of snowy mud.

"Stormsud." Mauger rose and held the mud close to his face. "Sacred home of my fathers' fathers, I have returned. Gods witness me. I swear I will not leave this realm alive unless the right to rule Skasgun has returned to House Hracour."

He kissed the clump of mud before scattering it on the road in front of him. Roltar dismounted his horse and clasped his son by the shoulder. Briefly, they embraced.

"Soon," Roltar said. "Soon, we will make this right."

"I know, Father." Mauger pulled out of the embrace.

Godfrey frowned. Did he have such dedication to Kovdor? Had he not told himself so many times that Bastogne was home?

They continued down the road for a few hours. The afternoon grew late. Eventually, the black knight stirred.

"You bring me before Skasgun's court to mock me?" he asked. "Spare me the dishonor, and leave me on the road to die a man's death."

"We take you to Skasgun to heal your wounds." Mauger gestured down the road.

"Slit my throat if you wish to extend mercy," the black knight grumbled. "I—"

"Spare us the melancholy," Godfrey cut in. "You saved our lives before, and we are returning the favor. You fought with honor and determination every time I have witnessed you. What have you to be ashamed of?"

For a moment, the captive said nothing. He turned his helmeted head away from Godfrey. What did a black knight without lands, titles, or even a name have left to be ashamed of?

"I still failed," the black knight sighed.

Godfrey bit his lip. The captive flexed his arms under his bonds, but they did not give. Godfrey's thoughts turned to Paschal as he looked the black knight up and down. Had he found redemption on Walaric's quest yet?

"You did not look beneath my helmet?" The black knight turned back to Godfrey.

"I swear by all that is sacred and divine, I did not." Godfrey placed his hand over his heart.

"I believe you," the black knight answered after a long moment. "Thank you for saving what little honor I have left in this world."

At last, Skasgun came into view. It was a newer castle. The crenellations along the parapet stuck up like sharp teeth. Its towers were round, and its walls were high. It was not mightier than Olso Fortress or Fuetoile Keep, but Godfrey certainly would not have wished to assault it without at least a few thousand men.

"New walls," Roltar marveled, "new towers, but the Nordsmen restored the original keep."

"It will be just like before Uncle Badian's death?" Godfrey asked.

"Mostly," Roltar answered with a humorless smile, "except without the old man himself."

"Right." Godfrey nodded.

Godfrey afforded himself a small smile. He never really knew Uncle Badian. He had only seen him a few times when he was very young, but his parents spoke fondly of him, and Roltar seemed to like the memory of *the old man* well enough, at least.

Skasgun's gate remained closed as Godfrey and the others approached it. They halted just in front of the portal and grimaced up at the battlements. Whatever sentinels watched over the approach to the castle remained out of sight. Godfrey cleared his throat.

"We have in our custody the black knight tasked with blocking our way across Harlstad Bridge," Godfrey called up to the crenellations. "We wish to return him to you so that he may receive a physician's attention."

Only the fluttering breeze whipping about the House Talhout banner planted above the gatehouse answered. It was the same black wolf passant against a white field that adorned Conrad the Wolf's shield and tabard. Godfrey clenched his jaw at the sight.

Godfrey fidgeted. Someone was watching them from the defenses, even if they remained unseen. Were they under orders not to let anyone in?

"I have a message from King Lothar." Godfrey took the parchment from his satchel and waved it up at the battlements. "By order of the King, you must let us in to deliver it to Lord Davin."

Again, no answer. The King's authority extended only as long as his arm once they had left the heart of Azgald. Still, Godfrey had to try.

Godfrey shook his head at Roltar and Mauger. The black knight shifted in Dash's saddle. Just as Godfrey was about to turn, the gates creaked open.

"Someone respects the King's authority if not the sacred rights of messengers." Mauger rolled his eyes.

Five House Talhout knights waited in the outer courtyard for them. Godfrey's jaw tightened as he recognized a few of them from the crusade. These were hard men. They bore the scars of more than one kind of campaign. Godfrey was sure they had no more desire to see him than he had to see them.

Two of the House Talhout warriors unbound the black knight and lowered him from Dash's saddle. As soon as they carried him off towards one of the halls lining the outer wall, the lead knight turned to Godfrey, Roltar, and Mauger. He was a tall, intimidating man Godfrey believed to have as much Gothian blood in his veins as he did Lortharainian.

"I am Sir Fedmar." The man crossed his arms. "Thank you for returning the black knight to us, but Lord Davin says you are not welcome here."

"I understand we are not welcome," Roltar replied smoothly, "but we have business with your lord whether he likes it or not."

"What business do you have?" Sir Fedmar raised an eyebrow at Roltar. "This is not your castle, and these are not your lands. Return to Vindholm."

"This is King Lothar's seal." Godfrey extended his scroll to Fedmar. "It's my task to ensure Lord Davin receives this message *now*."

Sir Fedmar examined the wax seal. He frowned before exchanging a glance with the knights on either side of him. They grumbled indistinctly with each other for a moment. At last, they murmured something in agreement.

"We will take you to Lord Davin," Fedmar answered, "but state your business quickly and be gone. Even King Lothar's seal does not make you any more welcome."

Skasgun's great hall fell silent as Godfrey, Roltar, and Mauger were escorted into the chamber by Sir Fedmar and his companions. Servants with trays of food and pitchers of mead stopped in their tracks at the sight. Lord Davin, a middle-aged man with greying hair and dark eyes, turned bright red as he shot up from his seat at the high table.

"I told you not to let them come in!" Davin slammed his fist against the table.

"Dear!" The young blonde woman who sat beside Davin trembled at his outburst.

"Not now, Wia!" Davin shot back. "These intruders seek to supplant me. I'll not stand for it."

"My lord." Fedmar bowed his head. "They carry a message with the King's seal on it."

"I don't care what poison you whispered in King Lothar's ear." Davin pointed an accusing finger at Roltar. "I know why you're here. Skasgun was bequeathed to me by Conrad the Wolf through right of conquest. If you want it, bring an army and take it. I'll not surrender what was justly appointed to me."

Mauger stepped forward to speak, but Roltar grabbed his son by the shoulder. Godfrey looked at the scroll in his hand, but Roltar waved for him to put it away. Quizzically, Godfrey glanced at his cousin.

"Stormsud was once a great land." Roltar gestured as he took a step towards the high table. "You have with you a few knights to defend Skasgun, but not enough to restore this realm to its former glory. What shall you do if the Nordsmen attack in the spring?"

"You have nothing to offer," Davin spat.

"Let us combine our strength." Roltar clenched his fist. "Allow House Hracour to return to our ancestral lands, and I can promise you and your men positions of power."

"I already rule this land," Davin crowed. "Why should I cede anything to you?"

"House Hracour may not have land or men, but we have wealth and friends." Roltar raised an eyebrow. "You have some land and some men, but neither wealth nor friends in Azgald. If we combine our resources, each of us may gain what he lacks."

Davin unclenched his fist and let his hand rest on the table. He took a long breath and shifted on his feet. At last, his eyes met the young woman's beside him.

"It may be worth hearing them out, husband." Wia stroked Davin's arm.

Davin grunted. A range of emotions crossed his face as he glanced between his wife and Roltar. He took another long breath before his gaze rested on Godfrey.

"I remember you well, Godfrey de Bastogne," Davin sneered. "Do not think I have forgotten the trouble you caused my lord, Conrad, on crusade."

"Leon de Valois came to my camp of his own accord," Godfrey snapped. "The rest of Conrad's trouble, he brought upon himself."

"What message do you bring from King Lothar?" Davin pressed. "What does he have to say about all of this?"

"Let's see if we can work out agreeable terms before we worry too much about the King." Roltar gestured for Godfrey to hush before he could even begin to respond. "It is best not to break the seal on that scroll until we have to."

Davin scowled, apparently deep in thought. He whispered something to his wife and one of the retainers on his other side. They replied in equally hushed tones. Distrust was etched on their faces.

"A trick?" Davin's eyes narrowed on the scroll still in Godfrey's hand. "Why not simply deliver King Lothar's words? His message is the only reason you stand before us in *my* great hall now."

"No trick," Roltar insisted. "But the King's message leaves no room for… compromise. I want to see if we can work out something more agreeable for both of us first."

Godfrey frowned at Roltar and Mauger. He hated these kinds of games. Then again, if they could resolve this without a trial by combat, surely the gods would favor the outcome more. Lord Davin exchanged a hard look with his wife. She shook her head.

"You have given me much to think about," Davin answered at last. "Come. Sit at my table. We were just about to start the evening meal."

Though the food at Skasgun was not nearly as sumptuous as what King Lothar served at Vindholm, it was far more filling than what Godfrey had been eating on the road. Davin and Roltar exchanged enough small talk to almost persuade Godfrey into thinking the two were old friends. Mauger's expression remained sullen, however. This was not the true nature of things.

Godfrey exchanged a glance with Mauger. Though no words were said, he thought he understood his kinsman. If this was going to end up being a trial by combat anyway, why delay any longer than necessary?

As the skies outside the windows grew dim, the black knight limped into the great hall. Lady Wia gasped at the sight, though Lord Davin and his armed retainers ignored him. Godfrey clenched his teeth. The black knight had to endure some shame after his failure.

He was still fully armored and hid his face behind his great helm as he filled his plate. Only as he left with a mug of ale in one hand and his food in the other did Davin acknowledge the black knight's presence with a barely contained sneer. He had failed, and now Lord Davin had to delicately balance a series of unknown quantities. Godfrey held his breath as the black knight exited the great hall. Only the gods could say what would happen from here.

After the meal had ended, Lord Davin waved his sojourners away for the evening before retiring from the great hall with Lady Wia. Sir Fedmar showed Godfrey, Roltar, and Mauger to one of the guest chambers on the keep's third floor. Wearily, Godfrey crashed on the closest bed after undressing for the night. His chin and arm still throbbed from his duel with the black knight earlier that day. More than one part of his body was bruised.

"What is our plan from here?" Mauger glared at his father as he sat on the second bed.

"We negotiate the best deal we can." Roltar smirked.

"But we told the King—" Mauger started.

"Not a word of that tonight," Roltar interrupted. "Assume every wall has ears."

"Yes, Father." Mauger swallowed.

"We only use *that* as a last resort," Roltar explained. "Davin does not know exactly what the letter states, and that's to our advantage for now. King Lothar won't care how we resolve the issue of Skasgun's rule, so long as it's resolved quickly enough. Godfrey, keep that scroll on you at all times. Don't show it to anyone."

"Right," Godfrey answered as he covered his head with his pillow. "I'll do whatever you say."

Godfrey took a deep breath as he stretched out under his blanket. He had spent weeks at Vindholm as Roltar negotiated there. How long would they spend at Skasgun in fruitless talks?

"Who is Lady Wia?" Godfrey sat up and turned to Roltar. "I didn't see her on crusade."

"Lady Wia is from House Drechov," Mauger explained. "The Duke of Friodlad married her off to Davin as soon as Skasgun fell into his hands."

"So, it would seem Davin is not entirely friendless in Azgald," Godfrey noted.

"The Duchy of Oblarv and Bochsogen Forest lie between Helsirki and Skasgun," Roltar answered. "There is enough distance between them to matter."

"It still sounds like a quick wedding if nothing else." Godfrey clenched his jaw.

Mauger nodded in agreement. Godfrey's thoughts turned to his own upcoming wedding. The snow was beginning to melt outside, if only ever so slightly. The first day of spring was coming sooner than later.

"I hope we can settle this quickly," Godfrey muttered. "I've been away from Kovdor too long."

Roltar sighed. Mauger grimaced. Godfrey lay back down in his bed and rolled to face the wall. He had suffered much for these kinsmen he barely knew. His thoughts turned to the other scroll in his satchel. The prophecy he had received from High Priest Throst was the only thing keeping him here after the way everything else had turned out thus far.

"Trust in my blood," Godfrey murmured as Roltar blew out the candles lighting the room.

Days passed uneventfully for Godfrey. Roltar presented many terms to Davin as he sought to restore Skasgun to House Hracour, but Davin flatly rejected almost every offer. He was not interested in serving as a chancellor, chamberlain, or some other high office at Skasgun. He would hardly entertain the notion of splitting Stormsud. Disgusted, Godfrey stopped attending these meetings after a while.

Soon, Godfrey took to long walks around Skasgun's courtyards and atop its battlements. It was cold, damp, and grey, but at least it was away from Roltar and Mauger. His resentment for his kin only grew the longer he stayed at Skasgun, and his feelings were hardly warm to begin with.

One morning, Godfrey caught the black knight standing atop the battlements at the outer gatehouse. His cloak fluttered in the breeze as he gazed at the land west.

Immediately next to Skasgun's walls, there was a small grove of trees, a frozen pond, and some rolling hills. Nothing special. Yet Godfrey sensed the black knight's yearning to go out there.

"Do you have any family in Azgald?" Godfrey stood beside the black knight. "Did they drive you into exile?"

For a long time, the black knight gave no reply.

"I had always viewed my house as a source of strength and comfort when I lived in Bastogne." Godfrey leaned against the crenellations. "But House Hracour has only asked for favors while offering nothing in return."

"I'm told your uncle was a good man," the black knight replied. "Azgald saw happier days when the old man, Badian, ruled Skasgun."

"I've been told much the same." Godfrey rolled his eyes. "I don't know if I feel the same about Roltar and Mauger. All they care about is getting this castle back."

"Grace Badian's son and grandson, out of respect for his memory, even if they are less deserving," the black knight admonished. "That is your duty now."

"How can you speak of duty or loyalty to kin?" Godfrey shook his head.

"Watch your tongue." The black knight turned sharply on Godfrey. "You don't know what I had to endure. The shame. The injustice."

Godfrey curled his lip into a frown but did not say more. A knight's honor was everything. Godfrey would rather have suffered the most grievous wounds than have his reputation tarnished.

"Will you be staying here for long?" Godfrey asked after a while. "Davin and his men don't seem very pleased with you now that we're here."

"No." The black knight shook his head. "I thank you for the pity you have shown my life, but now that I am recovered from our duel, I must press on."

"Kovdor is still in need of brave knights," Godfrey said. "You fought splendidly at Harlstad Bridge. Are you sure you will not join me at Olso Fortress?"

The black knight's gaze returned to the west. The edge of Bochsogen Forest lay near the horizon. Beyond that were the Irelven River, Oblarv, and, eventually, Kovdor.

"Where will you go?" Godfrey asked.

"Lubloin," the black knight answered curtly.

"That's a dangerous road." Godfrey furrowed his brow as they both turned their gaze to the east. "You'll have to travel between the Blighted Lands *and* orcish tribes to reach it from here."

"There will be work along the way," the black knight countered. "If I can earn enough coin, I can secure passage to anywhere I want to go from there."

"What about the twenty-five talents of gold you already earned ransoming Lord Storolf?" Godfrey wondered aloud. "Surely, that could take you anywhere in all of Aestas you could dream of?"

"That gold is intended to buy me a nice manor once I leave Azgald for good," the black knight explained.

"I'm sorry to hear Tyche has been so unkind to you here." Godfrey's lips creased into a frown. "Are you certain there is nothing to stay in Azgald for?"

The black knight made no reply. Though he briefly looked back west, his gaze soon returned to the east. There it remained fixed until Godfrey left.

By dawn the next day, the black knight rode his horse to the east, just as he had promised. Farewells from Lord Davin and his household were short. Only Lady Wia showed any signs of grief at his departure.

"Do you suppose there was any *courtly love* between him and Lady Wia?" Mauger indicated the black knight as he and Godfrey watched the dark figure vanish down the road from Skasgun's walls.

"Whatever it was, I'm sure it was honorable." Godfrey winced.

"I wouldn't have let him stay if I were Lord Davin," Mauger continued. "We all saw the way she looked at him whenever he came around."

"Women always seem to fancy whatever is just out of their reach." Godfrey shrugged. "The black knight turns their heads wherever he goes."

"True enough," Mauger sighed.

"Listen." Godfrey shifted awkwardly. "I need to start heading back to Kovdor."

"What?" Mauger scowled. "You're not going to see this through to the end?"

"I can leave the King's letter with you." Godfrey gestured to his satchel. "You and your father can entertain negotiations with Lord Davin for as long as you like before showing it to him, but I have a wedding to prepare for. Spring is almost here."

"That's pretty cowardly of you," Mauger spat. "I can't believe what I'm hearing."

"What else can I do?" Godfrey threw out his hands. "I'm not a part of your father's negotiations. I can't sway Davin. He hates me on account of Conrad the Wolf. What else am I supposed to do here at Skasgun?"

"You're supposed to support your family," Mauger scoffed. "You have a reputation for being this great chivalrous knight blessed by the gods, but I guess all that talk was just chaff in the wind."

"See here!" Godfrey fumed. "I have done my duty to you and your father—"

"Godfrey de Bastogne," Sir Fedmar interrupted as he approached from the gatehouse. "Lord Davin summons you. He wants to see King Lothar's letter immediately."

Godfrey and Mauger exchanged a glance. Scoffing, Godfrey stamped his way to the keep, and Mauger followed a pace behind him. Now the final card would be played, and Godfrey could return home. Let Roltar and Davin spill their blood, and the gods would decide who would rule Skasgun.

Once they entered the great hall, Davin ushered Godfrey and Mauger in. Dark circles hung under Roltar's eyes as if he had been up all night. Lady Wia and Lord Davin appeared no more rejuvenated this morning.

"Do you have King Lothar's letter?" Davin demanded. "Bring it to me now."

Godfrey took the sealed scroll from his satchel and stepped forward. Sir Fedmar ripped it from Godfrey's hand before giving it to his lord. Davin briefly examined the burgundy seal before breaking it.

Contempt racked Davin's face as his eyes scanned the letter. Godfrey swallowed hard. At least it would all be over quickly.

"King Lothar approves a trial by combat for the right to Skasgun!" Davin threw the letter down on the table. "This is preposterous."

"This is my ancestors' home." Roltar stood. "Louis the Blue slew the pale, twin-headed wyvern, Currog, here and built Skasgun on the very spot. My father, Badian, died defending this castle from orcs and Nordsmen. Do not tell me what is preposterous!"

"If you want a trial by combat, so be it!" Davin clenched his fist. "The winner will maintain the rights to Skasgun's lordship in perpetuity. The loser is bound as his servant forevermore."

"Let me fight him." Mauger stepped forward. "I swore that I would not leave here alive if I did not win Skasgun back for House Hracour."

Lord Davin sneered. He and Roltar appeared almost equal in vitality and vigor, but Mauger was younger, stronger, and faster. Only a fool could not see who would win that fight.

Davin looked around the room. Lady Wia pointed to Godfrey. Lord Davin smirked.

"I elect Godfrey de Bastogne as my champion," he announced.

"What?" Godfrey stammered.

"Roltar's son will fight as his champion, and Godfrey de Bastogne will fight as mine." Davin gestured between the two of them. "This will even the playing field."

Godfrey's heart sank. His love for Roltar and Mauger had only decreased over time, but he had no desire to actually fight them. There had to be another way.

"What if I refuse?" Godfrey snarled. "Or what if I lose on purpose?"

"You have too much honor to refuse a challenge when called upon." Davin raised his eyebrow. "We will bind both champions to a sacred oath that they will compete at their absolute best performance. You won't refuse the call to stand in as my champion, will you?"

Godfrey's hand trembled. Roltar's expression was resigned, but a fire burned in Mauger's eyes. He wanted this. He wanted the chance to beat Godfrey.

Godfrey set his jaw. He would show Mauger the price of his jealousy. He would put him in his place, kindred or not. He could not have come this far only to back down from the challenge now. He could not have his honor stained by refusing.

"I accept the challenge!" Godfrey roared.

"Excellent." Lord Davin clapped his hands.

Roltar's expression turned to dismay. Godfrey scoffed. If Roltar wanted Skasgun so badly, he would have to go through him to get it. The irony was not lost on him. The gods, too, were fond of a joke.

Chapter Seventeen

Sir Jordan lay in his hospital bed, moaning. The wound he had received in Gardesh the Pale's library had become infected not long after they hobbled out of the dungeon. Now, a fever drained the color from his face and left him in a cold sweat. Like it or not, the hospital in the Silver Suns' chapter house at Sval was Walaric's home for the time being.

"We're fortunate to have made it to Sval when we did." Izold crossed his arms. "Another day out in the wilderness, and he may have been entirely beyond the physicians' aid."

"Helios favored us." Walaric nodded as he sat at Jordan's bedside. "Will he make it?"

"The brethren of the Silver Suns tell me we'll know more in a day or two." Izold shook his head. "Their doctors don't believe it's ghoul rot, at any rate."

"Then, at least, he *can* be saved." Walaric grimaced.

"No need to put him out of his misery yet," Izold scoffed. "I think he'll make it."

A knock came at the door at the far end of Jordan's room. The hinges creaked as the door slid open, and Walaric raised his eyebrow at the sight of the man who entered. He wore the same blue and white twin-headed wyvern tabard over his chainmail hauberk that Godfrey's kinsmen, Roltar and Mauger, did, and the resemblance he bore to the other two was uncanny. His most distinguishing feature was the golden crown that sat atop his spangenhelm.

"My lord." Walaric stood and bowed his head as soon as the gleaming crown caught his eye.

"So, you are the heroes who destroyed Gardesh the Pale?" the crowned man asked. "That makes you eternal friends of Sval. I will make sure the bards here sing your names with honor for as long as I live."

Izold and Walaric nodded.

"I'm King Rivold," the man continued. "Forgive me for not coming sooner. I had to put down the last of Gardesh's cultists while they could still be found."

"You're of House Hracour?" Walaric asked.

"No." Rivold's lips tightened. "Though we are related. House Sval split from House Hracour generations ago."

"Do you know Roltar and Mauger from Azgald?" Walaric's excitement grew as he spoke. "My friend Godfrey is trying to help them reclaim Skasgun for House Hracour."

"We haven't had many dealings with House Hracour for a long time." Rivold frowned. "Sval has been its own kingdom for more than seventy-five years, and we harbor few good feelings towards our former brethren to the west. You three are an exception to such feelings, of course."

Walaric swallowed awkwardly. Upon closer inspection of the King's clothing, he frowned at Rivold's twin-headed wyvern tabard. While House Hracour's heraldic charge was blue on the viewer's left and white on the right, and the blazon mirrored these colors, House Sval had inverted this color scheme. Izold grimaced at Walaric as if silently telling him not to inquire further.

Pensively, Walaric held his tongue. Though the King's face was young, many grey hairs speckled his beard. Heavy was the crown that lay on his head.

"What business brings you to Sval?" Rivold cleared his throat. "I suspect the Silver Suns' remarkably expert doctors and famed hospitals were not what first drove you through the Tivelden Forest."

"We are merely passing through," Walaric answered. "As soon as our friend has recovered, we travel north against the Lenarm River to the Blighted Lands."

"To what end?" Rivold interjected.

"We must put the shade of Nera, the Great Witch of the North, to rest," Izold explained. "Walaric has studied the undead in great detail as well as the witch's writings. We believe we will find the key to sending her spirit beyond the mortal sphere in Mirtys."

"You seek out the Keeper of Souls, no doubt." Pursing his lips, the King shifted from one foot to the other.

"What can you tell us about it?" Walaric took a step towards Rivold. "I've never heard of such a being before coming across the name in Nera's journal."

"The Keeper of Souls has a name: Dolon." The King clenched his jaw. "Beyond that, none at Sval can say much of his origins. What we can say is that he is a powerful undead being that currently resides at the forbidden library in Mirtys. As his title implies, he traffics in the spirits of the dead, but to what end, none of my sages can guess."

"I was right!" Walaric rubbed the gold coin in his pouch that Dachlann had minted for him back at Olso Fortress. "I think I know how to unshackle Nera's spirit from the mortal sphere. Once Sir Jordan has recovered, we travel north."

"I cannot recommend traveling north." Rivold shook his head. "The undead there have not stirred with such vigor since the last eclipse."

"Eclipse?" Walaric asked.

"Twenty-five years ago, there was a great eclipse here." Rivold gestured around. "A foreign queen, Moswen, sought to use this ill portent as an opportunity to destroy Sval and give it over to the powers of undeath."

"How?" Walaric marveled.

"The story is long, and the details are sordid, as is the tragedy of every eclipse." The King waved a dismissive hand. "But it resulted in the deaths of my father and the Queen among many good knights, both of House Sval and the Silver Suns. Morgan the Bloodied is the only reason Sval still stands today."

"Morgan the Bloodied, as in the Grand Master of the Silver Suns?" Walaric's jaw dropped.

"He was not the Grand Master back then—and I was only three years old at the time—but that is the man." Rivold nodded.

"I am sorry to hear about your father." Walaric made a pious gesture.

"Don't be," Rivold snapped. "I am not my father, and I don't remember him. Save your pity."

Walaric's jaw gaped at this strange reaction. There was an intensity in the King's expression, but it soon faded. Izold cleared his throat.

"We owe you a debt of gratitude." Rivold sighed. "Fionn of Cromant was not the only Silver Sun we lost to Gardesh the Pale's predations."

"We lost friends as well." Walaric's voice trailed off. "Sir Paschal, Candac… young knights, brave knights. They had so much more to do in this life."

"But now the mists in Tivelden Forest subside, thanks to your bravery and sacrifice." Rivold dipped his head to the semiconscious Jordan lying fitfully in the bed before them. "Your man will be in my prayers, even if he hails from Azgald."

"His name is Sir Jordan," Walaric clarified.

"I will pray for Sir Jordan's speedy recovery," Rivold answered with a slight smile. "You may remain at the Silver Suns' chapter house as long as they welcome you, or you may stay at the citadel as my guest for as long as you'd like. May the gods watch over you all while you stay at Sval."

With that, King Rivold marched through the doorway. His footsteps echoed down the corridor for a long moment. After the sound of the King's steps had faded, Walaric rose from his seat before pushing the door closed. Shaking his head, he turned back to Izold.

"I wonder why he has so much hatred for his father." Walaric shook his head.

"I don't know." The paladin shrugged. "Some fathers hurt their sons in ways we may never fully understand. Some sons perceive such vicious attacks where none were made."

"I never knew my parents." Walaric bit his lip. "But I never thought anyone could hate a father he had no memory of. I don't understand."

"A touch of madness may be at work here," Izold cautioned. "Try not to read too deeply into it."

"Let's also pray for Sir Jordan's speedy recovery." Walaric turned back to the knight as he whimpered and struggled under his blankets. "We should not grow too comfortable here."

Days passed before Sir Jordan was well enough to eat a full meal. Even after that, the Silver Sun doctors recommended he spend most of his time resting. Jordan himself had no problem taking this advice and slept for long hours throughout the day as the physicians periodically changed his bandages and cleaned his leg wound. However, Walaric began to grow impatient and spent much of his time gazing north beyond the city walls. They were so close to the Blighted Lands.

"Let's visit Rivold's court," Walaric suggested to Izold over breakfast.

"Any particular reason?" The paladin looked up from his porridge as he hunched over the table they sat at.

"Boredom," Walaric confessed as he set his empty bowl and spoon on the long table. "We're so close to the Blighted Lands, yet we cannot move on while Sir Jordan is like this. I need to take my mind off it all. Aside from that, the King invited us, and it would be rude not to drop in for at least a short visit."

Izold grumbled something indistinct. Walaric looked about the hall where they ate their breakfast. Like most Silver Sun establishments he had visited, the chapter house at Sval had minimal adornment. The food was bland, and there was little in the way of entertainment.

Walaric might have chosen his words more carefully, but there were few Silver Suns in the chamber to offend, and these men rarely mingled with Walaric and Izold. Narlstad had been much more welcoming by comparison. He had to get out, even if it was just for a little while.

"Perhaps you have spent too much time in the luxury of lords' estates," the paladin suggested. "More time among humble surroundings might do you good."

"If you want to stay with the Silver Suns, that's fine." Walaric rose from his seat. "I won't be long."

"Remember we're on a quest." Izold tugged on Walaric's sleeve as he attempted to go. "And remember your priestly vows. We don't need any more distractions from beautiful young maidens."

Walaric flushed in embarrassment. For several weeks, Terrwyn had not come up in conversation. Though he had never divulged the whole story to Izold, the paladin had likely figured out much of what he had been unwilling to say. His head still spun at the memory of her hanging from the arm of that knight at Laht.

"I won't be looking for any of *those* kinds of distractions." Walaric pulled his arm away.

The priest was about to add that he had learned his lesson, but decided to hold his tongue before the words could form in his mouth. Before Terrwyn, there had been Elja. Would another young woman steal his heart after this?

"Be safe." Izold turned his attention back to his porridge. "Come back before dark."

"I will." Walaric barely stopped himself from rolling his eyes as he left the chamber.

Walaric chafed as the paternal sound of Izold's final words echoed in his mind. He huffed as he walked through the corridors to the chapter house's exit. The paladin meant well and had good reason to be concerned about Walaric. Still, all of the rules and vows began to suffocate him in a way he had never felt before this quest.

His mind raced as he stepped out into the bright morning sun. The cold bit his nose, though not as sharply as it did even a few days ago. His feet sloshed through melting snow, which soaked through his boots. Did he really even want to be a priest anymore?

He stopped in his tracks and wrapped his cloak about himself as he bit his lip. Sval's high city was grand, though not as grand as Laht, Vindholm, or anywhere back in the Ostlands he had seen. Wistfully, he turned his head to the mountains beyond Sval's gates. He had made solemn vows that could not be undone. It was too late.

Walaric sighed as he turned back to face the Silver Sun chapter house. The cylindrical stone building was fortified with crenellations, buttresses, and towers. What would Walaric be without the holy Church? What of the miracle he had performed with his star pendant to turn the undead in Gardesh the Pale's dungeon?

His gaze drifted to Rivold's citadel, and he started to walk towards it. He had faith. He could not abandon it. What was really bothering him? Was it still Terrwyn or Elja?

Walaric shook his head as he pressed towards the citadel. Gorgeous damsels were a temptation, and lately a stronger temptation than he had previously felt, but Bishop Clovis had warned him these feelings would come with manhood. His desire for these beautiful young maidens alone could not explain away his angst.

His feet sloshed through the muck and snow as he slowly made his way down the street. Was it Candac and Paschal's deaths that vexed him so? Though they died in the service of the gods, their fate was still horrid. Walaric never would have wished such deaths on anyone.

At last, Walaric reached the citadel, and he waved to the sentries at the entrance. The guards' House Sval heraldry still resembled House Hracour's too closely for Walaric to not be momentarily confused when he first saw them. Promptly, the sentries parted for Walaric and opened the citadel's gate.

"Welcome, Father Walaric," one of the guards chimed. "It's an honor to see you visit Sval's citadel."

"*Father* Walaric?" asked the other warrior. "I thought you were the paladin's squire."

Walaric paused, looking the man in the eye. Something rang true in what he said. Izold had spent much of his time with Walaric chastising him. It had slowly worn on him, he now realized. Was the answer that simple?

"I am Father Walaric," he said at last, "though Izold, the paladin, and I have been traveling together all winter."

"Travel around with a paladin long enough these days, and I suppose you'll start to look like one." The guard shrugged. "Come in. The King has been expecting you."

The citadel's great hall, like much of Sval, was impressive, though not as refined as Laht's. Walaric jolted as a herald announced his entrance into the chamber. He had never viewed himself as important enough to warrant having his presence announced before.

King Rivold gestured for Walaric to sit at the high table beside him as a hush fell over the courtiers watching his approach. The knights and dames tracked his every movement as he navigated to the King's table. Blushing,

Walaric made every effort to stand straight, step perfectly, and not awkwardly jostle into a table or chair.

"My lords and ladies," Rivold called out. "We are honored to have Father Walaric join us here today. A toast to his health, and a toast to all of his friends who helped Fionn of Cromant destroy Gardesh the Pale. Gods rest their souls in the celestial kingdoms."

"Hear! Hear!" One of Rivold's retainers enthusiastically lifted his mug.

The others present lifted their assorted mugs, goblets, and tankards. They took a deep swig of their drinks and hailed Walaric before slowly drifting back to the conversations they were previously holding. Walaric took a bow, then finished his walk to the high table.

"May I introduce Queen Jelske?" Rivold gestured to the crowned woman sitting beside him.

"Charmed." Walaric took the Queen's fair hand as she proffered it.

He lightly kissed the ruby ring on her finger ever so briefly before she batted her brown eyes at him. Walaric blinked. He had to have imagined it. Not every woman he met could fall for him so easily. Could they?

Queen Jelske's face gleamed like ivory beneath her delicate wimple. She was extremely beautiful. Walaric shook his head. There was no value in pursuing any such thoughts with a married woman, even if she was so close to his age.

Walaric took his seat on Rivold's other side. Jelske's eyes may have followed him the whole way around the table, but he ignored her. Nothing good could come of it.

No sooner had Walaric settled at the high table than the great hall grew quiet again. He squirmed uncomfortably in his chair. So many eyes were upon him.

"Father Walaric," a troubadour called from across the chamber. "Father Walaric, can you tell us how you defeated

Gardesh the Pale? I understand you were instrumental in his demise."

Several others in the great hall echoed the sentiment.

"Well." Walaric blushed as the chamber quieted down in apparent anticipation of his response. "I only played a small part. You should ask Izold or Sir Jordan for the full account."

"Such modesty!" Queen Jelske gestured to Walaric with a flattering hand. "But you do yourself and our court a disservice by not sharing your exploits in the Tivelden Forest. Our minstrels must hear this tale from you before composing their songs of Gardesh the Pale's undoing."

"If you insist, my lady." Walaric gulped at the Queen's sparkling eyes.

After clearing his throat, Walaric stood and did his best to account for his journey from Olso to Sval. His time preaching in Kovdor had improved his oratory considerably, but the audience was so thoroughly rapt with his story, he doubted such eloquence was needed. He only stumbled over one part.

While he was sure to give the full context of his quest to put Nera's shade to rest, he made no mention of Terrwyn or anything to do with her. There was no need to go over such things. Rivold's court was more interested in the parts about fighting undead monsters and cultists anyway.

Finally, Walaric finished elaborating all the details concerning Gardesh the Pale's dungeon, fighting the zombies there, and ultimately destroying the lich's phylactery. To his own surprise, he left nothing unsaid about Paschal or Candac's deaths. His voice trembled as he spoke. He could still hardly believe they were gone.

"How very hard this whole thing must have been for you." Jelske's eyes watered as Walaric resumed his seat. "We are so fortunate to have you among us."

"I did what I had to." Walaric looked at his feet.

Catching his wife's eye, Rivold tapped his fingers on the table. The King was not blind. No ruler could be and hope to survive long on the throne.

"We are all very touched." Rivold nodded tersely. "Thank you for sharing that story."

The King's eyes searched his courtiers. At last, they settled on a colorful jester dozing up in the minstrel's gallery. Rivold whistled, and the clown bolted upright in his seat.

"Majan," Rivold called up to the balcony. "Majan, come down. We need some entertainment."

"Right away, O King!" The jester's voice quivered as he jumped out of his chair.

The courtiers laughed at the spectacle of Majan frantically hobbling down from the minstrel's gallery to the chamber floor. In an exaggerated display, the jester slipped down the last few stairs before doing a cartwheel and landing on his feet. Even Walaric joined in the applause as he forgot his troubles.

The bells on the jester's bright red and green cap jingled as he took several long strides towards the high table. The aging retainer next to Walaric sniggered. Furrowing his brow, he turned to the grizzled knight.

"Lord Briac always enters court just like that," the retainer whispered as he pointed between the jester and one of the lords seated at a nearby table. "Majan the Fool does such a good impression."

"Oh," Walaric answered as a few more knights and dames laughed at the ridiculous display.

Lord Briac crossed his arms and scoffed.

"My king, I beseech thee!" The jester threw his arms out dramatically. "Only you can answer my prayer."

"What is it, Lord Majan?" Rivold cracked a smile.

"My dear wife has left me for another lover." Majan the Fool wiped false tears from his eyes.

"Who is it?" Rivold demanded. "Where did she go?"

"She can be found in the royal stables with the bravest knight in all the realm of Sval." The jester winked. "The King's horse!"

Most of the courtiers roared with laughter, but Lord Briac turned red as he sank deeper into his seat. Walaric also laughed at the absurdity, but Briac's indignant expression hinted at some deeper cut than what he could glean. Majan the Fool brayed and danced in a circle before taking a knee in front of the high table.

"Of course," Majan continued after the laughter had died down, "we cannot blame you, my king, for the fact that your bravest knight is your horse. I shudder to think of being called upon to face a death knight."

The jester rose and yelped as if quailing in terror. He spun and jumped as his eyes darted from one end of the great hall to the other. Walaric chuckled.

"Just keep giving your lands to the Silver Suns." Majan the Fool pointed an accusing finger at Rivold. "And they'll take on the fight."

Some laughed at this joke. Others, including Rivold, grew quiet. Walaric looked between the King and his retainer for some explanation, but none followed. Even Queen Jelske's face grew sour at this. The line between humor and insult was a fine one, indeed.

Walaric puzzled over this joke. The Silver Suns did have a large chapter house for the overall size of Sval. Perhaps Tyche had forced the King to give up more of his estates than he would have liked.

"Then again." The jester raised his eyebrow at Walaric. "Every season brings new ways. Perhaps the strength of the Silver Suns is all spent, if it takes a priest to vanquish a lich these days."

"I hardly really did anything." Walaric blushed amidst the laughter. "Fionn, Izold, Jordan, Candac; they were the real heroes in Gardesh's dungeon."

The greying retainer next to Walaric's seat nodded sympathetically, but no one else acknowledged his words. Majan the Fool proceeded with a series of bawdy jokes concerning other lords and ladies Walaric guessed were also in the crowd. Though Walaric flushed in embarrassment to hear such details concerning these people's love lives, their laughter rose as they all took turns as the punchline to the jester's quibbles.

"And let's not forget that harlot, Queen Moswen." The jester popped his hips in a way that might have been seductive were he a young woman and not a man approaching middle age.

"You would think a woman of the Sudlands would want a little warmth at night after coming this far north." Majan wagged his finger. "But something about the King's bed made her decide the dead were of greater worth."

Walaric snorted at the way Majan made *north* and *worth* rhyme. A few members of the audience sniggered at this joke, but most took note of the King's increasingly red face and refrained. Rivold gripped his mug so tightly that Walaric feared he might snap the handle off. The jester gasped, and his eyes widened as he met the King's gaze.

"But as our good lord can always be heard saying," the jester stammered, "he is not his father. Forgive Majan the Fool for this shame. It's not my lord's fault you share the same name."

"I am not my father," Rivold muttered under his breath before relaxing his grip on the handle of his mug.

Walaric leaned in close to the older knight who sat next to him. The situation was too awkward for him to ignore. Eventually, he tugged on the retainer's sleeve.

"Oh." The knight's wrinkled face contorted as the jester returned to his braying and dancing. "Rivold's father sided with Queen Moswen during the last eclipse. Morgan the Bloodied had to kill them both in the battle for Sval."

Walaric gasped. He turned to Rivold. The King once again was laughing with the audience at Majan the Fool's antics. He paid Walaric no attention.

"That's why he hates his father?" Walaric whispered back to the knight beside him.

"It's hardly a secret at Sval." The older retainer subtly nodded towards the King. "But he will live with this shame for all of his life. It's best not to bring it up if you can help it. There have been people at court who have used this information to their advantage."

"There's hardly any kingdom here to fight over," Walaric scoffed. "It's just one city."

The retainer snorted and sat up straight again. Walaric bit his lip. The old knight gave him a cold stare, but soon focused on the jester again and began chuckling at his latest impression of some other lord in the audience. Sval might not have been worth much to most people, but it was worth everything to these people.

Majan the Fool continued his performance for some time. Walaric laughed with the courtiers at some of the more absurd parts, but his lack of familiarity with Sval's aristocracy left him more confused when other gags were performed. To Walaric's relief, the tension in King Rivold's hand had lessened significantly since the joke about Queen Moswen preferring undead lovers to the last king. Perhaps now was a good time to make his exit.

"My king." Walaric nudged Rivold's hand. "It has been a pleasure to be entertained at your court."

"Leaving so soon?" The King clasped Walaric's hand. "Please come back any time you'd like. Remember, you will always be a friend of Sval."

"I won't forget it," the priest promised.

Walaric rose from his seat and left the high table. Queen Jelske's eyes followed him as he skirted the perimeter of the great hall. He gave a heavy sigh and pretended not to notice. Whatever she had in mind, he wanted no part of it.

Despite the chill, Walaric strode about the high city after exiting the citadel. Few shops were open, but the Sun was high in the air. Spring was coming.

Frowning, Walaric turned his gaze westward. Godfrey and Madeline's wedding would be soon. He was going to miss it. He knew, deep down, he would when he first set out on this quest, but now there was no doubt.

He shuddered as his thoughts turned to Dolon, Keeper of Souls. Somewhere in Mirtys, that accursed creature hid in the shadows. If Gardesh the Pale could prove the end of Paschal, Candac, Fionn of Cromant, and so many other noble warriors, what chance did Walaric, Jordan, and Izold have against the Keeper of Souls?

"Candac," Walaric groaned. "O cruel Fate. It should have been me instead of him. Surely, the gods had greater things in store?"

He turned to Sval's temple. It was a relatively austere structure, smaller than any of the temples at Vindholm, and much reduced in grandeur. The pediment's decorations were simpler, and the podium did not stand as tall as others. With a grimace, Walaric marched down the road to it.

Ascending the stairs, Walaric reflected on the first time he had climbed the steps to the Temple of Spes with Godfrey. This was not nearly as steep or as high. Almost everything about Sval paled in comparison to just about every other city he had visited. It was still a city, but a small grey one, at that.

Walaric pushed open the temple doors and was met by the gaze of a curious priest tending the fire of the sanctum's hearth. The old cleric frowned at him as he shut the doors. Finally, Walaric cleared his throat.

"Forgive the intrusion." Walaric bowed his head.

"Come in, brother." The older priest gestured for Walaric to step closer. "I am Father Nithard. You make no intrusion. We're just unaccustomed to many travelers here."

"Thank you for having me." Walaric made a pious gesture. "I am Walaric, *Father* Walaric, that is."

"You'll grow accustomed to the title in time." Nithard gave a faint smile.

"To whom is this temple dedicated?" Walaric asked as he looked over the statues behind the altar at the far end of the sanctum.

Two of the marble figures were winged angels, roughly the size of men. However, the central figure in the group stood about twelve feet tall and had the appearance of a young athletic man in a fine tunic. Walaric might have mistaken him for Helios were his hair not cut shorter than what was usually depicted adorning the Sun God.

"Aloeus," Nithard answered.

"A son of Helios." Walaric sighed in relief. "I should have come here when I first arrived. Many hard things have troubled my mind, and I have struggled through them without good counsel or divine guidance."

"There are many troubles in this world to darken the mind." The cleric's expression grew somber as he met Walaric's eyes.

"I am on a quest," Walaric explained, "and we have lost friends to Gardesh the Pale when we confronted the lich in his dungeon."

"The entire city speaks of the lich's demise and your great deeds." Father Nithard stroked his stubbled chin.

"Will you pray for my friends?" Walaric asked. "They died in a most gruesome manner."

"Of course," the cleric agreed.

"They were Sir Paschal and Sir Candac," Walaric said. "They were young, brave knights who fell too early."

He handed the old man all the silver coins he had left. Only the gold funerary coin that Walaric had Dachlann mint remained in his pouch. That was for Dolon, Keeper of Souls, Walaric mused as he glanced into the bag he had grabbed the other coins from.

"Please accept this silver for the sacrifices to be made in their names." Walaric held the silver out to the priest.

"Keep it." Nithard pushed the coins back with his bony hand. "You and your friends have certainly earned a sacrifice to Aloeus at the temple's expense."

"You're most kind." The silver clinked as Walaric dropped the coins back in his pouch. "What can you tell me about Dolon, the Keeper of Souls?"

"I'm afraid there is little I can tell you that others cannot." The old priest recoiled at the question. "He is truly ancient, even for an undead monster. His name is elvish, though none among the living have seen him well enough to say what his race truly is."

"There are undead elves?" Walaric raised an eyebrow.

"Certainly." Father Nithard swallowed. "Tales of dark elves can be found in a few books of arcane lore. We know they had a hand in bringing down the Empire more than six hundred years ago. Necromancers, warlocks, and other foul sorcerers were among them."

"I never read of the elves being anything other than an inherent force for good and order in the world." Walaric furrowed his brow.

"You would be mostly right," the venerable cleric agreed, "but even angels can fall from grace."

"My quest ultimately takes me to Dolon," Walaric explained. "He holds the key to the Great Witch of the North's ghost remaining in the mortal sphere. I must undo the curse that binds her here."

"The Blighted Lands are harsh." Nithard crossed his arms. "But Mirtys is the city of the damned. They say zombies and ghouls teem within its walls. From its towers, horrors watch that do not sleep. Death knights and worse patrol its withered hinterland. And vampires feast on human sacrifices every night in their high city."

"And I must go there as quickly as I can." Walaric clenched his jaw. "The Great Witch of the North's spirit is on her way there if she has not made it to Dolon already. Who can say what evil she will bring to this world if she is allowed to commune with the Keeper of Souls?"

For a moment, the gaunt, elderly cleric silently grimaced. Walaric knew the risk was great from the very beginning. Was the quest worth it?

"Allow me to leave you a blessing before we part." Father Nithard gestured for Walaric to come to the altar on the other side of the hearth.

Walaric's feet echoed against the stone floor as he approached the altar. Father Nithard positioned himself on the other side of the stone block just behind the outstretched arms of Aloeus' image. As Walaric knelt in front of the altar, Nithard placed his hands on the younger priest's head. The old cleric began to pray in the ancient celestial language, but Walaric knew it well.

"*Aloeus, son of Helios,*" Nithard spoke in the celestial tongue, "*You see a servant of your father on a perilous quest. He journeys to a place from whence few return. Grant him safety until he puts the shade of the Great Witch of the North to rest. Give him courage, though his traveling companions fall before him. Bless Walaric, servant of Helios, with these things. Amen.*"

"Amen." Walaric stood after Nithard removed his hands. "I think I can do this now. Waiting for Sir Jordan to recover won't be so bad."

"I do not suspect you will need to wait long." The old cleric smiled ruefully.

"I don't understand." Walaric crossed his arms as he glared at Sir Jordan, who was sitting up in his hospital bed. "You're not coming the rest of the way with us when we are so close to the Blighted Lands?"

"I'm not abandoning you." Jordan shifted with a pained expression. "I'm saying you two should go on without me."

"We've waited this long for you to recover." Walaric turned to Izold, who stood at the other end of Sir Jordan's bed. "What's a few more days?"

"The doctors did not say a few more days," Izold clarified. "They said he should not try to walk or ride until at least spring. That's further off than you think."

"You said haste was a priority," Jordan added. "We took the long road to the Blighted Lands, but now they are before you. Do not stand idle on my account."

"But we need you," Walaric protested. "Izold has been to the northern part of the Blighted Lands, but he doesn't know the Dovern Highlands."

"I don't know these lands either." Jordan shook his head. "I cannot guide you further. I'm sorry."

"What about your steel?" Walaric asked. "We need your shield and your mace. Paschal and Candac can't lend us theirs anymore."

"I don't know how well I could fight even after I am able to walk again." Jordan's gaze fell to his blanket. "I need to be able to run, jump, and surge forward and back in a fight. I could be limping for some time even after I can walk from one place to another."

Walaric sighed. Jordan had a good point. If only Madeline were here. Her healing fire could have closed the wound instantly and probably prevented the infection, too.

"And I agree we should go now." Izold nodded. "Tivelden Forest has been cleared of undead, but the Dovern Highlands have gotten worse. The necromancers' mists still spill down from those hills. Delaying for Sir Jordan's sake may hurt our overall chances of reaching Mirtys at all. We should leave now."

"Spoken true, as usual," Walaric sighed.

"Trust the gods," Izold insisted. "They have a plan."

"Candac died," Walaric murmured. "I thought they had a plan for him."

"He saved your life more than once." Izoldscolded. "Perhaps preserving your life was his greater purpose. Whether it was or not, he now rests in Spes with the celestial gods. Do not make his sacrifice for naught."

"Right again." Walaric frowned. "Did I not use those same arguments with Paschal earlier?"

"They will be missed." A single tear rolled down Jordan's cheek. "Go forth with haste. The Sun's blessing is upon you both."

Chapter Eighteen

After sipping her ice berry wine from the golden goblet she held, Madeline smacked her lips in satisfaction. The sweet aftertaste lingered well after she swallowed the crimson sour swig. It had been prepared with skill she had hardly conceived of before she reached Farthest Thule. Now, she could hardly remember the taste of the food and drink she had previously been accustomed to.

Fravash licked the corners of his mouth after gobbling up a slice of silky cheese from a small plate beside Madeline's. The mouse, like Madeline, had dined very well over the last few weeks in the chamber they now rested in. While the volume of food and drink could be called anything but plentiful, the flavor of even the most mundane meals was exquisite. Madeline's stomach never once grumbled from hunger before or after a meal, at any rate.

Across the table from Madeline sat a tall, proud elf lord. Much like the other elves she had met at Farthest Thule, his smooth skin shone almost as white as the unblemished ivory columns that lined the walls leading to the balcony outside. His hair was a sparkling silver, and his eyes a deep cerulean. His robes glittered red and gold like the ice berry wine in the goblet by his plate.

"Lord Bion." Madeline blushed between bites of succulent turkey. "We cannot thank you enough for hosting us while we await Anistemi."

"I am honored to fulfill this duty on behalf of the Queen." The elf's words rolled off his tongue like a flute's melody. "But you must understand that I am obliged to do everything in my power to stay in her good graces. Think nothing of it."

"Do you fear you may fall out of Queen Kypris' good graces?" Madeline raised an eyebrow.

"Opinions at the royal court are always shifting." Bion took a bite of his turkey. "Even in a realm as static as Vathepoli, one can never be too sure of his position."

"That sounds just like how affairs are run in the kingdoms of men." Madeline twirled a strand of her hair.

"Elves also have long memories." Bion gave a sympathetic look. "Favors are remembered, but faults, failings, and insults are remembered longer."

Madeline shivered.

"Forgive me for the cold," Bion added. "This house was built after the phoenix came to Vathepoli. It has not been strengthened against the cold like my last home."

A smile curled Madeline's lip. While the chamber's polished stone walls and floor were colder than she would have liked, the elvish dress she had been gifted was laced with strands of warm phoenix feathers. Madeline could not decide whether this marvel should be attributed to elvish craftsmanship, phoenix magic, or both.

"It's not been a bother to me," Madeline answered. "I'm as warm as anyone could hope to be in this weather. Besides, I'm told Anistemi will soon be strong enough to warm Farthest Thule. I will be fine until then."

Madeline paused awkwardly. She had wanted to ask this question since she first arrived at Farthest Thule. Dare she ask it now? Had she been among the elves long enough to gain their trust?

"Where is Kypris' husband?" Madeline blushed as she cast her eyes down at the table. "His throne still sits beside the Queen's in the palace. Yet he is nowhere to be seen. Surely, others would want to sit beside her."

Fravash coughed, but Madeline ignored him. She had to know. For a moment, Bion said nothing. Instead, he swirled the contents of his goblet with a soft roll of his wrist. A forlorn expression creased his face.

"We elves grieve loss far longer than men," Bion said at last. "The curse of our long lives is to witness so much change. We don't grow attached to much, but when we lose what we do love, that loss is always keenly felt. There are those who would like to take upon themselves the title King of Vathepoli, but none dare make a move while the Queen's heart is still broken."

"I see." Madeline frowned. "But what happened to the elf king? How long has he been gone?"

"His name was King Hagios." Bion folded his hands over the table. "He rose to save our people after the collapse of the Empire. With Fravash's help, he gained Anistemi's companionship and gathered as many of us to Vathepoli as were willing to go. He made our city the bastion it is today."

Madeline leaned forward in her seat, enamoured by Bion's story. Every word he spoke carried weight yet was delivered with sublime elegance. No mortal man she knew could mimic this art he performed so effortlessly.

"In the early days of his rule," Bion continued, "I was the captain of Hagios' picked swords. We drove back the trolls, the orcs, and the frost lions. Even the Nordsman Clans sang songs of terror about us in their halls."

His eyes growing dark, Bion turned away from Madeline for a moment. So much pain boiled just beneath the surface of his face. Madeline marveled at the level of control he was able to maintain.

"Your pain is a great burden." Madeline bit her lip. "A pity you must bear it alone."

"This truly could have been a great kingdom." Bion shook his head. "But the King unknowingly allowed Skodari into Vathepoli's gates."

"Skodari?" Madeline raised an eyebrow.

"Traitors." Bion scowled. "You would call them dark elves. They are hedonists beholden to foul rituals. They helped bring down the Empire from within, and they still seek to corrupt every haven of elvish civilization they can."

"There are still dark elves to be found?" Madeline pursed her lips.

"They are a rare sight these days, but not unknown among the elves," Fravash interjected. "They hide in pirate coves and black marshes, mostly."

"One of the Skodari," Bion continued, "Dolon, led an uprising not long after we had secured our borders. He murdered Hagios after leading astray many of our noble and great princes. We drove the traitors out, but at great cost."

"I heard a minstrel from Sval once mention a cadaverous beast named Dolon." Madeline tightly twisted a strand of her dark hair around her finger. "He was some terrifying necromancer of great power."

"Dolon was obsessed with the state of immortal souls for as long as I knew him." Bion shook his head. "Few in Vathepoli would be surprised to learn that obsession had eventually led him to necromancy."

Blinking, Madeline pondered this revelation for a long moment. She stabbed the last bite of her turkey with her fork before swallowing it. Even after sitting on her plate through the whole meal, it had not grown cold.

"The Queen does not have picked swordsmen of her own," Madeline noted. "I thought your people would all but refuse to abandon tradition."

"To my shame." Bion clenched his fists. "Some of the worst Skodari infiltrated the King's picked swords. Much blood was shed in the palace the night King Hagios was murdered on the throne. Queen Kypris disbanded the picked swords once we had crushed the rebellion."

"Oh." Madeline swallowed hard. "I am sorry to hear that. That was very unfair."

"Unfair is an understatement." Bion glowered.

Biting her lip, Madeline struggled to find anything meaningful to add. Though she was sure this rebellion and its fallout had concluded many years ago, the pain in Bion's voice was still fresh. Sometimes it was better to just nod in agreement and not say anything.

Madeline turned her attention to her goblet and drained the last of her ice berry wine. Soon, the evening meal concluded as a few elvish servants silently cleared away the dishes. Though just as regal in their overall appearance as any elves Madeline had seen in Farthest Thule, the servants' dress and hairstyles were simpler, and they maintained a deferential attitude. Some things stayed the same even across racial boundaries.

"Perhaps I could entertain you with a song?" Bion raised an eyebrow as the servants retreated with the last of the dirty dishes.

"Please do." Madeline leaned forward in her seat again, glad to see the elf lord's mood improve. "I love listening to your music."

Lord Bion grabbed a gilded ivory lyre from a wooden stand set against one of the walls. After tuning the strings, he began to strum an ancient melody. The tension in Madeline's muscles melted away as he began to sing a soothing countermelody.

Madeline sighed. Bion's song was as rich in its lyrics as it was in its chords. He was as much an artist as he was a warrior. Could any maiden ask for more?

Though Bion's song moved at a brisk pace, Madeline caught most of the elvish lyrics. Some nights, Bion sang songs about former glories and heroes long gone. Other nights, his songs were about the Wyrmwind Peaks and the isolation of Farthest Thule. Tonight, his song was about beauty and spring.

Fravash bounced his paw to the rhythm of Bion's verse. Madeline smirked. Just a few months ago, could she have imagined herself in Farthest Thule being sung to by a handsome elvish lord in the company of a talking mouse?

At last, Bion's final chorus came to an end. Madeline pouted. What a shame it could not continue longer.

"While you are guests in my house, Fravash..." Bion replaced his lyre on the wooden stand. "I wonder if I could trouble you to review a couple of works in my library this evening. I trust my sages were accurate in copying their manuscripts, but I have been vexed by certain discrepancies in the accounts. I would greatly appreciate any annotations you could offer."

"I would be happy to set the records straight." The mouse's ears perked up.

"Excellent." Bion clapped his hands. "Phlios will show you the way. He knows the books in question."

Fravash hopped off the table and scampered to the doorway, where another lithesome servant waited for him. Phlios cupped his hand and knelt. The mouse climbed into the elf's hand, and the two disappeared beyond the doorway. Now it was just Madeline and Bion alone.

"Let me escort you to your room, Lady Madeline." Bion extended his hand.

"Thank you, Lord Bion." Madeline bowed her head.

Madeline stood. She took a deep breath. Trembling, she extended her hand to Bion's. For a brief moment, her eyes met his. Frowning, she turned her attention to the doorway as they passed through it. She had best not let her imagination carry her too far.

"I am very glad Fravash brought you here," Bion beamed at Madeline. "It has been a very long time since we've had any visitors from among the children of men, and much longer since we've seen a talented sorceress such as you."

"Your people do not make it easy for us to visit you." Madeline raised an eyebrow.

"Not all of us would have it be that way." Bion shook his head. "But the fall of the Empire convinced most of my brethren that the affairs of men should no longer concern my people."

"Why is that?" Madeline stopped in her tracks.

The corridor to the guest chambers before her was long and dark. The light of the Moon and stars pierced only a few large windows. Small statues of nymphs and other fey creatures lined the alcoves. Staring into the inky darkness, Bion stopped beside her.

"We spent so long building the Empire." Bion opened a set of doors and stepped out onto a balcony running parallel to the corridor. "Men, elves, and dwarves all worked together. It seemed, for a time, that all of Aestas was within our grasp."

Madeline followed Bion as he led her by the hand onto the balcony. She shivered at the sight of the snow covering the rooftops and streets. All was still.

"Then, when times got hard, the dwarves retreated to their mountain halls." Bion gestured out to the Wyrmwind Peaks beyond Farthest Thule's walls. "The men became divided. The oligarchs' laws meant nothing, and the legions would just as soon raise kings unto themselves as they would put down a rebellion or stop an invasion."

"Begging your pardon," Madeline interjected, "but it sounds like those dark elves played a pretty large role in the unraveling of the Empire, too."

"I would agree." Bion gave a sad smile as he leaned against the balcony railing. "Many threats from within and without plagued the Empire for a long time. But most of my brethren blame men and dwarves for being ungrateful and not doing more to stop the crises. After all, we taught them our crafts, our laws, and our arts. Now your people remember almost nothing of them."

Bion sighed and stepped back into the house. He still gripped Madeline's hand with surprising firmness, and she was obliged to continue walking beside him. After a moment, he loosened his grip before stopping in front of a large window several paces away from the balcony.

"I believe there is still hope for our peoples despite the sorrow of the past." Bion's eyes gleamed as he glanced between the Moon's pale light in the starry sky and Madeline's face. "Selene favors me this night. The Moon's whispers cannot be ignored. You are the most beautiful woman I have seen in many centuries."

"That is quite the compliment." Madeline adjusted the engagement ring on her finger.

The Moon reflected in the elf's long, silvery hair through the hallway's spacious windows. His stance was firm, disciplined. Every move he made was decisive.

"If I may be so bold, Lady Madeline." Bion leaned against the windowsill just before the door to her bed chambers. "My wife, Kydilla, left us many seasons ago. I believe my season of grief is coming to an end. After having you in my home, I believe I am ready to move on."

"That is very bold." Madeline's leg wobbled.

"When you first came here, you spoke of renewing the elves of Vathepoli." Bion took a step closer to Madeline. "You asked why we idle away our lives when our survival hangs in the balance. The elves are not too haughty to see the danger we are in. But we often move too slowly to change the course of events in our favor."

Madeline gulped. Bion was tall and limber. His features were sophisticated beyond compare. Godfrey was strong and brave, but he was only modestly educated and only as refined as mortal men could be.

"We need new blood coursing through Vathepoli's veins." Bion stroked Madeline's cheek. "A marriage, sons, and daughters; you would have limitless access to the magic of my people. You would never want again."

"How generous!" Madeline gasped.

"Our half-elf children would spark the new life into our city it so desperately needs." Bion ran his fingers through Madeline's hair. "They would have the grace of the elves but the ferocity of mankind. They would be lions."

"And their lives?" Madeline pulled back a step. "What would their lives be like here?"

"Half-elves can easily live to be one hundred and fifty to two hundred years old." Bion frowned.

"That's a lot longer than men, but nowhere near the millennium that elves live." Madeline brushed Bion's hand away. "How would the elves of Farthest Thule see children of mixed blood?"

"They would grow to be accepted in time…" Bion's words trailed off. "But once they come into their own, they could be dynamic leaders; heroes of renown. The magic in your blood gives you a special place here. I can all but promise that gift would pass down to our children, too. Sorcerous abilities would gain them respect."

"That's a lot to think about." Madeline took a deep breath. "But I'm already promised to Godfrey de Bastogne. I cannot forget about that."

"I can offer you so much more than even the noblest of your race." Bion stepped to the side; the passion in his voice was quickly replaced by the stoicism she had grown to know so well among the elves. "But I am patient. Tell me when you have thought about it enough."

Blushing, Madeline swept past the elf lord and pushed open the door to her bed chambers. Her knees shaking, she closed it behind her with a thud. Her trembling hand reminded her too much of Godfrey's.

Two more days passed awkwardly for Madeline. Bion did not speak again of his proposal to her, but his burning question bored into her soul every time she spotted him. Beneath his steely gaze, whether in passing through a corridor, balcony, or his home's many luxurious chambers, she quivered at his desire.

Lord Bion had a library he often visited with more magical lore and books of poetry than she could have hoped to read in a lifetime. He spent his mornings training with the sword or practicing with the bow in his home's spacious courtyard. He had stables and proud horses he regularly took riding in Farthest Thule's hinterland. Madeline was always welcome to participate in any of these activities, though she had refrained since he asked her to marry him. Was Godfrey really the better match?

"You look troubled." Fravash twitched his whiskers as he stood on the balcony railing Madeline leaned against.

In the courtyard below, Lord Bion practiced his swordsmanship against a wood and sackcloth dummy. His movements were nimble and precise. His speed was unmatched. Surely, no man or beast could stand against him in single combat.

"I'm just anxious about Anistemi." Madeline turned towards the mouse. "What if she does not grant me an audience? What do we do then?"

"Don't worry about that." Fravash twitched his tail. "The guardians of the grove give all petitioners an honest appraisal. The phoenix will decide when she is ready."

"How will she decide without meeting me?" Madeline put her hands on her hips. "And I've barely had any interactions with Baucis or the other guardians of the grove. It all seems so arbitrary."

"Anistemi and her kind can see things most of us cannot," Fravash reassured her. "No one I know has ever pronounced a phoenix's judgment false."

"I guess that's comforting." She twirled a strand of her hair between her fingers.

For a long while, she leaned against the balcony's rail. The sky above was still dark even in the middle of the day. Could she get used to such long seasons of twilight?

"Fravash." Madeline squirmed as a knot twisted in her stomach. "If you had to choose between staying at Farthest Thule and returning to Olso Fortress, which would you decide on?"

"Well." Fravash cleared his throat. "Tying oneself to any particular spot is always a difficult choice. I'm just glad I'm more unfettered than most."

"I'm not asking because I thought it would be an easy choice." Madeline scolded. "Go on. Answer the question. Which would you pick?"

"If *I* had to choose between Farthest Thule and Olso Fortress, I would pick Farthest Thule." The mouse crossed his arms. "I am a magical creature and am more at home with elves than men. But I suspect your question is more about *you* than me."

"All right, if you were me, which would you choose?" Madeline crossed her arms.

For a moment, Madeline's gaze fell upon Lord Bion. Fravash's eyes followed. The rodent squeaked in what she decided was something close to contempt.

"You are of the race of men and belong with your kind," Fravash chirped. "You may find yourself a friend to the elves and a revered friend once you unlock the full potential of your magic. But you will never be one of them. The differences will always be too great to overcome."

"Did you not work so hard to persuade me to come to Farthest Thule in the first place?" Madeline raised an eyebrow. "Why do you now say I don't belong here?"

"Vathepoli is a refuge for elves," Fravash answered. "They have many lessons for you to learn about the arcane arts, but I never meant for us to stay forever."

Madeline sighed, deflated. The possibilities of Farthest Thule were endless. Was she ready for this answer?

"Some of the elves seem accepting enough." She frowned as Bion began to settle down from his exercises with slower repetitions of his sword forms. "Some have said that my magical abilities could give me a place of honor among the elves. Men fear me back home. Even Godfrey sometimes gets scared."

"Alas, that is your curse." Fravash put his paw on Madeline's hand. "A sorceress is never at home among her own people or abroad. You and you alone have to decide where your home truly is."

Madeline sighed as Bion handed his sword to a squire and left the courtyard. What did she really feel for Bion? Was it love? Infatuation? Or was it only Farthest Thule and the majesty of the elves she loved?

"Do you not love Godfrey, at least?" Fravash's gaze pierced Madeline to the core. "You came here to gain these powers to strengthen his realm."

"How do I know I'm in love?" Madeline stammered. "Sometimes I think I love Godfrey, but the more we're apart, the less sure I am."

"There are different kinds of love, Lady Madeline." Fravash gestured out to the courtyard. "You love ice berry wine because it tastes pleasant. You love the elves because they are beautiful and refined. These are very superficial kinds of love. If there were anything unpleasant about them, you would not love them anymore."

"I suppose you're right." Madeline nodded.

"You love your friends because they treat you well," Fravash continued, "but you love your brothers even when they don't behave as they should."

Madeline bit her lip. For all of Arius and Berig's faults, she did not truly wish any harm on them. If they disappeared, she would probably miss them, too.

"Deeper kinds of love are about more than beauty and pleasure," the mouse explained. "They're about sacrifice and commitment. Your father, though even more flawed than your brothers, would do anything within his power to keep you happy and safe, would he not?"

"Yes," Madeline agreed.

"Do you think Godfrey would do anything within his power to keep you happy and safe?" Fravash asked.

Madeline took a deep breath. Godfrey bested Conrad the Wolf for her hand. He rescued her from being sacrificed to Vozzab. He saved her from being ensnared by *The Book of Elder Wisdom* and risked his life for her on other occasions besides. He was determined to have her, at any rate.

"Most of the time, I think he loves me," Madeline answered at last. "But there was an uglier side of him I saw when Olso was under siege, and it seems that I'm only his highest priority until something else comes up."

"He's a young man and a new duke." The mouse shook his head. "He will learn the proper balance of all those things in time. Now, do you think you'd be willing to sacrifice something truly important for him, or do you just take pleasure in his company?"

Madeline furrowed her brow. She had risked exposing her magic back in Biorkon when she used it to heal Godfrey after the crusaders' arrival. She had crossed the Irelven with him in their efforts to find Farthest Thule. How much further would she go for him? What would she be willing to give up for him?

Baucis and Queen Kypris stood in the central hall of Bion's home. Somber expressions creased their faces. Bion's mood appeared no more pleasant. Madeline could only guess at the centuries-long history that defined their relationships. How many slights, insults, and other bitter exchanges did they still hold onto after all this time?

"How good of you to take care of Lady Madeline for us." The Queen frowned at Bion.

"It is *your* custom that the children of men should not stay in the palace," Bion answered stiffly. "I did everything I could to make her stay *here* enjoyable. Thank you for giving me the opportunity to prove my worth."

"You did well—" Kypris began.

"We certainly did enjoy our time here," Fravash cut in as he stood upright on Madeline's shoulder. "Lord Bion has been a most gracious host to us."

"He can be a gracious host when he wants to." The Queen's amethyst eyes gleamed at Lord Bion.

Briefly, Lord Bion bowed his head. Kypris' gaze had not faltered by the time he looked up again. The faintest smile cracked his lips before he cleared his throat.

Madeline blushed as Bion's eyes met hers. It had been almost a week, and she still had no answer for his proposal. She had not directly told Fravash about the exchange beyond her hints about staying in Farthest Thule. It should not have been such a difficult choice. Could she muster the courage to decide one way or the other?

"We have spoken with Anistemi." Kypris gestured to Madeline. "She will see you now."

Madeline sighed in relief. She would get her chance to commune with the phoenix. Would Anistemi prove just as proud as the elves she protected?

"Wonderful," the mouse answered. "We're ready to go see the phoenix right away."

"You must stay here, Fravash." Baucis shook her head. "I can only allow Lady Madeline to commune with the phoenix right now. She is still young and vulnerable."

"You don't trust *me?*" Fravash's eyes gaped. "I was hoping to mediate between Madeline and Anistemi."

"Take no offense," Baucis insisted. "We merely need to take extra precautions until Anistemi is fully matured. If Lady Madeline is to commune with the phoenix at this time, she must do so alone, and she may bring nothing with her but her staff."

The mouse crossed his arms. An indignant expression creased his face. However, his grimace subsided as Madeline sympathetically stroked the top of his head.

"It's all right, Fravash." Madeline exchanged a glance with the mouse as she gently grabbed him from her shoulder. "I understand."

Pursing her lips, Madeline knelt as she set Fravash on the perfectly smooth stone floor. It was cold to the touch. Briefly, he held onto her finger with his paws.

"Don't be scared." Fravash released her finger. "Ask your question, and the phoenix will answer. Be honest about everything she asks, and Anistemi will help us."

"Of course." Madeline smiled as she rose to her feet.

Though she still smiled as she turned to face the elves, panic gripped Madeline's heart. Was her motivation pure enough? Would the phoenix ask about Godfrey or Bion's marriage proposal? Would the phoenix want Madeline to stay in Farthest Thule or leave as quickly as possible?

Baucis pointed to the satyr's blade on Madeline's belt. Flushing, she hastily removed it and set it on one of the tables against the wall. She had forgotten it was there. Praise the gods she had not needed to use it while out in the Wyrmwind Peaks.

The guardian of the grove approached Madeline and briskly ran her hands over her arms and legs. Fuming, Madeline stammered at being searched so thoroughly in front of everyone present. However, Baucis' invasive touching was over after a short moment. "Why didn't you search me the first time I saw Anistemi?" Madeline clenched her jaw.

"The phoenix was already dying," Baucis scoffed. "You could not have changed that outcome. Anistemi, however, is young and not yet able to bear eggs. We must be much more thorough in our precautions now."

Satisfied, Baucis then gestured to the door leading outside. Queen Kypris began walking towards it. Madeline offered one last smile to Fravash, and the mouse winked. Bion cleared his throat as Madeline began to pass him by.

"If answering my question is too difficult..." Bion's cerulean eyes penetrated Madeline's very soul. "You don't need to say the words. I believe I already have my answer."

"Oh, Bion!" Madeline squeezed his hand. "I wish I could say, but I truly do not have an answer yet. Allow me to visit with Anistemi first. I think I will be able to speak more clearly after that."

"Of course, Lady Madeline." Bion bowed his head before releasing his hand from hers.

Queen Kypris and Baucis exchanged a glance with Lord Bion but said nothing. Madeline gulped as she regained her composure. How much of Bion's desires and schemes were they aware of?

The Queen, Baucis, and Madeline strolled through the gardens, colonnades, and forum of the high city before returning to the majestic palace. Despite the beauty, the skies were still dark. Ethereal light glowed from lamps lining the streets, but it was not nearly as good as true daylight. Could Madeline really live here?

Neither Queen Kypris nor Baucis spoke a word to Madeline or each other as they passed the mansions of the elf lords and ladies of the high city. She clenched her jaw. Bion had said her magical abilities would grant her acceptance among the elves, but she certainly did not feel that way now. Aloof glances were the best she could find here from most of Farthest Thule's residents. Maybe that would change after she spoke with the phoenix?

At last, they reached the palace. The guards Madeline had met the first time she arrived in Farthest Thule immediately parted for them after saluting the Queen. Kypris returned the gesture, and they entered the gilded halls without further obstacles.

As they marched through the palace's chambers, the Queen and Baucis exchanged cold glances. The gestures were so subtle, Madeline might not have noticed had she not been walking between the two. Perhaps the silent contempt she had observed on the journey between Lord Bion's manor and the royal palace was not directed at her so much as it was between them?

A pair of elves in cataphract armor stood near the entrance to the palace courtyard. They lightly bowed their heads to Madeline. At first, she did not recognize them, but she drew in a deep breath as comprehension dawned on her.

"Trophnus!" she cried. "Mygdon! I thought you were still on patrol out on the Great Ice."

"We were given permission to see you before your communion with Anistemi," Mygdon explained.

"I appreciate you coming." Madeline smiled. "Friends are a welcome sight here."

"It is a rare and significant event for anyone to be granted an audience before the phoenix, even among our own kind," Trophnus added.

"I do feel honored." Madeline's gaze shifted back to her staff. "So many things have led up to this. And I've been given so much help along the way."

"Your gratitude is noted." Kypris bowed her head. "If Anistemi approves of you, you may yet be called an elf friend in Vathepoli."

"I hope so." Madeline shifted uncertainly.

"Anistemi awaits." Baucis gestured to Madeline.

Waving farewell to Kypris, Trophnus, and Mygdon, Madeline followed Baucis out into the courtyard, where the phoenix's grove was planted. To Madeline's surprise, the courtyard was warm and humid. Not a single snowflake could be seen here.

Another pair of guardians of the grove appeared on Madeline's sides and brusquely searched her as Baucis had done at Lord Bion's home. She gritted her teeth. It was embarrassing to have a woman touch her in front of others. It was infuriating to have men handle her so, even if they were elegant and refined elves.

"A warning." Baucis took Madeline's hand as she led her to the hedge behind which the radiating phoenix rested. "Time passes differently when talking with Anistemi in her grove. A minute with her may be days for us. An hour could be years. It's unpredictable, but prudence suggests you keep your conversation brief if you have reason to care about the passage of time."

Madeline's jaw hung open. No one had told her about that before. It was too late now.

Beyond the hedge, Anistemi perched on a sturdy bough. Her orange, red, and yellow plumage was far brighter than her mother's in old age, though she was only two or three feet tall. Still, Madeline could not help but raise her eyebrow at how much the phoenix had grown from the copper egg she had seen but a few weeks prior.

Baucis bowed to the phoenix, gestured for Madeline to approach her, and then took several strides back until she was behind the hedge again. Anistemi cocked her head at her. Nervously, Madeline stepped forward a pace.

"Thank you for seeing me." Madeline bowed her head. "I have been eager to meet you for a long time."

"I have also been eager to meet you, Madeline of House Drois," the phoenix cooed. "A phoenix smiled upon your mothers long ago. Now I am curious to see if you are worthy of the blessing bestowed upon them."

"Was it you—I mean—your mother who gave my ancestors magic?" Madeline asked.

"Oh, I should think not." The phoenix hooted. "Anistemi spent much of her life in the service of Vathepoli and resided here long before your ancestors came to the Nordslands on their crusades."

"You know a great deal for one so young," Madeline squealed. "How is this possible?"

"A phoenix's mother imparts much wisdom upon her daughters even before they hatch," Anistemi chirped. "Now, I must ask some questions of you before too many more days pass."

Madeline's eyes bulged. She looked up at the sky. It was still twilight, but that did not say much in Farthest Thule from what she had seen. She had to stay focused.

"What do you hope to gain from one of my feathers?" the phoenix asked.

"Fravash the Bright says it could serve as the core of my staff." Madeline held the rod in front of her. "He says it can greatly enhance my powers."

"Fravash the Bright wants to enhance your powers." Anistemi hopped down from her perch and examined Madeline's staff more closely. "Is that what *you* want?"

"Well, yes." Madeline bit her lip. "Why wouldn't I want to reach my full potential?"

"Having even the slightest magical gifts already makes you more powerful than hundreds of thousands of other mortals." The phoenix turned her head this way and that as she continued looking over Madeline's staff. "Why do you need more power?"

"To help others." Madeline shifted on her feet. "Kovdor is beset by many foes. If I can grow as a sorceress, I can better protect my realm."

"Is Kovdor your realm?" The phoenix's dark eyes pierced Madeline's.

"Well, no." Madeline shook her head. "I am betrothed to Godfrey de Bastogne. Kovdor is his duchy."

"I see." Anistemi began preening the feathers on her back. "Do you want to return to the realm of men after seeing everything the elves have to offer?"

"Lord Bion proposed to me not long ago." Madeline averted her eyes. "He is handsome, strong, and refined, but I don't think I love him."

Madeline's gaze returned to the phoenix. The intensity in Anistemi's eyes was unmistakable. Madeline had to make a decision.

"I don't love him." Madeline nodded to herself as much as to the phoenix.

"Are you sure?" Anistemi tilted her head. "You hesitate to answer."

"I…" Madeline shifted her feet with her own conflicting thoughts. "I don't love him."

"Love is a strong consideration for your people when deciding whom to marry?" Anistemi clicked her tongue.

"It can be." Madeline swallowed. "It is for me."

"You don't have to marry a noble elf lord to stay in Vathepoli, should you desire it," the phoenix added. "It's not the elves' way to turn out guests after they are granted entry to Vathepoli. You could stay here your whole life without inconveniencing them."

"There are things that I love about Farthest Thule, but I don't know if I really belong here." Madeline grimaced. "The elves are proud, and their actions are motivated by histories too long for me to fathom. And I have friends at home. I'm starting to miss them."

Anistemi plucked a small feather from one of her wings with her beak. Then she did the same with a feather from her other wing before setting them on the ground in front of Madeline. Did she pass the test?

"This feather will help your fire burn hotter and reach farther." The phoenix indicated the feather on Madeline's left. "It can make you a true terror in battle. The other will help your healing magic mend bones and even regrow lost limbs. Which do you choose?"

"I can choose only one?" Madeline pursed her lips.

"Only one." Anistemi nodded. "Your staff can only contain a single feather as its core."

"Will amplifying the powers of one kind of fire hamper what I can do with the other?" Madeline took a step back from the phoenix.

"No," Anistemi answered. "Your choice will only help you in achieving your desires."

Madeline considered the two feathers for a long moment. There was merit in both options. She thought back to the siege of Olso Fortress, the Clan encampment just out of reach of her fireballs, and the old serf's missing hand. The choice was obvious.

"I want the feather that will improve my healing powers," Madeline answered at last.

"That is a wise choice," the phoenix cooed. "It is better to be loved than feared. You may take it."

"Thank you." Madeline grasped the feather on her right side. "This will be a blessing to everyone I know."

"Indeed it will," Anistemi agreed. "Now, I have much instruction to give you, and your time with me grows short. Pay close attention."

Chapter Nineteen

osy-fingered Dawn could not come early enough for Godfrey. He had slept little, but his eyes snapped open well before the roosters began to crow outside. He knelt beside his bed and offered a prayer to Loxias as he did every morning, but this one was shorter and unfocused. He had a duel to win. What else mattered today?

Mauger rose from his bed next to Godfrey's just as he had finished dressing in the full panoply of war. With a look of disdain, his kinsman began pulling his hauberk over his gambeson. The two had not spoken since they agreed to face each other in combat the previous day. Godfrey clenched his jaw as their eyes met.

"Don't hold back." Mauger glowered. "I won't, and I don't want anyone saying you did after I pummel you to the ground. Understand?"

"I wouldn't dream of it," Godfrey scoffed.

"Get a good breakfast, Mauger." Roltar crossed his arms on the other side of the room just as the first rays of the Sun crested the horizon. "We regain Skasgun and begin the reconquest of all of Stormsud today."

Godfrey frowned at being omitted, but he could hardly blame his cousin. They were at odds now. After so many slights and so much ingratitude, he fumed to think of Roltar and Mauger actually getting what they had set out for.

Mauger slid his tabard over his hauberk before tightening his sword belt across his waist. He scowled at Godfrey but said nothing else. Was there anything left to say after all this?

Without another word, Godfrey saw himself out of the guest chambers and down to the great hall. He clenched his fists and glowered as he stomped through the corridors. Some of Lord Davin's servants greeted him cheerfully at first, but recoiled as he glared at them. There were no friends here.

Down in the great hall, Lady Wia ordered her servants about as they prepared for breakfast. The smells of cooking sausage from the kitchen made Godfrey's mouth salivate and his stomach grumble as he entered the chamber. The welcoming aromas took some of the edge off his anger, and his mind began to wander.

"I am surprised to see you honor House Talhout as my husband's champion after all the contention between Conrad the Wolf and you." Wia placed her hands on her hips as Godfrey approached the hearth.

"I have little good to speak of concerning Conrad the Wolf," Godfrey confessed, "but he is not Lord Davin. He asked me to serve as his champion in this trial by combat, and it is an honorable request. How could I refuse after everything that led to this moment?"

"Does your service to my husband not dishonor your cousins' house?" Wia stirred the glowing coals in the hearth with a hot iron. "I am surprised you accepted the task so readily after everything you have done for them."

"My duty to the King requires me to ensure this trial by combat is conducted fairly." Godfrey bit his lip as the servants began setting platters of food on the tables. "Roltar understands this."

"I can hardly argue against that." Wia shrugged. "But Roltar will hold this against you. I understand he has coveted this fief for a very long time."

Godfrey squirmed uncomfortably.

"You may not have expected to hear this," Wia continued, "but Lord Davin is pleased to have you fighting for him. It is a great honor for us as well."

"I was wondering about that." Godfrey's stomach began to turn as he looked at the House Talhout knights entering the chamber and taking their seats. "Why me? Why not Sir Fedmar or some other knight proven to your cause?"

"You are a dragon-slayer." Wia gestured to Godfrey. "Your skill at arms is unquestioned. You also have a reputation for honesty and piety. No one could ask for a stronger champion."

Godfrey swallowed hard. For a long moment, he stared into the glowing coals of the hearth. He *was* pious and honest. Was it honest or pious for him to work against his cousin now? Could he hold onto the rage that spurred him to accept the challenge against Mauger yesterday?

"Come." Wia set her iron in a brass stand by the hearth and gestured for Godfrey to follow her.

The two made their way to the high table and sat after Lord Davin took his place. Godfrey frowned as Roltar and Mauger found their seats at a table near the back of the room. They could no longer be called *honored* guests if they ever were, but Godfrey still fidgeted in his chair next to Davin. He had journeyed all over Azgald with them. Should he not sit with them still?

He picked at his sausage and eggs. Mauger devoured his in great gulps. The words *don't hold back* echoed in Godfrey's mind. He set his fork down by his plate. What if he did lose on purpose for Roltar and Mauger's sake?

Mauger's eyes burned as they met Godfrey's from across the chamber. His kinsman's jealousy ran deeper than just a piece of land and a title. If given the chance during this duel, would Mauger kill him?

Godfrey shoveled his eggs down his throat. They were bland and already growing lukewarm. His stomach churned as his eyes refused to leave Roltar and Mauger, but he kept eating all the same. Too much was at stake now.

Grabbing his goblet, Godfrey stared at the cold, white milk inside. He swallowed several large draughts before his belly finally began to settle. He had to do this, not just for his own honor or fairness to Davin's cause, but for his very survival. Many a trial by combat ended in maiming, disfigurement, or death. The ferocity in Mauger's eyes said it all; *he* would not hold back.

After taking one last bite of greasy sausage, Godfrey pushed his plate away. Under normal circumstances, he would have eaten more, but too much was on his mind. He had forced as much food into his belly as he could, and it would have to be enough.

The others soon finished their food as well. Quickly, servants began clearing away dirty dishes and what food had not been eaten. After breakfast ended, the tables and benches out on the great hall's main floor were all pushed against the walls. Most of Lord Davin's retainers and other servants crowded around the edges of the chamber in a loose circle, facing the high table. They buzzed excitedly.

Mauger stood next to the hearth in his full armor with his sword and shield drawn. Squeezing Mauger's shoulder, his father whispered something in his ear. Godfrey held his breath as Mauger nodded.

"You all bear witness that Roltar of House Hracour has come to challenge me for the right to Skasgun and Stormsud through a trial by combat," Davin bellowed. "King Lothar sanctions it. None of us should be surprised that he favors another Azgaldian over us."

Davin paused and glowered. A murmur rolled through the great hall as Godfrey contemplated the dichotomy of native Azgaldians versus former crusaders still in the Nordslands.

At what point might he be called an Azgaldian and not seen as a foreign interloper?

"Roltar's son, Mauger, stands before us," Davin continued through gritted teeth, "defiant, ready to spill blood for his father's claim."

A series of hisses and boos escaped the crowd. Godfrey swallowed. He should have expected that reaction from these people.

"I accept this challenge." Davin spread his arms wide. "And Godfrey de Bastogne has agreed to act as my champion in this duel."

Some among the crowd cheered, but others cried out in uncertain or disapproving tones. Godfrey met several curious or accusatory glances among Davin's household. Godfrey winced. He was not sure if this was really the right place for him either.

"Father Jeustin will now administer the champions' oaths," Davin growled in response to the doubt apparently spread by his previous statement.

An elderly priest rose from the high table and gestured for Godfrey to stand next to Mauger by the hearth. Roltar withdrew to the side of the crowd directly opposite Lord Davin. Godfrey drew his sword and shield as he took Roltar's place at Mauger's side.

"I call upon Eleutherios, protector of oaths, as witness to this trial by combat," the priest's voice warbled as he called out for all in the chamber to hear. "Do you, Mauger of House Hracour, swear to fight with honor, to do so to the best of your ability, and to accept whatever results the gods grant you on this day?"

"I do." Mauger bowed his head.

"Do you, Godfrey de Bastogne, swear to fight with honor, to the best of your ability, and to accept whatever results the gods grant you this day?" Father Jeustin asked.

"I do." Godfrey bowed his head as Mauger had.

"Should either of you forswear your oaths," the old priest continued, "I call upon Horkos the all-seeing to mete out justice upon the guilty parties."

Godfrey swallowed hard at the mention of Horkos. Though Eleutherios, the father of many gods worshipped by mortals today, was deeply concerned with justice, he was also known to be merciful to mankind. His enforcer, Horkos, however, showed no sympathy for transgressors. Whether the punishment came swiftly in a terrible cataclysm or by smaller degrees over the course of generations, none could escape the god of oaths' wrath when provoked. There was no throwing the duel now.

"Excuse me." Godfrey held Uriel out to Father Jeustin. "This sword will give me an unfair advantage in the combat. I need another."

A groan washed through the audience as all eyes fell upon Uriel's sparkling blade. Frowning, Father Jeustin grabbed the sword by the hilt. Davin gestured to Sir Fedmar, and the knight handed Godfrey his own sword from its sheath.

With an uncertain grumble, Godfrey looked down at Sir Fedmar's sword. It was longer and a little heavier than what he was used to. There was no time to go through every sword in Skasgun, searching for a perfect match to Uriel's length and weight. Each sword was individually crafted to its owner's preferences. This would have to do.

"Satisfied?" Father Jeustin asked.

Godfrey nodded. Fedmar's blade would not be too much of a disadvantage. Better to fight in the sight of the gods slightly hindered than shamefully favored, he reasoned within himself.

"Roltar of House Hracour and Davin of House Talhout." Father Jeustin indicated each man in turn. "You stand under the same oaths as your champions, and you are charged as if you stood in place of them. Should you or your champions forswear these oaths, the judgment of Horkos will fall upon you and your champions. Understood?"

"Of course." Davin nodded.

"Yes," Roltar answered.

"Then, let us delay no further." The priest gestured to Godfrey and Mauger. "I ask each champion to take his place at the edge of the circle."

Mauger withdrew from the hearth and stood in front of Roltar near the circle's edge. Godfrey plodded several paces until he stood in front of the high table. Davin and Wia gave him reassuring smiles, but he ignored them as he turned to face Mauger.

Silence fell over the great hall. Mauger and Godfrey both turned to face Father Jeustin. With a grimace, Lord Davin nodded to the priest.

"Begin!" Father Jeustin shouted.

Mauger and Godfrey took turns shifting to the left and right of the circle. Godfrey could not be sure which way Mauger might try to engage him from around the hearth, and his kinsman's movements reflected a similar hesitation. His eyes were fixed on the fire pit's glowing orange coals in the center of the chamber. It was just large enough to make Godfrey cringe at the thought of falling in.

The crowd called out, cheered, and hissed with the combatants' movements. Their futures were also at stake. Godfrey owed it to them to do his best.

At last, Mauger rushed at Godfrey from his right side. Grunting, he turned his shield just in time to block Mauger's strike. He dodged a second and third blow before his kinsman lunged again.

Heaving, Godfrey parried the attack and launched an immediate riposte. Mauger turned the blade with his sword and bashed Godfrey in the face with his shield. Godfrey fell back a step. His vision blurred. The crowd shouted as Mauger leapt at him.

His heart pounding, Godfrey sidestepped Mauger's downward swing at the last second possible. He raised his sword, but Mauger batted it away with his shield. Fedmar's blade was just a little heavier than what he was accustomed to. He grimaced. It slowed his movements too much.

Gritting his teeth as he spotted an opening in Mauger's defenses, Godfrey thrust Fedmar's sword right at his kinsman's chest. The crowd cheered, but Mauger turned and jumped. He would not be caught so easily.

Silently, Godfrey cursed as Lord Davin's household murmured. A hair's breadth could make the difference between parrying a strike and kissing cold steel. He should have tried another blade before accepting Fedmar's. He frowned. Too late.

Relentlessly, Mauger swung again and again as he roared with the fury of a dragon. Godfrey's shield banged against his kinsman's blade as he shoved him back a pace. Twisting on his foot, Mauger narrowly dodged falling into the hearth. Lady Wia and Lord Davin shook their heads from the high table. The rest of the crowd murmured.

Godfrey slashed in a sweeping arc, but Mauger leapt over the fire pit. One of Davin's servants gasped at the sight. The two combatants circled for a long moment. The glowing coals reflected in Mauger's fiery eyes.

"I thought you were better than this." Mauger shook his head. "Where is the Godfrey de Bastogne who defeated the black knight? Where is the Godfrey de Bastogne who slew Vozzab and the vampire at Kurl Keep?"

Mauger's taunting boiled Godfrey's blood as the crowd muttered in obvious discontent. His kinsman was a mere man, and a flawed duelist at that. Perhaps he was more skilled at arms than other men he had recently faced, but Godfrey had only narrowly missed more than one opportunity to end this combat already.

With a yell, Godfrey jumped over the fire pit. His sword clashed against Mauger's. He pushed his kinsman, but Mauger's greater bulk and firm stance forced Godfrey back a pace, instead.

Panting, Godfrey stared Mauger down as they each subtly adjusted their stances to the other's movements. The ferocity still burned in Mauger's eyes. Eleutherios and Horkos watched from above. Was Godfrey willing to do what his oath required?

Mauger lunged at Godfrey once again, but he leapt out of his path. Godfrey struck Mauger on the side of the head with the pommel of his sword. Bawling, Mauger stumbled as the crowd whistled. Godfrey thrust his sword, but Mauger rolled out of the way. Fedmar's blade was still too heavy for Godfrey.

"I told you not to hold back," Mauger spat. "I've seen you do better than this."

Slashing Fedmar's unwieldy sword, Godfrey grunted. Mauger stepped aside and thrust. He had anticipated Godfrey's move too easily for comfort.

Mauger's blade ripped through the enarme of Godfrey's shield closer to his wrist. For a moment, it dangled off his arm, hanging only by the enarme near his elbow. Jumping back, Godfrey shook the shield loose from his arm, and it clattered to the floor.

Several of Lord Davin's retainers shouted and pointed. Many of the ladies' faces contorted as they sneered at the near miss. Godfrey's heart raced. His hand shook. Did some evil spirit curse his efforts?

Mauger leapt forward. Godfrey slashed. Steel rang against steel. Another clash. A line of blood streaked down Mauger's face.

Godfrey charged at Mauger. His kinsman swatted Fedmar's sword out of his hand, but Godfrey tackled him to the floor. He straddled Mauger across the waist and grasped his wrist with one hand while trying to beat away his kinsman's blows with the other. Mauger's sword clattered out of his hand, and Godfrey pummeled him in the face with his fists. Swallowing hard, Godfrey struggled to maintain his hold on Mauger as he writhed underneath him.

Heaving, Mauger shoved Godfrey off of him. The two rolled on the floor, panting, hitting, grunting, and kicking. Mauger slipped away from Godfrey's reach as he grasped his sword again. Gripping the weapon, Mauger fell on him. However, Godfrey clasped Mauger's wrist and forced the blade away. He head-butted Mauger and scrambled to the edge of the circle as his kinsman cursed.

Crawling on his hands and knees, Godfrey raced to Fedmar's blade. No sooner had his fingers wrapped around the hilt than he staggered to his feet. He turned to Mauger, who was already lurching towards him with sword in hand.

"I *thought* there was a warrior left in you," Mauger huffed. "Good… Good."

Godfrey parried another trio of blows as rapidly as they fell upon him. He twisted and turned. He thrust and slashed, but Mauger's blade and shield blocked every opening Godfrey sought.

Feinting, Godfrey elbowed Mauger in the gut. He dropped to the ground, but not before wrapping his arms around Godfrey's waist. A sharp pain jolted through Godfrey's spine as his head hit the floor with a thud. He was grappling with his kinsman next to the hearth before he could fully comprehend that he had fallen, too. However, both Mauger and Godfrey's movements slowed as exhaustion took its toll.

Wheezing, Mauger slipped from Godfrey's grasp and rose to his feet once again. Godfrey stood just in time to dodge another thrust of his kinsman's blade. Sweat dripped from Godfrey's brow. The taste of blood filled his mouth. He had to focus.

Mauger bashed Godfrey with his shield again. The steel-encased corner hit him square in the jaw. Yelping, Godfrey slipped back into the hearth. As the hot coals seared his foot, he cried out in pain. The crowd roared as he rolled out of the fire pit, clutching his scorched boot.

The tip of Mauger's blade touched Godfrey's neck as he lay on the floor. In a panic, Godfrey turned his face to the hearth. Sir Fedmar's blade rested in the middle of the crackling coals. He could not hope to pick it up without scalding his hand. It was over.

"I yield." Godfrey raised his hands, choking back tears of pain.

For a long moment, Mauger gave Godfrey a cold stare. Would he thrust his sword into Godfrey's throat? Lop off his head in a burst of fury? As the winner of this trial by combat, it was his right.

"Let it be known that I defeated Godfrey de Bastogne here in the home of my father's fathers." Mauger sheathed his sword. "You, all of you, and all of my ancestors bear witness to this deed today. Let no one dispute that the lordship of Skasgun and the realm of Stormsud has been rightfully returned to House Hracour."

Stunned silence fell over Lord Davin's household. The lord's face grew ashen, and Lady Wia clung to his arm with wide eyes. Godfrey's face throbbed, and his foot stung, but he sighed in relief. It was over. Now he could finally go home and leave all this behind.

Lord Davin glared at Godfrey as he lay in his bed with his bandaged foot propped up on a pillow. The man paced back and forth as Godfrey cringed under his gaze. There was nothing he could do to soothe his rage.

Sir Fedmar and Lady Wia also frowned at Godfrey. He averted his eyes. He had done his best. There was no way he could come out of this making everyone happy.

Only Roltar and Mauger, standing near the back of the guest chambers, appeared satisfied in the slightest. Their ancestral lands had been secured once more. They got what they wanted. Now Godfrey should be able to go home.

"You lost on purpose!" Davin spat. "I knew I shouldn't have trusted you."

"I swear, by Loxias, I did not." Godfrey raised his hands. "I gave it everything I had."

"Do you think my cousin would have thrown himself into the fire on purpose if he had intended to lose from the beginning?" Roltar gestured to Godfrey.

"He also nearly sliced my head off." Mauger pointed to the fresh scar on his face.

"You all swore the oath." Father Jeustin indicated Godfrey, Mauger, Davin, and Roltar in turn. "You must abide by the results of the trial."

"But you heard him." Davin pointed at Mauger. "He accused Godfrey of holding back during the trial. He said he wasn't fighting as well as he could have."

Godfrey clenched his teeth as Father Jeustin stroked his chin. His honor was at stake. Should he mention Fedmar's sword being too heavy for him, or would that only come across as an excuse?

"You lost." Roltar wagged his finger at Davin. "You've done everything you can. All that's left for you to do is concede with what little dignity you have left."

"Not everything!" Davin shot back.

"What do you propose?" Father Jeustin raised an eyebrow at his lord.

Wia grabbed Davin's shoulder. She pulled him in and whispered something frantic in his ear. With a smirk, Davin turned back to the old priest.

"Another trial," Davin demanded.

"Horkos frowns upon those who will not abide by the results of a trial performed under oath," Father Jeustin warned. "Do not tempt the gods."

"A different trial." Davin cleared his throat. "Against Godfrey. I declare he did not act in good faith."

Roltar groaned.

"But *you* selected Godfrey de Bastogne as your champion, my lord." Father Jeustin raised an eyebrow at Davin. "Should you not bear the blame if his performance was less than satisfactory?"

"We all saw him." Fedmar glared. "His movements were slow, too slow for a seasoned knight."

"This is ridiculous," Godfrey sputtered. "How many ordeals do you intend to put me through?"

"You will not rob us again!" Mauger shook with fury.

Roltar, Lord Davin, Mauger, and Lady Wia began shouting over each other all at once. Godfrey clenched his jaw as he threw his head back against his pillow. He covered his ears and closed his eyes, but the bickering would not cease. It had to end. Why could it not end?

"I'm not doing another ordeal by combat with a burned foot!" Godfrey shook his head in protest. "I did everything asked of me and more. House Hracour won. House Talhout lost. And now I need to go back to Olso Fortress as soon as my wound heals."

The room was silent for a long moment. What was Godfrey's honor really worth? So what if some distant relations to Conrad the Wolf called Godfrey a liar or craven?

"I'm not suggesting another trial by combat," Lord Davin corrected. "This will be an ordeal by water."

"An ordeal by water?" Roltar gasped. "In this weather? You're mad!"

All eyes fell on Father Jeustin. Why everyone should defer to his judgment on this matter was beyond Godfrey. He had as much to lose or gain in this as his lord.

"Do you accept the challenge to go through a trial by water?" Father Jeustin tilted his head at Godfrey. "It is your prerogative to decline."

Slowly, Godfrey sighed. An ordeal by water was dangerous, too. At least, it was not by fire.

"Decline," Roltar insisted. "Godfrey has nothing left to prove to Davin or anyone else here."

"If Godfrey acted with pure intent, why should he be afraid to prove it?" Wia answered.

"A trial to prove the legitimacy of another trial?" Mauger reeled. "This is unheard of. The gods already said their piece back in the hearth!"

"It is unusual but not unheard of," the old priest corrected Mauger. "I think the particular circumstances of this trial merit a further sign from the gods. But as I already said, it is Godfrey's choice to accept or decline this second ordeal."

Godfrey's eyes locked with Lord Davin's, then Lady Wia's. Their expressions were smug, as if daring Godfrey to back down. He bit his lip. What harm could they imagine if he refused this latest gamble?

"I will not let a shadow hang over my head concerning the trial by combat," Godfrey began.

"No!" Mauger interrupted. "Don't be a fool. There is nothing to gain by this."

"What do I have if not my honor?" Godfrey shot back. "I will undergo the ordeal by water, but let that be the end of this. If I pass the challenge, may no one question my efforts to uphold Lord Davin's cause in the trial by combat. If I fail, then may the gods themselves call me a deceiver."

"Godfrey…" Roltar moaned.

"It is settled, then." Father Jeustin raised a hand. "The trial by water will take place in three days. Prepare yourselves against that time."

The priest led Davin, Wia, and Fedmar out of the guest chambers. The door ominously latched behind them with a heavy clank. Roltar's gaze turned from the door to Godfrey. A glower etched across his face.

"That was very stupid of you," Roltar scoffed. "Have the gods cursed you with madness? We won the trial by combat. King Lothar will honor the results."

"If I had backed down from this ordeal," Godfrey explained, "people would be questioning me for the rest of my life. I don't see how I could not go through with it."

"Let those fools question your honor," Roltar spat. "Their opinion means nothing."

"But others will hear their version of these events," Godfrey countered. "I have to prove myself."

"At the risk of delegitimizing the last trial." Roltar clenched his jaw. "I won't lose everything we had just won."

"This is not a test of strength, skill, or wit." Mauger shook his head. "This ordeal will only prove if you sink or float in a freezing pond. How confident are you about that?"

"My heart is pure." Godfrey pointed to his chest. "I hate to admit it, but I really did my best against you, Mauger. The gods themselves must have hindered me."

Mauger's nostrils flared as he let out a heavy sigh.

"If they were with you today," Godfrey continued, "surely, they will be with me in three days. The water will accept me. Have faith."

"At least no one will question your piety," Roltar grumbled. "Gods be with us until then."

Though the weather had been generally getting warmer over the last few weeks, a heavy snowstorm fell over Skasgun on the morning of Godfrey's trial by water. Only a few vague grey shapes hid behind the icy curtain that veiled the landscape as Godfrey peered through the window in his chamber. Mauger approached him as he sat at the windowsill, a grim expression on his kinsman's face.

"Should we ask to postpone this to another day?" Godfrey's kinsman crossed his arms.

"No." Godfrey rose to his feet. "My burns have healed. This is the appointed time. Whatever the outcome, I need to go back to Olso after this."

For a long moment, Mauger's gaze turned to the window. He furrowed his brow at the falling snow. Eventually, it began to subside.

"I'm sorry for what I said earlier." Mauger looked at his feet. "You're not a coward. You've done a lot for Father and me; far more than we initially asked."

"At Vindholm, I asked High Priest Throst for a prophecy." Godfrey took the scroll from his satchel. "It told me to trust in my blood. I didn't know why it said that at the time. I always believed I needed to be loyal to my family, but the weeks since then have tested this belief more than I would've imagined."

Mauger nodded. Letting out a heavy sigh, he toyed with the signet ring on his finger. The House Hracour crest etched in the ring's face gleamed in the dim morning light. At last, his eyes met Godfrey's.

"We will repay you." Mauger clasped Godfrey's arm. "Someday, somehow, House Hracour will make you realize that loyalty was not misplaced."

Godfrey looked Mauger up and down from head to toe. The tension was still in his muscles, and stress beyond his years aged his face, but the spite had left his eyes. Perhaps Godfrey would eventually find a friend in that gaze.

"It's time, Godfrey." The bed chamber door creaked open as Roltar entered. "I hope you said a special prayer to Boreas this morning. It's cold out there."

"Loxias knows my needs," Godfrey answered. "I'll leave it to him and his angels to sort things out with the North Wind this morning."

Roltar and Mauger followed Godfrey out of the guest chambers, where they were met by Father Jeustin, Sir Fedmar, and a few House Talhout men-at-arms. Without a word, the priest gestured for Godfrey to proceed down the corridor. He took a few steps forward, but the Talhout men-at-arms seized him by the shoulders.

"Don't struggle," Father Jeustin warned as Sir Fedmar bound Godfrey's hands with tight cords.

Clenching his jaw, Godfrey made no reply. He had seen others' hands and feet tied together with ropes as they were led to their ordeals. Why should he be treated differently from his peers?

Before long, Godfrey found himself marching through the snow to the pond on the western side of the castle. The grove of trees next to it was enshrouded in frost, while the pond itself was only partly covered by ice at the far end. Davin, Wia, and the rest of his household waited a few paces away from the water's edge as Godrey was led there by Father Jeustin and Sir Fedmar's men. Roltar and Mauger followed closely but said little. Godfrey gave a heavy sigh at their lack of confidence.

Then again, Godfrey mused to himself, was he tempting Horkos? Would the gods be offended by seeking a sign to confirm a previous omen? If only Walaric were here.

"Lord Davin has challenged the integrity of Godfrey de Bastogne's performance in his trial by combat against Mauger of House Hracour three days ago," Jeustin announced after they had reached the crowd. "I have determined that this claim has merit and deserves petitioning for further signs from the gods."

Godfrey cringed as he stared into the murky depths of the pond. Though the blizzard had stopped, the cold still bit his nose, and he shivered. Davin smirked at him. It was too late to change his mind. Everyone was watching.

"Godfrey de Bastogne has agreed that this ordeal should proceed, so that the question of his honor in the previous matter may be made known to all." Father Jeustin gestured to the assembled men, women, and children. "He will be pushed into this pond, and we will all observe what happens. Water is the purest substance in all of Aestas. If it accepts him, he will sink to the bottom of the pool. If it rejects him, he will float."

Everyone in the crowd exchanged hard glances. The last time Godfrey went swimming—years ago—floating came easily enough. His jaw tightening, he turned to Roltar. Godfrey had never actively tried to sink before. The gods would have to intervene.

Fedmar's men-at-arms dragged Godfrey to the water's edge. They sneered and mumbled quips to each other. Godfrey held his breath as he waited for them to shove him into the pond.

"A word with my cousin before the ordeal." Roltar raised his hand.

"As you will," Jeustin answered after exchanging a glance with his lord.

Lord Davin and Lady Wia's mouths moved quickly as they whispered to each other. The rest of the crowd also started mumbling as Roltar approached Godfrey. Mauger crossed his arms with a curious expression etched across his face. What did the head of House Hracour have to say?

Roltar's face was impassive. Godfrey cried out in agony as he punched him hard in the gut. Gasps raced from the crowd. Grunting, Roltar then shoved him with both hands.

Still reeling from the blow, Godfrey fell back a step and tumbled into the water before he could take a breath.

Searing pain jolted through every inch of him as Godfrey plunged beneath the surface of the pond. He sucked in icy water as he thrashed about. He struggled against the ropes, holding his wrists together, but they remained firm. He was going to drown.

His heart raced as he panicked. He kicked but continued sinking. He was not even sure which way was up anymore. He turned his head. It was too dark for him to know which way to try to swim.

His movements grew sluggish as he hit the bottom of the pond. He had to get up, but his strength was sapped. His arms were too heavy. He was going to drown. The thought repeated in his mind over and over again.

His legs were numb and as heavy as lead. His arms were immobile under the weight of his bonds. A small bubble tickled Godfrey's nose as it raced to the surface, but he could barely twitch in response. His vision grew dim. He was going to drown.

The next thing Godfrey knew, he was choking, gasping for breath as he coughed uncontrollably. He lay on the cold, muddy edge of the pond, surrounded by Lord Davin's household. Mauger hovered over Godfrey, also soaking wet and retching.

"The water has accepted him." Jeustin gestured to Godfrey with a clenched jaw. "Let the matter of Skasgun's lordship—and Godfrey de Bastogne's honor—come to a close. Dry them off. Get them inside before they freeze."

Roltar threw his cloak over Mauger, and Fedmar cut Godfrey's bonds with a knife. Fedmar lifted Godfrey off the ground before wrapping his own cloak over the young man's shoulders. Shivering, Godfrey stopped in front of Lord Davin before proceeding back to the castle.

"May no one *ever* sing a shameful song about me." Godfrey glared at Davin between dripping locks of hair.

"No, they won't." Lord Davin glowered.

"You saved me." Godfrey shivered. "Thank you, Mauger. I thought I was going to drown."

"I wasn't going to let you," Mauger stuttered as they marched back to the castle. "You've come this far with us."

"Well, as soon as I'm dry, I'm going back to Kovdor." Godfrey's teeth chattered as he looked up at Skasgun's walls. "Not after lunch. Not first light tomorrow. Now. I won't let any bonds of kinship or powers of the Abyss stop that."

Chapter Twenty

Once Walaric and Izold decided not to wait for Sir Jordan's leg to recover, they could find no reason to remain at Sval. Though there were considerably more comforts to be enjoyed between Rivold's citadel and the Silver Suns' chapter house than the wilderness beyond the city walls, their quest called. There had been too many sacrifices to delay any longer than they had to.

King Rivold, some of his retainers, Father Nithard, and the Silver Suns' ranking knight at Sval, Marshal Gunteric, escorted Walaric and Izold to the city's eastern outer gate. Every man's face among them was bleak. They all knew what lay ahead.

"Follow the Lenarm River for about twelve days," King Rivold advised. "Once you find the headwaters in the midst of the Dovern Highlands, Mirtys will be about another day north of that."

"The waters of the river grow bitterer the closer you get to its source," Marshal Gunteric warned. "It is cursed, so do not drink of the Lenarm once you are in the mountains. Melt the snow off the ground instead."

"Understood." Izold frowned.

"Are you certain you want to take that horse with you?" Rivold pointed to Izold's steed as he gripped the horse's reins. "The Dovern Highlands are dangerous."

"We've been through worse." Izold shook his head. "Vielantiu and I go everywhere together. At least, above ground, that is."

"Gardesh the Pale's dungeon would not have been a good place to take him." Walaric rolled his eyes.

"Indeed." The King frowned. "It was barely suitable for men to travel through."

"That reminds me of something." Walaric reached into his coin purse. "See that Jordan is given a good horse to take him back to Kovdor once he regains his strength. He lost his mount, Boreas, earlier in our travels, and he sorely misses the beast."

"The Temple of Aloeus will bear the cost of Sir Jordan's new horse." Father Nithard waved a dismissive hand at Walaric before he could withdraw the coins from his pouch. "We will not so soon forget his role in destroying Gardesh the Pale."

"Allow the Silver Suns to purchase Sir Jordan's new horse," Marshal Gunteric insisted. "He is in our care, and we will see him returned to Azgald safely."

"He lost his horse on account of *my* quest," Walaric protested. "I feel responsible."

"Let the people of Sval repay you and your friends," Father Nithard insisted. "We can afford it more than you."

Walaric let the coins in his hand slide back to the bottom of the pouch at his belt. The generosity of Sval's people was hard to overstate since they had arrived. He doubted he really had enough money to buy a steed anyway.

"Gods be with you both." Rivold gestured to the open gate. "Come back safe and victorious."

"Safe and victorious," Walaric repeated as he and the paladin waved farewell.

Izold led Vielantiu through the gate, and Walaric walked on the other side of the paladin. His gaze turned to the

Dovern Highlands up north. The danger would only get worse from here.

Beyond Sval's outer gate lay a cluster of docks and warehouses that had been built up along the Lenarm's western bank. Curiously, Walaric tilted his head at the sight. Some cities he had visited with Bishop Clovis back in Lortharain encompassed their docks behind the walls. However, the people who built Sval obviously feared being attacked from the river more than they valued protecting their commerce. A strange choice by Walaric's estimation.

No boats plied the river's course, as Walaric might expect in this season, and the docks were empty. That would change soon enough. Spring was coming.

"I'm going to miss Godfrey and Madeline's wedding," Walaric sighed as he and Izold marched past the docks and warehouses.

Vielantiu groaned.

"They understand you would be there if you could," Izold reassured him. "I don't think we'll come to regret going to the Blighted Lands. We're on the cusp of discovering whatever wicked magic binds the Great Witch of the North to the mortal sphere."

"I think so too." Walaric rubbed the gold funerary coin in his pouch. "But it's lamentable that I can't be there after they have spent all these months preparing for it."

"Duty before all else." The paladin sighed. "Our vocation demands it."

"*Our* vocation?" Walaric raised an eyebrow.

"Though you have no formal training as a knight, your skill at arms has grown during this quest." Izold gestured to him. "You could learn something more of obedience to the Church's rules, but the gods themselves have witnessed that your heart is right down in the lich's dungeon. In time, you could make a great paladin."

"A paladin?" Walaric blinked uncomfortably. "I'm not sure if that's what I really want."

"There are many ways you could serve the gods, Walaric, and I'm not sure if a priest's office is right for you." The paladin shook his head as they followed the Lenarm's western bank across the snowy fields.

"I've already made my vows." Walaric gestured to the sky. "My options are limited."

"They're not as limited as you might think." Izold furrowed his brow. "Talk to your bishop once this quest is over. Either way, you're too tempted by beautiful maidens to endure a celibate life in a chapel forever."

Walaric flushed in embarrassment.

"Trials and temptations have to be endured," he stammered. "That is the way of life."

"I won't tell you what to do with your life when this is over, but consider becoming my squire." Izold turned his gaze to the Dovern Highlands ahead. "I will give you all the training you need to become a paladin."

"How can a paladin start a family when he's expected to travel the whole world in search of evil to vanquish?" Walaric asked.

"Some great lord—say the Duke of Kovdor—may host you at his court on a more permanent basis." Izold patted Vielantiu's neck. "And the scope of your travels may become limited enough to permit you a family."

"That's something to think about." Walaric pursed his lips. "After our quest is over, of course."

Soon, Sval disappeared into the distance behind rugged hills. Izold and Walaric followed the Lenarm's bank as the river gradually turned west. By the time they made camp, their course nearly faced the setting Sun.

"It feels like we're going backwards," Walaric moaned as he threw some sticks onto their campfire.

"This river twists and turns, but we've gone uphill the whole day," Izold noted. "Water follows the path of least resistance."

"That's true." Walaric looked back downstream before frowning at the steeper hills to the north. "I guess following the Lenarm is easier than going up and down hills and mountains all day."

"It's probably a little faster too, even if it's not as direct," Izold added as he began fixing a skinned rabbit he had caught earlier that day to a spit.

The evening meal went quickly. They said little as they ate the rabbit Izold had roasted over the fire. As dusk's shadows grew longer and darker, Walaric's unease only increased. They skirted the edges of the Blighted Lands now and would inevitably turn directly into them as they followed the river. Things would only get worse.

Walaric tossed and turned in his bedroll as he slept that night. Phantoms haunted his dreams, and more than once, he awoke with the distinct impression some invisible malevolent being lurked just beyond his tent door. Swallowing hard, he threw open the canvas covering. Only the smoldering fire pit, Izold's tent, and Vielantiu's slumbering form beside it greeted him in the inky darkness. Still, he could calm himself only after muttering a prayer of warding before slowly drifting back to sleep.

The next day passed much as the first had after they had left Sval. The foothills grew steeper and the land greyer as they followed the Lenarm's winding course northwest. Birds, hares, and other game became scarcer, so Walaric and Izold had to increasingly rely on trail rations for meals. It did not take long for the tough, salted meat, hard bread, and nuts to grow stale in Walaric's mouth after eating so much of the same all winter.

The wind blew down from the Dovern Highlands that night as if carrying the whispers of dead lips. The mists, though faint, spilled over the foothills like a ghastly sheet over a table. Walaric shuddered. He continually glanced over his shoulder or past Izold as they sat at the campfire. Would some terrifying monster jump out of the shadows at any minute?

"Am I the only one hearing noises out there?" Walaric gestured to the darkness beyond the light of the fire.

"A foul wind is in the air tonight." Izold frowned. "I had to make sure Vielantiu's reins were secure a moment ago. He's afraid."

"It's like ghosts are mumbling hexes at us," Walaric gasped. "How do you remain so calm?"

For a moment, Izold warmed his hands at the fire without speaking. His expression was stoic. Walaric shivered as a gust of wind rasped down his neck.

"You can endure much if you have hope," Izold said at last. "Arktos shows us that the celestial gods will not fail in the end. These evil days will pass soon enough."

"It's hard not to forget all the horrors we've already suffered." Walaric's heart raced as his imagination began to run wild. "What if some revenant should stumble across our camp in the middle of the night or a vampire or a wraith?"

"Or a death knight or a dragon?" Izold raised an eyebrow at Walaric from across the flames. "Take no thought for tomorrow. For tomorrow shall take thought for the things of itself."

"Sufficient unto the day is the evil thereof," Walaric muttered. "Ironic that *I* should need to have scripture quoted to me at a time like this."

By their third day following the Lenarm from Sval, the river abruptly turned north into the mountains. Walaric's legs ached as they marched uphill, and Izold led Vielantiu by the reins rather than risk his steed slipping in the mud and snow with him in the saddle. There were fewer shrubs and trees here. Walaric grimaced at the overcast sky.

"We must be in the Dovern Highlands by now," Walaric said. "The land is so desolate."

"We have entered the Blighted Lands." Izold patted Vielantiu's flank. "Courage, friend."

"Courage," Walaric repeated in a strained voice.

The Lenarm grew murkier as they traveled along its western bank. Its color was bilious, and what few tree stumps littered the bank were rotting away. Walaric swallowed hard as he remembered Marshal Gunteric's warning not to drink from it once they reached the Dovern Highlands. He clenched his jaw at the filth he imagined just beneath the water's surface. There was no temptation to disregard the Silver Sun's words, especially now that he saw what the waters had become.

As they continued up the bank, Walaric glanced at some strange white stones jutting from the mud. Some were small and oblong. Others were large and round. He stopped in his tracks. His stomach sank as he recognized what lay before him.

"Bones." Walaric set his jaw. "Men's bones."

"Hurry." Izold shook his head as he continued leading Vielantiu along. "Let's not linger here."

Walaric swallowed hard before picking up the pace to rejoin the paladin and his horse. Were these the victims of some senseless act of violence? A dark ritual? He shuddered. There was no time to dwell on it.

Tightening his lips, Walaric glanced from place to place as he marched beside Izold. The air grew colder, and ice formed on the edges of the Lenarm's banks. Walaric's breath came in sharp, shallow gasps. Vielantiu whinnied, his muscles tensing. Izold hushed his steed with a reassuring pat on the side of the stallion's neck.

"Something's not right," Walaric muttered.

"Quiet!" Izold hissed as he threw his great helm onto his head. "Be still."

Walaric scanned his surroundings. A thicket lay directly ahead, but the growing fog and rolling hills concealed much beyond that on the western bank. On the eastern bank, a crumbling stone castle stood sentinel on one of the taller hills closest to the Lenarm. It was little more than lichen-covered walls, broken towers, and a neglected keep, yet Walaric shuddered at the sight. Surely, something vile made that awful place its home.

Footsteps squelched through the mud on the other side of the thicket ahead of them. Walaric gulped. The paladin nodded at him. Izold drew his war hammer and shield. Walaric grabbed the hilt of the sword at his belt.

His hands trembling, Walaric drew a sharp breath as a skeletal figure emerged from the thicket along the bank. It wore a faded blue surcoat and a tarnished spangenhelm. In one hand, it carried a large heater shield with the image of a horned cyclopean skull emblazoned upon it. In the other hand, it carried a heavy, stained mace. Its chainmail hauberk clinked with each step the monster took.

"Can you pay the toll?" The beast's pin-prick glowing eyes met Walaric's as it pointed its mace at him.

"Toll?" Walaric stammered.

"We pay no toll to the likes of you, death knight." Izold's grip tightened around his war hammer.

"I am Sir Luthren," the death knight seethed as his mindless skeletal minions emerged from the thicket and from beneath the putrid surface of the Lenarm itself. "All pay me the toll. One way or another."

A skeleton wearing a chainmail shirt thrust its rusting blade at Walaric. He dodged the blow as he grabbed his shield from his back. He raised it just in time to meet another sword strike. The steel clanged off the rim of his shield. With a yell, Walaric struck out against the undead.

The pommel of Walaric's weapon cracked the jaw of the nearest monster, and it fell back into the river's murky depths. Izold's war hammer shattered the exposed rib cage of another skeleton. More undead lurched forward to take the places of their fallen kindred.

Roaring, Vielantiu bucked and kicked at the skeletons around him. His powerful hooves easily smashed skulls and broke arms, legs, and ribs. His eyes bulged. His nostrils flared. He was every bit as dangerous as Izold.

The death knight lunged at Walaric, but he fell back before Luthren's mace could connect to his skull. Slipping in the cold mud, he hit the ground hard. Leering down at him, Luthren raised his hefty weapon.

Bellowing, Izold rushed the death knight. Luthren turned as the paladin swung his war hammer. The weapon thumped against the death knight's shield. With the monster distracted, Walaric scrambled to his feet.

Another skeleton charged Walaric, but he deftly severed its skull from its neck as it attempted to impale him. It was hard to tell exactly how many there were. For every one Walaric destroyed, another emerged from the river, thicket, or over the hills.

Izold's war hammer smashed a skeleton's shoulder as he blocked Luthren's mace with his shield. The death knight swung his heavy weapon again and again. Though his attacks forced the paladin back several paces, Luthren howled as Izold repelled his strikes. Despite this, the death knight's gaze repeatedly fell on Walaric. Luthren wanted him, and Izold was all that stood between them.

A skeleton batted Walaric's sword out of his hand. He fumbled to retrieve it, but his foe furiously slashed at him. Walaric gasped as an idea struck him. Stepping back from the undead, he grabbed his star pendant by the chain and held it aloft. To his surprise, Luthren cackled in response at the sight of the holy symbol.

"Oh, so your friend is a priest of the celestial gods?" the death knight jeered as he continued exchanging blows with

Izold. "These grounds are desecrated, fool. Your gods have no power in the Blighted Lands."

Grimacing, Walaric bashed the skeleton in front of him with his shield and dove for his sword. Sliding through the mud, he grasped the hilt and slashed at the monster's leg. The creature fell, and Walaric broke its jaw with his sword pommel.

Vielantiu continued biting, kicking, and thrashing at everything around him. Bones fractured, cracked, or were smashed under the warhorse's hooves. The monsters' strikes had ripped the steed's caparison, exposing his chainmail barding. Blood leaked from minor cuts, but Vielantiu lashed out, defiant as ever. Soon, the undead surrounding the steed became little more than heaps of bone fragments and discarded weapons and armor.

Izold swept at Luthren with his war hammer. The shining metal head struck the death knight's spangenhelm. The helmet went careening off into the river with a splash, and the creature's skull split at the point of impact. Hissing, the death knight fell back a pace. Luthren locked eyes with Walaric before attempting to surge past the paladin.

"The celestial gods shall have no power here!" the death knight wailed.

Walaric jumped back from the undead warrior as the monster snapped its teeth at him. Izold came from behind and hit the horrid thing again. Luthren collapsed in the mud. A final blow from Izold smashed the death knight's face. Walaric released a long, steamy breath.

Black ethereal fumes sizzled from Luthren's broken form lying on the riverbank. His remaining skeletal minions slunk back to the shadows and the Lenarm's foul waters. Walaric huffed as he looked about. Izold kicked the death knight's inert bones. The danger had passed.

"I suppose that's it, then." Walaric frowned at the thought of the other skeletons lurking just out of sight.

"For the moment only." Izold shook his head.

"Why was he so interested in me?" Walaric sheathed his sword. "The death knight should've kept attacking you."

"A touch of madness?" Izold began tending to Vielantiu. "All undead suffer from that curse. Whatever the cause, his poor choice in tactics likely saved our lives."

"No doubt there," Walaric agreed. "Do you think Sir Luthren understood something of our quest?"

"Foresight is not a gift commonly bestowed upon death knights." Izold gently led Vielantiu past the thicket next to the riverbank. "They are powerful warriors and can command lesser undead, but they do not possess any great magical abilities."

"Strange." Walaric pursed his lips as he followed Izold past Sir Luthren's remains. "Perhaps he just had a special hatred for celestial priests."

"It would seem that way." Izold's pace quickened once he had cleared the thicket. "But why he would hate a cleric more than a paladin is a mystery we may never know the answer to."

As the day wore on, Walaric's fatigue grew. The march uphill grew steeper. They saw no sign of more undead, but a chill ran down Walaric's spine every time he glanced back to the ruined castle on the eastern side of the Lenarm. He had to put as much distance as he could between himself and that awful fortress. Izold showed no signs of wanting to explore that wretched place, either.

After cresting a particularly large hill, Walaric stopped to catch his breath. He blinked, then blinked again. To his surprise, a small village surrounded by farms occupied the valley before them. Smoke billowed from the chimneys of the cottages, and lights gleamed from their windows as the Sun sank lower in the sky.

"People!" Walaric pointed down to the cluster of houses in the valley. "Look at that. I didn't think anyone would *choose* to live here."

"We'll stop there for the night," Izold answered.

Walaric and Izold descended the hill to the village. Even from this distance, the crumbling keep they had passed after fighting the death knight was still visible. With a sigh, Walaric nodded to himself. The castle had been placed to overlook both the Lenarm and this village.

Only a few tired, greying farmers were out and about at this late hour. Of those few, most ignored Walaric and Izold or scowled at them as they approached the cottages. Vielantiu snorted in what Walaric could have mistaken for contempt at this reception.

"Travelers," an old man grumbled as Walaric and Izold reached the middle of the village. "What business have you here in Madsorn?"

"I am Izold, son of Kolen, and this is Father Walaric," The paladin said. "The hour grows late, and we seek lodging for the night."

The old man rolled his eyes. There was little charity in his demeanor, even in the presence of a paladin. The Dovern Highlands were grim, indeed.

"We'll pay for our room and board," Walaric added hastily. "We won't be a burden."

Walaric took out the few silver coins he had left in his pouch. The old man snatched them from the priest's hand as soon as the coins' luster reflected in his greedy eyes. Now Walaric was reduced to the one gold coin Dachlann had minted for him back at Olso.

Walaric frowned at the old man as he counted the silver cupped in his hand. His tunic and cloak were only slightly better quality than what most of the commoners wore. He must have been a village elder.

After inspecting the coins, the old man snorted as he placed them in the pouch at his belt. Grunting, he turned from the village center and waved for them to follow him. Walaric exchanged a hard glance with Izold. The paladin shrugged in response. Madsorn was far from welcoming.

The elder led them to one of the larger cottages on the opposite end of the village from where they had entered. He signaled to a young farmer near a stable next to the cottage. With a grimace, the farmer took several reluctant strides towards them.

"Alpin, take this horse and feed it well," the old man barked as he gestured to Vielantiu. "These men are staying with us tonight."

"Yes, Father." The younger man took Vielantiu's reins from Izold before leading the horse to the stable.

The farmer bore some resemblance to the elder both in physical characteristics and mannerisms. Most people in smaller villages and hamlets looked somewhat alike, from what Walaric had seen. No doubt, everyone in Madsorn came from just a few different families.

"I didn't catch your name." Walaric raised an eyebrow as the elder showed them the door to his cottage.

"Uvan," the elder growled.

The old man opened the door and gestured for them to enter. A dim light glowed from the hearth just inside. Izold scanned the room before entering, and Walaric followed him closely.

"Ethne," Uvan called into the chamber. "Ethne. We have guests, dear."

"So I see." An old woman sneered from the far side of the chamber. "And you didn't think to ask me before inviting them in, did you?"

Walaric glanced between Uvan and Ethne. The elder's cheeks glowed red as his lips curled into a frown. Ethne put her hands on her hips as if readying herself for whatever excuses he would make. The two had the appearance of an old married couple who often sought occasion to exchange such barbs. Walaric shifted his weight uncomfortably from one foot to the other as he stepped aside from the simmering quarrel.

"They offered us *money*, Ethne." Uvan held out the silver Walaric had given him just a few minutes before.

"Well, money is good, Uvan." Ethne furrowed her brow. "But who are these men coming into my home with swords and shields and armor?"

"Don't be stupid, Ethne." Uvan pointed at Izold. "This one's a paladin, and that one's a priest. Haven't you heard about the knights who bear the fleur-de-lis?"

"I've heard that their kind always causes trouble around here." Ethne shook her head.

"I noticed there is no shrine in this village." Walaric cleared his throat. "How do the people of Madsorn worship the gods without a shrine?"

Uvan and Ethne exchanged a glance. The old woman leered at her husband as if silently berating him. Surely, Walaric was not the first traveler to ask about such a curious absence from Madsorn? Walaric turned to Izold. Then again, travelers to the Blighted Lands had to be well-armed if they intended to leave alive.

"Lord Giric doesn't permit us a shrine," Uvan answered at last. "If we won't worship Athanatos at Madsorn Keep, we can't worship any god."

"Athanatos." Walaric bit his lip. "Only a truly cursed realm openly worships the god of undeath."

"And it is a cursed realm," Uvan reassured them. "Lord Giric sees to that."

"And who is Lord Giric?" Izold asked.

"Now you've got them asking questions." Ethne pointed a scolding finger at Uvan. "Don't tell them any more about us or this place. I told you they'd just cause trouble for us.

The only people who come to the Dovern Highlands are the ones always look for trouble."

"I assumed they paid Sir Luthren the toll." The old man turned to Walaric with a frenzied expression. "They should know Lord Giric is the Baron of Madsorn. Didn't Sir Luthren tell you this at the river?"

"We met him." Izold crossed his arms. "But Sir Luthren was a death knight. Paladins can have no peaceful dealings with such abominations."

"What do you mean?" Uvan's eyes went wide.

"We were not about to pay a toll to that kind of monster," Izold explained. "We destroyed the death knight and all of his minions that we could."

"You *destroyed* Sir Luthren?" The elder's face went pale. "How could you do that? No one has ever—"

"See!" Ethne's voice grew shrill. "I told you they were here to cause trouble. Now think what Lord Giric will do when he sees them here!"

"I didn't know." Uvan shook his head.

"You never do!" Ethne sneered.

The elder's shock turned to rage as his focus shifted from his wife to Walaric and Izold. Walaric winced. Uvan bared his teeth and puffed out his chest as he waved his hands at the two of them.

"You have to leave." Uvan shook all over. "You have to leave Madsorn now. Get out of my home. Get out of this village. Get out! Get out!"

The elder reached into his pouch and threw Walaric's coins back at him. He was so stunned by the sudden outburst that he let the silver hit his chest and clink against the floor without picking it up. The old couple began pushing Walaric and Izold out of the room, and they hastily stepped back through the front door without the money.

"Alpin!" Uvan hobbled to the stable once they were all outside. "Alpin, get that man's horse you just put up. They have to leave right now."

The farmer tugged on Vielantiu's reins as he led the steed out into the twilight. Whinnying, the horse stopped in his tracks. A chill ran down Walaric's spine as he turned to face the direction Alpin's mouth gaped at.

Atop a withered undead stallion sat a skeletal cavalier that bore a striking resemblance to Sir Luthren and shared the death knight's heraldry. Beside him, a similar undead horror held three iron chains fastened around the collars of a trio of emaciated hounds. Behind them stood at least a dozen lesser skeleton warriors armed with swords, shields, and spears.

"Lord Giric!" Uvan fell on his face.

The elder's wife and son also immediately prostrated themselves in the frigid slush before the monsters. The undead hounds snarled at Walaric and Izold as their handler leered at them with eyes made from a cold, unholy light. Walaric's heart pounded as he looked at Izold. The paladin's hand was on the grip of his war hammer.

"These are the criminals who did not pay the toll to pass by Madsorn Keep." The cadaverous beast handler turned to the mounted death knight.

"Are these the fools who killed Sir Luthren?" Lord Giric hissed. "Are these the fools who slew my brother?"

"I am Izold, son of Kolen." The paladin stepped forward. "I destroyed the death knight. I vanquished your foul-spawned brother."

"And you harbor this paladin and his cleric, Uvan?" The death knight spurred his ghastly steed forward a pace. "How many more of your sons must I take to teach you your place in my realm?"

"No!" Drawing his war hammer, Izold stepped between Giric and Uvan. "Your quarrel is with me, death knight. Leave them alone."

"You sought sanctuary here." Giric drew his sword. "You wished to gain food, warmth, and shelter from my subjects. This cannot be allowed."

Shifting in his saddle, the death knight turned to his undead henchmen. A cold fire burned in his eyes. The other skeletal creatures stood motionless, yet ready to vault at Giric's command.

"Make an example of these wretches." Giric waved his sword at Walaric, Izold, and the villagers with them. "Kill them all. Avenge my brother!"

The hounds rushed Walaric first. He drew his sword just in time to sever the snout of one of the fetid canines. However, the other two pounced and tackled him to the ground. Shaking their heads vigorously, the beasts growled as they ripped at his cloak and habit. Walaric cried out in anguish as teeth sank into his arm and leg.

Running at a full gallop, Vielantiu trampled the hound biting Walaric's arm. Releasing Walaric's limb, it squealed as the warhorse's hooves crushed its back. A sickly stench escaped the undead animal's carcass as its putrid innards spilled out into the snow and mud.

Rolling over, Walaric drove his sword through the last hound's neck. The creature whimpered and slumped on top of him. Thick ichor seeped from its matted fur as Walaric shoved the limp remains to the side.

Izold swung his war hammer in a wide arc. The weapon's heavy, metal head connected to the beast handler's shoulder with a crack. As its back was shattered, the undead monster crumpled under the force of the blow.

Giric gave a shriek and trampled his horse over Ethne as she turned to flee from him. Walaric's jaw dropped at the gory sight. Weeping for his mother, Alpin rushed to her broken body, but the death knight skewered him with his blade. Cursing, Uvan raised his fist, but the death knight struck him hard in the face with his sword pommel. Gushing blood from the wound, the old man fell in the snow, crying out.

For a moment, Walaric stood in stunned silence. A whole family had been murdered before his eyes. Others in nearby cottages peered at the unfolding battle through their windows, but none dared to leave the safety of their homes.

Vielantiu bit and kicked at the skeletons surrounding him. However, the undead monsters presented a hedge of spears on all sides. They stabbed again and again. The warhorse cried out and fell in a bloody mass.

Roaring, Izold struck the nearest skeleton. Its bones snapped. He deflected a spear thrust with his shield and pounded another monster's face into splinters. Walaric gasped at the paladin's fury. He was growing reckless.

The death knight charged Izold from behind. Lifting his sword overhead, Lord Giric howled. Twisting on the spot, the paladin raised his shield.

"Watch out!" Walaric rushed forward.

Giric's attack bounced off the paladin's shield just as Walaric's blade pierced the undead stallion's muzzle. Shrieking, the monstrous steed reared, and the death knight fell from the saddle. Izold pounced.

As the paladin repeatedly struck Giric with his war hammer, the death knight's efforts to rise and lash out soon proved futile. The death knight could neither stand nor raise his weapon under the ferocity of Izold's attacks. After one final wail, Lord Giric crumpled under the heavy blows before he could even recover from falling out of the saddle.

Madsorn village was still. Lord Giric and his cursed steed lay cold and silent. All of the other undead either were destroyed or had disappeared into the night. Izold sobbed over Vielantiu. Several deep wounds to the noble steed's sides oozed blood. The cost of victory was steep.

Walaric grimaced at the death knight's broken form. No final words. No last efforts at retaliation. Only an ignominious pummeling after falling from the saddle.

"Thus to all tyrants." Uvan spat on Lord Giric's remains as he stumbled to his feet. "Now, get out of Madsorn. Don't come back here ever again. You've caused enough trouble here."

Chapter Twenty-One

oaring, Tancred burst into the great hall of Olso Fortress' keep. He stomped past the hearth as servants recoiled and fled before him. A sharp squeal abruptly silenced the soft melody Macsen the Elgunian had been playing on his flute while sitting in his chair. With a yelp, he spilled out of his seat at the sight of the enraged duke.

Briefly, Tancred paused at the sight of the minstrel picking himself up off the floor. He had paid good money for Macsen the Elgunian to perform at Madeline's wedding. But all the world's riches would not matter if there was no wedding.

Arius and Berig exchanged terrified glances and quivered as they backed against the high table at their father's approach. He sneered at them. It took every ounce of strength in him not to strangle the twins.

"Where is she?" Tancred bellowed.

"Who?" Arius gave a nervous chuckle.

Scowling, Berig punched his brother's shoulder.

"Madeline took the griffin a couple of weeks ago." Arius winced. "One of her handmaidens found a note saying something about Fathest Thule, but we don't *know* where she went."

"You don't know where she went?" Tancred fumed. "You didn't send anyone after her?"

"What horse could hope to keep pace with a griffin?" Berig shook his head. "Spathi leaves no trail to follow. By the time we knew she wasn't here, it was too late. And good luck finding Farthest Thule in winter, if that's where she really went."

"Why did I make you two counts if you weren't going to keep an eye on your sister?" Spit flew from Tancred's mouth into Arius' face. "Where is the boy?"

"Lord Godfrey also left." Arius flinched. "He went with Roltar of House Hracour to Vindholm a while ago to press his claim on Skasgun. It turns out they're related on his mother's side."

"He should be back any day now," Berig added.

"Should be back any day now?" Tancred repeated, clenching his jaw as he turned back to the wedding guests slowly trailing into the chamber behind him.

"He should've already been back," Arius corrected.

The elderly Bishop Manfred gave Tancred a quizzical look as he took a few tentative steps into the room. Tancred's sisters, Moschia and Annina, entered a few paces behind. Their faces were cross.

"He *should* be back any day now." Tancred threw out his hands. "I can't believe this. All this time gathering the guests, arranging food and entertainment…"

Moschia and Annina's smaller children entered the chamber and began running and playing in the great hall. Tancred's jaw tightened as the noise grew. He had to think.

"I told you Conrad the Wolf would've been a better match." Moschia wagged her finger. "That young man knew what he wanted. Or Cedwyn of Twyl would've been a respectable choice."

"Tybalt of House Norfulk would've been an even better choice." Annina sighed. "The man had brains and brawn. Cardigal isn't that far away from Azgald. Madeline could've learned to be happy with him."

"But Godfrey can't say no to anyone," Moschia continued, "and now look at what's happened! Madeline ran off because he left her at the altar."

"Who got left at the altar?" a small, blonde child asked. "Why would Lord Godfrey do that?"

"No one got left at the altar." Annina shot her husband a vicious look. "Folcard, take the children somewhere else to play while we discuss this matter."

"Where do you want me to take them?" Annina's husband, Folcard, stretched out his arms with an exasperated expression.

"Out of the great hall, *dear.*" Annina's jaw tightened.

Grumbling, Folcard grabbed the blonde girl by the wrist and gestured for his other children to follow. Slowly, the children complied, but not before many threats of punishment passed through Folcard's gritted teeth. At last, the door closed behind Tancred's nieces and nephews.

"You don't know where Madeline went?" Tancred turned back to Arius and Berig. "What about Sister Vanya, Elja, or Thieda? Someone has to know."

"We asked them," Berig explained. "One of Godfrey's rangers saw Madeline take the griffin. She had her magic staff with her."

"Staff?" Tancred interjected.

"Madeline has been building a magic staff all winter." Arius stood upright. "We think she was trying to get the elves of Farthest Thule to help her finish constructing it."

"Didn't she run off with Godfrey, trying to find that place earlier?" Moschia raised an eyebrow.

"Did the Great Witch of the North put some curse on her?" Moschia's husband, Whichmann, crossed his arms as he joined them. "Why does she keep trying to go to Farthest Thule? No man has been to that place since…"

"She has a spell familiar guiding her there." Berig cringed. "Sister Vanya told us about him."

"So, you see why we couldn't go after Madeline?" Arius gestured to the chamber doors. "We have no idea how to get to Farthest Thule, if that's where she even went in the first place."

"A spell familiar?" Tancred groaned. "This is getting worse by the minute. Next time I see Godfrey, I'm going to wring his neck so hard that boy will regret ever having laid eyes on my daughter."

"To be fair, the spell familiar doesn't sound like it had anything to do with Godfrey de Bastogne." An older woman approached the high table.

The venerable matron glided across the floor in a blue and gold gown with all the ease of gilded royalty. Her gaze was stern and her features regal, not unlike Sister Vanya's, though her face was not darkened by years of disappointment as the old librarian's usually was. For a moment, her eyes met Tancred's.

"Mother." Tancred bowed his head as she stopped in front of the table. "What should we do?"

"We still have a little time before the first day of spring." Tancred's mother tapped her finger against the table. "My granddaughter knows when her birthday is. She will either be here for her wedding or she won't. We'll continue preparing as if she will come."

"Her wedding dress hasn't even been fitted yet," Moschia objected.

"I suppose we could fit it to her friend, Elja," Tancred conceded. "She's about Madeline's size."

"What if Godfrey doesn't make it to the wedding on time?" Berig grimaced.

"Then I'll personally skin the boy alive." Tancred's mother shook her fist.

Resting against the balcony of Lord Bion's home, Madeline squinted at the sky above. Though the Sun still hung low near the mountaintops, true daylight had at last returned. She sighed in relief. Spring was almost here.

Only a light morning frost covered the ground of the courtyard below. As Anistemi matured, her heat radiated more strongly across Farthest Thule. It was warmer here than it was farther south in Azgald, Madeline mused.

Fravash skittered across the railing and stood on his hind legs. The mouse's whiskers twitched as he gazed into Madeline's eyes. She smiled in return.

"Good morning, my lady." The rodent bowed his head. "Did you sleep well?"

"Yes," Madeline answered. "Thank you."

"I just checked on your staff." Fravash's expression grew serious. "It's ready."

Madeline nodded. She held out her hand, and Fravash scampered up her sleeve before coming to rest on her shoulder. With the mouse gently gripping the fabric of her dress in his paws, Madeline made her way to the inner chambers of Lord Bion's home.

Rays of morning light gleamed through the windows as Madeline walked into the central hall. Lord Bion stood at the entrance, ready to receive her. His expression was aloof with only the vaguest hints of affection stirring beneath his cold exterior.

Madeline blushed as the elf lord took her hand. She had never given him a direct answer to his marriage proposal. However, deep down, she knew the longer she went without answering him, the more firmly she was telling him no, through inaction if not by words.

Biting her lip, Madeline allowed Bion to lead her to a table set in the middle of the chamber. She had already promised herself to Godfrey. Why did she still even entertain the thought of marrying Bion?

On the table before Madeline, the shaft of her staff rested on an embroidered silk cloth. The spells, incantations, and potions the wood had been subjected to gave it the appearance of polished white stone. Next to the head of the staff lay the silver end cap and the feather Anistemi had gifted her. Her jaw tightened in anticipation. So much preparation had led up to this moment.

The faintest rustling Madeline could imagine pricked her ears. Her eyes darted to the far end of the chamber. Her hair glowing in the morning sun, Queen Kypris strode into the hall. Gasping, Madeline bowed. Fravash and Bion followed suit.

"This is a special occasion today, young sorceress." The Queen bade Madeline to rise. "Do not think I would neglect this moment."

"You honor me, your majesty." Madeline curtsied.

Fravash scurried onto Bion's shoulder, and the elf lord took his place by the Queen on the opposite side of the table from Madeline. Bion and Kypris exchanged a glance almost too subtle for Madeline to notice. A smile passed between them. Perhaps they were not irreconcilable after all?

Madeline grinned at the spell familiar before turning back to Kypris. Fravash nodded encouragingly. Finally, the Queen gestured for her to proceed.

Taking a deep breath, Madeline grabbed the phoenix feather from the table. She concentrated all her thoughts on her healing fire. Briefly, the feather glowed as bright as a lit candle before fading back to normal.

Next, Madeline grabbed the staff and inserted the feather into the hole drilled into the top. Once it was completely inside the shaft, Madeline screwed the silver end cap onto the top. She stopped only after it was secured as tightly as she could twist it.

"It is finished," Madeline beamed.

"Not yet." Kypris raised her hand.

With her other hand, the elf Queen produced a large jewel resting in an open velvet-lined box. It was amber fashioned in the likeness of a flaming sphere. Kypris extended the jewel to Madeline.

"How can I accept this gift after already being shown so much hospitality?" Madeline asked.

"Graciously." The Queen smiled.

"You are too kind." Madeline bowed her head once again. "I am forever in your debt."

With a trembling hand, Madeline snatched the amber from its box. The jewel was soft and brittle to the touch. To her surprise, it had warmed in her hand after just a moment.

"Fashion it to the end cap," Kypris instructed.

Madeline examined the amber. A grooved hole had been carved into the bottom of the jewel that was large enough to fit over the top of the staff. With minimal effort, she twisted it in place.

"There!" Madeline held the completed staff at arm's length. "Thank you all for the help you've given. I couldn't have done it without you."

"What will you name your staff?" Bion asked.

Madeline frowned curiously.

"It's tradition that every magician names her wand or staff upon its completion," Fravash explained.

With the amber secured to the top of the staff's end cap, it almost had the appearance of a long torch. Madeline scoffed. Knights gave names to their swords. Ship masters gave names to their boats. Why should Madeline's staff not have a name worthy of great deeds?

"Pyrsos," Madeline said at last.

"That is well." Queen Kypris smiled in agreement. "May your staff help light the way through all of your journeys from this day forward."

Bion and Fravash nodded in agreement.

A tingling sensation trickled from Madeline's fingertips through her arms to her entire body. It was as if some invisible power coursed from her staff through her veins. She began to shake but quickly regained control. Her jaw gaped at the staff. Never had she felt so keenly aware of everything around her.

"You can already feel Pyrsos amplifying your powers?" Fravash asked.

"I think so." Madeline trembled.

"You'll only get stronger from here," the mouse reassured her. "Don't worry if it feels strange at first."

"I'm not worried." Madeline shook her head.

"Good." Fravash twitched his tail. "This is only the beginning of better things to come."

Over the next few days, Fravash had Madeline experiment more with her spellcasting. He had not only tested the limits of her raw power but her finesse and control as well. Though the exercises left Madeline exhausted at the end of each session, she could not help but smile at the thought of just how far she had come so quickly.

At the end of one of these lessons, Madeline wiped perspiration from her brow as she stood in a muddy field outside of Farthest Thule's gates. She frowned at her feet. The snow was beginning to melt at last.

"That is good," Fravash chirped. "You're getting used to the staff's power now."

"It's almost too much to handle." Madeline gazed at the sparkling amber atop her staff. "It's like trying to ride a minotaur in a thunderstorm."

"You're already beginning to tame Pyrsos," Fravash answered. "A little more practice, and we'll be able to start learning more advanced techniques."

"Can I learn about different kinds of magic?" Madeline wondered. "Nera's magic seemed different from my phoenix fire, and there are other sorts of wizards, warlocks, and spellcasters I've been reading about."

"Some kinds of magic may come more easily than others," Fravash explained, "but with enough time and effort, I don't think anything is beyond your reach."

"Anistemi seemed to think so too." Madeline nodded. "She says I have great potential."

A pair of elvish cataphracts trotted their horses up to Madeline as they approached Farthest Thule's gate. She smiled as she recognized Trophnus and Mygdon saluting them. Any familiar face was a welcome sight.

"It's been a while." Madeline leaned against her staff as the elves stopped next to them. "Back for a visit?"

"Our patrol is over." Trophnus shook his head.

"The flying cataphracts are on duty for the spring." Mygdon gestured to the sky overhead. "Griffins, hippogriffs, and their kind fly more easily in warmer air currents."

A trio of snowy white griffins similar to Spathi screeched as they soared over the city's towers. Their riders' armor and brass scale barding glimmered in the late afternoon sun before they disappeared behind the Wyrmwind Peaks. Slowly, Madeline's thoughts drifted from the griffin riders to Farthest Thule to Olso Fortress.

"Spathi!" Madeline furrowed her brow as she looked down at the emerald engagement ring on her finger. "It's not the first day of spring, is it?"

"We have a few days before spring still," Trophnus explained. "The flying cataphracts are a bit zealous for elves, and they like an early start."

"Oh, we may be too late already." Madeline turned to the mouse. "Fravash… I need to make a decision. And I need to make it now."

The spell familiar twitched his head.

"Lord Bion offered to marry me," Madeline confessed. "I don't think I love him, but I do love studying magic and being at Farthest Thule."

"Many a maiden *learns* to love her husband over time." Mygdon pursed his lips. "Lord Bion is one of the great princes of Vathepoli. He will treat you kindly, and you have other friends in the city as well."

"Don't encourage her." Trophnus shot Mygdon a dark look. "Lord Bion is out of the Queen's favor. The damsel needs to go back to her own kind."

"You're letting your feelings against the children of men cloud your judgment," Mygdon countered. "Besides, Lord Bion may not always be out of the Queen's favor."

"As of now, many at Vathepoli still do not care for Lord Bion… *or* the children of men." Trophnus shifted in his saddle. "Lady Madeline is a guest but cannot be more."

"Fravash?" Madeline grimaced at the mouse. "Will I be able to study magic with the same ease at Olso Fortress as I have here now that Pyrsos is complete?"

"The elves have greater access to magic." Fravash shook his head. "It flows more naturally in their presence, and they have a greater abundance of lore than can be found in the libraries of Azgald. That's why I wanted to spend a little more time here."

Madeline bit her lip.

"But completing your staff is what we came here to do," the familiar continued. "Though the journey is long and difficult, we can always come back to Vathepoli another time. If you want to marry Godfrey, we have to leave now."

"There's one more thing I need to do before we go, then." Madeline took a deep breath. "Fravash, can you get Spathi ready? I need to talk to Lord Bion."

"We'll take Fravash to the stables." Mygdon offered his hand to Madeline.

"We were already on our way there." Trophnus rolled his eyes as the familiar climbed from Madeline's shoulder into Mygdon's hand.

After curtsying to the cataphracts, Madeline raced through the gates and the lower city. The Sun was already beginning to set. She owed Bion an answer, but time was short.

Though her legs ached from exertion, it did not take long for Madeline to reach Lord Bion's home in the high city. She knew the way. The lovely sights, soothing sounds, and fragrant smells of Farthest Thule had become all too familiar to her.

Upon reaching the home's entrance, Madeline paused to brush her hair out of her face. Normally, other women would care more about a slightly disheveled appearance than men, but all elves, male and female, took note when anything about Madeline's appearance was out of place. She could not really spend the rest of her life here among so many judgmental stares.

After checking and rechecking her appearance, Madeline walked through the entrance of Lord Bion's home. Bion's servant, Phlios, raised his eyebrow ever so slightly as he held the door for her. Madeline blushed. A tiny spot of mud from the grounds beyond the city gate stained the hem of her dress, and she had not noticed until now. It was ridiculous how effortlessly they could see those kinds of imperfections.

"May I see Lord Bion?" Still out of breath and flustered, Madeline raised herself to as dignified a posture as she could manage.

"My lord left for the Queen's palace not long ago." Phlios gestured back outside. "You have an invitation to join them for the evening meal."

For a moment, Madeline frowned. The Queen's palace was not far, but it was growing late. There was little light left outside for flying.

"Of course." Madeline nodded.

Making her way back outside, Madeline repeated the words she would say to Bion. He would understand. She had already all but told him.

Though twilight was fast approaching, the palace hummed with activity. Madeline raised her eyebrow at all of the servants and guests moving to and fro about the grounds. Something special was happening tonight.

"Excuse me," Madeline addressed one of the guards as she approached the palace gate. "What's happening here? I've never seen so much excitement at the palace before."

"Queen Kypris is going to make an announcement to the lords and ladies of Vathepoli tonight," the guard answered. "Please proceed to the dining hall, Lady Madeline. The Queen is expecting you."

The guards parted for Madeline, and another servant escorted her through the palace. Their course to the dining hall soon took them through the throne room. For a moment, Madeline paused at King Hagios' empty chair next to Kypris'. Something was different about it. Madeline could not say what it was. She was obliged to move on to the next chamber.

In the dining hall, a grand feast lay before Madeline, scattered across the tables. The sights and smells made her salivate. Though it was difficult for her to take in the bewildering array of dishes all at once, what was clear was that this was extravagant even for elfkind.

A number of guests mingled in the chamber, including Baucis and other elf lords and ladies Madeline had become acquainted with during her stay at Farthest Thule. Musicians played harps, flutes, and other refined instruments worthy of some momentous occasion. Their faces were all unusually bright compared to the somber moods Madeline had grown accustomed to seeing in the city.

At the high table, Lord Bion sat next to Queen Kypris with a goblet of ice berry wine in hand. His eyes sparkled as they met Madeline's. What had she walked into?

"Your majesty." Madeline curtsied to the Queen before turning to Bion. "Please excuse my haste, but time is short. My lord, Bion, may I speak with you alone for a moment? It's urgent."

"Alone?" Bion raised an eyebrow. "There are no secrets in this house tonight. We are in the midst of a celebration, you see."

"You have me at a disadvantage." Madeline tilted her head. "What do I see, Lord Bion?"

"You just missed the official announcement, but the Queen and I are now reconciled." Bion took Kypris' hand as she beamed at him. "And our houses are to be joined in marriage."

"You two are getting married?" Madeline's mouth hung open. "Congratulations are in order."

"The future King of Vathepoli is before you," Kypris explained. "Give him your due respect."

"Of course!" Madeline bowed.

Madeline's breathing grew shallow as she gazed at Bion and Kypris. Her stomach sank. She had already decided she would pick Godfrey. She was about to leave Farthest Thule. Why did this news sting so much?

"Please." Bion gestured to an empty seat at the high table. "Join us for dinner. We are just beginning the feast."

"With all due respect, Lord Bion." Madeline wiped the tears from her eyes. "I have to go now."

Whatever protests Lord Bion and Queen Kypris made, Madeline did not hear. She tore through the dining hall and back into the throne room. Huffing, she stopped to inspect Hagios' throne more closely. Now she recognized what had changed. The former king's crest had been replaced by Lord Bion's.

Shaking her head, Madeline pressed on. This was not her world. This was not her people. Silently, she scolded herself for making a scene in front of them all.

She left the palace without saying another word to anyone. She still had difficulty articulating why she felt so hurt by Bion and Kypris' decision to get married. Did this not make it that much easier for Madeline to leave?

At last, she found herself in front of the stables where Spathi had been kept. Fravash rested on top of the griffin's saddle. It was dark now.

"Perhaps we should wait for tomorrow morning," the mouse suggested.

"I have my staff." Madeline tapped Pyrsos against the ground. "Spathi has sufficient provisions in his saddlebag. We don't need anything else."

"Are you sure?" Fravash cocked his head.

"My eighteenth birthday is in less than three days," Madeline said. "If I've learned anything important while at Farthest Thule, it wasn't about magic. It was about not letting the best opportunities pass us by."

"Godfrey is Duke of Kovdor." Fravash twitched his tail. "He's in a very important position. He won't remain unmarried for long, whether you're at the altar or not."

"I can't let it be someone else." Madeline climbed into the saddle. "Spathi, fly hard for me."

Fravash clutched Madeline's cloak as she tugged on the griffin's reins. Spathi galloped forward several paces before kicking off the ground. His wings flapping hard, he screeched as he slowly climbed through the air.

Soon, Farthest Thule grew more distant amidst the Wyrmwind Peaks. Madeline frowned at the twinkling lights of the elf city below. Would she ever really have the chance to visit the elves again?

It did not take long for Spathi's pace to begin to grow sluggish. The air was cold and heavy beneath his wings. The griffin's eyelids lazily began to open and close. Even Fravash stifled a yawn. They could not go for much longer at this rate.

Madeline took a sharp breath as an idea struck her. Her healing fire could now not only close wounds but also mend bones and regrow missing limbs. What could it do for weary muscles and tired minds?

The amber at the top of Pyrsos began to glow as Madeline focused her thoughts on her staff. Sparks began to radiate off the jewel as if they were glowing snowflakes. As the sparks struck Spathi's feathers, the griffin's speed increased. One splintered into magical glowing dust as it hit the tip of Fravash's nose, and the mouse quickly blinked several times. Another hit Madeline, and whatever weariness caused her shoulders to droop instantly vanished.

"Now we can fly!" Madeline called out. "We can do this all night, Spathi."

"Maybe not all night," Fravash warned. "You'll still need to sleep eventually, at least once your staff is drained of its power."

Chapter Twenty-Two

Godfrey rode Dash down the muddy road to Olso Fortress. The horse's hooves squelched along the path as a chill wind carried a few small snowflakes southward. Sardonically, he smiled down at the steed from the saddle. Only within the last few days could he say the horse truly had been broken in. Either way, Dash would be Sigibald of Fulda's problem soon enough.

Frowning, Godfrey tugged on Dash's reins, and the horse stopped as Kolsmarden Forest came into view. The misty trees were just as dark and menacing as he remembered. Had the ghouls left of their own accord or cannibalized themselves as Varin had hoped?

Olso Fortress was just on the other side of the dark woods. It was less than a day's journey to go around. Godfrey could go around. His heart sank as the misty trees beckoned to him. No, he could not go around.

"We have to make sure whatever evil is in that forest has been put to rest for good." Godfrey stroked Dash behind the ear. "I don't like it any more than you, but Kovdor is my realm. This is my duty."

The horse snorted in reply.

"Varin said to stay out, but I've never known the forces of darkness to just disappear on their own." Godfrey scolded. "If it will not be us to drive the ghouls out, then who will? If not now, then when?"

Spurring Dash forward, Godfrey unsheathed his sword and drew his shield. He would rather have had Spathi with him. He would rather have had thirty knights with him, too. Neither was a possibility at the moment.

Slowly, Dash trotted off the road into the trees. The air suddenly grew far colder than it had been outside the forest a moment ago. Godfrey shivered and let out a steamy breath. The curse of undeath was still strong here in Kolsmarden Forest.

Before long, Godfrey watched from the corner of his eye as a shadowy figure began stalking him through the mist. A moment later, two more creatures began following him from the other side. Soon, more undead approached from the sides and behind as Dash trotted through the trees. There were at least eight or nine of them now. Their pale bodies and hunched shuffling instantly gave them away as ghouls.

"Take heart, Dash." Godfrey tightened his grip on Uriel as a trio of ghouls blocked the path ahead. "They have all of this, and yet they still can't overcome us."

Bellowing, Godfrey charged the ghouls in front of him. Dash trampled two of them as Godfrey carved through the third. The other monsters rushed them from all sides. Godfrey cut and thrust. Dash kicked and bit.

Each blow felled a raking claw or snapping jaw, but every monster they destroyed was replaced by at least one or two more ghouls shambling through the fog. He spurred the steed deeper into the woods. Did some malignant force not draw these creatures to Kolsmarden Forest? He had to find the source of this scourge if it was to come to an end.

The ghouls chased Godfrey and Dash with surprising speed. He dared not push the stallion harder for fear of tripping over some unseen branch or root. That would bring both rider and steed to a sudden grisly end.

Godfrey lashed out with Uriel whenever a ghoul's reach came too close, but his attention was divided between riding, fighting, and scanning the trees for anything out of place. His heart stopped as Dash's gallop came dangerously close to a fallen log. The horse jumped over it, barely.

Without warning, the ground disappeared beneath Dash's hooves. The stallion cried out, and his eyes bulged as he tumbled into a narrow ditch on the other side of the log he had just jumped over. A sharp pain blurred Godfrey's vision. He blinked and found both himself and Dash lying on their sides. Panicking, Godfrey grasped his sword and rose to his feet as quickly as he could.

"Hurry, Dash!" Godfrey winced. "Get up!"

The ghouls clambered over the log, and Godfrey threw himself at them. One, two, three monsters fell as Uriel's blade flashed with as many strokes. He had to buy the steed a moment if he could.

Godfrey hacked and slashed as Dash rose to his feet. The horse snorted and shook himself off. Then he began to hobble away from the undead. Godfrey's jaw dropped. Of all the selfish acts...

"No!" Godfrey limped after Dash. "Wait for me!"

The horse struggled up the side of the ditch, and Godfrey latched onto Dash's saddle. Heaving, he pulled himself up. Dash brayed in apparent protest but steadied himself as Godfrey found his seat. The steed kicked its rear leg, shattering the skull of a ghoul as it lurched at them.

"Now go," Godfrey urged as more undead chasing them came into view. "Hurry!"

Godfrey's head, leg, and side throbbed as Dash galloped through the woods. Silently, he thanked Loxias that was the worst that had happened. A moment longer in that ditch, and they would have been ripped to shreds.

Scanning the forest ahead, Godfrey clenched his jaw. Nothing but trees, mist, and skulking ghouls lay in front of him. He could not even be sure this was the right direction. He huffed. There had to be something sustaining the undead in the forest.

Godfrey slashed at the outstretched claw of a threatening ghoul as Dash ran past it. The creature squealed as it hit the ground. He bashed another with his shield as it rushed in from the other side.

"There's more ahead of us now than behind." Godfrey looked over his shoulder. "I think that means we're going the right way."

Before long, Godfrey spotted it. At the top of a small hill ahead stood a frosty runestone not unlike the one Alvir had erected in his camp during the siege. The grey monolith had heaps of bones piled around it. More than a dozen, if not twenty, ghouls surrounded the vile object, swaying as if entranced by it.

"Drive through them!" Godfrey urged.

At a full gallop, Dash trampled the monsters in his path. Some were crushed under hoof. Others fell to the sides. Godfrey swept his sword wide to catch any foes that dared to close in. The thrill reminded Godfrey of riding his old steed, Baruch, into battle.

Though at least five or six ghouls had been crushed, knocked over, or sliced through in Dash's initial charge, the remaining undead had stirred from their trance and now pressed in. Groaning, the steed reared and kicked a cadaverous husk down the hill. Godfrey thrust Uriel into the putrid face of another. Still more pressed in. There were too many for Godfrey to count.

"We have to knock it down." Godfrey pointed Uriel at the runestone.

Godfrey cut through another ghoul and urged Dash forward. The horse stepped closer to the runestone with each attack Godfrey made. They now stood next to it. His skin crawled. To his surprise, the steed turned on the spot and kicked out with his hind legs.

The runestone tipped over and shattered into several large chunks with a heavy thud. Hissing, the ghouls scattered in every direction. The air immediately grew warmer. With a sigh, Godfrey sheathed Uriel. It was over.

"Good boy." Godfrey patted Dash's neck. "Now I'm almost sorry to give you to Sigibald of Fulda."

Slowly, Godfrey's breathing steadied. All was quiet. The awful sensation of dread he had experienced when the runestone stood erect was gone.

Muttering aloud to himself, Godfrey continued to ponder the ruined form of the dark relic before him. The monolith lay shattered just as Dash had left it. Though he could not read the abyssal runes etched into the broken pieces, he had no doubt the runestone had been dedicated to Athanatos.

"But who would build such an awful thing in the middle of the forest like this?" Godfrey wondered aloud.

Godfrey still ached as he entered Olso Fortress through the outer gatehouse. His hands, feet, and nose had grown numb as darkness crept over the land. Even if it was night and few people were out and about, the familiar surroundings of the castle brought him some measure of comfort.

Sniffling in the cold air, Godfrey spent little time meandering about the grounds. His fatigue was too great to take the time to fully appreciate all the sights and sounds of his return home. Still, he smiled softly at Drogon's blacksmith shop before taking Dash to the stables. After leading the steed into his stall, he left a generous helping of oats in the trough in front of it. With that, he patted the horse's neck in farewell.

"Good work, Dash," Godfrey beamed as he left the stables. "You'll make a fine warhorse yet."

Then, Godfrey made his way to the keep. It was tall and imposing, and he recalled how threatening Olso Fortress first appeared to him when he was tasked with rescuing Madeline from it. Ironic that this was now home.

As he entered the keep's great hall, slowly, the warmth of the hearth began to penetrate his fingers and toes. His only thoughts were of the glowing fire, a hot slice of venison, and a tall mug of ale. Nothing else mattered.

"Thieda," Godfrey called as he spotted the maidservant talking with Vonig the Cold. "Some ale and venison, if we have any, please."

"Of course, my lord." Thieda blushed and made her way back to the kitchen.

"My lord." Vonig the Cold strode to the hearth, where he clasped Godfrey's hand. "At last, you've returned. We have much to discuss."

"In a moment." Godfrey raised his hand before signaling to Sigibald of Fulda from across the chamber. "I want to tell Sigibald of a wonderful gift I have for him. Don't worry. I'll have one just like it soon enough for you."

"My lord, that's a most gracious offer." Vonig cleared his throat. "But Lady Madeline. Her father—"

"Oh, I'm sure he's furious with me!" Godfrey shook his head. "That business with House Hracour took far too long for my liking."

"I wouldn't worry about how furious I am nearly as much as I would worry about how furious Madeline must be with you." Tancred emerged from the shadows.

Sigibald of Fulda stopped where he was, a few paces from the high table. Pursing his lips, he slinked away as he watched the exchange between Godfrey and Tancred unfold. Though

Sigibald had saved his life during the siege, Godfrey could hardly blame him for backing down from this confrontation. His hand trembled. If only he could also back away unnoticed.

"Right." Godfrey lowered his eyes. "The wedding's in a couple of days, and—"

"Oh, it is?" Tancred crossed his arms.

"Is it not?" Godfrey's heart jumped.

"Lady Madeline has been gone for some weeks now," Vonig explained as he met Godfrey's gaze. "We don't know where she went or when to expect her back."

"She's gone." Godfrey's jaw tightened. "No one told me. Where did she go? Do we have any leads?"

"If she didn't tell you, then she didn't tell anyone." Tancred sneered. "She must be very upset to leave like this right before the wedding."

"I had to go to Vindholm on my kinsmen's business," Godfrey stammered. "Then I was obliged to see that business through at Skasgun. I didn't want to go."

"Did you bother to write a letter telling anyone here you would be delayed so long?" Tancred scoffed.

Godfrey mumbled indistinctly. There had been so much going on all winter. There had been so much frustration. So many delays and other obstacles. At so many points in his journey, he thought he was just about to return to Olso Fortress anyway.

"My daughter is missing two days before her wedding." Tancred wildly gesticulated. "As far as I can see, this is your fault. What are *you* going to do about it?"

Tancred's piercing gaze bored into Godfrey's very soul. He shrank back. There was too much truth in Tancred's words. He should have stayed. He should never have gone with Roltar and Mauger.

"I'll take Spathi." Godfrey swallowed hard. "I'll go right now and search everywhere his wings will take me. I won't rest until she's found."

"Lady Madeline took the griffin," Vonig interjected. "Otherwise, we would have done that already."

"She took Spathi." Godfrey raised an eyebrow.

Godfrey's thoughts raced. He had not seen the griffin in his pen next to the stables, now that he thought about it. He was too tired to have noticed before.

"Then it must have been important," he continued.

"More important than marrying you, it seems." Tancred glowered. "Trust young people to make their own decisions, and look what they do. I knew I should have made her pick Conrad the Wolf."

Godfrey flinched. Had Tancred said any other name, he might have agreed in his moment of shame, but not Conrad the Wolf. No one deserved him for a husband.

"I'll send out riders at first light," Godfrey answered through gritted teeth. "We'll find her. I promise I'll turn over every stone in Azgald myself if I have to."

"I already sent Arius and Berig out to find her when I arrived," Tancred added. "They had talked to Elja and Thieda and some of your men, and they were under the impression she had left for Farthest Thule."

"Farthest Thule?" Godfrey's jaw hung open. "I couldn't get Spathi to take me there or the Watch Tower of Uvalin when I tried, even after I had already met Uvalin's lord, Luka."

"Wherever she went, if Madeline is not back here at Olso Fortress by her eighteenth birthday, this wedding is off." Tancred waved his hand in obvious frustration. "I have given you men and lands, and you repay me by going over my head to King Lothar for titles you have not earned."

Godfrey cringed at this accusation but made no reply. It was completely unfair. He was the son of a duke. More than that, he had earned his title not just by birth but by deeds. King Lothar saw it that way.

"I hire renowned minstrels," Tancred continued, "pay for an elaborate feast, make travel arrangements for wedding guests from far and wide, and you think you can just drop in right before—"

"I've had enough of this." Godfrey cut in, his blood boiling. "I have spent all winter traveling the length and breadth of Azgald, fighting monsters, being robbed by Nordsmen, and undergoing all manner of trials for kinsmen I didn't even know I had before going to Pskov. Everything I have done was in the name of duty."

Tancred's face grew red. He drew in a deep breath as if he were about to reprimand Godfrey in the most severe language possible. However, Godfrey raised his hand and turned to Vonig before Tancred could get a word in.

"Have Thieda take dinner to my room upstairs." Godfrey clenched his fist. "It's been a long day, and I need to set out before dawn. Have Varin meet me up there as soon as he can."

"Understood, my lord." Vonig bowed before marching off to the kitchen.

Godfrey stormed past Tancred out of the great hall, though he refused to meet the older man's gaze. He did not deserve this. He had not come so far and sacrificed so much to be scolded like a child.

As he climbed the spiral staircase leading up to his bed chambers, Godfrey stopped in front of the window overlooking the stables and Spathi's pen. It seemed not so long ago, he had sat on these very steps, talking with Madeline about their future. He had no doubt then that Madeline was going to be a part of that future, wherever it led.

Godfrey frowned as he recalled Sister Vanya's shrill voice interrupting the tender moment he had shared with her.

While the old librarian was clearly against Godfrey and Madeline at the time, her reaction to Sister Vanya's accusations seemed extreme. Whatever the case, Godfrey's stomach sank as he remembered the disappointment in Madeline's eye as he skulked away from that confrontation. Should he have done more to come to his betrothed's defense in that moment? Could he have done anything differently in retrospect?

With a sigh, Godfrey continued up the stairs. Every less-than-perfect interaction he had with Madeline vividly replayed itself in his mind. Was there one particular moment that had driven her away from him, or was it the slow culmination of many small acts?

At last, Godfrey came to the top floor, where the bed chambers were. His gaze first fell on Madeline's empty room. The door stood ajar, and her belongings lay scattered about in the darkness as if someone had recently searched it. Or as if she had left in a hurry, Godfrey darkly thought.

Next to Madeline's door was Turpin's old bed chamber. Godfrey's thoughts still drifted to the deceased chaplain from time to time. The grizzled man was more warrior than holy man by far, but he was Godfrey's last true link to Bastogne. His hand shook. With Turpin's death, a part of Godfrey was also lost forever.

Godfrey drew in a sharp breath as Father Edric emerged from Turpin's doorway. The priest blinked at Godfrey in confusion but soon regained his composure. However, Godfrey's teeth were still clenched.

"Welcome back, Lord Godfrey." Edric yawned.

"Are you staying in *that* room now?" Godfrey furrowed his brow. "It was my former chaplain's."

"Yes." Father Edric frowned. "I was told it was unoccupied, and I didn't want to take Walaric's since you're anticipating he'll return sooner than later."

"Of course." Godfrey slowly nodded.

With effort, Godfrey released the tension in his muscles. This was no dishonor to the chaplain's memory. Someone was going to take Turpin's room, eventually. Everything changes. Nothing stands still.

"Any word from Walaric?" Godfrey asked.

"No." Edric shook his head. "No word from any of them as far as I'm aware."

"Let's be sure to remember them in our prayers." Godfrey's eye briefly turned to Walaric's door next to his. "They've been gone a long while now."

"Your piety is commendable." Edric gave a small smile. "I haven't forgotten Walaric, Izold, or their companions in my prayers."

"I appreciate that." Godfrey nodded.

Godfrey's thoughts turned dark. He had not thought about Walaric, Candac, Paschal, Jordan, or Izold nearly so much as Father Edric must have. There was so much to do with Roltar and Mauger, and now Madeline was missing.

Edric looked Godfrey up and down. He shifted on his feet. Deliberately, he let out a long breath.

"You look unhappy." The priest tilted his head at Godfrey. "What troubles you?"

"Madeline is gone." Godfrey gestured to her bed chambers. "The wedding is supposed to be in two days, and Tancred is blaming all of this misfortune on me. Of course, I'm unhappy."

"I have yet to see a wedding where everything went right." Edric patted Godfrey's shoulder. "Live long enough, and you'll see it happen in your sons' and daughters' weddings, too. Some of these brides make such elaborate plans. They want the flowers to match the napkins. They want the wine to have been laid down the same year they were born. Yet it can't all go precisely according to plan. No one else even notices all these trivial details."

"They'll notice if the bride's not here." Godfrey raised an eyebrow.

"Young ladies sometimes get cold feet," Edric muttered. "But if she really wants to marry you, she'll be back in time."

"Her father said he will cancel the wedding if she doesn't come back in time." Godfrey gesticulated. "He never favored me."

"What Lady Madeline really wants and what Tancred of House Drois thinks of you are things that are really beyond your control." The priest shrugged. "Try not to worry about what you can't control."

"Don't worry?" Godfrey rolled his eyes. "I don't even know where she went. She could be hurt or held hostage by the most—"

"I don't think she's in any danger." Edric waved his hand dismissively. "Lady Madeline is quite capable, and your griffin is a rather fierce traveling companion."

"You're right." Godfrey sighed as Thieda and Vonig the Cold brought his dinner up the stairs from behind him. "I appreciate the talk, but I have to eat before Varin comes."

"It will all work out for the best." The priest winked at him. "If not Madeline, another young maiden will come your way soon. You are the Duke of Kovdor, after all."

Godfrey shifted uncomfortably at this thought. Lady Isbeil of House Perch, Aethling Lili, Elna of House Merrich, or one of a dozen other beautiful and well-connected maidens could become Godfrey's wife easily enough. Yet he only wanted Madeline.

A knock came at Godfrey's door just as he was finishing the last of the ale in his mug. Only a few crumbs remained on his plate. He had eaten quickly. Varin would not take long to answer his summons even after dark.

"Come in." Godfrey drained the last of his ale.

With a creak, the door leading into the bed chamber opened. Varin entered, casting furtive glances about the room. The ranger never could trust anything or anyone, for that matter.

"Is this about Lady Madeline?" Varin asked.

"That isn't why I summoned you." Godfrey rose as he set his mug on the table he had been sitting at. "But if you know anything or can think of a way to help find her, I'd be glad to hear it."

"I saw her take Spathi the day she left." Varin gulped.

"And you didn't tell anyone?" Godfrey clenched his jaw. "What were you thinking?"

"Forgive me, Lord." Varin bowed his head. "You must understand it is a difficult position for a servant to have a lord and lady at cross purposes."

"You saw her, then." Godfrey took a deep breath. "Where was she going? What did she tell you?"

"They were going to Farthest Thule to finish constructing Lady Madeline's staff," Varin answered. "The mouse seemed to know the way."

"The mouse?" Godfrey raised an eyebrow. "Staff?"

"Oh, Lady Madeline has been busy while you were away, Lord." The ranger gestured around the room. "She got a talking mouse to help her learn magic, and they were insisting they needed to go to Farthest Thule to finish making her staff."

"I'm sorry." Godfrey frantically began clenching and unclenching his fists. "I don't like the sound of any of this. You let her leave Olso Fortress with a talking mouse."

"She seemed determined to go whether I let her or not," Varin said. "She had her things packed, and there was no stopping her so far as I could see."

"Varin." Godfrey grabbed the ranger by the shoulder. "How do you know this mouse wasn't some demon or other malevolent being?"

"It didn't have an evil look about it," Varin insisted. "Anyway, the little rodent spoke quite kindly to me. I was sure I must have lost my head and was imagining the whole thing until after it was all over."

"You're lucky I'm not inclined to remove your head myself." Godfrey released Varin's shoulder from his grip as his hand began to shake. "You're sure they were going to Farthest Thule? Is there any way we could catch her?"

"Spathi can fly three times faster than a horse can run." Varin shook his head. "No one can catch her trail."

After he took a few deep breaths, Godfrey's hand stopped shaking. Whatever the circumstances were, Madeline had seemed to go with this mouse willingly, if it was even really a mouse at all. Still, Godfrey could not help but be reminded of the disaster surrounding *The Book of Elder Wisdom*. His jaw tightened again. So many strange and unknowable entities preyed upon the souls of the innocent.

"Did she say anything about the wedding?" Godfrey asked at last. "Was Madeline upset with me?"

"I can't recall Lady Madeline talking about either of those things." Varin shrugged. "Now, what *did* you want to talk with me about, Lord?"

"Oh, right." Godfrey bit his lip. "I ventured back into Kolsmarden Forest. There were still dozens of ghouls there. I found a runestone in their midst and destroyed it."

"The magic of wicked runestones can sustain undead abominations in the absence of flesh and bone to feast upon." Varin's eyes flashed in apparent understanding. "I had been wondering why their numbers only seemed to grow over time."

"Someone set up that runestone," Godfrey said. "They don't just spring out of the ground."

"I will discover who did it," the ranger promised.

"Could it be some orcs or those dark satyrs that were part of High Warlord Alvir's forces?" Godfrey wondered aloud.

"I suspect we would have already found some trace of them if any of their ilk had lingered." Varin shook his head. "It's probably a local cult taken hold of the villagers."

Chapter Twenty-Three

The Blighted Lands only grew greyer and more desolate the deeper Walaric and Izold traveled through them. They continued following the Lenarm for another week, though they did their best to avoid the few castles and villages they came across. More harm than good came from their stop at Madsorn.

Neither Walaric nor Izold had said much since their confrontation with Lord Giric. Uvan had lost his wife and son. Izold had lost Vielantiu. Was it worth it? Would anyone in the Blighted Lands even notice the destruction of Sir Luthren and Lord Giric with so much evil all around?

"How do you think Madsorn is faring now?" Walaric asked as he and Izold trudged up the foothills of the Dovern Highlands. "Do you think things are better for them now that we've destroyed those two death knights?"

"Death knights are powerful beings that have a fearful reputation in their own right," Izold explained, "but sometimes they are no more than minions to even greater undead monsters."

"So, you think Lord Giric might have been replaced by something even worse?" Walaric swallowed hard at the thought.

"I'd like to think not." Izold shook his head. "But it's a possibility. That village elder didn't give me a good impression of the state of that realm."

"Uvan and Ethne didn't want to tell us much about their dreary little village." Walaric kicked at a rock in their path. "Didn't seem like they trusted outsiders at all."

"If only we had the chance to explore Madsorn Keep," Izold lamented. "Then we could have been sure that the taint was cleansed."

"I think there might be too much taint in the Blighted Lands for the two of us to cleanse by ourselves." Walaric shrugged.

Izold grunted in reply.

Walaric stared long and hard at the paladin as he led the way up the foothills. He could not say Izold was ever jovial or even happy, but his mood had taken a turn for the worse ever since they destroyed Lord Giric. No doubt Vielantiu's absence gnawed at his thoughts night and day.

"Should we go back?" Walaric bit his lip.

"No." The paladin cleared his throat. "We have sacrificed too much on this quest already. We cannot afford more diversions."

"But what about Gardesh the Pale?" Walaric glanced over his shoulder. "That lich haunting Tivelden Forest wasn't part of our quest."

"The road only grows more dangerous with each step we take deeper into the Blighted Lands," Izold answered. "We have no friends here. Besides, time is of the essence."

"True enough," Walaric answered. "Who can say what Nera's shade will do if given enough time?"

They continued marching in silence for a long while. The skies overhead had been almost perpetually overcast since they entered the Dovern Highlands. The air itself felt clammy with gloom. No birds sang, and Walaric's skin constantly crawled as if he was being watched. Could his prayers even reach Helios from here?

The camp was somber that night as it had been every night since they left Sval. No game could be found, so yet again, Walaric and Izold were obliged to eat their trail rations by the campfire. The very act of chewing on the hard biscuits from Walaric's pouch had grown so laborious that spiting them out almost would have been preferable.

"We should be reaching the Lenarm's headwaters soon." Walaric absently threw a stick into the fire. "Isn't that what King Rivold said?"

"About twelve days following the river is what they said back at Sval," Izold agreed. "It should be soon."

"Do you think Sir Jordan's doing all right?" Walaric watched the coals of the campfire pop and crackle.

"If he has been resting as the doctors instructed…" Izold raised an eyebrow. "He should be able to start walking soon. Spring is almost here."

"You could've fooled me," Walaric muttered. "Everything is so dark and grey."

"We are in the Dovern Highlands." Izold shrugged. "It seems that the Blighted Lands' reputation is well deserved, from all we've experienced."

Softly, Walaric began humming a hymn. It was so easy to dwell on evil thoughts in this cursed realm. He had to find something to take comfort in.

Before long, Izold gruffly started singing the words to the tune. Walaric met the paladin's eyes and also began to sing. Sacred music had a way of lifting people's spirits when nothing else could.

Eventually, Izold threw a large handful of melting snow onto the fire and retired to his tent. Walaric grimaced. The cold and despair seeped through the night air once more. With a curt nod, the priest also withdrew to his tent.

Walaric's thoughts continuously drifted back to Terrwyn as he tossed and turned in his bedroll that night. Did she cuddle next to that handsome knight he last saw her with at a warm hearth in Laht's citadel even now? Or, ever the opportunist, when things soured with the first knight, did she take solace in the arms of that half-orc retainer that was also at Raymond of Wrehst's court?

Stretching, Walaric ground his teeth at the possibilities. There was no way for him to know these things without going back to Laht. However, he was in no hurry to go back there either, even with Mirtys as the alternative.

Walaric rolled over on his side. There was also Elja. He would have to go back to Olso Fortress eventually, if he survived this dreadful place. How would she receive him there when that day came?

In the gloom, Walaric's eyes popped open. His shield rested next to him. The white griffin rampant of Godfrey's coat of arms faintly stared back at him. If a fleur-de-lis emblazoned his shield instead, it could make his troubles with maidens more tolerable. He frowned.

"That's not a good reason to become a paladin," he scolded himself aloud. "Loxias, forgive me for the thought!"

Rolling over on his other side, Walaric closed his eyes again. A paladin's life was unenviable at best. To be a roaming warrior without lands or titles, relying solely on the charity of others… Only if he limited his service to the realm of a great lord and gained his patronage could Walaric imagine supporting himself and a family as a paladin. Yet his training as a priest had taught him he could not be fully dedicated to the gods *and* have a family to care for.

Tossing and turning, Walaric tried to clear his thoughts. He could not be a paladin. Izold must not have been thinking clearly when he suggested it.

Breakfast the next morning was light, as it had been since Walaric and Izold began following the Lenarm upstream.

With a scowl, Walaric tightened his belt. This was not the first time he had to do this since he had first gone on crusade with Godfrey, but he could never have been described as heavy to begin with.

For much of the day, Walaric and Izold marched through the hills as they had previously until several taller peaks came into view. Ahead, the Lenarm turned sharply up into the mountains until it disappeared amidst the craggy heights. Walaric gave a heavy sigh.

"That's it." Izold gestured to the headwaters. "That's the end of the Lenarm River. Now we go straight north from here for another day, and then we should be at Mirtys. Gods protect us."

"Gods protect us," Walaric muttered.

Above the Lenarm River's headwaters, the land grew even more sickly and decayed than Walaric had previously noted. The vegetation between the icy patches of snow was sparse, and the mud was sallow. A few carrion birds huddled on dead trees, but even these scavengers were unusually brittle and bony.

Walaric resumed singing the hymn he had started beside the campfire with Izold last night. Though the paladin was quick to pick up the tune as well, Walaric faltered as crows began circling overhead. Izold stopped as well as he turned to follow Walaric's gaze.

"A bad omen." Walaric pointed up at the birds.

"Did you expect a good omen in the realm of Athanatos?" Izold rolled his eyes at the crows. "Do not trouble your heart over birds and their signs."

The paladin resumed walking and began singing one of the old Gothian marching tunes he had sung with Paschal, Candac, and Jordan earlier in their quest. Walaric smiled at the memory of them all singing together on the way to Narlstad. How happy those days seemed compared to Walaric and Izold's time in the Blighted Lands.

"Should we even be singing at all in a place like this?" Walaric glanced over the eerie hills and mountains. "I wouldn't want to attract another death knight."

Izold abruptly halted and stopped singing. His head tilted this way and that as he surveyed the ridges and slopes around them. There were few signs of life—or *unlife,* for that matter—but sound could carry far through the hills.

"You're probably right," the paladin murmured. "But nothing is stopping you from remembering bright songs and better days as we continue. We're going to need something to take comfort in as we get closer to Mirtys."

"Right." Walaric gulped.

They marched in silence for a long while. A few bones of men and beasts occasionally jutted from the ground in different spots, but these sightings grew in frequency the farther they went. Had they ever received a proper burial, Walaric could not say. However, so many dead never properly receiving their last rites, or having their graves desecrated, would help explain why the Blighted Lands were cursed. It was too much evil for anyone to undo. Walaric clenched his jaw.

As they crested a larger hill, the light began to fade. Walaric drew in a sharp breath. A dilapidated village lay before them with broken-down hovels and shambling, cadaverous denizens. The fields below were rocky and smelled sour, yet a team of skeletal oxen pulled a plow across the furrows. Walaric gulped at the pale, undead farmer pushing the rusting plow.

"He carries no grain." Walaric pointed to the plowman's torn and empty sack in his bony hand. "He's not sowing anything."

"But if he had crops to plant, this would be a late start for him," Izold mused. "I saw many such undead villages south of Kirnu along the Amurd River. It is the fate of all Aestas at the dawn of Ragnarok."

Walaric grimaced at the hideous parody of life before him. Other necrotic farmers and villagers milled about the broken-down hovels, shops, and less discernible edifices. A skeletal smith hammered at a black piece of iron in a cold forge. Gaunt weavers with matted, patchy hair worked at looms with moldering linen. Somehow, these futile efforts to complete various chores were more unsettling to Walaric than Gardesh the Pale's dungeon or the mist-shrouded Bochsogen Forest.

"Let's go around," Walaric begged.

"No need to seek out trouble here," Izold agreed.

They went back up the ridge they had just crested. However, with the light fading, it was harder for Walaric to keep his bearings. Even Izold's steps seemed less certain as they attempted to circumnavigate the village through the darkening shadows.

"It's hard to say when we've gone far enough around that village." Izold stared into the menacing gloom. "I don't know these lands. It's too easy to get lost in the dark."

"We can't stop so close to that village for the night," Walaric insisted.

"Do you want to press on?" the paladin asked. "There's no telling what we will stumble across."

"We should be close to Mirtys," Walaric answered.

"I suppose it makes no difference to the undead if we attempt to breach their city under cover of darkness or light of day." Izold shrugged.

As the last vestiges of twilight disappeared, a starless night blanketed the sky. Walaric and Izold trudged up and down the slopes, but the going was slow. Walaric half expected to walk right into that necrotic plowman and his team of skeletal oxen from the village every time he and Izold descended a hill. He shuddered at the thought of the undead vainly attempting to engage in the chores of living villagers preparing for spring. Were they trapped in some irresistible macabre dance against their will, or did they unknowingly pantomime the routines they once performed in life?

Walaric kicked at a fallen log as they ascended another hill. He stopped and frowned at its vaguely familiar shape. Had they passed it before?

"We're walking in circles," Walaric moaned. "I've seen this log at least twice now. Maybe we *should* stop."

The paladin gave an exasperated sigh as if he agreed with Walaric. So much extra effort. What a waste to just keep ending up in the same spot.

"Look there." Izold pointed to a faint light glowing from somewhere over the ridges in front of them. "What do you make of that?"

Walaric squinted. The dim green light was barely perceptible in the darkness. He blinked several times to be sure his eyes were not playing tricks on him.

"Is it the northern lights?" Walaric shrugged. "Godfrey and Madeline told me about them when we first came to Azgald."

"No," Izold huffed. "This is something foul. Come. I think we found Mirtys."

Walaric and Izold drew their weapons and shields as they made their way towards the light. Though still not bright by Walaric's estimation, it gradually grew more distinct the closer they came to its source. The snow and ice grew thicker as well.

At last, they stopped as the dark shapes of ruined walls and towers came into view from the valley below. The pale green light they had been following glowed from unholy torches and braziers dotting the streets. Painful moans and wails echoed from the shadows. Walaric shuddered. What woeful things lurked in that vile place?

"How should we approach it?" Walaric stammered.

"There is an open gate," Izold noted, "but I can promise you it will be watched. Let's circle and see if there is another way in."

"Where do you suppose the Keeper of Souls is?" Walaric whispered.

"No doubt he resides in the high city," Izold grumbled. "In a necropolis such as this, such a singular individual will certainly have a place among the vampires, liches, and other undead aristocrats."

"In the very heart of Mirtys." Walaric glowered.

Descending into the valley, they crept closer to the necropolis. Walaric hardly dared to breathe as they circled its walls. Mirtys' eerie lights illuminated their surroundings just enough to convince him that searching for a suitable gap in the crumbling stonework was not quite suicide.

"Here?" The paladin stopped in front of a pile of rubble next to a partially collapsed wall section.

The rubble was high enough for Walaric to envision himself clambering most of the way to the top of the wall, but he would still need to find some sort of foothold to scale the last ten feet or so.

"I'm not much of a climber." Walaric bit his lip. "Maybe there's an easier way we haven't found yet?"

"I'll go first." Izold shook his head.

The paladin put on his helmet and scrambled up the heap of broken masonry. His dexterous steps quickly led him to the top of the pile. Twisting on the spot, Izold gestured for Walaric to hurry after him.

Holding his breath, Walaric tried the best he could to follow the course Izold had taken. His feet slipped and twisted over the uneven rocks. With a grunt, he fell to his knees after his foot dislodged a broken stone from the rubble heap. His sword clanged as it hit the masonry. Biting back the pain, he tensed as the rock clattered against the other stones on its way to the ground. Walaric's eyes bulged.

For an agonizingly long moment, Walaric clenched his jaw. He was sure every monster in the necropolis heard him. Izold froze in place, too.

After several tense heartbeats passed in dread silence, Walaric eventually let out the breath he was holding. The paladin took one last glance at his surroundings. With an equally relieved sigh, Izold at last took a few tentative steps down to Walaric and helped him to his feet. His knees and the palms of his hands throbbed, but he did not see any blood. He had that much to be thankful for, at least.

"Be more careful," the paladin hissed.

With Izold guiding his steps, Walaric gingerly walked over the top of the rubble pile where the stones rested against the wall. The paladin glanced around before sliding his shield over his back and hooking his war hammer to his belt. Likewise, Walaric sheathed his sword and pulled his shield's guige over his neck.

"Right after me." Izold gestured to Walaric. "Ready?"

"I have to be," Walaric answered.

After grabbing a small handhold, the paladin pulled himself up to the next one and the next. Before long, Izold stood atop the wall with his war hammer and shield drawn once again. He made it look so effortless. Walaric shook. He had never attempted anything like this.

"Loxias," Walaric whispered, "Averruncus, Clarius, or whatever other name the Sun wishes to go by today, if you can hear me in this awful place, don't let me fall."

Seizing the stone Izold had grabbed a moment before, Walaric let out a grunt as he pulled himself up to the next foothold. He did not hesitate or look down as he climbed. He kept all his focus on gripping what little pieces of the wall he could and reaching for the next handhold. There was no time to doubt. Only swift action would see him to the end.

Before Walaric realized it, Izold was pulling him up the last few feet of the wall. He gasped. He could hardly believe he had done it. Silently, he muttered a prayer of thanksgiving to the Sun. Such a feat, Walaric could never have imagined himself pulling off without divine aid.

"Come look at this." The paladin pointed down to the city beyond the wall.

Walaric frowned. Moaning zombies listlessly wandered through the streets as he might have expected, but in an open area next to what appeared to be the main gatehouse, stood thousands of armored skeletons. Their swords, spears, and axes were as tarnished as their helmets and hauberks, but they were arrayed in disciplined ranks that would have impressed Walaric even if they were living. At the head of these ranks, wight lords and death knights inspected their soldiers without a word escaping their lips.

"There are thousands of them," Walaric marveled. "What are they all doing down there? I've never seen so many skeletons all in one place like this."

"They're assembling an army," Izold explained. "They're getting ready to invade Azgald; maybe Sval too."

"Invade?" Walaric gripped his sword tightly.

"It all finally makes sense." Izold shook his head. "The mists, the ghouls, the Great Witch of the North's lingering shade; Athanatos is readying his servants to attack the lands of the living."

"How soon will they be ready?" Walaric fidgeted.

"Hard to say from what we can see here," Izold confessed. "But I don't think even this would account for their entire army if they are really planning an attack."

"There could be dozens of other armies just like this throughout the Blighted Lands, waiting for the command to strike," Walaric agreed. "Undead hosts can grow to be tens of thousands strong. We have to warn everybody."

"We still have to fulfill our quest." Izold planted his foot where he stood. "We're too close to finding the Keeper of Souls to turn around now."

Walaric gulped. This was a major discovery, but it was not what they had set out to do. They had to put Nera's shade to rest.

"Right." Walaric nodded.

Izold clambered over the broken wall until he found a portion of the parapet that was still intact. Walaric shuffled close behind. Once his feet stood atop more solid stonework, he let out a long breath.

Ahead, a pair of skeletal spearmen stared beyond the outer wall through empty eye sockets. Izold gestured for Walaric to stay put. The paladin crept behind them and pounced. Two well-placed hammer strikes shattered their skulls in quick succession. Walaric tensed at the noise of the scattering bones, but it ended just as quickly as it began.

"Hurry." Izold gestured to a set of stairs descending from the battlements.

They raced down the stairs as noiselessly as possible, but their steps still attracted the attention of a curious ghoul. Izold smashed the putrid creature's brains in before it had the chance to cry out, but the groans of other undead monsters drew near. Walaric's heart pounded.

"Quickly now." Izold scampered down the street.

Walaric ran down the tight, twisting streets as fast as he dared without making too much noise. The old stone ruins on either side of them were little more than crumbling arches, walls, and pillars. Occasional torches or braziers lit the way with their sickly green flames, but too much was obscured in blackness for Walaric's liking.

Without warning, Izold dove into the shadows behind an open doorway. Walaric leapt after him. The paladin gestured for silence as Walaric gasped from exertion.

With cracking frost preceding it, a mounted death knight slowly rode down the winding street. The hooves of its skeletal steed clopped against the broken cobblestones. A chilling silence fell as the death knight stopped just in front of the doorway Walaric and Izold hid behind before the knight's unholy steed snorted and shook its head.

A cold sweat trickled down Walaric's face as he held his breath. The death knight's piercing gaze searched the darkness. For a moment, the pinprick lights in the monster's eye sockets stared straight at Walaric. However, the undead creature's head soon turned to other corners and shadows before it spurred its mount farther down the street. Only after it was out of sight did Walaric release his breath.

"He almost saw us." Walaric trembled. "Do you think they know we're here?"

"I don't know," Izold confessed.

"We took out two of those horrid things back at Madsorn." Walaric grimaced. "Don't you think we could've destroyed that one, too?"

"Those two death knights at Madsorn almost killed us." The paladin shook his head. "More importantly, we don't want to draw any unwanted attention here."

They scrambled through the ruins away from the street the death knight patrolled while they moved deeper into the necropolis. More than once, Walaric froze at some noise or movement he perceived from the corner of his eye. Izold was quick to turn and twist at each of these as if he were a hare in the field on the alert for some clawed beast.

Though they flitted from one dark crevice to the next, progress was slow. Walaric heaved and perspired. Even Izold's breathing grew ragged.

"Rest," Izold gasped. "For just a few moments."

Walaric leaned against a pillar. The cool stone was weathered and cracked. The roof of the building they stood in had likely collapsed long ago. How long had it been since Mirtys was populated by living people?

"We're almost to the citadel." Izold peered through the broken columns ahead. "There's no inner wall."

"Praise Helios, we don't have to climb another wall." Walaric staggered forward a pace as he wiped his brow with his sleeve.

A pair of cold, pale arms grasped at Walaric from the shadows. He yelped and slashed them with his sword. Its rancid breath churning Walaric's stomach, the now armless zombie fell forward. With a few quick strokes, he cut the creature to pieces before it could attempt to rise. Yet his skin crawled at the groans of more zombies approaching from the darkness.

Izold struck a pasty corpse as it emerged from the gloom. Walaric hacked at another as it reached for him. More came from every direction.

"To the citadel!" the paladin urged.

Swinging his war hammer left and right, Izold surged through the broken columns towards the heart of Mirtys. Walaric cut down the zombies in their path. Izold's strikes sent more undead sprawling to the ground, but the tide of cadaverous foes was endless. It was impossible to tell just how many there were.

Finally, Mirtys' citadel came into view. It was an ancient, crumbling structure far older than even Madsorn Keep, if Walaric had to guess. However, there was little time for the priest to focus his attention on the architectural details of the edifice. He had to keep blocking the zombies' attacks with his shield while striking out with his sword and trying to keep pace with Izold. He dared not remind himself of the grisly fate that awaited him should he stumble over some broken stonework.

They stopped in front of the citadel's wall. It was low and narrow but smoother than the city's outer walls. They glanced to the left, then right. Walaric cringed. There were no good handholds he could see.

A zombie lurched at the paladin from the shadows. Izold bashed the cadaver with his shield before striking it down with his war hammer. Walaric lashed out at a second and third zombie as they grasped at his habit. More shambled forward. His heart froze at the sound of hooves trotting across the cobblestone.

"Up and over the wall." Izold dropped his war hammer and knitted his fingers.

The paladin lowered his clasped hands, and Walaric stepped into them with one foot. Heaving, Izold boosted Walaric over the wall. He fell into a dark courtyard with a clatter. After he brushed himself off, Walaric looked to where he had just fallen in anticipation.

"Izold?" Walaric whispered.

An ear-piercing shriek came in reply. The sound of the hooves now came at a full gallop as they drew nearer. Steel rang against steel. A dull thud was followed by some grunts. Walaric's jaw tightened as he tried to make sense of the struggle he was hearing.

A horse whinnied. Metal scraped against metal. After another moment of grunts, clangs, and thuds, Izold cried out. Something heavy hit the ground. Walaric bit his lip.

There was a brief pause. Then the horse snorted, and the hooves slowly clicked against the street, growing fainter with each step. Then silence followed. Walaric gulped. Only the occasional anguished moans of moldering zombies filled the air now.

Walaric stared into the darkness for a long time. Fearing giving away his position to the monsters in the dark, he refused to call out to the paladin. He kept imagining Izold would clamber over the wall beside him at any moment. No matter how many times he did this or silently prayed that Izold would somehow be all right, he still knew what really happened. He was all alone now.

With his fingers growing numb, Walaric began to shiver. He was completely alone. No paladins or knights could protect or guide him now. He could not stay long where he was. Something would find him.

In the distance, the sobbing of what sounded like a small child echoed through the streets. Walaric bit his lip as the noise drew closer. He was sure he did not want to find out what that thing really was.

"Courage," Walaric mumbled to himself as he touched the star pendant hanging over his breast.

Slowly, Walaric stumbled through the black. Dead, overgrown shrubbery and gargoyles filled much of the garden he had landed in. A few neglected edifices stood against other parts of the wall in the courtyard, but the grounds were otherwise empty aside from the citadel itself.

Setting his jaw, Walaric marched towards a shadowy portal that looked like a servant's entrance to the citadel. After he took a few steps forward, his gaze met the unsettling green glow of lights somewhere inside. There was no door, Walaric mused. It must have fallen off long ago.

With his sword gripped tightly in his hand, Walaric raised his shield and cautiously pressed through the entrance. The chamber before him was small and cramped. Shelves lined the walls, filled with dust-covered pottery. A few small gardening tools also rested on the shelves, but rust had corroded them beyond any but the bluntest uses. No one had been in here for a long time.

A corridor ran perpendicular to the exit at the far end of the chamber. Walaric pressed towards it. He peered down the passageway. A few bone-white candles glowed in a set of alcoves that lined the hall.

Definitely necromancy, Walaric silently murmured as he inspected the green flames licking the candle wicks.

The priest looked to his left, then his right down the corridor. There was no way to know which way might lead to the citadel's library, if the citadel even had one at all. If he found it and discovered the Keeper of Souls after all of this, would he be able to confront him alone?

"Left is always right," Walaric quietly scoffed.

Turning down the passageway, Walaric kept his sword and shield raised. Something terrible could pounce from the shadows at any moment. If the denizens of Mirtys could kill Izold, what chance did he have?

Before long, Walaric found a crooked set of spiral stairs leading up to the next level. He stopped. Was some divine force telling him to go up the stairs, or was he just following every random hunch that came to mind?

His doubts notwithstanding, Walaric began climbing the stairs. The green light emanating from the candles in the alcoves nauseated him. His legs wobbled. His eyelids grew heavy. Only with great effort did he continue past the second-floor landing, and he leaned against the wall.

Blearily, he stumbled onto the third-floor landing. Walaric gasped as his gaze met the hollow eye sockets of a robed skeleton clutching a large scroll. Walaric blinked incredulously. The creature screeched.

Fear jolted through Walaric, banishing any thought of rest. His heart pounded once more. Acting on little more than instinct, he knocked out several of the monster's teeth with his sword pommel before severing its neck with his blade. The creature's bones clattered against the floor. Walaric cringed.

Something clanged from the stairwell above Walaric. Bone scratched against stone from the far end of the passageway. Blindly, he rushed down the corridor away from the sounds of pursuit. His eyes darted frantically in search of anywhere to hide. Nowhere in the moldy hallway looked particularly inviting.

After rounding a corner, Walaric lunged at the nearest door. It did not matter where it led. Skittering footfalls came from too close behind for him to think.

Shaking all over, Walaric barely jostled the door open and slammed it behind him. He held his breath as he pressed against the closed portal. The muffled noise of hurried steps scampered past the door. Walaric sighed. He had lost whatever was chasing him.

The chamber before Walaric was a dank archive. Blackened tomes filled the shelves set before him. A few pale lanterns lit the room, not unlike much of what illuminated most of the necropolis.

"The library of Mirtys," Walaric's mouth gaped wide. "My thanks, Helios. The gods guided my steps after all."

Grimacing, Walaric took a few steps into the room. A dark shape moved from the corner. Walaric tensed.

Suddenly, a tall, withered figure loomed over him. A large metal key ring dangled from the belt, holding together its tattered robes. Underneath its dark hood, unholy fire lit its eyes. Shivering, Walaric recoiled a step. Hate burned in those flaming eyes.

Finding his resolve, Walaric made to pounce at the undead creature. However, the figure waved his hand, and an unseen force slammed into Walaric's face. Walaric hit his head hard against the floor. His ears rang, and blood trickled from his nose. Slowly, he got back to his feet.

"Dolon, Keeper of Souls," Walaric stammered.

"Sheathe your blade, boy." The creature chuckled. "Swords will do you no good here."

Incredulously, Walaric blinked. The monster smirked but took on a relaxed posture. It was not about to strike again so far as he could tell.

"You're not going to kill me?" Walaric asked.

"Far worse than you has sought to vanquish me in ages past." Dolon shook his head. "You're powerless against me here. There's no need to destroy you yet."

Walaric frowned at his weapon for a moment. It was not blessed by the gods like Uriel. Aside from that, destroying the Keeper of Souls was not the purpose of his quest, even if he was an abomination worthy of such an end.

Dolon leered at Walaric as he fidgeted. His head still throbbed from hitting the floor. Reluctantly, he sheathed his sword as instructed. He had to complete his quest before he could think of anything else.

"Curious to see the living this deep in the Blighted Lands." The undead being glided across the floor towards an open codex resting on one of the desks in the middle of the chamber. "What brings you to me at this hour?"

"Nera, the Great Witch of the North." Walaric gulped. "She was slain some time ago, yet her spirit haunted Olso Fortress for many weeks after, despite my efforts to exorcise her from the castle."

"I know Nera," the Keeper of Souls acknowledged.

The undead creature studied the pages of the book in front of him. Walaric recognized the script as abyssal runes. His skin crawled at the sight.

"She made a pact with you to prevent her shade from moving on to the afterlife." Walaric set his shield down at a desk next to him.

"So she did," Dolon acknowledged.

"As a priest of Helios, I am here to send the witch's spirit to the afterlife." Walaric's jaw tightened.

"What makes you think you have the authority to do that in the Blighted Lands?" The Keeper of Souls chortled.

"Your pact with Nera cannot be eternal," Walaric argued. "It can last only as long as the conditions are met. Afterwards, every soul must eventually go to its master."

"You're hardly one to lecture me about the trafficking of souls." Dolon snorted. "I've made my business with gods and devils for centuries."

The Keeper of Souls closed the book in front of him before examining the keys on his belt. There were at least a dozen. Though each of the long iron keys had many subtle differences, they looked far too similar to Walaric to readily tell them all apart.

"I came here to put Nera's shade to rest," Walaric insisted. "Perhaps there is something I can offer you to speed her along to her final destination."

"She schemes and plans her return even now," Dolon rasped. "She has long supplicated the lords of Mirtys in the hopes of avenging herself. But only our pact binds her to the mortal sphere as of now. What can you offer as sufficient payment against our pact?"

"This." Walaric produced the gold funerary coin from his pouch. "I seek to pay passage for the Great Witch of the North to the underworld."

"Exquisite." Dolon clasped the gold coin in his bony, clawed hand. "It is a handsome fee, indeed."

"Will you accept this payment as the last rite to see Nera's shade to the Abyss?" Walaric asked.

"An infernal pact cannot be undone so easily in the Blighted Lands," Dolon rasped. "Even Tyche herself cannot break such a bond without true recompense. Perhaps we could trade your soul for hers?"

Walaric gulped.

"You're a lonely young man," the Keeper of Souls continued. "You fear abandonment. If you serve me willingly, I can promise you immortality, beautiful women, and anything else your heart desires."

"The gift of the enemy is not a gift." Walaric shook as his heart raced. "You can only offer undeath. Nothing more or less."

"What you offer me is insufficient to end my pact with the Great Witch of the North," Dolon answered.

"Look closer at the coin," Walaric pointed out. "It was made from the holy symbol of Turpin, a chaplain sacrificed by High Warlord Alvir on Nera's behalf. His blood marks that gold you touch."

"So it does." Dolon held the coin close to his face between his fingers. "The price is just."

With his other hand, the Keeper of Souls pinched one of the keys on his ring before making his way to the back of the archive. Walaric followed. They stopped in front of a large desk filled with several locked drawers.

Dolon unlocked one of the drawers and removed a small scroll. He took a quill from an ink bottle filled with dark blood. Walaric swallowed as the Keeper of Souls scrawled something onto the bottom of the parchment. Finally, Dolon replaced the scroll in the drawer before locking it again. It seemed too easy.

"Her price is paid," Dolon announced. "My pact with the Great Witch of the North is undone."

No sooner had the Keeper of Souls placed the gold in a pouch at his belt than a horrid wailing filled the chamber. Walaric jumped. Terror clutched his heart.

"That would be her now." Dolon waved a dismissive hand as the screeching grew louder.

The vague ethereal shapes of a skeletal woman being pursued by three large hounds floated over Walaric's head. His jaw hung open at the spectacle of her shooting cloudy streams of arcane energy at the beasts. One wispy hound vanished in a puff of smoke as the spell struck it, but the other two snarling creatures pounced on the witch's shade. The hellhounds ripped and tore at Nera. Her eyes met Walaric's as she uttered one final curse before the whole scene faded into thin air.

Silence filled the archive for a long moment. Walaric sighed. The hellhounds had dragged Nera to the Abyss, and it was finally over.

"They always fear the afterlife so much." Dolon turned to Walaric. "But you are right. Every soul must eventually go to its master."

"Every soul but yours?" Walaric tightened the grip on the hilt of his sword.

"No, no, you are mistaken." Dolon sneered as he stretched a claw out to Walaric. "I have no soul."

Walaric drew his sword, and the undead monster snarled. He swiped at Dolon's outstretched claw and batted it away, but another blast of unseen force knocked him off his feet. The Keeper of Souls took a step forward and leered down at Walaric. He tried to stand, but Dolon stepped on his chest with a bony foot, pinning him to the floor. He would die here alone in the city of the damned.

Chapter Twenty-Four

Night settled over the Wyrmwind Peaks. Tiny lights twinkled from Olso Fortress' windows and the village below. Painfully, Madeline's lips cracked as she let out the faintest smile from Spathi's saddle. She had flown the griffin from Farthest Thule almost nonstop since they left Queen Kypris' palace. Now, home was finally in sight.

Madeline's fingers were white and numb as she gripped Spathi's reins. Her hair was unkempt. The ceaseless wind had all but deafened her. However, none of that mattered. Home was finally in sight.

With a sad smile, Madeline's thoughts drifted from Olso Fortress back to Farthest Thule. For all the fabled city's splendor, it was not home. Even Mendelpav, back in Pavik, was no longer home. Six months at Olso Fortress and the promise of a future finally in sight made this castle home.

"Just in time." Fravash pointed to the keep from Madeline's shoulder as they drew closer. "I told you we wouldn't miss the wedding."

"Let's hope you're right," Madeline agreed.

Spathi flared his wings as he descended into his pen. The griffin's landing was no harder than usual, but Madeline's stiff body jolted at the impact. Groaning, she rose from the saddle and stretched.

The few horses in the stables next to the griffin's pen quietly snored, and one or two grunted as Madeline and Spathi's rustling disturbed their sleep. She undid the griffin's saddle but left it next to the pen's gate. Someone else would put it away in the morning.

The griffin circled in place a couple of times before settling down in a bed of straw. Spathi stretched and yawned, but soon curled into a ball with his eyes closed. Madeline had half a mind to do the same.

They left Spathi in his pen and took a few steps out into the castle's inner courtyard. A golden light glowed from the window of Drogon's home next to the gatehouse. Otherwise, the only sources of warmth and light emanated from the keep.

"It's still pretty cold out." Madeline drew her cloak around herself as she surveyed the dark courtyard. "I guess everyone must be inside."

"Not everyone." Fravash pointed towards the keep.

From the shadows, Madeline's father strode towards them. His fists were clenched. His nostrils flared. Rage contorted his face. Madeline glanced nervously at Fravash.

"I don't think I can help you much with this problem," the mouse squeaked. "I'll go look after Spathi."

"What are you doing, Fravash?" Madeline hissed as the rodent leapt from her shoulder and scampered away. "Come back here, you coward!"

Madeline blinked, and the mouse had already disappeared. Now her father towered over her. His arms were crossed. His face was red. Madeline gulped.

"Hello, Father." Madeline winced.

A mix of emotions boiled under the surface of Tancred's face. Anger, disappointment, relief, and a few other feelings Madeline had difficulty identifying washed over her father too quickly for her to fully account for. It was rare for the Duke of Pavik to appear vulnerable to anyone, even his only daughter.

"The night watch just told me you arrived." Tancred squeezed her in a tight embrace. "We were so worried. The twins said you were gone for weeks. No one could say for sure where you went. We had no way to follow or make sure you were safe. The boy didn't even know you had left until I told him."

"Godfrey?" Madeline started.

"Never mind him." Tancred pulled back from his embrace. "He doesn't know you're back yet. If you don't want to marry Godfrey de Bastogne, I won't allow it."

"You're calling off the wedding?" Madeline gasped.

"Not yet." Tancred's eyes narrowed. "But if you left because you're not sure about this, I will call the whole thing off right now."

"No, Father." Madeline shook her head. "That's precisely why I came back. I do want to marry him."

Tancred's eyes fell on Madeline's fine elvish gown, her magic staff in hand, and the satyr's sword on her belt. With a sigh, he frowned at her. Madeline grimaced.

"You accomplished what you set out to do?" Tancred indicated the staff.

"Yes." Madeline nodded.

"Your mother and I could never have imagined you becoming so great a sorceress." Tancred furrowed his brow. "And you still want to marry him?"

"Why are you so against us?" Madeline gestured to the stone keep behind him.

"He's young and foolish." Her father crossed his arms again. "He's headstrong and selfish. You could easily marry someone better: Tybalt of House Norfulk, Conrad the Wolf. You could even marry—"

"I could even marry an elf prince if I wanted to." Madeline raised an eyebrow. "Father, opportunities are always coming and going. Some are better. Some are worse. How can any of us say what the best choice really is until after it's already been made?"

"I only want what's best for you," Tancred grumbled. "Godfrey de Bastogne is barely a man. Kovdor is barely a duchy. His knights are few, and he holds onto this realm by a mere thread."

"It's still my choice to make." Madeline put her hand on Tancred's shoulder. "And I say Godfrey de Bastogne is the best choice. He is brave, kind, and pious. He has performed great deeds, including saving my life on more than one occasion. And he loves me. How many suitors have we entertained who can say that?"

Madeline gazed into her father's eyes. His expression softened. With a smile, she kissed his forehead.

"His heart's in the right place, if nothing else," Madeline continued. "Pavik's not far, and the twins are here. If trouble comes, I know where to turn."

"I don't want to see you repeat my mistakes," Tancred said brusquely. "The wedding is set for tomorrow morning, and Godfrey only returned from his errand with House Hracour just before you. It hardly seems like either of you is ready."

"Let me speak with him," Madeline pleaded. "If he is not ready, I'll call it off. I promise."

"Eighteen years old tomorrow." Tancred gave a humorless smile. "Look at how you've grown. You are of age. I suppose you're old enough to make your own decisions now."

Tancred and Madeline embraced once again. He kissed her on the cheek and squeezed her hand. She blinked, and a warm spark flashed in between their palms. Her father's face brightened. It was the strongest approval she could have asked for.

Tancred escorted Madeline to the keep's entrance. The guards' jaws dropped as their eyes fell on her in the dim torchlight. Madeline glowered. She should have expected this. News of her return would not remain a secret for long.

"Lady Madeline!" One of the sentinels gawked. "You've come back at last."

"Where is Lord Godfrey?" she asked.

"In the chapel," the guard stammered.

"Good." Madeline winked. "Don't tell anyone I'm here yet, including him. Understood?"

The footmen slowly nodded at the same time. Madeline held her breath and turned invisible. The guards blinked incredulously before gaping at her father.

"You heard her." Tancred wagged his finger. "Don't tell anyone she's here, or it's your heads."

Madeline jogged from the anteroom next to the entrance into the great hall. The blazing hearth warmed her fingers and toes. The smells of hot food and the sounds of joyful banter soothed her spirits.

Inadvertently, she let out a sigh. To her shock, she remained invisible despite having taken a breath. Her magic staff must have enhanced her stealth. Madeline was sure this was going to be far from the last surprise Pyrsos gifted her. How she would once again become visible, she would have to figure out in a moment.

Next to the hearth, Macsen the Elgunian strummed a lute as Madeline's younger cousins sang along to the tune he played. Aunts Moschia and Annina watched over the children from a table farther back in the chamber as their husbands swapped stories over large tankards of ale. Madeline frowned. Aunt Moschia had been very set on her marrying Cedwyn of Twyl and was very vocal in her disappointment when that arrangement had fallen through. What did they think of her decision to marry Godfrey?

Not far from Moschia and Annina sat Grandmother Annora. She cradled a baby in her arms whom Madeline did not recognize. Beyond the friends and family she had directly invited, a small host of more distantly related kinsmen and acquaintances also filled the chamber. Some, Madeline knew only by sight. Others, she did not really know at all.

Aunt Collette chattered in a corner with Uncle Gerold. Madeline thought to approach them and drop her invisibility, but hesitated. Her few interactions with her mother's side of the family had been fairly positive, but she did not really know them all that well.

Some of Godfrey's vassals and retainers also mingled with Madeline's guests. Crocus the Entillan played a game of chess with one of Aunt Moschia's older daughters at a table in the corner opposite Aunt Collette and Uncle Gerold. Sir Magnus and Berold approached some of the damsels of House Merrich and House Falserd. Madeline smirked. No doubt this was a happy occasion.

Slowly, Madeline drifted within earshot of Elja as she talked with Sir Segeric. The conversation was only idle chatter concerning falconry, horses, and hunting, but the two hung onto each other's words with all the intensity of passionate lovers. With a rueful smile, Madeline nodded at the exchange. It was best for Elja to forget about Walaric.

"She's *great* with child." Elja indicated someone over Segeric's shoulder.

The knight and Madeline turned to follow Elja's gaze. A young cavalier clad in Broguish arms and armor helped a maiden a few years younger than him into her seat at one of the feasting tables. The beautiful maiden was fair and very thin, save for her protruding belly.

"That's Liam of Cavard and his wife, Fial," Elja explained. "She should be due in a couple of months."

"I'm surprised they came to Olso Fortress with how pregnant she is." Segeric raised an eyebrow. "How are they related to Lady Madeline?"

"I'm not sure." Elja shrugged. "A friend of House Drois? I don't really remember if they were even on the guest list, to be honest. It seems that every noble is connected to every other noble by blood or marriage if you search hard enough."

Segeric grunted in reply.

"Have you ever thought about having children?" Elja raised an eyebrow at the knight.

Blushing, Segeric spluttered something nonsensical. Madeline laughed but quickly covered her mouth. Elja's eyes darted in her direction for the briefest moment before returning to Segeric. To Madeline's relief, she was still invisible when she looked down at herself. Clenching her teeth, she took a step back all the same.

Madeline glanced at Fial as Liam of Cavard began pouring wine into her goblet from a pitcher. The fair noblewoman was right about Madeline's age, if not a little younger. Though Elja and Segeric's conversation took an awkward turn, the point was not invalid. Children followed marriage. It was the next step. Was Madeline ready to be a *mother* and a wife, too?

With a grimace, Madeline began marching to the chamber's exit leading to the chapel. She had been invisible for at least a few minutes, and she was unsure how much longer it would last. Best not to waste too much more time.

Madeline raised an eyebrow as she passed Karl the Hammer and Alpia de Toron, who were eating and drinking at a nearby table. Thieda and Vonig the Cold now openly held hands not far from them. More than one other wedding would likely soon follow.

Near the exit, one of Godfrey's barons, Renaud of Vosg, crossed his arms as he talked with one of Queen Noela's ladies in waiting. Madeline tried to squeeze past them, but the gap to the doorway was too narrow. Scoffing, she took a step back and crossed her arms, too.

"Can you believe Lady Madeline ran out on Duke Godfrey just before the wedding like this?" the woman asked. "The scandal!"

"Irene, Duke Godfrey has suffered much," Renaud groaned, "and he is young. Don't be too hard on him if he has not always endured the trials of the crusade very well."

"Well," the woman named Irene continued, "I think it's just as well she ran off on him."

"The wedding's not until tomorrow." Renaud shifted his weight from one foot to the other. "She could still come back before it's too late."

The lady in waiting rolled her eyes.

"But I admit the chances are low." Renaud looked at his feet. "Madeline of House Drois can be wild, too. She's a witch. That means there's at least a touch of madness in her. Everyone, including Lord Godfrey, is right to fear her untamed powers."

"Wasn't she making some arcane staff?" the woman asked. "Perhaps the thing possessed her."

"None can say." Renaud shook his head. "But perhaps it is better if Lord Godfrey marries a *normal* maiden instead of Lady Madeline."

At this, Madeline clenched her jaw. More than one conversation in her proximity revolved around Godfrey, Madeline, or both, not really being prepared for marriage yet. Some blamed her for being too caught up in arcane studies. Others blamed him for being away all winter or for his poor leadership during the siege. Still others could not fathom his willingness to marry a witch.

Sparks flew from Madeline's eyes, and her invisibility dropped. Renaud of Vosg and Queen Noela's lady in waiting jumped back at her appearance. Their faces grew pale as Madeline huffed.

"My lady!" Renaud quickly bowed. "You're back!"

A sudden hush fell over the great hall. Macsen the Elgunian's lute gave a flat twang before falling silent. All eyes were on Madeline.

"Irene of House Falserd." Madeline glowered at the Queen's lady in waiting. "Is Godfrey still in that chapel?"

"Yes, my lady." Irene curtsied.

"I need to talk with him," Madeline answered.

Irene took a step away from the chapel's entrance. Everyone else in the chamber continued to gawk at Madeline. She sniffed.

"The rest of you continue as you were." Madeline awkwardly gestured with her hand as she left the great hall.

A wave of excited prattling filled the chamber. She clasped the heavy ring handle to the chapel door and pulled it open. With great effort, she closed it as quickly and quietly as she could behind her.

The chapel was dimly lit by a few candles, both on the altar and in alcoves lining the wall. Before her, Godfrey knelt at the altar with his hands raised in an attitude of prayer. His cloak was damp at the edges as if he had just come inside, and he wore his full panoply. She twisted the engagement ring on her finger. Now was the time to decide.

"Is everything ready?" Madeline took a few quiet steps towards Godfrey.

Godfrey's eyes flashed open. He stood up beside her almost immediately. Gripping her in a tight embrace, they exchanged a long kiss.

"A few guests aren't due to arrive until tomorrow morning still," Godfrey said, "but now that the bride is here, I think everything's ready."

"Do you really want this?" Madeline asked. "Everyone out there seems to think we're not really ready to be married yet."

"Of course I want this." Godfrey took Madeline by the hand. "I spent most of the last two days looking for you after

I got back. I only came back to Olso tonight, hoping you would still want this, too."

"But the others—" Madeline tugged at a strand of her hair.

"Who cares about the others?" Godfrey shrugged. "We don't need their approval to be happy."

"Will we be happy?" Tears welled in Madeline's eyes. "You've had a habit of letting so many things get in the way of this wedding."

"House Hracour is family." Godfrey clenched his jaw. "I didn't want to go with Roltar and Mauger. Besides, where were you all this time?"

"I—" Madeline gestured to her staff in her hand. "I thought I was doing this for us. But now I don't know…"

Madeline sniffled, and tears rolled down her cheeks. Godfrey had done so much for her, yet she could not help but feel as if he was putting her last. It was all right for him to go on some stupid errand for family, but she could not leave Olso Fortress for a once-in-a-lifetime opportunity?

His expression softening, Godfrey reached out for Madeline's shoulder. Biting her lip, she pulled back before he could touch her. He frowned.

For a moment, the two said nothing. Godfrey's hand still hung limply in front of him as if he did not know what to do with it after Madeline rejected his caress. With a heavy sigh, she leaned against her staff.

"What do you call it?" Godfrey gestured to Madeline's staff. "I hear you spent a long time making it."

"Pyrsos," Madeline answered. "A spell familiar, Fravash the Bright, helped me make it."

"Fravash the Bright is trustworthy?" Godfrey raised an eyebrow. "You've had some bad luck with magical beings in the past."

"Oh, yes, he's trustworthy." Madeline nodded. "He's friends with the elves of Farthest Thule."

"Did you see Luka at the Watch Tower of Uvalin?" Godfrey's jaw hung open.

"No." Madeline shook her head. "But I think I met some friends of his when we took Spathi to Farthest Thule."

"So, he does know the way." Godfrey pursed his lips.

"Not really," Madeline corrected. "Fravash directed us most of the way, and it would be difficult to do it again without his help."

"I see," Godfrey slowly answered.

"Godfrey." Madeline focused her gaze on his hazel eyes. "How important am I to you, really? Am I just a pretty face, or do you want to spend the rest of our lives together?"

"Of course I want to be together forever." Godfrey's voice strained with the words. "You keep asking if I want this, but I don't know how else to prove it to you."

"May I interject?" Father Edric walked up to the altar from the back of the chapel.

Godfrey cleared his throat and straightened up. Madeline also straightened up. Their time so far with the new cleric had been short, and, while a venerable priest like Father Edric certainly deserved respect, it was hard to be open with hm.

"Whom do you love the most?" Father Edric gestured to Godfrey as he stood in front of the altar.

"Madeline," Godfrey quickly replied.

"More than the gods?" Edric tilted his head.

"Well, I guess not *more* than the gods," Godfrey corrected after a moment's thought. "But I love her more than any other mortal."

"And Lady Madeline?" The priest gestured to her.

"Yes," Madeline answered. "I love Godfrey more than any other mortal."

Father Edric gestured for Madeline and Godfrey to kneel at the altar. Madeline set her staff down on the front pew and then knelt with Godfrey in front of the priest. Father Edric joined their hands with his and looked them both in the eye.

"Only the gods can love perfectly," the priest explained, "and only the gods can be loved perfectly. You're both young and full of faults. But if you put the gods first in your marriage, you will overcome those faults together."

Godfrey turned to Madeline. He smiled, and she blushed in return. Then, remembering why she had doubted him in the first place, she glowered.

"Am I the most important person in your life?" Madeline pointed her finger at Godfrey.

"First is my duty to the gods." Godfrey looked at Father Edric, then at Madeline. "Second shall be my duty to my wife. Everything else comes after that."

"Including if your cousin comes with a quest?" Madeline raised an eyebrow.

"Including if my cousin comes with a quest," Godfrey agreed.

Slowly, Madeline nodded. She should not have doubted. Godfrey's piety was without question. With the gods' help, this marriage could work.

Chapter Twenty-Five

Godfrey awoke well before sunrise, though he spent much of the night tossing and turning in his bed. Today was the day. Today, he and Madeline would finally be married. Unless more trouble came. He grimaced.

Pushing dark thoughts aside, Godfrey rummaged through the clothes in his armoire. He snatched his best tunic and slipped it over his bare chest. It was his only silk garment. Next, he put on a pair of clean trousers that had been washed specifically for the wedding. Then, he found his new boots, which had been made for today.

Next, Godfrey put on his gambeson, armor, tabard, and cloak. His gambeson had to be thoroughly washed the night before, and his cloak and tabard were hastily mended. He had stayed up very late polishing his chainmail and spangenhelm. After so much travel all winter, the steel had begun to stain in spots. That would not do for today.

Lastly, Godfrey grabbed his sword and shield. They had also been repaired and cleaned late last night. He snorted at the irony that, despite how long they had been preparing for the wedding, certain tasks could not be completed until the last moment. In either case, he did not expect any violence at the wedding, but these were symbols of his office. He could hardly imagine going anywhere without Uriel in its scabbard at his belt.

Down in the chapel, Godfrey smiled as he recognized Leon de Valois, Osvald of House Rime Wyrm, and Karl the Hammer in the pews for the morning prayer service. However, Madeline, Tancred, Elja, Thieda, and some of the other members of House Drois were conspicuously absent. Godfrey clenched his jaw.

"Where is Lady Madeline?" Godfrey asked Sir Magnus as he stopped beside his pew.

"It's tradition for the groom not to see the bride until the wedding, my lord." Magnus shrugged. "Bishop Manfred should be conducting a private prayer service for Lady Madeline's family in her chambers right now."

"Oh." Godfrey sighed. "I forgot about that. For a moment, I was worried she might've run off again."

Godfrey chuckled awkwardly, but Sir Magnus only nodded in response. It was supposed to be a joke, but the knight apparently saw no humor in it. Godfrey cleared his throat and decided it was best to drop that line of thinking, even if it was only in jest.

"I didn't think they were actually going to go through with that tradition," Godfrey continued. "Seems rather silly since I already know what Madeline looks like, right?"

"They say it's bad luck," Magnus answered.

"If they insist." Godfrey rolled his eyes.

"From the few weddings I've been to," Magnus added, "it seems best to just smile and agree with everything the bride says. Some of these maidens have had their wedding days planned out their whole lives."

"Right." Godfrey nodded.

As he found his seat in the front pew, Godfrey still pondered Magnus' words about agreeing with all of Madeline's choices concerning the wedding. Much of what she said seemed unimportant at the time, and he had quickly agreed to most, if not all of it. The more important details Godfrey had been concerned with were things like how many knights Arius and Berig would be bringing from House Drois, what titles he would have to give them, and what Kovdor's position would be relative to Pavik. Little of that actually had anything to do with the wedding itself. At last, Godfrey could understand some of Madeline's frustration with him.

Sitting alone in the front pew as Father Edric began the prayer service, Godfrey quickly looked at the others present in the chapel. Vonig the Cold, Sigibald of Fulda, Sir Berold, and the other household knights who had remained with him since the crusade first captured Olso Fortress were there. A few of the guests Godfrey had invited, mostly his vassals from other parts of Kovdor, also sat in the pews. Yet he keenly felt Madeline's absence at the seat beside him. No other maiden could fill that seat.

The prayer service dragged on as Godfrey tapped his foot. He had tried to listen for any particular message the gods may have had for him in the sermon, but his thoughts kept drifting to the wedding just a few hours ahead. Whenever he was not thinking of that, he could not help but dwell on Father Edric standing in Walaric's place at the altar.

Once again, Godfrey scanned the faces of everyone in the chapel. He sighed. No word had come from Walaric, Izold, or the others. They should have made it to the Blighted Lands by now. If he did not hear anything soon, he would have to take Spathi and fly there.

Breakfast in the great hall also passed without Madeline or her closest family's presence. However, this went by much more quickly than the prayer service. Renaud of Vosg and Sir Govran had to discuss some minor business with him regarding livestock in Vardo, and Godfrey passed the rest of the time entertaining the guests as they arrived.

"It's snowing?" Godfrey laughed as Varin entered the great hall with thick flurries clinging to his cloak. "Madeline will love this."

Godfrey looked through the nearest window. Sure enough, countless white snowflakes fell from the clouds overhead. Maybe it would stop in time for the ceremony out in the courtyard.

Melting snow dripped from Varin's cloak and boots as he marched to the high table. A fierce look creased the ranger's face. Godfrey gave a low groan. It was not like Varin to walk amidst so many people without good cause. What evil tidings did he bring?

"Any leads on who erected the runestone in Kolsmarden Forest?" Godfrey asked as Varin approached the high table. "Any clues?"

"None yet, my lord." Varin lowered his eyes. "It appears that the runestone was set up earlier than I initially thought. Evidence of who built it may prove too difficult to find now that winter has come and gone."

"You don't suppose High Warlord Alvir set it up out there during the siege?" Godfrey wondered.

"Perhaps," Varin conceded. "But if he did, he must not have intended the siege to last much longer than autumn. Ghouls would've spooked Nordsmen in a siege camp just as easily as Ostmen."

"Right," Godfrey answered.

"Actually." Varin shifted his weight from one foot to the other. "I came to tell you we slew a great stag this morning out on our hunt. Life is returning to Kolsmarden Forest already. The butcher is preparing the stag for the wedding feast as we speak."

"Many thanks, Varin." Godfrey smirked. "I'm all right with you giving me good news once in a while. Try to do it more often."

"Of course, my lord." Varin bowed his head before slinking out of the great hall.

Godfrey frowned after the ranger as he left the chamber, still dripping snow. Of course, Varin was invited to the wedding like every other member of the household, but Godfrey wondered if he could stand being around so many people long enough to endure it. Time would tell one way or the other.

Not long after Varin left, a few more wedding guests entered the great hall. Arthur of House Drechov, Victor of the Great Hunt, came to represent the Duchy of Friodlad. Duke Odoin and Duchess Gelvira, the rulers of Austlad, then arrived with their young children. To Godfrey's chagrin, Hugo of House Merrich came to represent the Duchy of Gotlad. He wasted no time pretending not to notice Hugo's entrance.

"So, this is spring in Azgald?" a red-clad knight asked Godfrey as he approached the high table.

"Fallard?" Godfrey blinked several times at the snow-covered knight. "You made it. Good to have you. I didn't see you come in!"

"I wouldn't miss this for anything." Godfrey's cousin smiled. "But don't take on the Nordsman practice of polygamy. Passage by ship can get pretty expensive."

"Perhaps there is no need to go back to Lortharain." Godfrey raised an eyebrow. "Kovdor is in need of good, strong knights, and I can think of none better than the one for whom I squired."

"A generous offer." Fallard bowed his head. "But my estates in Tyrol keep me busy enough. In fact, we have come to persuade you to come home after the wedding."

"We?" Godfrey asked.

A man in a black surcoat approached the high table. His heraldry depicted a black eagle set against a per pale yellow and black field. Holding his arm was a regal blonde woman in her early forties. Godfrey knew them. There was no mistake about it.

"Lady Seda Eist." Godfrey's jaw dropped.

"You remember my husband, Rodolf." Seda nodded.

"Yes." Godfrey swallowed. "I didn't expect to see you here in Kovdor."

"This is a day for celebration, Godfrey, and we have no desire to detract from the occasion," Seda explained, "but Bastogne's need is dire."

"Your letters gave me that impression." Godfrey frowned. "It causes me great pain to hear Simon of House Gramon is making such an inadequate duke."

"That's quite the understatement." Rodolf gestured to the great hall's exit. "King Wilhelm's reign has turned tyrannical. His nephew, Simon, is but a pawn in his schemes. Many in Bastogne, Tyrol, and Ghend stand ready to remove House Gramon and receive the true heir of Bastogne."

"Many of my father's knights just returned to Bastogne and now serve under Duke Simon," Godfrey pointed out. "How many of them might I have to slay to liberate Bastogne from House Gramon?"

"Their loyalty is to you, not King Wilhelm's house." Seda took on a reassuring tone. "Your deeds are great. Your heart is great. Bastogne will know whom to follow when the time comes. Do not doubt your father's men."

"Other lords may follow if sufficiently persuaded." Fallard raised an eyebrow. "But we need a leader to unite behind. No one has been more wronged by the King than you. The duchies will unite behind you."

"I'm not sure what to say," Godfrey stammered. "I already renounced my claims to Bastogne, and my duty is to Kovdor now. We have a few knights here, and I don't want to set myself against the friends and kinsmen I stood beside just a few months ago."

"With luck, you might not have to slay any of your friends or kin." Fallard crossed his arms. "Duke Simon is even more unpopular than King Wilhelm."

"Simon must have some friends willing to stand by him." Godfrey waved his hand dismissively. "He will not be ousted from Fuetoile Keep without a fight. I need time to prepare for a campaign, *if* I am to go at all. We endured a hard siege here not long ago, and there's trouble brewing with the undead."

Before Rodolf, Fallard, or Seda could respond, a pair of trumpeters blasted their horns from the great hall's entrance. All fell silent as they turned their heads to the open doorway. A herald entered and puffed out his chest.

"All rise for his majesty, Lothar, King of Azgald, and Queen Noela the Sornian," the herald boomed. "Hail King Lothar! Hail Queen Noela!"

"Hail King Lothar!" Godfrey stood and chorused with everyone else in the chamber. "Hail Queen Noela!"

Though every lord present wore his finest tabard and had his armor polished to its brightest shine, the King's panoply outdid them all. The Queen's gown was no less impressive. Surely, she was the envy of every damsel, maiden, and old woman in the chamber. Yet all the Queen's splendor was no match for the beauty of the elves of Farthest Thule, if Godfrey could believe Madeline's account. One day, he would have to see it for himself.

Godfrey considered the golden crown set atop King Lothar's spangenhelm. Then his eyes fell back on Lord and Lady Eist's expectant faces. Were Azgald's concerns not far more important than anything back in Bastogne now?

The King and Queen slowly made their way to the high table, stopping to greet individual lords and ladies as they crossed their path. Seda exchanged a glance with her husband. Fallard scowled. Godfrey shook his head. Could he neglect their suffering after they had come so far?

"I'm the Duke of Kovdor now." Godfrey cringed. "My first duty is to this realm and then to the King of Azgald after that. I'm not saying I won't help, but it's a lot to think about right now."

Fallard nodded. A sad smile crossed his face. If anyone understood Godfrey's heart, it was he.

"Let's talk more about this later," Fallard suggested. "There's enough for Godfrey to worry about now. Let's not spoil his wedding day."

Lord and Lady Eist curtly nodded. Fallard briefly embraced Godfrey before he found a seat at the table that Rodolf and Seda ambled to nearby. At last, Lothar and Noela stood before Godfrey with several of the King and Queen's retainers trailing them. He recognized many of their faces, but he still had trouble putting names to all of them. Constable Magneric, Steward Durand, and Chamberlain Fulrad, among others, were still mostly just names he had merely overheard at Vindholm that he had little chance of getting to know today.

Godfrey walked in front of the high table and bowed to the King and Queen. Lothar bid Godfrey to rise and clasped his hand. Smiling, Godfrey took a step back after the King released his grip.

"Congratulations are in order," Lothar said.

"The wedding hasn't happened yet, my lord." Godfrey blushed. "But that's going to start momentarily."

"He wasn't meaning the wedding," Noela corrected him. "He was talking about Skasgun."

"Oh." Godfrey took a sharp breath.

"That was a difficult situation," Lothar confessed, "but it seems you have been able to return Skasgun to House Hracour's control without losing Lord Davin in the process. I might need to send you on more diplomatic quests in the future."

"As long as they don't involve more ordeals by water." Godfrey shifted his weight from one foot to the other. "One in the dead of winter is plenty."

"I should hope not." Lothar gave a humorless smile. "But I can't make any promises."

Godfrey chuckled nervously. The King and Queen both laughed. They had to laugh, Godfrey mused. It was all he could do not to cry. What else could they do?

"Thank you again." Mauger emerged from behind the King before clasping Godfrey's hand. "It was hard to see it at the time, but you saved House Hracour from fading into darkness. The day is not far when Stormsud will prosper as in the former days."

"I'm shocked to see you here," Godfrey admitted.

"I already said House Hracour owes you greatly." Mauger gestured to him. "There's no reason to continue to carry the enmity of the past. Aside from that, you may recall we were on the guest list from the beginning."

"It was a difficult journey for all of us." Godfrey pursed his lips as he struggled to remember any details about the guest list Madeline had put together for the wedding. "The outcome was less than certain for most of it. I just hope we don't have to repeat such a trek."

"We won't put you through that again." Mauger shook his head. "Father sends his regards. He would've come, but there is still much to put in order at Skasgun."

"May Stormsud prosper under his reign and yours after as it never has before." Godfrey embraced Mauger.

For a long moment, Godfrey looked into his kinsman's eyes. The jealousy, anger, and bitterness were all gone. All of that was replaced by the gratitude and goodwill Godfrey might have otherwise expected to see in Mauger from the beginning of their quest. Ruefully, Godfrey smiled. One day, he thought, he might find a true friend in Mauger.

"It is time," Father Edric called out as he gestured for everyone to begin exiting the great hall.

After bowing to the King and Queen and clasping Mauger's arm one last time, Godfrey joined the crowd making their way to the chamber's exit. Godfrey's hand twitched. It was time.

As he walked out into the snowstorm in the castle's inner courtyard, Vonig the Cold pulled Godfrey to his place next to Bishop Manfred on the keep's steps. Perhaps Karl the Hammer or Leon de Valois might have made for a better best man. Both Karl and Leon were more skilled warriors. However, Vonig was the de facto castellan of Olso Fortress whenever he and Madeline were absent. With luck, none of the guests—including Hugo of House Merrich—would disrupt the wedding or attempt to kidnap the bride, Godfrey hoped.

"Madeline is sure going to love this." Godfrey gestured to the falling snowflakes.

"Oh, she's livid," Vonig answered as he took his spot at Godfrey's side.

Soon, the bridesmaids and groomsmen took their places on the steps around Godfrey and Bishop Manfred. Thieda and Elja were among the bridesmaids, as well as a few of Madeline's cousins near her age. It was only as he noticed Elja stood closest to Bishop Manfred that Godfrey realized she must be the maid of honor.

Godfrey glanced at his groomsmen. Next to Vonig the Cold stood Karl the Hammer, Leon de Valois, Sigibald of Fulda, and Sir Berold. Others could have stood in their places. Godfrey's only previous thoughts were to ask the knights he felt closer to and to make sure there were enough of them to match the number of bridesmaids.

A long aisle divided the guests in the courtyard. Madeline's guests congregated on one side of the courtyard, a few paces away from the stairs, while Godfrey's guests occupied the other side. Benches had been set out for the guests to sit on, but most preferred to stand rather than sit in the snow left on the benches by the unexpected blizzard.

However, Arius and Berig cleared a seat for a woman close to Tancred's age. She wore a clean and colorful gown, though it was not as refined as a true noblewoman's. Godfrey raised an eyebrow at her.

Arius wiped the snow off the bench before Berig laid his cloak down on it for the woman to sit on. Godfrey frowned. It was perhaps the first act of genuine kindness he had seen from the twins.

"Sennin," Bishop Manfred whispered to Godfrey in response to his inquisitive glance. "She's the twins' mother."

"I was told about her." Godfrey nodded as he tried to recall the details. "But Lissette of House Vred was Madeline's mother?"

"Sennin was not Madeline's mother." The old bishop shook his head. "You can imagine she's been treated as something of a pariah by most of Madeline's kindred since they arrived here."

"A pity." Godfrey frowned. "Fate can be so cruel."

"It's a tragic story." Manfred sighed. "Tancred was not unfaithful, at least in his mind. I could say more, but it's also not my place to speak of it. When I was Tancred's chaplain, he confessed to everything, but the scars still run deep after all these years."

"I see." Godfrey took a deep breath.

At last, the snowfall died down, and most of the wedding guests slowly took their seats after clearing them of precipitation. They talked excitedly for a few moments, but pipes and strings began to play from behind them. The guests fell silent.

One of Madeline's younger cousins walked up the aisle with two golden rings resting on a crimson pillow. Godfrey had been told the child's name at one point, but he had quickly forgotten it. After handing Bishop Manfred the pillow bearing the rings, she wailed and ran back down the aisle to her mother in the crowd as fast as her legs would take her. Everyone chuckled. No amount of preparation could account for the equally innocent and wild outbursts of small children put in front of large crowds.

Soon, the musicians' tune changed from a prelude to a proper wedding march, and silence fell over the audience once again. Two knights strode up the aisle side by side. One, Sir Halinard, carried the House Cretus banner. The other knight, one of Tancred's retainers, carried the House Drois banner. In unison, the banner bearers stopped at the bottom of the keep's stairs and turned to face the crowd.

Finally, Duke Tancred led Madeline up the aisle. One of her hands clutched her father's. The other carried her staff. Her wedding gown shimmered silver and blue, not unlike the colors of Godfrey's house. No doubt such an exquisite dress—that even put Queen Noela's gown to shame—was a gift from the elves of Farthest Thule.

Madeline glided up the snowy aisle effortlessly. Her every move was flawless. Fortunately, the snow went up only to her ankles. Tyche could have been less kind, Godfrey reminded himself. He had almost forgotten how cold Azgaldian springs could be.

Madeline's veiled face glistened like white marble. Her aunt, Collette, began to sob uncontrollably at the sight. Many of the other women also shed tears. Ironic that so many warriors had bled and died here just a few months before during High Warlord Alvir's final assault on Olso Fortress. Now many of those same people cried for joy.

Godfrey's jaw hung open as Madeline drew nearer. Never had he seen her so resplendent. He could hardly believe it. Vonig cleared his throat, and Godfrey swallowed. Straightening himself to his full height, he attempted to maintain the most dignified posture he could manage.

At last, Madeline and her father reached the top of the stairs, and Tancred placed her hand in Godfrey's. The Duke of Pavik and he exchanged the briefest glance. Godfrey swallowed again. Had he really won her father's approval? Tancred had already begun walking down to the bench closest to the bottom of the stairs before Godfrey could decide what it was he saw in the man's eye.

Madeline handed her staff to Elja, who took the magical device with some reluctance. Godfrey shook his head, but, in truth, he could not blame her. He would have hesitated to touch it, too.

Once Tancred was in his seat next to Arius, the processional music stopped. Godfrey tilted his head at them. He thought Tancred would have sat between one of the twins and Sennin instead. Did he not care for her? Did he merely want to appear not to care for her?

Godfrey shook his head. That was none of his business. He had other things to focus on. His eyes briefly met Lady Eist's in the crowd. Clearing his throat, he tried not to think of *that* business either.

Still holding the pillow with the wedding rings resting on it, Bishop Manfred began his homily prior to exchanging vows. Godfrey blinked. He had to pay attention to this.

"A marriage built on a foundation of faith cannot fail," Bishop Manfred explained. "The gods have ordained marriage between man and woman as a sacred responsibility to care for one another, to build one another up, and to bring precious children into the world."

Godfrey squeezed Madeline's hand. She squeezed his hand in return. Beneath her veil, a faint smile cracked her lips. His heart fluttered. So much lay in store for the future.

"Not every day will be easy," the Bishop continued. "You will find patience and understanding to be your strongest allies. As you seek out these allies in your relationship, you will find that the gods are refining you as a smith refines gold in the fire."

Godfrey's thoughts had already begun drifting to children. He would have many sons, he was sure. He would have to name his eldest Ulric after his father. Perhaps he would name his second son after himself and then his third after Fallard or King Lothar. Time would tell.

To Godfrey's relief, Bishop Manfred's homily soon wound down. He was sure he would make a good husband. He had no doubt Madeline would make an excellent wife.

"Does anyone object to the union of this couple?" Manfred asked after clearing his throat.

Godfrey looked over the crowd. No one said a word. Not even Hugo of House Merrich.

"Then let us proceed." Bishop Manfred turned to her. "Madeline of House Drois, do you, of your own free will, vow to honor and obey your husband as he honors and obeys the gods above? Do you vow to always love and cherish him as he shall love and cherish you through sickness, health, poverty, and wealth?"

"I do." Madeline bowed her head.

"Godfrey de Bastogne." The Bishop turned to him. "Do you, of your own free will, vow to lead your wife in love and righteousness as the gods lead you in love and righteousness? Do you vow to always love and cherish her as she shall love and cherish you through sickness, health, poverty, and wealth?"

"I do." Godfrey bowed his head.

"Now, my children, take the rings." Manfred indicated the pillow in his hands.

Madeline grabbed one of the bands from the pillow, and Godfrey took the other. He removed the mailed glove covering his left hand, and Vonig the Cold took it. Once they had taken both rings, the Bishop indicated Madeline.

"With this ring, I do thee wed." Madeline placed the plain gold band on Godfrey's fourth finger.

"With this ring, I do thee wed." Godfrey placed the ring on Madeline's finger.

For a moment, Madeline stared at the ring. Where her emerald and silver engagement ring had been, now rested a sapphire and gold wedding ring. It sparkled in the emerging sunlight as the clouds floated beyond the Wyrmwind Peaks.

"You may now kiss the bride." Bishop Manfred gestured to Godfrey.

Godfrey lifted Madeline's veil. Tears welled in her sparkling grey eyes. Grabbing her around the waist, Godfrey pulled her in for a long kiss.

A significantly longer feast followed. Gifts were showered on them for hours after. King Lothar officially pronounced Madeline Duchess of Kovdor late that afternoon, and even more food and drink gifted from the royal stores followed.

By sunset, Godfrey grew so full, he was certain his stomach would burst if he ate another bite. Rising from his chair at the high table, he stretched his legs. His eyes narrowed as something dark flitted into the shadows.

"Mice," Godfrey muttered. "We'll need to get a cat."

"Not for that one." Madeline winked.

If you enjoyed what you read, please post a review online. Your input is greatly appreciated!

THE SAGA CONTINUES

GODFREY AND THE SONS OF BASTOGNE

THE FOURTH NOVEL IN THE GRIFFIN LEGENDS

2027

Acknowledgments

I can't thank my wife, Summer, enough for all of the sacrifices she has made to help bring this book to you. Many weekends and late nights had to be put on the altar to bring Godfrey Before the Phoenix to the public, and she has never once complained about time lost or chores left undone. She also continues to be my first and most valuable editor. Her unique insights have only ever improved my work, and it brings me great joy to collaborate with her on stories in this setting.

I would also like to thank my beta readers, Shawn and Tyler, for their feedback throughout the writing process. It's rare to find friends who share complementary passions and expertise, and I am blessed to have them take the time out of their busy schedules to help me make this story the best that it can be.

My editor, Michael, also deserves special praise. Over the years, I would like to think we have developed a genuine friendship, and I've come to value his opinion on more than just grammar and syntax.

My new cover artist, Dave, has also done a wonderful job on *Godfrey Before the Phoenix*. While a flashy cover can't make up for a lackluster story, we all know that good-quality art is the first step to catching a potential reader's eye.

I am grateful to also count my parents among my greatest supporters. There might have been less stress and hardship while raising a young family if I had just become a doctor, but they always trusted that I would do what I believed was best.

Finally, I would like to thank all of my other friends, family, and supporters, and especially my readers! In some ways, writing gets easier with each new book, but discouraging experiences, moments of doubt, and other challenges never cease to impede finishing such an undertaking. When such obstacles rear their ugly heads, I remind myself that there are people out there who are truly eager for the next installment of Godfrey de Bastogne's adventures. No matter how many or few you may be, I owe it to you to see this through!

Thank you all!

About the Author

Mark Howard lives in Ohio with his wife and four children. When he is not writing or taking care of his family, he enjoys reading, biking, playing board games, and going on other imaginative adventures.

For regular updates on Howard's latest works, follow him on Facebook and Twitter, and check out his latest fiction on his website:

www.thegriffinlegends.com

www.ingramcontent.com/pod-product-compliance
Lightning Source LLC
Chambersburg PA
CBHW032138050726
47591CB00001B/6